Clockwork Bread

By: Peter Evan Fatouros

Peter Evan Fatouros

This is a work of fiction. Names, characters, places, and incidents either are the product of the author's imagination or are used fictitiously. Any resemblance to actual persons, living or dead is entirely coincidental.

Copyright © 2022 by Peter Evan Fatouros

First paperback edition December 2022

Paperback ISBN: 978-1-0689095-0-4
eBook ASIN: B0BPQB997R

Chapter 1
Oct 14th, 1932

Abigail walked into her boss' office & handed the tall man his date book. She was eager to leave for the weekend. He took the book from her & looked at her intensely.

"The meeting with the managers from the Hudson Bay Company?"

Abigail pointed to his book.

"Monday afternoon, at two o'clock."

"Excellent miss Oldman. You're the only person that I know who can get those guys to agree to a Monday meeting on Friday afternoon. enjoy your weekend."

"Thank you sir."

Abigail then turned on her heels & marched out the door. A moment later, she was outside & walking down the street from the bank in Soho to her little apartment in Hell's Kitchen. As she walked, she reached up behind her & loosened the bun in her raven black hair. As it slipped, her shoulder length hair fell free, earning a whistle from a teenage boy who happened to be walking past. Abigail could hear the sound of his mother's hand slapping his cheek as she walked on.

Walking down the street, Abigail knew that this weekend was going to be a good one. She didn't have to go to the diner with the other secretaries, she didn't have to check in with her mission contact, she had nowhere that she needed to be. She could simply lock her door, close her curtains, open her jewelry box & take out her music pod.

The only reason that the mission designers had allowed her to take it with her was because it had been disguised to look like a fragment of broken jewellery. Worthless to anyone who came across it, it was the only thing keeping her going some days.

Abigail had spent years training for this mission. Learning how to talk, how to walk, how to dress & how to act in order to blend in perfectly. She had thought that she was ready, but she was wrong. None of the simulations could prepare her for living in the 1930s. It had been one thing when she could simply leave the simulator & be back to modern life. But after almost two years here, she was almost ready to call it quits on some days. There had been a day or two when the only reason that she didn't go home was because she couldn't. Until someone built a gateway in the past, she would have to get back home to 2088 the long way.

Turning the corner on her way home, Abigail was dismayed when she saw that the road she normally used to get home was blocked off by construction crews. Seeing a police officer standing on the corner, she went up to him & asked him what had happened. He answered with a thick English accent.

"Public works miss. People have been complaining about the state of this road for years, especially since it was made for horses & not cars."

"So they're just digging it up?"

"Yes mam. Part of the mayor's public works initiative to put some people back to work & improve the state of the city. In a few weeks, this road will be one that the rest of the city wishes that they could live on."

The officer was beaming with pride while he stood there in his dark blue coat & trousers. Abigail figured that he lived on this street & that this pride was his way of dealing with the inconvenience of living on a construction site.

"Is there any way that I can get down that road?"

"Sorry miss. Local residents only. I'm afraid that if you don't live here, you'll need to find another way."

"I'm trying to get to Hell's Kitchen."

"Now what's a lovely young English lass like you doing living in an Irish neighborhood like Hell's Kitchen?"

Practically needing to bite her tongue to stop herself from telling him that he shouldn't put down the Irish like that, she composed herself before answering.

"Cheap rent."

"Ah yes. Can't be too picky with the state of the world these days. Whole damn thing gave like a house of cards."

"It'll get better. This too shall pass officer."

"Aye I hope so. Anyways, you can probably make it home along eighth avenue just as easily."

"Thank you officer."

Abigail then turned towards eighth avenue & continued on her way. Annoyed that the path that she normally walked was going to be unavailable for a few weeks, she continued down the street, distracted by thoughts of being able to dance in her apartment to her favourite bands. While she was deciding if she should listen to cyber chill or elf punk, she was brought back to reality by the smell of freshly baked bread. Realizing that she was standing on the corner of 24th street, she turned to see Rodin Bakery with it's door propped open to attract customers with the wonderful, heart lifting smell of freshly baked bread. While Abigail was absolutely certain that she wouldn't be able to get dark rainbow bagels with pumpkin spice infusions, she decided that fresh bagels would be a good way to start the weekend & a good reward for making it through another week in the great depression.

Stepping inside the warm bakery was like walking into heaven, or as close to heaven as something outside of virtual reality could get. Still, after being in the great depression for almost three years, this was wonderful. Abigail walked up to the counter where another woman was facing the kitchen & arguing with a much older man in French. When the woman noticed a customer, she said something to the older man that caused him to raise his hand to his head. She then turned around & time seemed to slow down for Abigail.

The woman's dirty blonde hair seemed to flow like a river that finally settled into place like a halo around the young woman's face. Her pale, flawless skin seemed to shine in the light from the one electric lamp on the counter. Her Apron seemed to hug her body & called out to Abigail to be untied. But what really drew Abigail in was her eyes. The woman's eyes were a deep, vibrant green. Abigail had never seen eyes like that in the real world, not in the 2080s & not in the 1930s. They almost caused Abigail to blow her cover by asking if the woman was another operative from the future, since eyes that green could not possibly be natural. When the woman spoke, Abigail was entranced by the sound of her voice.

"How can I help you?"

"Bagels."

Abigail shook her head, causing time to speed up again & her heart to start beating a little more normally. The woman with her French accent looked at Abigail confused.

"Bagels… miss?"

"Yes, sorry. I got distracted. I'd like some bagels please."

The woman blushed.

"You are very fortunate, my father Maurice just finished baking some. How many would you like?"

"Umm, three. Yes, three."

"One moment. Papa, trois bagels pour la jolie fille!"

"Did you just call me cute?"

The French girl blushed again.

"You speak French?"

"I used to have a… friend… who taught me enough words to know when someone calls me a cute girl."

"Ah. Yes, sorry."

"Don't be sorry. My name is Abigail. Abigail Oldman."

"It is nice to meet miss Oldman. I'm Renee Rodin. My father Maurice owns the bakery. Do you live near here?"

"No, I'm up in Hell's Kitchen, but this place is on my new way to work."

"New way? What happened to the old way?"

"It didn't have a decent bakery along it."

Renee smiled.

"Does that mean that I expect to see you here again?"

Maurice came forward from the back & handed Abigail a bag with three freshly baked bagels, still warm from the oven.

"Tu as raison, elle est mignonne."

Renee slapped her father & pointed him back to the kitchen. Abigail watched him grin & head back to his fresh batch of baked goods.

"What did he say?"

"He said… he said that he hopes you enjoy his bagels."

Abigail looked at the French woman.

"He didn't say that did he?"

"No."

Both women laughed as Abigail paid for her bagels.

"I look forward to seeing you in here again miss Oldman."

"Call me Abigail."

///

Abigail made it the rest of the way home with a new skip in her step. She hadn't felt like this in years. Even before she stepped through that gateway into the past of a parallel timeline, it had been years since she felt giddy just from meeting a girl. She certainly hadn't been expecting it in this decade. Abigail had never thought that a fully organic human with no augments could make her feel this way, but here she was, a bag of bagels in her hand & the depressing world of the 1930s seeming a little less depressing.

She opened the front door to her apartment building & bounded up the stairs. As she was walking up to her door, the door to the apartment across the hall from her door opened up & a plump older woman walked out of the apartment. She was wearing an old toque hat that had fallen out of fashion a few years ago & by the way she wore it, it was clear that she was trying to hide the fact that her blonde hair was starting to turn white. She saw Abigail beaming & with an Irish accent; she made an enquiry of her neighbor.

"Well, don't you look like the cat that caught the canary. What's got you grinning like a fool in a funhouse?"

"Hello Lola, I guess it's just a very good day."

"Oh? What's so good about it miss Abigail?"

Abigail could sense that Lola was fishing for gossip. That was her thing in the world, uncovering her neighbor's secrets & being the first to spread them around. Made it easy to learn about anyone that was moving into the building, but it made it a lot harder to come & go unnoticed. She had complained to her handler that she needed a better home with a better neighbor more than once.

"Well, it's Friday, that's always a good thing."

"True enough, what's that in your hand?"

"Oh, I had to take a detour around construction on my way home & I stumbled on this wonderful little bakery. Would you like a fresh bagel? I bought three without realizing how many I was ordering."

"No but thank you for the offer. What had you so distracted that you didn't realize how many bagels you were buying? A handsome young man perhaps?"

"Good night, Lola."

Abigail then slipped into her apartment before she would have to lie about who she was distracted by at the bakery. Her home was small. This wasn't something new to her. Back home, her apartment had been about the same size & layout as this place. A decently sized main room with a small kitchenette in the corner, a small bedroom & a cramped bathroom. Remarkably similar to what she had had back home, only back home, she was allowed to have a full VR suite installed in her head. Small homes weren't so bad when you could lie down & slip away into virtual reality for a few hours. No such luxury here. No augments allowed until 2030.

"Home sweet home."

Abigail then went to her bedroom & opened up her jewelry box. The small device looked like it had once been a misshapen pearl that had been set in necklace or an earring. In actuality, it was her music pod. She popped the fitted device into her ear & a second later, she heard the pleasant tone that meant that it was awaiting instructions. In the same jewelry box, there was what looked like a clunky bracelet. Also made to look worthless, it was actually the music pod's charger & controller. Abigail took it out & set it on the table in the kitchenette underneath one of her lights. It would turn the lamp light into electricity that it would later use to charge the music pod. With everything set up, she looked to the little bracelet shaped device & told it what to do.

"Play elf punk symphony of the heart playlist."

A second later, she could hear the faint sounds of an electric violin being lightly played before a symphony of Elf Punk started playing for her. Abigail then went about preparing a simple spaghetti dinner for herself while she listened to some of her favorite bands from the early 2080s & the late 2070s. How she wished that she could slip into VR & watch a performance in a virtual opera house. How she wished that she had a mission that required a partner. It would be wonderful for her to have someone that she could talk about future stuff with.

Oct 19th, 1932

It was days like this Amelia wished that she could afford a cab. The rain was coming down in sheets. Her umbrella was taking a beating as she spent an hour & a half walking to work like she did five days a week. It felt like New York was getting all of its rain for October in one downfall. More than one person on her route to work told her that if this kept up, they would need boats instead of cars to get home. The chilly weather wasn't helping either. Abigail was huddled up under her umbrella, struggling to stay warm as the icy wind blew the pouring rain.

When she saw Rodin bakery up ahead, she smiled & navigated her way there. The little bell over the door greeted her as she slipped into the warm bakery. As she breathed in the smell of fresh bread, her heart was warming faster than her body.

"Well, if it isn't my favorite new customer. One bagel fresh from the oven to start your day?"

Renee was waiting there with a bag in her hand ready to go. It was Wednesday morning & this was the third time this week that Abigail had stopped by. She knew that she wasn't supposed to become too familiar with anyone in the past. She was supposed to just keep her head down, not cause trouble & wait to light her beacon. Still, she couldn't resist Renee's smile lighting up her day each morning. That cute French accent was better than any alarm clock that Amelia had ever had.

She fished a nickel out of her pocket for her morning bagel & took the warm bag from Renee. It was fresh alright; it drove the cold right out of her fingers.

"Oh my, your hands are freezing! Is it that cold out there?"

Abigail had opened the small bag & taken a bite of the delicious warmth that was a Rodin bagel. Everything seemed to slow down as she enjoyed the delicious bagel in front of this beautiful French woman that she was certain that she was falling for.

"It's not the cold that's the problem. It the cold wind & the cold rain. I fear that I might have a thin coating of ice on my legs by the time I reach the office."

Renee shook her head.

"If the rain is so bad, then stay here for a few minutes & warm up before you head back out there."

Abigail smiled.

"As much as I would love to, I can't afford to be late for work. My boss might understand, but his boss wouldn't."

"Your Bosses boss sounds like piece of work. Very well, then I shall wish you the best of luck on your trip into work."

"Thanks Renee."

Abigail finished her bagel as more customers came in. As Renee worked to tend to them, Abigail slipped back into the pouring rain & began making her way to work.

Oct 20th, 1932

What a wretched day. Despite her training in early twentieth century gender politics, it still sucked for her when she had to sit there & pretend that she didn't mind every prick in a three-piece suit trying to convince her that he was the best of the strutting peacocks. She had lost count of how many hands had slapped her Ass & it was driving her crazy. Lunch was the worst part. Her boss had taken a prospective investor out to lunch & that investor had grabbed her, patted her, & brushed up against her so many times that she was on the verge snapping. By the time he left, Abigail was about ready to blow her cover by demonstrating eight forms of martial arts in a brutal display.

When the worst Thursday ever was finally at an end, she decided that she needed another pick me up. Normally the other secretaries would have invited her to dinner, but they could see that she was not in a mood to be around people, so they wished her a safe trip home & reminded her that she was always more than welcome to come & join them after work for a meal.

Abigail began the long march home & when she reached Rodin bakery, she went right in. When the little bell rang, Renee quickly walked in from the back where she had clearly just been near an open oven. Renee wiped a bit of sweat & a lock of her dirty blonde hair out of her eyes before seeing Abigail there.

"Well, hello again. Bad day at work?"

"One of the worst yet. I think that I might need more than a bagel tonight."

Renee called back to her father & then proceeded to chat with Abigail in between customers. After a few minutes, Maurice emerged from the kitchen with a fresh Baguette. Abigail paid for the freshly baked bread & thanked Renee & Maurice before heading home.

A while later, Abigail was walking through the lobby door when she saw Lola coming down the stairs.

"Hello, miss Oldman, another trip to the new bakery of yours I see."

"Hi Lola, yeah, A bit of warm bread felt like just the thing to brighten my day."

"I'm sure. This wouldn't have anything to do with a handsome young man working at this bakery now, would it?"

"I've already told you Lola, there's no handsome young man. The man who owns the place is twenty years older than me."

Lola looked at the baguette & thought about things for a moment as she stood on the stairs, blocking the way up.

"I suppose that without whiskey, fresh bread would be the next best thing for warming a person up. God, I haven't had a decent nip of a good whiskey since twenty-seven."

Abigail was about to ask Lola if she could pass when she stopped for a second.

"Prohibition started in 1920, right around the time that you moved here. Where did you get whiskey in 1927?"

"What are you a prohis now?"

"Enjoy your night out Lola, where are you heading anyway?"

"I'm heading out to the pictures with a few friends of mine. Enjoy your baguette miss Oldman."

Abigail watched as Lola left & then headed upstairs to make herself dinner while wondering how many of her neighbors had been misinformed by Lola into believing that she had some young suitor in the bakery.

Peter Evan Fatouros

Oct 28th, 1932

Abigail was sitting in the diner down the street from where she worked. The place smelled of grease, sausage, bacon & eggs. Abigail was playing with the fries that had come with her lunch, mindlessly thinking about all of the ingredients that this place used that would be banned over the next century & the ones that people would start using. Abigail would literally kill for either a plant-based burger or a lab grown patty. The irony of her willingness to kill for cruelty free meat was not lost on her.

"Abigail… Abigail… Abigail!"

Abigail snapped out of her trance & remembered that she was having lunch with another one of the bank's secretaries.

"Sorry Grace, I got lost in my head."

"Yeah, you do that sometimes. Where do you go when you slip away like that?"

"The future."

"Well from what I can see, the future doesn't look too good. Can't earn enough to live on my own, can't find a boyfriend rich enough to marry & we're not even allowed to drink."

"This'll all-pass Grace, you'll see. It'll get worse at first, but things will get back on track."

"Well, I'll believe that when I see it. Do you want another coffee?"

"No thanks, I've probably had more than enough today."

As grace flagged down a waitress, Abigail wondered how many times Grace had actually called her name before she snapped out of it. Maybe if Abigail were her real name, she would have woken up faster. She missed using her real name, but the names that people used in the 2080s would not work back here. Abigail wondered how long it would be until she could hear someone use her real name again.

"Future looking any better there Abigail?"

Chapter 2
Nov 10th, 1932

Abigail was sitting at her desk, typing up a report for her boss when his door opened. The young couple that had gone in half an hour earlier walked out. The man in his mid-twenties had a grim look on his face while his wife, who was clearly a few months pregnant was fighting to hold back her tears. With one hand on her shoulder, the young man turned to Mr. Parker.

"How could this have happened? How can it all be gone? We've got a kid on the way."

"I'm sorry Jeremy. I wish I could help you, but there's nothing that I can do."

The woman broke out into sobs as her & her husband walked her away. Once they were gone, Abigail followed her boss back into his office & sat opposite him at his desk.

"That looks like it was particularly horrible."

"Godawful. Her father had made some very strategic investments when she was a child. He had left it in his will that the two of them would inherit the bulk of it when their first child was born. They had been counting on it. They bought a house that they couldn't afford, a cottage that they really couldn't afford & all kinds of expensive things thinking that as soon as their baby is born, the bills would be dealt with."

"The market collapsed three years ago. Didn't they think that they should check if everything was alright?"

Mr. Parker sat back in his chair, eyeing the bottom drawer where he kept the emergency bottle of scotch.

"Nope. They figured that her father was brilliant & that this whole market thing that they had heard about wouldn't really affect them. They were stunned when I told them that all of the companies that her father had invested in had gone under & that the thousands of dollars that they had been counting on wouldn't be there."

Abigail sat there for a moment, not admitting that a small part of her no longer felt so sorry for these people who saw the market collapse around them & thought that their investments would be untouched.

"Now, miss Oldman, I'm fairly certain that you didn't just come in here to talk about my bad day. What can I do for you?"

"The reports that you gave me to type up this morning, I was wondering if you needed them all tonight?"

"Sadly, yes. I know that it's a lot of typing that will probably keep you here rather late, but I need to present them first thing tomorrow morning."

"Alright. I'll get back to work then."

"I'm sorry Abigail, I know that it's a lot, but on the bright side, we'll both be able to leave early tomorrow. Early start to the weekend."

"No need to apologize. Just leave your door unlocked so I can leave the reports on your desk."

"Of course, lock up when you're done. Can I ask, why do you never seem to mind working late? Wouldn't you rather get a bite to eat with the other secretaries?"

"The two-day weekends are worth a bit of Thursday overtime. As for the other secretaries, if I'm working this late, odds are that most of them are working a bit late as well."

"True enough. Now as much as I would prefer to spend the rest of my day in your fair company, my next appointment seems to be waiting at your desk."

///

Over the next several hours, Abigail would have killed for a camera or a document scanner. Everyone knew that she was the fastest typist in the building, but they had no idea how fast. When Mr. Parker finally went home for the night, he gave her one last report to type up & an apology to go along with it. Once Abigail was certain that nobody around her would notice how fast she could type, she went at it. By eight o'clock, she was done. She wondered how late she would have had to work if she typed normally. Fortunately, unlike the other women who only started learning how to type in high school or even later in life, Abigail had started typing on keyboards & touchscreens from early childhood.

Still, it took ages for her to work her way through the pile of paperwork to type up. When she eventually worked her way to the end of the pile, she stapled the appropriate pages together & walked into her boss's office to leave them on his desk.

Checking to make sure that nobody was around, she then searched through his files for a few key pieces of information. It was times like these that she missed having servers & search engines. Finding two potential files, she took them to her desk & started copying them. Her handler had told her that she could just write the information out, but her handwriting had always been terrible, so she continued typing away.

Eventually, when even the janitors were finishing up, Abigail put her boss's original files away & locked up his office. She then took her copied files & the ribbon from her typewriter. Slipping it all into her purse, she replaced the ribbon in her typewriter & headed home. Just another Thursday night.

Nov 12th, 1932

The blonde wig itched. She hated wearing it. Abigail didn't really feel the need to wear it, but her handler insisted. He had a point. She didn't visit him very often, but it was often enough that some of his coworkers might notice. So she wore a different wig each time that she went. Today, she was wearing a blonde wig done up in a matronly bun. Combined with a set of matronly looking glasses, it was enough to make her look quite different & a little older than she actually was.

The post office was packed. Despite the cool temperatures outside, it was sweltering inside. From some of the snippets of conversation that she was hearing, it seemed that nearly everyone hear was trying to send letters & small packages overseas to Europe for Christmas or Hanukkah or a variety of other holidays. It seemed a bit early to her, but it would take two weeks to get across the Atlantic by boat & after that, it might take anywhere from days to weeks for it to get from mail service to mail service. It would be even longer if it were going to some small village in the middle of Europe or Asia or the middle East.

After what felt like a small eternity in the intense humidity that was building up in the room, she was finally at the front of the line. The man in front of her, after taking his sweet time understanding how many stamps it would take to send his package to his small hometown in Lithuania left the front counter. Abigail walked up to the man behind the counter & smiled when she saw that it was her contact. He stood there, tall, resolute & with a touch of grey in his black hair.

"Welcome to the US postal service, how can I help you?"

"I'd like to buy a pack of 21 century stamps."

"Of course, miss."

He then handed her an envelope with a slip of paper in it. Nobody noticed that she hadn't paid for anything. She then walked away & left the post office. The woman behind her was clearly grateful that she hadn't taken to long.

Once Abigail had gotten outside & taken a second to enjoy the relief from the thick air of the post office, she opened the envelope. Inside, the slip of paper had contained an address & a time. An hour later, she walked into the building at that address, a café down the road. She ordered a cup of coffee & found a nice little table for two that was out of the way.

While she waited for her handler to show up, a man with a bit of a belly asked if he could join her & needed to be told a few times that the second seat was taken. He walked away, muttering some barely heard profanity under his breath when Alex showed up.

With his olive skin & his dark hair & his strong arms, most people mistook Alex Xenas for an Italian or Greek immigrant. In reality, his grandfather was going to be a Greek immigrant in about a hundred years. He sat down opposite Abigail & put his cup of coffee down next to hers & he put his briefcase down on the table.

"Hello Abigail, how are you doing today?"

"Homesick."

Alex chuckled.

"Yeah, I know the feeling. I've been here since the end of World War 1. What I wouldn't give to have my phone back."

Abigail smiled & reached into her purse. She pulled out a small bundle wrapped up in newspaper designed to look like a gift & handed it to Alex as he opened his briefcase.

"Seems heavy."

"I've got twenty files on paper in there & three typewriter ribbon segments that you'll have to retype. There's about another dozen files on the ribbons. Things have been getting worse every week."

"That was to be expected, the great depression is in full swing & won't reach its worst until next year."

"Think that you'll be able to recruit anyone in those files?"

"Probably not, but if they're in financial trouble, we might be able to acquire a good deal of resources & property from them. Even with what we were expecting, this is a good haul. Is anybody at work getting suspicious?"

"Nope. My boss trusts me enough to leave his office door unlocked when I tell him that I have to work late."

"How did you achieve that so quickly? You didn't have to… you know…"

"No, no. Nothing like that. He's just a good guy. If I had gotten the guy in the next office over, then I probably would have had to, but Mr. parker is a nice guy."

"That's good to know. How's your home life? Friends? Romantic partners? Neighbors?"

"My friends are good. These days, I end up going out to dinner with some of my coworkers about once a week & it's actually a little fun. I can't wait until the end of next year when we can all go out for drinks."

Alex grinned. As much money as some of their agents made in the dangerous work of bootlegging, he knew that a lot of his charges would be much happier when they could go to a bar & order a drink.

"As for my neighbors, they're alright, they don't intrude too much, except for Lola. I'd like to remind you once again that I'm living next to the gossip queen of Hell's Kitchen. Not exactly great for undercover work."

"I understand, but properties can be difficult to come across, especially for a single woman with one job. Not to mention the fact that there are always high priorities that need a place. If something that could be believably in your price range comes up, I'll see that it goes to you."

"You'd better. Sometimes I think that Lola waits at her front door so that she can be conveniently walking out as I get home."

"Good friends & nosey neighbors. Anything else that I should know about? Boyfriend, girlfriend, sex cult?"

"Nothing so fun. Although there is a girl. She works in a bakery along my new route to work."

"Anything serious?"

"Not really, I'm just sort of a customer that she knows by name."

"Do you want it to be serious?"

"Hell yes. She's like a little French angel that smells like freshly baked bread."

"Abigail, I think that you just described one of my three perfect women. Let me know if you intend to start anything with her so I can look her up, make sure that a relationship with her won't change anything."

"I know, I know. Protocol 2 avoid, unauthorized changes to the past. I remember that getting involved with a local can change things in ways that are unpredictable."

"Good to know that you paid attention to your training. So why did you need a new route to work?"

"There was construction on the one that I was taking."

"Yeah, a few of our people have had a similar situation."

Alex took a sip of his coffee before continuing.

"So, how's the beacon holding up? Any issues?"

"No problems. I ran a diagnostic on its systems last night, all green."

"That's good, life will get a lot easier for us when those are all up & running."

"I know that they're supposed to make it easier to target specific dates, but there's already a dozen of them in place, are they really that important?"

"Yes. Even with the ones in place, someone from home jumping to today could be off by as much as two weeks. When I first arrived, I got here five weeks after I was supposed to. Missed the window of opportunity for the job that I was supposed to get. There were ten beacons back then."

"Wow, how far off the mark were the first travelers?"

"That info is classified level six."

"Level six!"

They both looked around for a second to make sure that they hadn't drawn any attention to themselves.

"Yeah, level six. I heard from a friend of a friend in the tech division that the first team targeted this century & got scattered across the 14th century. That's just a rumor though. The earliest beacon that we have online is in 1890."

The two of them sipped their coffees together.

"So Abigail, anything else that I can do for you?"

"Can you get me a neural VR suite?"

"I can't even get myself one."

They both chuckled & finished their coffees before heading out separately.

Dec 16th, 1932

"One more week!"

Abigail smiled as Molly, one of the secretaries that she worked with threw her fists into the air & celebrated the second to last Friday of the working year. Tonight was going to be the last hooray for the small swarm of secretaries this year. Next week was the last week before the bank closed for the holidays. It was going to be a brutal week. The last week of the year was always bad, but with the economic downturns of the last two & a half years, it was going to be worse. It was going to be five days of foreclosures & bankruptcies just days before Christmas.

After next week, they would probably be too tired & dejected to celebrate, so they were heading out tonight. It was Friday, the five of them all got to leave on time, thanks to their bosses' good will, & they were going to have some fun. Molly's cheer was infectious, soon the five of them were cheering as they made their way to a nearby diner to grab a bite before they headed off to go dancing.

They only had to go two blocks before they found the diner that they were looking for. Once inside, they made their way to one of the large booths & crowded in. In the minute that it took for a waitress to get to them, they let the weariness from the week evaporate away. The waitress showed up & asked them what they wanted.

"The biggest plate of food on your menu!"

Grace & Abigail looked to the slightly older woman. Grace spoke while Abigail shook her head.

"Sandra, how can you eat like that before we go dancing?"

"Doesn't bother me."

"Yeah, but how are you ever going to land a husband if you keep stuffing your face like that?"

"Hey, if a man can't handle my fat arse, he sure as hell can't handle the rest of me."

The five secretaries all laughed while the waitress taking their orders smiled. A minute later, she was off with their orders & the five of them sat back in the cushioned seats of the round booth. Grace then turned to Abigail.

"Speaking of finding a husband, any luck with finding one of your own there Abigail?"

"Who? Me?"

"No, the other person here named Abigail. Yes, you. You can't tell me that there aren't any guys trying to stir something up."

Abigail laughed. Not for the first time in the last three years, she wondered how much longer she could remain single & not attract any attention.

"Nobody is stirring anything up."

"Yeah, that's the problem Abigail."

Abigail laughed with all the others while Jasmin pointed her finger at Grace.

"I don't see anyone knocking on your door on Saturday night Grace."

"Hopefully, that changes tonight."

"You think that you're going to find a husband at a dance club?"

"No, I think that I'm going to stir something up!"

Laughter broke out among them once more as their mostly small meals arrived rather quickly. They quickly ate their food & paid their bill. As nice as it was to sit down & eat, they wanted to dance. They stood outside where a young cop almost walked into a lamp post because he couldn't keep his eyes off of them.

They picked a club that a was a good way away. Sandra wasn't happy about needing to head so far when there were clubs that were much closer. Still, she understood the logic, it was closest to all of their apartments. Which would be useful when their feet were screaming from the dancing. An added benefit in Abigail's mind was that every few dances, this club would kick the men off the dance floor.

Some women liked it because they could tease the men who were standing off by the side, watching. Other women liked it because it meant that they could just dance for a few minutes without some guy trying to grind against them. Rumor had it that the cops had once raided the place thinking that it was a lesbian club. The attempted lawsuit that supposedly followed kept them from ever trying again, or so the rumor had it.

They caught a bus that was heading in that direction so that they wouldn't have to spend half an hour walking. Once inside, the music quickly called them to the dance floor.

They then proceeded to spend the next hour dancing like fiends. They danced with each other, they danced alone, they danced with men, they danced with women, they danced. Saxophones, trumpets & trombones as well as guitars & drums & men that hugged the microphone stand as if it were a woman filled the hall with music.

While the others sat at their table, Abigail & Jasmin were dancing with an incredibly happy accountant between them. Just as he was starting to drift a little too close for Abigail's comfort, the music came to an end.

"Alright folks, some of our horn players need to catch their breath & grab a smoke, so cool your feet for a moment & feel free to grab a virgin rum & coke. We'll be back in a few minutes with a song for the ladies."

Abigail started walking over to the table where most of her friends were kicking back with their own cokes. As much fun as she was having, she was starting to feel exhausted & home was a good way away. She was about to call it a night when someone tapped on her shoulder. Thinking that it was Jasmin, she turned around to see Renee standing there, flushed & breathing deeply.

"Renee? What are you doing here?"

"I was over there dancing on my own when I saw you. So I thought that I would come & say hi."

Renee's voice was a little bit raspier than normal as she had probably been dancing for a while.

"I was just dancing with a few friends from work. Care to join us for a bit Renee?"

"Sure."

Renee followed Abigail to the table & sat down as Abigail introduced her to her coworkers. They all welcomed her one by one. Once the introductions were out of the way, it was Molly who turned to Abigail.

"That guy that you & Jasmin were dancing with, did you see which way he went?"

"That way."

"Thanks. Renee, it was night to meet you, but that guy looked like I could bounce a dime off of his ass, so if I don't come back, I'm sorry to say hi & run off."

Renee laughed.

"I understand, go, before another woman finds a dime."

Renee & the others all laughed as Molly ran off after the man that filled out a pair of blue jeans quite well. The new combination of five women started talking & enjoying their drinks until the band got back on stage. Grace, Sandra & Jasmin saw no need to get up just yet, but Abigail saw a chance & decided to take it.

"Looks like the band is getting ready to go again. Up for a dance Renee?"

"Hmm, sure. Ladies, I'll be back."

Renee followed Abigail onto the dance floor & as the band came on with a song for the women, the two of them started dancing as a saxophone sounded the start of the song. As the song went on, they danced next to each other, laughing & smiling & getting close to one another. Abigail hadn't been this happy since she arrived in this decade.

When the song eventually ended & the next one began, men flowed onto the dance floor. A few of them tried to dance with Abigail or Renee, but the two of them stayed close together as they kept dancing. Renee had a bunch of chances to pair up with a handsome or cute man, instead, she stuck with Abigail through each song until the band needed to take another break.

The two of them headed back to the table where they found Jasmin sitting there, looking exhausted. As they sat down, Abigail looked around for their friends.

"Where did Grace & Sandra go?"

"They headed home half an hour ago. You two have been out there for ages, dancing away."

Renee's eyes opened wide.

"How long have we been dancing?"

"I don't know, well over an hour, that's for sure."

"Merde!"

Abigail turned to face Renee.

"What's wrong?"

"I was only supposed to stay for a few songs. My father is probably worried sick. I have to go."

"Do you need help getting home?"

"Merci, but I live three blocks away, I'll be home in no time. Take care you two."

They both wished her well as she rushed off into the night. Abigail sat down, disappointed that she wouldn't get to walk Renee back home & talk along the way.

"Abigail, do you live near here?"

"Not really, why?"

"I'm fairly sure that the last bus has come & gone by now & my place is an hour away on the bus."

"Well I'm probably about an hour from here on foot, do you want to stay at my place tonight?"

"It's not any trouble, is it?"

"Well it's not like I'm getting anything stirred up tonight."

They both laughed & walked out of the club on sore feet. Jasmin had been right; the last bus had come & gone. They then walked over to Abigail's apartment in the cool night air that was just a few degrees above freezing, huddling up when the wind blew.

Dec 17th, 1932

When Jasmin woke up, it took her a solid minute to remember whose couch she was sleeping on. If she had gone home with a guy, she would be in his bed. The smell of coffee was enough to get her mind started on remembering where she had ended up. She sat up & as her feet reminded her of how much dancing she had done the night before, Abigail walked in with two hot cups of coffee.

"Thank god. Coffee."

"Here you go Jasmin, careful, it's hot."

"Thanks, we didn't disturb your roommate when we got home, did we?"

"I don't have any roommates, it's just me here."

Jasmin looked around the apartment. It wasn't massive, just a few rooms with peeling wallpaper. Still, there was no way that she could afford such a place on her own.

"It's just you in this place. How do you afford it?"

Abigail sat down next to Jasmin & sipped her coffee in order to give herself a second to collect herself.

"We're in Hell's Kitchen, it's not exactly expensive to live here."

"Still, I don't see a single woman affording her own place that's this big, even if we're in a neighborhood for Irish immigrants. I couldn't afford a place like this unless I was willing to *earn a raise.*"

Jasmin had emphasized the last bit of her sentence to imply something indecent. Abigail laughed.

"It's not like that. Even if I were willing, Mr. Parker wouldn't do that."

"Does he not like girls? So how can you afford this place Abigail?"

"When my father passed, he left me a bit of money. Not much, but enough to help me live until I find a husband."

"Oh. I'm sorry, I forgot that you lost your parents."

"That's alright Jasmin."

"So how long can you go before it becomes an issue?"

"If the economy doesn't get to much worse, a few more years. Then I'll either need a roommate or a significant raise."

"Or a husband."

"Right, one of those could work I suppose."

Jasmin laughed before she continued drinking her coffee.

"So you said that Renee works at a bakery?"

"Yeah, it's on my way into work, so sometimes I stop in for a bagel or some bread or something."

"She seems nice. She can certainly dance, that's for sure."

"Yeah."

"Thanks again Abigail, for letting me sleep here. My place is ages away. I'd still be walking."

"No problem, Jasmin."

The two of them sat together sipping their coffee for a while until eventually Jasmin had to leave. She didn't want her roommate to worry & she still had to do her weekend chores. The two of them hugged each other goodbye & Jasmin went off to find a bus for the long ride home.

Abigail waited for half an hour before getting to work on what she had to do today. She drew the curtains closed & made sure her door was locked. She then went to her bedroom & opened her closet. Hidden among various items was what looked like a thermos. She took it out of its hiding spot, took it to the kitchen table & carefully unscrewed the cap.

The inside was lined with all kinds of circuitry. A small LED light was the only thing giving off light at the moment in order to discharge any static that built up. Inside the thermos, there was a cylinder that rose from the bottom & didn't touch the sides. The top of this cylinder had two buttons & half a dozen LED lights.

The beacon. The device that she had been sent here to activate in 1935. It would create a unique signal in the timeline that would act like a lighthouse, helping other travelers to navigate the timeline. She very carefully pressed the button marked test.

The six LEDs turned on & turned yellow. The system was booting up just enough to run a self-diagnostic, the same self-diagnostic that Abigail had run every single week since she first arrived in 1930. In a minute, the lights would change color one by one. If they all turned green, all was well. If one of them turned red, she was to get into contact with her handler immediately.

One by one, five of the lights turned green. So far, all was well. The sixth light always drove her crazy, needing twice as long as the others. It was the most nerve-racking moment of every week. Eventually it turned green & once again, Abigail breathed a sigh of relief.

Chapter 3
Feb 14th, 1933

Sally's Diner was packed tight for a Tuesday. Probably something to do with it being Valentine's Day & a greasy diner being the only thing that a lot of couples could afford. As Abigail & Jasmin sat there getting a lot of strange looks, several young men were promising their girlfriends & wives that next year, they would get to go to a proper restaurant. Abigail wished that she could tell them that while this year was the worst that it was going to be, it would be a long time before it was right again. Then they would have to contend with the second world war.

Just as she was beginning to wonder where the others were, Renee & Molly walked in & joined them. The individuals that had been eyeing the two women suspiciously turned their gazes away, satisfied that it was just a bunch of friends getting together. A group of dateless women that didn't want to be alone on Valentine's Day. Molly smiled as they sat down.

"Hi guys, sorry we're late, there was some sort of police raid downtown & we had to go around."

Jasmin perked up.

"What were they raiding?"

"Some warehouse that was stocked to the gills with Caribbean rum & Canadian whiskey."

Jasmin shook her head before continuing.

"So much for the war on alcohol, a few years ago, those bootleggers wouldn't have dared store a single bottle in Soho, now they have warehouses full of the stuff."

"Yeah well, the war might be over soon enough."

"What do you mean Molly?"

"I overheard my boss talking with a congressman, it seems that the federal government is getting sick of dealing with the effects of prohibition. They've finally realized that it hasn't reduced crime & improved society like it was supposed to."

"It took them 13 years to figure that out?"

It was now Renee's turn to shake her head before taking over the conversation.

"Don't go joking about the prohis, they raided the bakery last year."

The others all looked at her. It was Abigail who spoke up first.

"They raided the bakery?"

"Yes, they were suspicious because we weren't losing business as quickly as everyone else. Half the shops on our street went under, but we were still able to earn a very narrow profit."

"What happened?"

"They burst in, they harassed our customers & they did about three hundred dollars' worth of damage, which nearly put us out of business."

Abigail put her hand on Renee's arm while Molly put her hand on Renee's shoulder & asked the question that was on her mind.

"Did they find anything?"

"Non, we sold the last bottle that we could afford to get our hands on back in 31."

They all laughed. Eventually they got their meals & the four of them enjoyed a Valentine's Supper together. A little later, Molly had to head home since they all had to work tomorrow. A while after that, Jasmin left so that she wouldn't have to use Abigail's couch again. Once again, Abigail was getting strange looks for sitting at the table with another woman on Valentine's Day. The only difference was that this time, she was sitting with Renee. Together, they ordered desserts & coffee & chatted away for a while until the dinner started emptying out. Since they both lived in the same direction, Abigail offered to walk Renee home & was thrilled when Renee agreed.

"Oui mon cher ami."

Together, they trudged through the snow & the slush towards the bakery. Once they were certain that they were out of earshot of anyone at the diner, Abigail walked a little closer to Renee before asking the question that had been on her mind since they paid their bill.

"Did you see the look that the waitress was giving us. I know that we didn't tip much, but what the heck was that look about?"

"Well, it was probably something to do with it being just the two of us together, on Valentine's Day."

"What does that have to do with it?"

Renee almost stopped for a second as she looked at her new friend.

"Sweet, innocent, Abigail. Too women, staying late, enjoying coffee & deserts on Valentine's Day with all of the loving couples. She probably thought that we were queer."

"Oh, right. I see. I'm not so innocent by the way."

"Really? You didn't realize that they thought you were a tommy?"

"No, I didn't catch on that they thought that we were carpet munchers."

Renee laughed in the chilly wind.

"Perhaps you are not as innocent as I thought. Still, you did not see what they were thinking. It was perfectly clear after Molly & Jasmin left that everyone thought that we were a pair of folles."

"Couldn't help it, for a second, I was having so much fun that I forgot that people in this…"

Abigail damn near bit her tongue. She had almost said the words *in this time*. She would have had a hard time explaining that to Renee.

"Abigail? Are you well? You stopped talking."

"Sorry, lost my… train of thought."

"Ah, I see. Your innocent mind was imagining what they would have done if we had done something crazy."

"Crazy like what?"

"You're the one who says that she is not innocent. Imagine it for yourself."

Abigail thought for a second & saw an opportunity. She then grabbed Renee & planted a quick peck on the French girls' lips. Renee panicked & looked around to make sure that they hadn't been seen.

"Mon dieu! Are you trying to get us arrested?"

Renee kept looking around until she was satisfied that nobody had seen anything while Abigail laughed.

"Still think that I'm innocent?"

"Non, I think you are crazy."

"Does that mean that you don't want me to walk you home?"

"Non. But be more careful you little Tommy."

Abigail held her arm out & Renee slipped her arm though it so that they could walk through the slippery, wintery mess together without slipping & sliding.

Mar 21st, 1933

Sometimes, the greatest gift that a person can get is to have a boss who has no idea how long it actually takes to do a task. Once again, Abigail was staying late at work to copy files. She had actually finished all of her actual work an hour before Mr. Parker had left for the night, but that was something that he didn't need to know. Once again, he had trusted her with full access to his office & once again, she was using that trust to acquire useful information that her handler & his bosses could use. Infiltrating the past isn't easy after all.

With only a few documents to type up tonight, she was finished in no time. Looking at the clock on her boss's wall, Abigail congratulated herself on having finished so quickly. She put her boss's files away & locked up his office before making her way towards the main entrance. It was early enough that the evening security guard was probably still at his post.

Turning around a corner on her way to the stairs, she saw that there was a light coming from an open office door. Not the first time that this has happened. It's a bank in the worst part of the great depression. Damn near everyone works insane hours from time to time. Most of her coworkers had seen her leaving far later than this without raising any suspicion. She simply walked calmly down the hall, planning on waving & saying goodnight to whoever was in their office.

It looked like Mr. Halls office. One of the older bankers, practically an institution himself. Abigail recalled the stories about how he's been in that office since Victoria was still Queen. Abigail wasn't too fond of Mr. Halls. He was usually polite enough, at least with his words. His hands seemed to get around a bit. Abigail was planning on ignoring him unless he called out to say something along the lines of are you still here. That was the plan, until she got close to his door & heard something.

It sounded like someone had shoved a desk. Not wanting to get involved if he was upset, she kept walking, her feet barely making a sound as she approached his open door. When she was about to walk in front of the door, that was when she heard the grunting. It took her a second to recognize the sounds of a man grunting & flesh slapping against flesh. She closed her eyes & hoped that he wasn't rubbing one out in there. He wouldn't be the first guy to get in trouble for that. Then she heard another voice. It was small & quick. Somewhere between a gasp & cry. It certainly didn't belong to Mr. Hall.

Approaching the door more closely, Abigail could clearly hear the sound of two people rutting. Thinking that it was probably against her better judgement, she braced herself & peeked into the open door.

There was Bess, Mr. Hall's secretary, without a single stitch of clothing on her. She was bent over her desk with an impatient look on her face. Her perky Breasts with their little pink Nipples were bouncing as behind her, Mr. Hall was pumping his hips forward & back.

Abigail was shocked. Judging by the look on Bess's face, she was not enjoying herself. Not hard to imagine, Mr. Hall wasn't ugly, but it had been a good long time since he had been what women would want bending them over a desk.

As Abigail watched, she saw that Mr. Hall was completely fixated on Bess's Ass. Her wide Ass had always been the target of pinches & gropes in the office, but now it was bare, bouncing, & in Mr. Hall's grasp as he kneaded the rounded flesh. After a moment of watching this, Bess looked up through her mop of blonde hair & saw Abigail standing there.

Mr. Hall was too enraptured by Bess's rear to notice that they weren't alone. Abigail reached into her bag & grabbed the first thing that her hand found that was tougher than paper. Pulling it out, she saw that she had grabbed a whistle. Abigail wished that it were a stunner, or an emergency beacon, or even just a can of good old-fashioned pepper spray. Still, if she blew her whistle, the security guards would come running to see why someone was blowing a whistle in the bank at this late hour.

She put the whistle to her lips & was about to let loose an ear-splitting screech when Bess shook her head. Abigail drew in a large breath, but Bess shook her head again. It seemed clear that Bess didn't want Abigail to get involved. Abigail watched as the naked girl simply endured this man's lust. Bess pointed to Abigail & then pointed to her side, indicating that Abigail should leave.

Abigail drew in another breath when Bess put her finger to her lips, silently shushing Abigail & again, indicating that she should leave. Mr. Hall started grunting more loudly. He screwed his eyes shut & pulled Bess into a standing position as he cried out in climax.

As Bess stood there, nude & on full display in front of Abigail, she jerked her thumb in the direction of the stairs in a gesture that clearly meant one thing. Scram. Abigail left, putting the whistle back in her handbag & getting out of sight before Mr. Hall finally realized that he had been seen.

Not sure what was going on, Abigail hoped that it had been something… consensual as she said goodnight to the guard at the door & headed home. She barely slept a wink that night.

///

The next day, Abigail came into work, not knowing what to expect. She said hello to Molly & Jasmin as she passed them by in the hallways. When she walked past Mr. Hall's office, she saw Bess, at her desk, typing something up as if nothing were wrong. Seeing that the door to Mr. Hall's office was closed, Abigail walked in & walked up to Bess. All that she could see was Bess naked from last night, standing there on full display with Mr. Hall's hands on her.

"Hello Abigail, what can I do for you?"

Abigail managed to find some words.

"Hi… Bess… Listen… about… late last night…"

"Did something happen here? I left early yesterday."

She was pretending it hadn't happened. Was she scared? Embarrassed? Humiliated? Was she actually into letting old men strip her down & bend her over the table? Abigail understood that everyone had their own kinks, but Bess hadn't looked like she was getting off. Still, what could Abigail do? Technically, she shouldn't get involved, it would be a violation of her operational protocols. Something that she had completely forgotten last night.

"Nothing Bess, my mistake I guess."

Abigail turned around to head to her desk when Bess interrupted her.

"Abigail?"

"Yes Bess?"

"You want to… get lunch together later? There's a café down the street. Some company might be… nice…"

"Sure Bess."

///

A few hours later, Abigail walked into the café & ordered a pair of sandwiches & some coffees. She had just sat down at a little table for two in the corner when Bess walked in & made her way over.

"Thanks for meeting me, Abigail. I didn't want to talk at work."

"I get it Bess. I wouldn't want to be overheard talking about something like that either. Speaking of that, what the hell was that? Are you alright?"

"I'm alright. He wasn't forcing himself on me. Not really anyway."

"Not really?"

"It's complicated Abigail."

"Trust me Bess, I can handle complicated. What I can't handle is not knowing if one of my friends is being… violated. Please, tell me what's going on."

Bess took a sip of her coffee before taking a deep breath, preparing to bare her soul like never before.

"I guess that it all started about four months ago."

"He's been doing this to you for four months?"

"No, that's more recent. For the last few years, my mother has been getting… forgetful. It was small things at first, forgetting her keys, forgetting why she walked into a room. Then it got worse. She would go to work & get lost. She would put on something to boil or to cook & completely forget about it."

Abigail cringed silently. She recognized the symptoms. Back home, everyone knew about Alzheimer's disease. But back here, there would have been next to no help. Abigail kept quiet & let Bess continue.

"About four months ago, it got so bad that my sister & I had to make a choice. We could either take her to an asylum, or one of us would have to take care of her. We've heard about what happens to women in asylums & long-term hospitals. Even if we could afford a private hospital, we couldn't do that to her. Since my sister wasn't having any luck finding work, she moved back in with Mom & started taking care of her. Now I have to support the three of us. After a few weeks, I moved back in with Mom & my sister as well, that way I could save on the cost of rent."

Bess took a minute to take a small bite out of her sandwich.

"That sounds hard Bess, but I still don't see how that translates into you letting Mr. Hall… you know…"

"Bend me over my own desk like a two-penny whore. I'm getting to that."

Bess took a deep breath before continuing while Abigail sat there stunned.

"Even having moved in with my family, I'm still barely getting by. It doesn't help that I rarely get to sleep through the night since Mom wakes up & forgets where she is. Between work, money, Mom & not being able to always sleep through the night, it's been hard to focus on my job. About two months ago, I started making mistakes. Big mistakes. The kind of mistakes that can result in becoming unemployed."

Abigail knew how hard it was to hold down a job in this decade. There were thousands of people living in tents in Central Park, there were hundreds of thousands that needed a job. There was no such thing as job security. Everyone was expendable. Bess continued.

"After about a week of putting up with my constant mistakes, Mr. Hall got mad when I accidentally mailed an internal expense report to one of his clients & gave him the client's monthly statement for the board meeting that he was supposed to present at."

"Crap. I remember that day, he came downstairs fuming."

"Yeah, I got an earful. He told me to pack my shit & get out. That's when I begged him for a second chance. I told him that I needed this job to support my family & then I said something very stupid."

"What did you say?"

"I said that I would do anything."

It suddenly clicked for Abigail. Bess was letting Mr. Hall use her for his own pleasure in exchange for keeping her job.

"That was when he told me to meet him at his desk after hours. He closed the door behind him, made me take my clothes off &…"

Bess started tearing up. Abigail pulled out a handkerchief so that Bess wouldn't turn into a blubbering mess.

"I was just trying to take care of my mom. Now I'm a… I'm a… I'm a… a…"

Abigail put her hand on Bess' arm. Bess didn't need to finish her sentence. Abigail wanted to throw her arms around Bess & tell her that it would all be okay. She wanted to sit there with her friend & figure out a way that Bess could get out of this situation. But she couldn't. She had rules to follow. Protocols.

Abigail remembered sitting in classrooms, both real & in virtual reality, where her teachers made her memorize the protocols of working in the past until she could recite them backwards in her sleep. She remembered protocol 4. Do NOT get involved in civil, political, social, or domestic issues unless ordered to. Getting involved could mean altering history in unpredictable ways which would violate protocol two. It would draw unwanted attention onto her, which would put her identity at risk, which would be a violation of protocol three. Most importantly, it would distract her from the mission, which would be a violation of protocol one, the mission comes first.

Still, as Bess silently sobbed next to her, she had to do or say something. Anything. She couldn't just let this sweet girl go through this alone.

"Listen Bess, I know a guy, he's good at finding jobs for people. He got me the job at the bank. I can't promise anything, but next time I see him in a few weeks, I could ask if he has anything for you."

Bess' eyes lit up.

"Do you think that he can get me out of this?"

"I don't know, I don't want to risk getting your hopes up for nothing, but I'll see what he can do."

Bess turned around & hugged Abigail. Abigail hoped that she hadn't just gotten herself into all kinds of trouble on her first mission.

Mar 30th, 1939

The next week had not been easy for Abigail. The knowledge of what one of her friends was doing in order to keep her job was like a constant reminder of how different this world was from home. Abigail didn't know how Bess could keep coming into work with a smile on her face. Nor did she know how she had spent so many weeks not noticing how strained that smile was on some days. Abigail made it a point to take Bess out to lunch more often. She also tried to think about how she was going to ask Alex for help in this matter.

The experience of not being able to immediately help Bess had Abigail missing life back home. While Abigail was going through her normal Saturday routines, her mind just kept drifting. She thought about how back home, there would have been a treatment for Bess's mother & it wouldn't have cost her a thing. She imagined what would happen if a man tried to take advantage of Bess's situation & she arrived at the conclusion that the man would end up in jail.

While Abigail was buying some groceries, she remembered the words of her instructors echoing in her mind again. Sitting at a desk in a virtual reality simulation, nothing around her but white nothingness as she took notes while her professor stood in front of a chalk board. She remembered the man's tall avatar with the young face & the old eyes.

"Abigail, the next few simulations that you will be going through over the next few days are designed to familiarize you with protocol 4. You've heard the protocol before a hundred times by now, so you know what it basically means."

"Don't get involved."

"Exactly. This is going to be one of the hardest things that you'll have to deal with if it comes up. You'll want to try to change society, wake them up to how barbaric they are. You'll want to help people out of troubling situations. You'll want to help people with their problems. But you can't. We need to maintain low profiles & we need to avoid making too many changes until we have enough beacons to come & go with ease."

Some of the simulations that they had put her through had been rough, but this was going to be far harder. This arrangement that Bess was in could go on for years. Abigail would need to spend at least the next few years going to work while knowing what was going on & not getting involved. Except that, she was involved.

When she got home with her fresh groceries, she put them away & then waited a little while before performing the Beacon diagnostic. She missed her quad. The candidates in the training program weren't supposed to fraternize, but all of the higher ups usually turned a blind eye, as long as it didn't affect your training. In the middle of her training, Abigail had been invited into a throuple consisting of two women & a man who were all going through the training program. Together, they became a quad that held together through the rest of the training program.

Now the four of them were all on missions, scattered across the 20th century & around the world. Thoughts of her quad soon led her to thoughts of Renee. Even if it were safe to get into a relationship with Renee, & even if Renee were interested in women, Abigail had no idea how she would go about finding out if Renee were interested in her.

Abigail's train of thought then went all over the place. Eventually she shook the thoughts of the moment from her mind & focused on performing the Beacon diagnostic.

Chapter 4
Apr 9th, 1933

The blasted curls from the red wig that Abigail was wearing was driving her crazy. The one that kept hanging in front of her eye was driving her particularly crazy. No matter how many times she brushed it back, there it was, sitting right in front of her eye. If she could get her hands on a pair of scissors, she would have cut the damn curl off by this point.

Telling herself to try & ignore it, she took a deep breath as Alex walked into the café. Her handler looked exhausted. He sat down across from her & unceremoniously dropped his briefcase down on the table between them. She could see the bags under his eyes.

"You alright Alex? You look like crap."

"Good to see you too Abigail. My neighbors just had their first kid a few weeks ago. Apparently, he's destined to be a soccer announcer."

"Ah, I see. So other than that, how are things going?"

"Can't complain too much. Work is exhausting, but it keeps me out of trouble. Speaking of work?"

Abigail opened her purse & handed over a thick envelope that was crammed full of paperwork. He took it, felt the weight of it & slipped it into his briefcase.

"I hope that you didn't have any trouble acquiring this."

"No trouble."

"Now that that's out of the way, how are you doing Abigail? You still interested in that girl? The French baker if I remember right."

"Very much so."

"Does this girl have a name?"

"Renee. Renee Rodin."

Alex smiled a bit.

"Renee Rodin. I love it when a person's names start with the same letter. I'll look into her, see if interacting with her will be any problem."

"Thanks Alex."

"So how's work going? Still hanging out with your friends?"

"Yeah… uhm… I've been meaning to ask you a question about one of my work friends."

"Okay, this sounds serious. What's up?"

"One of my friends, Bess, is in a bit of a situation & I was wondering… if there was… anyway that we could… help… her… out…"

Alex looked at Abigail suspiciously.

"Help her how, exactly?"

"By maybe getting her a new job?"

Alex's eyes widened.

"I don't think that I quite heard you right. You want me to find your friend a job."

"I wanted to know if it was an option."

"No. It isn't. You should know this. Aside from the minimal changes that our mere presence demands, we can't change anything."

"I know Alex, I know."

"If you know, then why are you asking about this?"

"It's just, when I found out what was happening to her, we talked about it &… I could hear my instructors in my head reminding me about protocol 4. Don't get involved, but… I…"

Alex suddenly took on a look of sympathy for the woman in front of him. He reached out & put his hand on hers.

"I get it. It's hard to develop social connections & not get involved. Honestly, protocol 4 is the one that gives us the most trouble. The need to help them, to save them from what they're enduring. I get it, but we can't help her. Our job is to light the beacons & to gather intel."

Abigail slumped in her chair. She had known that it was a long shot, but she had hoped that there was a chance that he would say yes.

"Look, Abigail, since all that you did was to ask me if there were any options, I won't report this, but I need to know that you can hold it together until your beacon is lit."

Abigail looked up at her handler & took a deep breath.

"I can do it. It's just another two years. I can manage."

"Well if you can't, let me know, I can relocate you without too much trouble if it's affecting your mission."

"I can handle it. I just don't know how I'll tell her that I couldn't help her in the end."

May 20th, 1933

Abigail walked into the apartment building with two large bags full of groceries. Carefully balancing as she climbed the stairs, she put her bags down & began fumbling in her purse for her key. As she kindly remembered life back home where her groceries would be delivered by a cute little drone & her apartment door would open automatically for her, she heard the door behind her open as Lola appeared.

"Oh, Abigail, fancy meeting you here."

Abigail was glad that Lola couldn't see her eyes rolling. Instead, she turned around with her best fake smile.

"It's good to see you, Lola. What's happening?"

"Oh not much. I just thought that I would go for a walk. Are you expecting company?"

"No, why?"

"Oh, well, it's just that you have a lot of groceries there. I know that that many eggs would have cost you quite a bit."

"Oh, no. I got them cheap because they were mislabeled. The man at the market thought that they were about to spoil."

"Ah. Still, it can't be easy affording so much food when you're paying rent on your own. Have you thought about getting a roommate?"

Just as Abigail had suspected. Lola was on another fishing expedition, looking for any good gossip. Abigail wondered if Lola knew how bloody obvious it was.

"No, Lola, no roommate in my near future."

Lola screwed up her face a bit.

"Sometimes, I wonder how a young girl like you makes rent & puts food onto her table. Most of the apartments in this building have three or four tenets paying their way."

Abigail wished that it could be socially acceptable to just back out of an awkward conversation. It would be so much easier than dealing with a nosy neighbor while she was trying to conduct clandestine missions.

"Oh, I just scrimp & save wherever I can. A penny saved is a penny earned after all."

Lola eyed the groceries as if they were a testament to Abigail lying.

"I know Lola, looks like a lot, but half of it will spoil by this time tomorrow."

"Going to be baking & preserving a few things then."

"Yeah, something like that. Anyway, Lola, I have to get some of this in the icebox."

"Oh, yes, of course, I won't take up more of your time, I'm just going to go check my mail."

"I thought that you said that you were going for a walk?"

"Yes, I'm going to walk to my mailbox. Take care Abigail."

"You too Lola."

Abigail opened her door & headed inside, grateful that Lola hadn't found some excuse to look into her bags. Abigail then quickly put her fresh groceries away & began the process of turning some of her new fruits & berries into preserves & pies in case Lola came sniffing around. At least it gave her something to do for the rest of the day.

///

Over the next few days, Abigail kept running into Lola a lot. She always ran into the snooping woman at least once or twice a week, but now it was more like once or twice a day.

On Sunday, Lola asked about the preserves. On Monday, Lola was walking out her door just as Abigail was leaving for work & coming home. On Tuesday, Lola just so happened to be getting her mail at the same time the Abigail was coming home & checking her mail. On Wednesday, Abigail actually caught Lola with her ear to Abigail's door. That was it. On Thursday, Abigail was able to get her boss to let her leave early. She then headed down to the post office after work. With some luck & some patience, she made it to the counter where Alex was working & she gave him the code which meant that she needed to talk to him tonight.

A few hours later, Abigail was sitting on a bench in a park. She had been sitting there for so long that the sun had set & she was worried that she might be arrested by the police as a prostitute looking for clients in the park when Alex walked up to the bench & sat beside her.

"Where the hell have you been Alex? You're shift ended three hours ago."

"Sorry Abigail, you're not my only agent that's having issues this week. What's the problem?"

Abigail took a second to calm herself down. Sometimes she forgot that Alex had several agents, maybe dozens that he watched over. That could be exhausting.

"Do you remember my nosey neighbor?"

"Yeah, uh, Lulu or Lily or Lilah…"

"Lola. She's becoming a problem."

"How much of a problem Abigail?"

"She's suspicious about my money situation. She started asking how I can afford that apartment on my own & I guess that my answer didn't satisfy her. She's been snooping around me like crazy. I run into her at least twice a day & yesterday, I caught her with her ear against my door. At this point, I wouldn't be surprised if she were rummaging through my trash."

"That does sound like a problem."

"One that could easily be solved by a change of address or a partner."

"We've been through this Abigail. Your mission doesn't require a partner. As for a change of address, I have no locations that I could stick a single working woman in right now."

"Well then, there's only one option, I have to kill Lola."

"Before you violate protocol 2 by killing her & potentially changing the future, maybe we could try something less desperate Abigail."

"Like what."

Alex leaned back & looked up at the stars as he thought about it.

"You said that she has no idea how you can afford to live?"

"That's right."

"Okay Abigail, here's what we'll do. Tomorrow, I'll mail you a fake cheque from your… What does Lola know about your backstory?"

"She knows that Abigail Oldman came to this country from a small town just North of London. That's it."

"Okay, so tomorrow, I'll mail you a fake cheque from Abigail Oldman's brother. Doctor… I'll make up a name in the morning Oldman. You let Lola *accidentally* see the cheque & tell her that your remarkably successful doctor helps his family out by sending everyone a few pounds a month."

"What kind of doctor is he?"

"Nothing specific, a general practitioner."

"Alright, thank you Alex."

"That's what I'm here for."

///

The next day, as she was getting home, Abigail went to her mailbox & sure enough, there was the check. She opened the envelope & read the check & sure enough, it legitimately looked like a check from her newly invented brother. She stood at the mailbox for a few minutes to lure Lola out & sure enough, out she came, like a cautious cat.

"Oh, hello there Abigail."

Abigail pretended to jump in surprise & dropped the check. She then pretended not to notice that the check had fallen to the ground.

"Lola, you scared me."

"Sorry Abigail, I believe that you dropped something."

"Did I?"

Abigail was thumbing through a few other fake bits of mail that Alex had been smart enough to include.

"Yes, here."

Lola bent over, picked up the envelope & saw the check.

"Gary Oldman? You're father?"

"What? Oh, how did that… Sorry, can I…"

Lola gave the check back to Abigail.

"Sorry Lola, Gary is my older brother. He's a family doctor in London. Ever since the market crash, he's been sending the rest of the family a few pounds every month to help out."

"Ahh. I see."

Abigail could see the little grin that was spreading on Lola's face. It was only there for a moment, but it said everything. The gossip queen of Hell's Kitchen was satisfied & Abigail could go back to flying under the radar.

Jun 16th, 1933

A long day at the end of another long week had not left Abigail disheartened. It was Friday afternoon & like many people who were fortunate enough to only have a five-day work week, Abigail was looking forward to the weekend. A weekend that was starting with taking Renee out to supper. Sure, it was just as friends, & it was just at a greasy diner, but it was supper.

Abigail wished that it could be a proper date, so that at the end of the evening, she could kiss Renee good night. It was just a few days ago that Alex's research had come back with a confirmation that getting into a relationship with Renee wouldn't screw anything up. According to his research, she never marries, never has kids & after her father died, she apparently went home to France to live with some relative. There were no records of her after World War two.

Highly confident that a relationship with her wouldn't disrupt history to any great extent, Alex gave her the green light. Still, she couldn't actually ask Renee out on a date. Everything would have to be as friends. Abigail had stopped by the bakery a day ago & asked Renee if she would like to get something to eat tonight, just the two of them. After asking her father if he could manage the store on his own, he waved her off & told her that she needed to get out more.

So tonight, they were having supper. As friends. Abigail wondered if Renee's lips tasted like freshly baked bread. Abigail was walking towards the diner as fast as she could, resisting the urge to break out into a run. She got to the diner just in time to see Renee walking up. Abigail's jaw almost dropped.

Renee was walking up to the diner dressed in a dark teal jumpsuit. The suit hugged her slim waist while draping her legs in the billowing teal fabric. The half sleeves showed off Renee's slender arms & the gathered bust drew just enough attention to Renee's chest for it to be noticed without showing off. Abigail wasn't the only one who noticed Renee walking down the street.

Abigail saw that broad, teal belt & wished that she could unfasten it as Renee walked up to her.

"Wow… Renee… just… wow."

"Do you like it? I was worried that it would be a bit much for eating at a diner, but everyone is wearing jumpsuits, so I thought that it might be alright."

"It's great. You look stunning."

"Thank you, I can't even remember the last time I wore it. Shall we head inside?"

It took a second for Abigail to remember that she was standing outside on the sidewalk. A gentle breeze was causing the vast fabric around Renee's legs to billow & it had caught Abigail off-guard.

"Yeah, sure, let's head inside."

They headed in together & they managed to find a table that wasn't being occupied by another bunch of friends that were kicking back after a long week. They both ordered their meals & as the exhausted waitress left, Renee turned to Abigail.

"So, how was your day?"

"Up until now, it wasn't so great."

"What happened?"

Abigail smiled; it was nice having someone to talk to about her everyday issues. Someone who was concerned.

"Not much, just another week of people losing their homes & everything that they've ever had. It's hard working in a bank, knowing that a large part of your job, or your boss's job is telling people that there's nothing left for them to do but to take up a place in Hooverville."

Renee cringed a bit when she heard mention of the shanty town in central park. Nobody wanted to end up in those slums.

"That's awful, Abigail. I don't think that I could work at a bank."

"It's challenging, but it's over for a few days, for me at least. Tell me about your day. I didn't drag you out here just to depress you."

Renee smiled. She then began recounting the events of her last few days. From baking wedding cakes to chasing out a guy that tried to pocket some day-old rolls. Abigail listened intently to every word. When their food arrived, they dug into it. They then had a cup of coffee before leaving to take a stroll in the evening. Their conversation continued with Abigail stealing the occasional glance as Renee talked.

"Did you hear about the raid in Queens?"

Abigail looked up, drawing her eyes away from Renee's slender fingers.

"What raid in Queens?"

"Mon Dieu. It is in all of the papers. The prohis raided a warehouse in Queens, but the people inside all had military machine guns."

Abigail almost stopped in her tracks. It was usual for local era gangsters to have a Thomson submachine gun or two, but actual military style machine guns, that sounded like something more future related to her. Even still, her people would only use weaponry like that around a major base of operations.

"Did the papers say what happened?"

"Apparently, the prohis weren't ready for something like that."

"Jesus, Renee, what happened?"

"According to the papers, the prohis retreated for a minute to regroup & figure out how to go about dealing with the bootleggers when a fire started."

"A fire?"

"Oui, a roaring blaze started that consumed the entire warehouse before the firefighters could get there."

That settled it in Abigail's mind, that sounded like standard operating procedure for a compromised outpost. Keep the enemy out, & then burn it to the ground so that they can't discover anything. It couldn't have been a primary base, otherwise she would have gotten an alert within the hour. It had to be something less vital.

"That sounds incredible Renee."

"Yes, fortunately, nobody was hurt."

For the next little while, it was difficult for Abigail to concentrate on what was going on in the conversation as she wondered if she was going to be getting a coded message soon telling her about what's happening. After a little while, she was able to put it out of her mind & focus on her conversation with Renee.

A long while later, they were walking up to the bakery where a closed sign was hanging in the window. There was a single candle lit in one of the windows where Renee's father was probably relaxing after a long day in front of the ovens.

"Thank you, Abigail. It is not often that I go out. I enjoyed out little walk tonight."

"I had fun too Renee."

Renee then turned around & planted a quick kiss on Abigail's cheek. Abigail wished that she could have turned her head & tasted Renee's lips. Judging by last time however, Renee would freak out again, so she simply enjoyed feeling Renee's cheek press against hers.

"Goodnight, Abigail. I hope that you don't have to wait long for your bus."

"Goodnight, Renee, I'm sure that it won't be long."

The two women parted ways & Abigail made her slow way home on the bus. The whole way home, Abigail was in her own little world in her head where Renee had come home with her & they were now in the middle of slipping their hands under each other's clothes.

As Abigail got off of the bus, she tried to shake these thoughts from her head. Renee was a friend & there was no indication that that would be changing anytime soon.

When Abigail got to the lobby of her apartment, she checked her mail & found exactly one thing waiting for her. A postcard from London showing an image of the tower bridge. It was marked as being from her brother, who didn't exist, meaning that it was a coded message. She took it into her apartment, lit a lamp & quickly decoded the message.

SECONDARY EVAC SITE NY-Q COMPROMISED. PRIMARY EVAC SITE STILL GREEN. IF UNABLE TO REACH PRIMARY SITE, DIVERT TO SECONDARY SITE NY-B.

That settled it, the secondary outpost in Queens was lost & if anything went wrong, her new secondary evac site was the location in the Bronx. Abigail double checked her decoding to make sure that she hadn't made a mistake. Once confirmed, she shredded the postcard & burned the pieces in her kitchen sink.

Jul 5th, 1933

Abigail walked into the bathroom at work with a throbbing headache. Memories of celebrating the 4th of July with some of her friends came back to her with a fresh throbbing of pain that was radiating from the left side of her head & pounding on the right side like a drum. The bathroom was the only quiet place in the building, so she had retreated there to let the aspirins that she had just taken have the time that they needed to take effect.

It took her a moment to notice the sound & the smell of someone throwing up in one of the stalls. She turned to face the stall a little too quickly & felt a fresh stab of pain in her temple.

"Are you alright in there?"

In between heaves, Bess answered.

"No, I'm not."

"Did you party last night as well or are you sick?"

"I'm sick, sort of."

"Sort of? Bess, is something wrong?"

"Yes, oh… … can we talk later… at lunch…"

"Sure Bess, can I get you anything?"

"No… Thanks…"

Abigail then returned to her desk, hoping that Bess was going to be alright.

An hour later, Abigail was walking into the nearby café to get lunch with Bess. Over the last few months, the two of them had gotten together here once or twice a week to talk. Bess was already seated & had ordered their usuals for them. Despite the state she had been in an hour ago, she was now acting as if she were ravenous, constantly looking to the kitchen for their order. Abigail sat down across from her.

"Are you alright Bess? This morning you were rejecting breakfast, now you look like you could eat a horse."

"I'm not doing to good Abigail."

"What's wrong?"

Bess took a deep breath to calm herself.

"I'm… pregnant."

Abigail almost reflexively said congratulations. Fortunately, she realized who the father must be before she said anything. She stayed quiet while their food arrived before continuing with the only thing that she could think to say.

"Are you sure?"

"Yeah, I'm sure. I'm about two months late & the small bump that's starting to show is undeniable."

Abigail suddenly realized that despite it being July, Bess had started wearing bulkier clothes. She looked at Bess who was eyeing her sandwich & asked the question with the obvious answer.

"I assume that it's… his…"

"Yeah, Mr. Hall. I wouldn't think that a man his age was up to the task. Guess I was wrong."

They both then took a tentative bite of their sandwiches before Abigail worked up the nerve to ask the question that didn't have an obvious answer.

"So… what are you going to do?"

"I don't know Abigail. I can't exactly afford to support it on my own & I don't think that Mr. Hall will like the idea of me giving it away. Sure, he'll never acknowledge it, but how likely am I to keep my job if I leave his kid in an orphanage?"

Bess took another bite before continuing.

"I figure that my only real option is to ask him to help support me, which means that I'll either have to keep earning my job here or become his kept mistress. Maybe I'll get lucky & he'll just pay me to stay home & raise the kid."

"Is that what you want?"

"It's the best that I can hope for Abigail."

"I get that Bess, but what would you like to do if you could?"

Bess needed a minute to think about it.

"If I could, I'd quit this job, not tell him about the baby, then in a few months, after I had it, I'd get a job somewhere else where I could make enough money to support my family."

"What would you need for that?"

"Are you kidding Abigail? I'd need a few thousand dollars to support my family while I gave birth & then got a job. I don't suppose that you have that kind of money just lying around?"

"Can't say that I do?"

Abigail really couldn't say that she could get her hands on that kind of money. She had access to an emergency fund, but that was only supposed to be for mission purposes. Helping Bess was not part of her mission & would violate protocol 4. Bess looked down at her sandwich.

"I guess that my only real option is to tell Mr. Hall. I should probably do it in the next few days before he notices. I think that I'll tell him on Friday, he always works late on Fridays, probably why he doesn't have any kids with his wife."

///

That night, Abigail couldn't sleep. All that she had to do was go to the bank down the road where she didn't work & cash one of the blank cheques that Alex had given her. The account had all of the paperwork & permissions on file for a woman to be able to withdraw large sums of money without Alex being there. The only problem was that he would be notified within a few hours & he would immediately want to know why Abigail had accessed thousands of dollars from the emergency account.

She tossed & turned all night; her mind & dreams were plagued by nightmares of all the things that could go horribly wrong when a mistress tells the married man that she's pregnant. Finally, at two in the morning, she swore that she would get Bess the money & finally, she could sleep.

///

The bills sat heavy in her purse. Alex had probably already been informed & was sending out coded phone calls & letters to have other agents find out what was happening with Abigail. A beacon deployer accessing half of her emergency funds out of the blue, Alex's boss probably already knew about it. Hell, his boss probably already knew. As she was walking past Bess's desk, she asked Bess to meet her in the bathroom in twenty minutes with her purse. Bess looked at her confused but nodded her head in agreement.

When Bess arrived in the bathroom, Abigail did a quick check to make sure that they were alone, which had Bess even more confused.

"Abigail, what is going on?"

Abigail then locked the door.

"I didn't want anyone to disturb us when I gave you this."

Abigail then opened her purse & produced the money that she had withdrawn from the bank.

"Christ! Abigail, did you rob a bank or something? How much is here?"

"Five thousand dollars."

"Five thousand dollars! Where the hell did you get this?"

"It doesn't matter, look, take the money, put it into your purse, walk into Mr. Hall's office & tell him that you're quitting, effective immediately."

Bess was stunned.

"Abigail… I… I can't take this…"

"Look, I can't explain it Bess & if anyone asks, you didn't get it from me. Tell them an uncle died & left it to you or something. Just take the money, quit this job & next year, after the baby is born, get a job as a waitress or something. You can do it."

"But… where did you get five thousand dollars?"

"I told you; I can't tell you that."

"Are you going to be in trouble?"

"Don't worry Bess, it's all good. The money is yours."

Bess looked at the money. It was freedom & security being handed to her. Before she realized it, she was shoveling it into her purse.

"What do I tell my family?"

"Tell them that you got pregnant by your boss & this is him paying you off to keep quiet, so that his wife doesn't find out."

"Abigail… how… how can I ever thank you?"

"By being frugal with it, this is a one-time thing, I won't be able to do this again without getting into serious trouble."

"Are you in trouble now?"

"I imagine that a stern talking to is in my immediate future. Don't worry, I'll be fine. I promise. Now go & quit."

Bess threw her arms around Abigail & hugged her tight. Words couldn't describe how happy she was. She then unlocked the bathroom door & marched off to tell her boss that she was done here.

About half an hour later, a man in a crisp grey suit walked up to Abigail's desk with an envelope & a folded piece of paper in his hand. Abigail just knew that he was another agent from the future that Alex had sent to check on her workplace.

"Ms. Oldman, I have a registered letter here for you, I'll be needing your signature."

Abigail took the piece of paper & signed it A. Oldman, her alias, indicating that all was well. Inside the envelope was a coded message from Alex telling her to call him on the delta number if everything was alright & the omega number if it wasn't.

She took a deep breath & picked up the phone on her desk.

Nov 25th, 1933

Abigail had been on probation for 142 days. She supposed that she should count herself lucky to still be on the mission at all. Probably her only saving grace had been that changing Bess's fate didn't seem to be too big of a deal. The people back home who were going over these things said that it would make no real difference. Still, she was on probation, & on thin ice.

She had to check in with her handler every single week instead of once a month. On top of that, her music player had been locked remotely & her application for a VR implant had been rejected. As if all of that weren't enough, if she broke one more protocol before December 6th, she would be taken off of the mission & sent to a tertiary safe house somewhere in the country where she would have to wait out the centuries until she got home & could be relieved.

Abigail missed her music player. She was a century away from elf punk bands & she was tired of needing to go to a club to hear some music. Still, today would be better than most of her recent days.

As people crowded into the theater, she stood at the entrance waiting for Renee. When Renee finally showed up, she was bundled up in a cute little brown coat against the November chill. Abigail wrapped her arms around her friend, wishing that she could let her hands wander over Renee's body.

"I'm not late, am I?"

"No Renee, the movie is still a few minutes away from starting."

"Thank goodness. I wanted to see this movie ever since I heard that it was coming out. You know that the novel was written by H. G. Wells?"

Abigail looked at Renee for a second with a surprised expression.

"I didn't realize that you read science fiction."

"Oui, when I was a girl, I read my father's copy of De la Terre à la Lune."

Abigail just looked at Renee for a moment.

"Oh, ah, in English, it would be… From the Earth to the Moon. It was written by Jules Verne. Ever since then, I've liked reading science fiction."

"Have you ever read the Time Machine?"

"Of course, it is one of my favorites."

The Time Machine was one of her favorite books. Abigail was almost convinced to take it as a sign from the universe that Renee was her Weena. Of course, she was also thinking about the 2048 movie where the time traveler & Weena fall madly in love. Still, it was almost like the universe was teasing her. The two of them then walked up to the ticket booth & ordered two tickets to see the Invisible Man.

Throughout the movie, Abigail was repeatedly surprised by the quality of the image & the special effects. They weren't anything like what she was used to seeing back home, but having seen some older movies before she left, she was expecting to see something blurry & cheap.

While she had been admiring the quality of the movie & laughing at the old woman that screamed like a banshee every time that the invisible man made his presence known, Renee was terrified by some of the things that the invisible man was doing. At one point, when the invisible man was strangling someone, she turned her face away & buried it in Abigail's shoulder. Abigail felt like she could hear a voice whispering in her ear to put her arm around Renee's shoulders.

Nervously, Abigail reached her arm around Renee's shoulder & held her. Coming to her senses for a moment, she turned her head to make sure that nobody was watching. Fortunately, the only people who might have noticed were people like her, people who were hoping not to get caught in an inappropriate moment with an inappropriate person.

When Renee came back up from hiding from the screen, she thanked Abigail. Abigail then pulled her arm back, hoping that she hadn't just made things weird between them.

Later, after the movie, Abigail was walking Renee home while Renee was talking about the special effects in the movie.

"Mon Dieu, when he took the bandages off & there was nothing there. I almost fainted. I've never seen anything like it! The scene where the footprints in the snow appeared, it was like there was really an invisible man walking through the snow."

Abigail grinned. It had been impressive, not because of what she saw on screen. Abigail had spent most of her life watching far more impressive effects in movies. It was amazing because they had done it without any CGI, no computers, nothing. Just physical props & tricks with the film.

"It was pretty incredible Renee."

"I know, it was like it was real. Thank you, Abigail."

"For what?"

"For talking me into coming out tonight. It's been ages since I've seen a movie & I am really enjoying our time together."

"I'm enjoying it too Renee. Our friendship has been the best thing that's happened to me since I came here."

"Really?"

"Yeah, I haven't had this much fun since I left… England."

Abigail had needed a second to recall where her cover identity had come from. Fortunately, Renee didn't notice. A minute later, they reached Renee's home. The bakery was closed, but there was a light on upstairs where her father was writing letters back home according to Renee.

"This is where my night ends. Thank you again Abigail. Are you sure that you don't want to stay for the night? It's a long way back to Hell's Kitchen from here & it's a bit late to be on your own."

"Thank you for the offer, Renee, but…"

Abigail needed a reason to leave & again, it took a second to come to her.

"Yes?"

"I've got to do my laundry in the morning, I was supposed to do it today, but shopping for the groceries took longer than I thought."

"Ah. Okay, well I hope that you get home safe."

Renee then spread her arms & hugged Abigail. Abigail returned the hug eagerly.

"Thank you, Renee. God, even your hair smells like fresh bread."

Renee laughed as Abigail held her close until it was about to become awkward. Renee then kissed Abigail on the cheek before she headed into the dark bakery to see what her father was up to.

Abigail turned around & with an almost noticeable skip in her step, she headed home. Along the way, she wished that she could turn her music player on. The songs from one of her favorite bands, Lonely Reaper, was running through her mind. The album in her mind was basically a series of songs about spirits that were in love with people that couldn't see them. More than one person along her path noticed her humming the odd tunes to herself as she longed for Renee to kiss her lips next time instead of her cheek.

Dec 5th, 1933

Abigail was staring out of her living room window. The city below her was waking up to a chilly December day, a day that promised to be unlike any other day in American history. Today was the day that prohibition was coming to an end. Some forms of beer had been legal for a few months, but tonight, all of the restrictions would be gone as impromptu parties kicked off all over the country to celebrate the end of prohibition.

Abigail had been invited by her friends at work to an 18th amendment farewell celebration. She accepted the night of drunken partying on a Tuesday because it would distract her from the final hours of her punishment.

Abigail had been on probation since July & it was coming to an end tomorrow. Tomorrow, her music player would unlock, her news privileges would be restored & she would only have to meet up with her handler on a monthly basis instead of a weekly basis. No more worrying that at any moment, she could be reassigned to take care of a tertiary safe house out in the countryside, miles from her nearest neighbor.

It was now just a matter of counting the hours until her probation ended & seeing as how prohibition was ending a day sooner, what better way to get her mind off of things then mingling with a massive crowd of people who would be getting their first tastes of real booze in 13 years.

Abigail set out for work & no sooner had she gotten there than Jasmin was at her desk.

"Tonight is going to be legendary."

Abigail nodded her head. In her mission briefing, she had been shown several photos of tonight's celebrations. It was going to be legendary all right. Abigail put her purse down & sat down properly at her desk before answering.

"Definitely, a lot of livers are going to be sore by dawn."

"Including ours!"

Abigail shushed Jasmin since they were working in a bank. She calmed herself down & leaned in closer to Abigail.

"It's too bad that it's happening on a Tuesday. Who came up with that idea?"

"It's probably genius."

"How do you figure Abigail?"

"Think about it, if they did it on Saturday, half the city would be dead from alcohol poisoning by Monday. This way, people have to moderate themselves in order to show up to work the next day."

"Yeah, that does make sense. Anyway, you're still coming tonight, right Abigail?"

"Yes Jasmin, I'll be there, throwing them back with the rest of you."

///

True to her word, Abigail got out of work & headed straight for the bar down the street. Wedging her way through the crowds, she got inside just in time. She reached her table where a pint of beer & a shot of Canadian whisky was waiting for her with her coworkers. Everyone in the bar had a drink, but nobody was drinking just yet.

Everybody watched breathlessly as the bartender pulled out an old bottle of rum. He wiped the dust off of it & uncorked it. He then held the bottle of rum up high & gave a small speech.

"I received a delivery of rum from the Caribbean the day before those idiots in the government announced prohibition. I'm not going to lie, when I heard the news, I was tempted to drown in that shipment of rum. Instead I sold all but one bottle off as fast as I could. I kept this bottle in a very safe place that the prohis would never be able to find where it could wait for this glorious day. 13 years dry, that's how long it's been for most of the people in this room. No more. Join me in toasting tonight ladies & gentlemen, to the end of the 18th amendment!"

The entire bar shouted out his last line as he took a swig from his bottle of Caribbean rum & everyone else took a shot of Canadian whiskey.

That was the start of the night. As the next few hours wore on, Abigail & the girls partied into the caliginous night. At a time when they would normally be crawling into bed, they were just stumbling out of the bar in order to head home.

Jasmin headed off with another pair of women who lived in the same direction that she did. Grace & Sandra headed off together & Molly walked along with Abigail for a while.

"Abigail… who… who was that guy… that I was… dancing with?"

"That was the coat rack."

"That explains why he was so stiff on his feet."

Abigail laughed. She had held back compared to everyone else & she was drunk. Half the people leaving the bar could barely stand upright. She saw Molly staggering & wrapped her arm around her shoulder to help Molly stay up.

"Well aren't you Prince Charming!"

Molly then grabbed the front of Abigail's shirt & pulled her in for a sloppy kiss. A second later, when Abigail's brain caught up & she realized what was happening, she pulled Molly off of her.

"You're drunk as a skunk Molly."

"Abigail? Where's Prince Charming, he was helping me walk a minute ago."

"That was me. I'm helping you walk."

"Ahh, you're such a good friend, let me give you a kiss."

Abigail was grateful that Molly lived relatively close. She got Molly to her apartment where half of her roommates were in a similar state. With help, she got Molly into bed. Molly's roommates then offered her the couch when they found out that she lived in Hell's Kitchen. They reasoned that here in Molly's apartment, she was closer to work & would have an easier time getting in though the hangover. Abigail accepted & crashed on their surprisingly comfortable couch.

///

In the early hours of the morning, Abigail woke up with a mind-splitting headache & three couch springs digging into her back from the world's lumpiest couch. How had she not noticed the springs last night?

She climbed to her feet, grateful that she had been offered the couch to crash on since it meant that she was an hour closer to work than she otherwise would have been.

As she looked out the Kitchen window, Abigail thought about how in her apartment, her music player was unlocked for the first time in months.

Chapter 5
Feb 14th, 1934

The sign next to the dance hall entrance read Singles Valentines Dance. While all of the people that were fortunate enough to be in a relationship were celebrating Valentine's Day, the people pouring into this dance club were the ones that were dateless & in the mood to dance. Since Abigail & Renee were both without a significant other, Renee had agreed to go dancing with Abigail.

As much as Abigail secretly wished once again that this was a proper date, or even a secret date, she was starting to accept that Renee was never going to see her as anything more than a friend. Still, at least they could dance together. Abigail had gotten off of work & made her way to the dance hall where she found Renee waiting just inside the hall in a simple blue dress with a wide blue belt that wrapped around her waist.

"Renee! I hope you haven't been waiting long."

The two women then hugged before they started walking into the main dance hall.

"Not at all, it's only been a few minutes."

"Ready to dance your feet off?"

"Bien sûr. Of course."

In the hall, people were dancing everywhere to the Jazz that the band was playing. Nobody seemed to be pairing off as they normally would. Instead, everyone was just dancing on the floor, except for the folks who were taking a breather & having a drink. It almost reminded Abigail of the last rave that she went to before she travelled a century & a half into the past. There were a few differences of course. Everyone here was still fully clothed & they were listening to a jazz band instead of a vampire synth band. Still, Abigail was willing to take what she could get.

They made their way onto the dance floor & found themselves dancing in a crowd of people who mostly didn't seem to care about who they were dancing with. Every now & then, some complete stranger would come to Abigail & dance next to her. Sometimes she would turn from Renee & dance with them for a minute or two before turning back to her friend. When Abigail wasn't dancing with someone else, she found herself being mesmerized as Renee's dirty blonde hair flowed around her, & she wasn't the only one.

"Renee! You've got a trio of guys over there that wishing they were over here!"

Renee turned & saw them all look away, feigning disinterest. Abigail laughed before pointing out their nervousness.

"They look scared of coming over here."

Renee laughed.

"It is a shame; they are kind of cute."

"Thinking about leaving me here to go & dance with them Renee?"

"Non, not a chance. If they want to dance with me, they have to come here, like this man behind you."

Abigail turned to see a man with bulging biceps & a caramel complexion that was waving her over, inviting her to dance next to him. For the rest of the song, Abigail found herself impressed by his moves as more than one woman wondered why she got to be so lucky. When the song ended, Abigail pouted as he backed away. When the next song started, Abigail saw him dancing on his own next to a man that looked like he was about to have a panic attack as he danced alone next to Mr. Caramel complexion. Abigail wondered for a second if that was the same kind of fear that Renee had experienced that one time that she had jokingly kissed her so long ago.

Despite the number of men that had come to them throughout the night, they were both still alone two hours later when they made their way off the dance floor & headed over to the bar for a drink. When Abigail reached into her annoyingly small pocket for the handful of bills that she could cram in there, Renee waved her hand in refusal. She then pulled some bills of her own out of a very discreet little pocket that Abigail couldn't even see because it was hidden under the wide belt.

"You're always taking me out & paying for everything. Let me buy the drinks tonight."

"If you insist Renee."

The two of them then threw back a few drinks before deciding that their feet were too sore for another hour of dancing. Feeling a

little tipsy, the two of them got their coats from the coat check &
headed out into the chilly night. Along the way, they got to talking.

"Thank you again Abigail."

"For what?"

"For dragging me out. My father is right when he says that I
don't get out much. I really like it when you ask me to go dancing or
to go to a movie or to go & get something to eat. It's always fun."

"Well, you're very welcome. I gotta say though, I don't know
why more people don't ask you out. You're all kinds of fun to spend
time with."

"Probably because I am always working, or maybe because I'm
very shy."

"You're not that shy with me."

"No, I'm not."

Renee then smiled as the two of them continued on their walk.

"You know, Abigail, my favorite part of the day is when you
walk into the bakery for your morning bagel."

"Really? I had no idea."

"Yes, it's always fun to talk to you & sometimes, you give me a
reason to leave the apartment & have some fun."

"Well, Renee, I have to say that it is the best part of my day as
well."

"You're not just saying that?"

"Of course not. The smell of the bread that you just finished
baking, your cute little smile, getting to talk to you before the
morning rush comes in. It always makes my morning a little
brighter."

Renee smiled while Abigail wondered why she was opening up
like this. She never opened up; it was part of her training to avoid
opening up. If she opened up too much, it made it extremely easy to
accidentally let something slip out. She should stop talking so much.

"You know Renee, I sometimes wonder how I made it through
all those days before I stumbled on your bakery."

Abigail put her arm around Renee's shoulder, partly to hold
Renee close & partly to support herself along the slippery sidewalk.
Eventually, they reached the bakery where they would have to part
ways.

"Thank you again Abigail. I had so much fun."

"I'm glad."

Renee then turned to face Abigail so that she could give her a kiss on the cheek goodnight. When Abigail saw it coming in, she threw caution to the wind. She would later blame it on the booze even though she was basically sober by this point. She turned her head at the very last second & for the second time, their lips met. Renee, seeing what was going on, pulled back after a second.

"Sorry Renee, I don't know why I…"

Abigail's half cooked excuse was interrupted when Renee leaned forwards & pressed their lips together. Abigail was stunned. She was confused. She tasted fresh bread.

Standing there in the middle of the street on a cloudy Valentine's Day eve, Renee had her hands planted on Abigail's shoulders & her eyes closed as they kissed each other. This was no quick peck on the lips, this was long & slow. Abigail felt like time was moving slow for a moment.

Renee then pulled back, her hands still on Abigail's shoulders. She then opened her eyes to see a stunned Abigail standing there nearly speechless.

"Wow… Renee… wow… that was just… wow…"

Abigail stopped herself from saying anything else as she heard her practiced English accent start to waiver a bit. Renee suddenly seemed to panic as she realized that she had just kissed another woman. She started looking around to see if anyone else had seen them. Hoping that nobody had seen it, Renee stepped back from Abigail.

"Sorry Abigail… I… I don't know why I… "

Renee then turned & ran back into the bakery while Abigail called after her.

"Renee! Wait… I…"

It was too late. The only thing that Abigail could do was turn around & head home, replaying the kiss in her head while she hoped that Renee would soon be alright.

Mar 19th, 1934

Abigail wasn't quite running late just yet, but a few more minutes & she would be. Abigail was having one of those mornings where nothing was going right & as she was fumbling with the key to lock her apartment door, she was desperately hoping that nothing else slowed her down. The end of March was not a good time of year to be late for work. As people all over the city were starting to file their taxes before April, banks were getting busy.

Having finally gotten her door locked, she turned around to see Lola walking towards her from the stairs. Abigail cursed in her head, quickly plastered on her best fake smile & hoped that Lola would understand that she was in a rush.

"Good morning, Abigail."

So much for understanding.

"Morning Lola, can I just get by you?"

"Is everything alright? You look upset."

"Do I?"

"Yes, in fact you've been looking upset for a few weeks now. Is everything alright?"

Abigail didn't have time for this. The truth was that she had been upset for a while now. After Valentine's Day, her relationship with Renee had gotten very awkward & she missed spending time with her friend. Her friend that she secretly had a major crush on. Still, even if Abigail had the time, she wasn't going to talk about it with Lola of all people.

"I'm alright Lola, I'm just very tired from work most days. It is tax season after all. As for this morning, I must just have a case of the Mondays."

"Ah, I see."

"Yeah, speaking of work, I'm actually running a little late."

"Oh, sorry, let me get out of your way."

Lola stepped aside & Abigail said goodbye to the older woman as she rushed off to work. Along her way to work, Abigail was wondering if she should stop by the bakery. As much as she wanted to, she had been trying to give Renee some space to work through her issues with the kiss. For the last month, Abigail had only been going twice a week, on Monday & Thursday mornings. Abigail didn't want to run the risk of being late for work, but she didn't want Renee to think that she was cutting her out of her life by skipping a Monday.

As she approached the bakery, she decided that she wanted to see Renee. Over the last few weeks, Renee had been shy, awkward, distracted & sometimes absent minded. Abigail wasn't trying to put pressure on her, but she needed Renee to see that she wasn't going to let one wonderful little kiss come between their friendship. She told herself that she had to be quick today & she walked into the bakery.

As it had so many times before, the smell of fresh bread pulled Abigail out of her head & warmed her soul. Abigail walked up to the counter where Renee was finishing up with another early customer.

"Hi Renee."

"Abigail, hi… can I… can I get you your usual?"

"Please."

Renee walked over to one of the shelves with fresh bagels & wrapped a few of them up for Abigail.

"Here you go."

"Thanks Renee."

"Abigail…"

Abigail turned around, hoping that this wasn't Renee telling her to stop coming by.

"Abigail… are you in a rush… right now…"

Abigail almost said no, remembering just in time that she was already running late for work.

"Yeah, I've got to get to work. What's up?"

"I was just wondering… if we could… talk… maybe after work?"

"Sure, I can stop by after work."

"You don't have to… if you don't want to…"

"I'd like to Renee. I'll see you after work."

Renee smiled before Abigail had to turn to head off to work.

///

Knowing that Renee wanted to talk to her seemed to make the day drag on endlessly. Working late didn't make things any better. By the time that she got out of the office, the sun was setting & she was rushing to get to the bakery in the hopes that Renee wasn't upset about having to wait so long.

When she finally got there, Renee was dealing with one of the last customers of the day. Abigail waved & walked up to the bakery where she met Renee at the door.

"Sorry I'm so late. Work was insane today. There's less than a month before everyone's taxes will be due."

Renee waived it off, understanding why she had been waiting for so long for Abigail to show up.

"I should have realized this is a busy time of year for you. I'll admit, I was starting to worry."

"Sorry Renee. So, you said that you wanted to talk."

"Yes, Please, come inside."

Abigail followed Renee inside. Renee then turned the open sign to closed & locked the door. She then checked to make sure that her father had gone upstairs to relax after a day in front of the ovens. Certain that they were alone, she walked up to Abigail & took a deep breath.

"I wanted to apologize to you Abigail."

"What for? The kiss?"

Renee blushed.

"Yes… the kiss… I'm sorry... I honestly don't know what came over me. I'm sorry that I upset you."

"You didn't upset me, Renee."

Renee was surprised by that one.

"But… you stopped coming here every day, I thought that I had ruined our friendship."

"No Renee, I just figured that you needed a bit of time to sort some things out. I was just trying to give you a bit of space."

"Dieu merci, je pensais que j'avais perdu mon meilleur ami."

"You lost me there Renee."

"Sorry, I was saying that I thought I had lost my best friend."

"Well, you haven't."

"So you're not upset that I kissed you?"

"Not at all Renee."

"Thank god, I was so worried that I had ruined our friendship. The truth is that I've missed you these last few weeks. I've missed dancing & going to movies with my friend."

"I've missed it too Renee."

Renee then wrapped her arms around Abigail & pulled her in for a long hug. Abigail then decided to go against her better judgement & try to push things a bit further. While holding Renee in her arms, she chose her words & hoped that they wouldn't drive Renee away again.

"I don't mind that you kissed me & for future reference, if you ever feel the desire again, I won't mind if you kiss me again."

Renee blushed a bit & got a bit nervous before Abigail let her go & asked Renee if she would like to hit the diner a few blocks over that was open late. Renee agreed & after telling her father that she was going out, they were off to catch up on the last month of their lives.

May 10th, 1934

How anyone had ever managed to keep track of what was in this account was beyond Abigail. Abigail had a stack of folders on her desk from a small family run bank that had failed a few weeks ago. The bank's assets & accounts had been bought by the bank that Abigail worked for & now on top of all of their normal workload, the secretaries had to make copies of all of the active accounts.

Apparently, the small family bank that had gone under had never upgraded to typewriters. All of the ledgers & accounts had been written in by hand & Abigail was struggling to read the chicken scratch writing that in some cases dated back to the last century. She had been working on them for days & would be working on them for weeks most likely.

When she finally got to the end of the account that she had been working on, she took the last sheet of paper out of the typewriter & after making sure that nobody was looking, she typed the words *End of Account 19040417*. Even without any paper, it would show up on the typewriter ribbon, making it easier for whatever agent receiving the ribbon to know when he had reached the end of the account.

Abigail finished the ninth such file of her day & seeing that it was six o'clock, she went ahead & changed out the typewriter ribbon from her typewriter with a new one. When Jasmin saw her, she wasn't suspicious at all. They all had to change their ribbons from time to time, especially since they were all working so hard to copy the new files & get their normal work done. What Jasmin didn't see was when Abigail slipped the old ribbon into her purse instead of throwing it out.

Abigail then left with the other secretaries. It was the first time in the last two weeks that they were leaving before 8. Even their bosses realized that from time to time, people need to leave work at a reasonable hour. Of course the only real reason that they were being allowed to leave at normal hours tonight & tomorrow was because they had all agreed to come in on Saturday & focus on nothing but these new files.

Abigail promised the girls that she would go out with them to celebrate tomorrow. She then left the group to whatever they had planned while Abigail made her way over to her favorite bakery.

Abigail walked up to the bakery to find Renee walking out the door, her loose dress fluttering in the wind & her hair free from the bun that Renee usually liked to wear. Her father was standing in the doorway promising that he would be fine & that she should have fun with her friend. He then pointed to Abigail & told his daughter to go. She gave him a quick kiss on the cheek & then dashed over to Abigail.

"Ready Renee?"

"Yes, come on, the restaurant is just around the corner."

A few minutes later, they were walking into the dimly lit restaurant. The place had a bit of a romantic feel to it. Small candles at each table providing most of the dim lighting in the private little tables & booths where a young couple could enjoy some privacy. The two women sat down in one of the dark little booths & quickly ordered from the menus. When the waiter left, Renee smiled.

"So how was your day?"

"Exhausting. We bought the accounts of a bank that went tits up a few weeks ago & now, on top of my normal work, I've got to copy the account info & history of hundreds of accounts."

"That sounds exhausting. How are you going to get it all done?"

"By going in on Saturday."

Renee reached over & patted Abigail's hand. Normally she would have made some comment about how the bakery is open every day of the week, instead, she just sought to comfort her friend.

"What about you Renee? How's life in the bakery?"

Renee then began telling Abigail about her last few days. As their food arrived & they slowly ate, the two women talked endlessly about all of the things going on in their lives. They talked about work, their families & friends, what movies would be showing up in the theaters in the next few weeks that they might like to see. They talked about how desperate some people were getting & Franklin Roosevelt's new deal.

They talked endlessly into the night until eventually, their waiter brought them their bill & told them that the restaurant was closing for the night. At the realization of how late it was getting, they paid their rather expensive bill, finished the last of their drinks & headed out into the night. With both women a little tipsy, they locked arms as they headed back to the bakery.

"I can't believe how late it is Renee. I can't remember the last time that I closed a place out like that."

Renee looked at Abigail funny for a second.

"What's up Renee?"

"Your accent went a little funny there."

"My accent isn't funny!"

Renee laughed & let it drop before looking back at the restaurant for a second.

"That was a lot more expensive than I thought that it would be. Are you sure that you don't mind how much of the bill you paid Abigail?"

"I don't mind Renee. It was worth it for a night out with you."

Abigail then leaned in & kissed Renee on the cheek.

"Thank you, Abigail. It was a nice restaurant."

"It was, although, I have to say, I didn't think that it was going to be so… romantic."

"It wasn't romantic, it was… it was… intimate."

They reached the bakery & Renee unlocked the front door so that they could spend a few minutes together inside.

"Intimate is just a polite way of saying romantic. Nearly every other couple in there probably ended up kissing goodnight."

Abigail then puckered her lips, mockingly waiting for a goodnight kiss. Renee gave her a gentle push back as they laughed.

"Do you have to go home now Abigail, or would you like to stay for a few minutes & have some tea or coffee or something?"

"Thanks Renee, but I should be good to get home. Why are you looking at me like that again?"

"Your accent went funny again."

"I think you're the one that needs coffee, or a bed. Goodnight, Renee."

Abigail pursed her lips mockingly again. She was surprised when Renee walked forward & kissed her lips. Confused, she pulled back in a small panic. Last time that they had kissed, it had left Renee freaked out for months & nearly ruined their friendship.

"Renee... I was..."

Abigail couldn't finish as Renee grabbed her blouse & pulled her forward, pressing their lips together. Still a little nervous that this could backfire on their friendship again, Abigail nevertheless didn't resist as Renee's inexperienced lips explored hers. A minute later, when Abigail was starting to feel warm, Renee finally pulled back & opened her eyes.

"Abigail... I..."

"It's alright Renee. I told you a few weeks ago. I don't mind if you want to kiss me. You don't have to..."

Again, Abigail couldn't finish her sentence. Renee pulled her forward once more into another kiss. This time, Abigail wasn't nervous at all. Soon her tongue was probing for entrance into Renee's mouth as they wrapped their arms around each other. Renee found herself taking slow steps backwards with Abigail in her arms until her back was against a display case that was normally full of croissants & muffins.

When their kiss came to an end, they stayed nose to nose, breathing heavily for a moment before Abigail asked the question that was burning in her mind.

"Renee, are you alright?"

"S'il te plait ne t'arrête pas."

"Either your accent is the one that's going funny, or I need to learn some French."

"Please don't stop."

"Alright."

Abigail brought her lips to Renee's & soon; they were kissing once more. Renee felt her heart beating like a drum when Abigail's hands started caressing her back, one of her hands slowly finding its way further down while the other buried itself in Renee's hair. Abigail felt her own pulse quickening as Renee's hands slowly started to move, gently circling & caressing her back.

When Abigail's hand slid over the slight curve of Renee's buttocks, Renee gasped, breaking their kiss for a moment. Abigail caressed the soft flesh for a moment longer before she started using her hand to gently pull the fabric of Renee's dress up her legs. Renee barely even noticed that her dress was being pulled up, her mind was too occupied by heavenly sensations & devilish lips.

Abigail finally succeeded in bringing the hem of Renee's dress within reach. As Renee gasped & moaned, Abigail's fingers brushed against the top of Renee's stockings & the pale skin of Renee's thigh. The sudden contact was like an electric shock for Renee. Her eyes flew open as she suddenly realized what she was doing & just how far it had actually gone.

She broke the kiss & pushed Abigail back with just enough force for Abigail to realize that a line may have been crossed. Abigail stood there as Renee rested against the display case, breathing deeply.

"Renee… are you alright?"

"Yes… I just… I…"

Abigail understood. For Renee, this was all too new. She wasn't ready to be with a woman, let alone a friend, let alone to be ravaged against the display case of her father's bakery by her best friend.

"I don't… I… I can't… I…"

"Shh. It's alright Renee. We don't have to go any further. We can talk tomorrow when we're sober or whenever you're ready."

"I'm… I'm sorry Abigail…"

"You don't need to be sorry. I'll see you tomorrow. Don't forget to lock up."

Renee nodded her head, standing there confused about what had just happened & grateful that Abigail seemed to understand.

Aug 11th, 1934

Abigail was sitting at the small little table in the café a mile away from where Alex worked. The black wig that she was wearing was the exact same color as her own natural raven locks, but it was about a foot longer & it didn't itch. She had braided it into a long ponytail & put on a pair of fake glasses to wait for her handler. He walked in twenty minutes late & wearing a blue suit & a striped tie. More than one woman gave him a once over before he sat down across from Abigail.

"What? No neon sign to point you out?"

"Very funny Abigail, this happens to be rather fashionable these days. Sometimes you have to be seen to blend in."

He sat down & ordered a sandwich with decaf coffee. Abigail looked at him as if he had just started talking backwards.

"Since when do you order decaf?"

"Since the field medic told me that I'm only a few more cups of caffeine away from a coronary."

"Really?"

"Yeah, wasn't expecting to hear that at 54. I was hoping to make it into my sixties before they told me to start slowing down. But this era ages you fast."

"Can't you get treatment from home?"

"Yeah, cardiac rejuvenation nanites. The order has been put in, but the drop off isn't for another month. So until then, got to try & kick some old habits."

"Wow."

The waitress then showed up with his order, Alex took the cup of coffee & his meager meal from her & thanked her. Sipping the coffee, he scrunched up his face, missing the kick of caffeine.

"So, how's the beacon holding up?"

"All green, as usual."

"That's good to hear. Less than a year to go before you deploy. Nervous?"

"Not at all."

"Liar. Everyone gets nervous. Anyway, I have preliminary confirmation, your primary activation site is still a go. I'll keep you informed as we get closer to the day if there's any change."

Alex then looked around discreetly to make sure that nobody was coming up on them. He then nodded his head. Abigail then took her satchel from between her legs & handed it to Alex.

"Pretty heavy, you must have been putting in a ton of overtime to get all this."

"You have no idea. I would legitimately kill for some sort of discreet scanner so that I wouldn't need to copy all of this stuff out when nobody is looking."

"I'd love to oblige you, but you know that getting permission for non-local tech is nearly impossible."

"Yeah, I know."

Alex put the satchel between his own feet, confident that nobody had noticed the handoff.

"So, Abigail, other than working yourself into the grave, how's life? Is your neighbor Lola still giving you grief?"

"It hasn't been so bad lately. The guys that moved in down the hall are clearly more than just friends, so she's become so preoccupied with them that she barely remembers that I exist most days."

"That's good to hear, so I can tell the boys in the resources department that your request to relocate is now a low priority."

Abigail gave him a look that could curdle milk from ten paces.

"Don't. You. Dare. Old Man."

"Just playing Abigail. I've got no caffeine, no greasy or salty food & a neighbor with a screaming toddler. You can take a joke for my sake."

"As long as it's just a joke."

He grinned before sipping his coffee again.

"So, how are things going with Renee? Has she finally decided about how she feels about you touching her leg?"

"Yeah, it only took three months."

"I'm guessing by your lack of a smile that it's not good news."

"A few days ago, I met her after work. We talked in the alley behind the bakery. She said that she doesn't know where these urges keep coming from & that she doesn't feel it's right to keep inflicting them on her only real friend."

"Ouch, friendzone."

"Yeah. The thing is, I don't know if she's scared of being with another woman, or if she's scared that she's confusing friendship for desire."

"Did you try asking her?"

"I couldn't. Once she said her piece, she didn't want to talk about it anymore."

"I see. So what are you going to do?"

"I don't know. Should I just accept that she's a friend that'll occasionally kiss me, or should I do something bold?"

"Well, officially, I should be telling you to do whatever allows you to better focus on your mission, which would be to get comfortable in the friendzone."

"But unofficially?"

"Unofficially, I would say that if you think it might work, go bold. Just come to a decision soon Abigail. If you're going to make a move, you might want to do it fast."

"What difference does it make if I take my time?"

"Your next mission, that's the difference."

Abigail opened her mouth to respond but didn't say anything. As she closed her mouth, Alex went on.

"Your current mission concludes in ten months. After that, you'll be reassigned, possibly to another state, possibly within weeks or days. If you're going to be bold, do it sooner rather than later, because throwing yourself at her & opening her world up to so many new possibilities, only to leave her a few weeks later, would be cruel."

Alex finished the last of his meal & coffee before grabbing the satchel & paying the bill. He then stood up & readjusted his tie.

"I won't tell you what to do Abigail. I also won't tell you to choose wisely. That would be nearly impossible."

"So what do I do?"

"Be kind by choosing quickly."

He then tipped an imaginary hat & walked away, off to his normal life or possibly to deal with another agent. Abigail ordered another cup of coffee & sat there for a while, thinking about her mission, how long it might be before she gets reassigned & if she would be risking her friendship with her best friend by being bold.

Chapter 6
Jan 18th, 1935

Abigail stared at her reflection in the mirror over her bathroom sink. After five years in this era, the reflection that stared back at her was still unfamiliar. She wished, like she did many days, that she could see her rainbow hair once again, cut short on one side & shoulder length on the other. She wished that she could have her bionic eyes back, with all of their capabilities & enhancements. Instead, it was the same reflection staring back at her once more. A simple woman in a desperate age.

"Today's the day. You've trained for this. Nine minutes of pandemonium, then a quick chat with the cops, then it's back to your normal life as Abigail Oldman."

On top of the normal stresses of maintaining her cover, the bank that she worked at was going to be robbed today. At 10:37 am, half a dozen robbers were going to come in with rifles. Nine minutes later, they would be leaving with about forty thousand dollars. No casualties, no injuries. She just had to remain calm at her seat & not draw the attention of the two men that would come upstairs. Easy enough. Abigail finished working on her makeup, another thing that took ages in this century, & set off for work.

She stopped by the bakery as she normally did on Friday mornings & as usual, she spent a few minutes talking to Renee before the morning rush flooded into the place. It was hard acting normally when she knew that she was a few hours away from being in the same room as desperate men with rifles.

After taking a second too long to say goodbye to Renee, she walked out the door & made her way to the office. It was incredible how everything was so normal. Everyone was just going about their business, blissfully unaware of what was coming. Ten o'clock passed by, then ten thirty. As the last few minutes ticked away over what felt like days, Abigail felt herself tense up as she watched the clock. She watched it reach 10:37, then 10:38, then 10:39. She kept watching it right until eleven.

Something was wrong.

It would be one thing if they were a minute or two off, this was long before clocks could be digitally synced. But it was nearly half an hour at this point. The two that were caught in the getaway should already be getting booked at the precinct. Abigail was about to call her emergency number. She had to let whoever it was that reported to her handler know that there was a problem. Then it happened.

The deafening sound of a shotgun being fired up into the air, followed by the sound of a man shouting.

"Everyone! Get your hands up in the air! This is a robbery!"

Something was wrong.

It took a few seconds for Abigail to remember. Her briefing for this event had said rifles, there wasn't supposed to be a shotgun involved. She stood up & went to where the second floor looked out over the bank lobby below. Something was definitely wrong. There were eight men with guns when there should only be six.

"Shit."

Three of them came upstairs to make sure that nobody was calling the police. They started waving their guns around while telling everyone what to do.

"All of you, here, where we can see you from the lobby. Now!"

Everyone got up & moved to where Abigail was standing, many of them with their hands up. When they had gathered together, one of the gunmen gave a signal to the man in charge downstairs. He then pointed his shotgun in the face of one of the tellers.

"Take us to the vault, now!"

Abigail wanted to curse. They weren't supposed to be going for the vault, they were supposed to be smart & timid enough to just grab what was in the registers. In & out & most of them get away. But now they were going for the vault. Abigail watched as the teller, in a state of near panic, escorted three of the men to the vault. A moment later, the three of them cheered as they started ransacking the contents of the vault. The whole time that this was going on, Abigail was sneaking glances at the clock on the wall. Seven minutes in, everything went from bad to worse.

The police had arrived. Everyone could tell because their sirens were blaring. Someone in the bank, or next door, must have called them right away at the sound of the shotgun blast. Apparently, nothing gets cops moving faster in this decade than gunshots at a bank.

Now the robbers were panicking. Shots were fired. The police reacted. More shots were fired. After a minute, everything calmed down. One of the bank's security guards was injured & the robbers were ordering everyone brought down to the lobby. Abigail almost cursed. The in & out bank robbery was quickly turning into a hostage situation & she was going to be one of the hostages.

A few minutes later, Abigail was sitting on the floor with some of the tellers & secretaries when the phone rang. Judging by what she heard, it was the police calling to talk to the robbers. By this point, her handler would know that something had gone wrong, simply because she hadn't called her emergency contact with the signal that all was good. Not that it would make a difference if they knew. It wasn't like an emergency incursion team could get past the police & storm the bank unnoticed. She would just have to wait for this to play out.

It was around noon that things started to get tense. Rifle 1 had been getting antsy for some time. He was talking rather loudly with Shotgun 2 about how they were supposed to be in & out, but Shotgun 1 just had to make an entrance. Rifle 3 & Rifle 4 were nervous as hell since they were near the door, the first line of defense if the police tried something.

When the phone rang with the police calling again, Shotgun 1 went to answer it. That was when Rifle 2 decided that Shotgun 1 had lost control of the situation. The phone kept ringing while they argued. One of them reached for the phone & the two broke into a fistfight. Rifle 2 dropped his gun. It went off. The next few minutes were chaos. The police stormed in, bullets flew, Abigail tried to stay down & then there was a loud bang.

Abigail never did find out what the bang was. The next thing that she knew, she was on her feet, stumbling as someone helped her forward. She was outside in the bright light, near an ambulance, throwing up as the sun blinded her. Then her vision went wonky for a minute & the next thing that she knew, Alex Xenas, her handler, was waving his hand in front of her face.

"Abigail! Are you with me?"

"What… what happened?"

"No idea. The robbery did not go according to history & somehow, you've ended up with a moderate concussion."

"Something hit my head… or… my head hit… something…"

"Yeah Abigail, that's generally how concussions happen. Now listen, you should be coming out of it in a minute. This tall man to my right, he's one of our field medics. I gave emergency authorization to use advanced meds. He gave you something for your concussion. You should already be fine."

As Alex was talking, Abigail's mind cleared right up & she found that she could get up on her own.

"Thanks Alex."

"No problem. Now listen, you're going to go home, get some rest, tomorrow when we meet up at the café, I'm going to need a full debrief of everything that you remember."

"Understood."

"Good. Now your boss is sending everyone home, everyone that wasn't carted off to a hospital or a precinct that is. Check in with him, then head home. Our medic friend here says that you're good to go, I'll see you tomorrow morning, ten a.m., sharp."

"Understood."

The two of them left before they were noticed. Abigail then checked in with her boss who, seeing that she was on her feet, told her to go home & get some rest. She walked away from the calming chaos & started making her way home.

///

An hour later, she found herself in front of the bakery once again. Walking in, she found Renee finishing up with a customer. Renee quickly saw her as well & as soon as she was done with the man in front of her, she walked over to Abigail.

"Abigail, what are you doing here so early, it's not even three in the afternoon."

Abigail wondered if perhaps the something that she had been given for the concussion had completely worked. As she saw Renee standing there concerned, words started coming out before she could think about them.

"Everyone was sent home early today."

"Why would a bank send everyone home early on Friday?"

"We were robbed."

"What?!"

Abigail couldn't respond. She suddenly felt a surge of tears welling up & overcoming her.

"Abigail!"

Renee's father Maurice came out from the back to see Renee holding Abigail who was crying on Renee's shoulder. He signaled to her that he would man the store alone for a bit. Renee then brought Abigail out the back door into the alleyway next to the bakery. By the time that they got there, Abigail was already getting herself under control.

"Abigail. What happened? Are you alright?"

"No, we we're robbed, but it didn't go right. It wasn't supposed to be so long."

"What do you mean it wasn't supposed to be so long?"

"There were too many of them. They were supposed to be in & out, but one of them fired a shot, & the police came rushing in."

"Mon Dieu! Abigail, are you alright?"

"No, I hit my head… I think… There wasn't supposed to be shooting… I'm sorry Renee."

"It's okay."

"No! It's not okay, they were supposed to be in & out in nine minutes!"

Renee looked confused.

"What do you mean? How could you know how long they were supposed to take to do a robbery?"

Abigail finally came back around & started thinking a little more closely. Alex was going to get a talking to the next day. That field medic should have warned her not to talk to anybody, that she might lose control for a second. As Renee looked at her confused, Abigail held her head in her hands & pretended that she had a throbbing headache.

"Sorry Renee, what did you just say?"

"I said, how could you know that they were only supposed to take nine minutes?"

"Nine minutes? What? Sorry, my head. I think I hit it hard."

"Here, just a second Abigail."

Renee then looked around & found a small crate. She put it against the brick wall of the bakery & had Abigail sit down.

"There, now sit here & tell me what happened, slowly."

Abigail then took a deep breath & proceeded to spend the next few minutes slowly telling Renee about what had happened in the bank, without any more indications that she knew something was going to happen ahead of time. In the end, Renee ended up passing off the nine-minute mark as shock, or Abigail hitting her head.

What Abigail didn't know was that Renee's mind was bringing up all of her other little inconsistencies, like those times when Abigail's accent went funny.

Mar 23rd, 1935

Bullets were flying, people were screaming, a siren was blaring, the bank staff were panicking, something slammed into the back of Abigail's head & she bolted awake. She was sitting upright in her bed, drenched in a cold sweat. Looking over to the alarm clock, she saw that it was two in the morning. After a quick change out of her damp clothes, she climbed back into bed, hoping that she could make it the rest of the way to morning without a repeat.

For the last two months, the dreams had been plaguing her. For a while, they would haunt her every single night, but lately, it had gotten less frequent. Still, she wondered how it could possibly be that they had been that far off on what was going to happen. Sure, there were always the occasional details that weren't exactly like they should be. That's just what happens when you're getting your information from predigital records that are well over a century old, but this was ridiculous.

When morning finally came around, Abigail woke up properly & started in her normal Saturday routine. She made herself breakfast, listened to music on her earbuds & performed the weekly beacon test. Just like every time before, all six indicator lights were green. She cleaned the apartment a bit, got dressed for an early spring walk in the park & headed out her door. After getting some of the most recent gossip from Lola about how the young couple on the fourth floor was pregnant yet again, Abigail was out the door with a satchel over her shoulder.

A few minutes later, she snuck into a café, slipped into the bathroom & donned her short blonde wig. An hour later, she was sitting on a park bench, watching children play & old men feeding the pigeons. She wondered for a moment if these pigeons were the ancestors of the ones that would one day be cursed by people who had just gotten a car wash in her time.

Just as she was starting to get impatient, Alex showed up in a tweed jacket & a blonde wig of his own. The idea was that anyone passing them by would think that they were a father & daughter. He sat down next to her.

"Good morning, Abigail."

"Morning? It's almost the afternoon."

"Yeah, well, I'm older & slower now that I'm off of caffeine."

"Didn't you get your heart treatment Alex?"

"Yeah, but the medic said that I should still limit my consumption. Afterall, I don't get to rejuvenate until 1945. Got to keep myself in good health until then."

"Damn, so they're going to let you get right up to retirement age before rejuvenating you?"

"That's the idea, once I reach retirement age, my cover identity is going to 'retire' somewhere nice. I'll get rejuvenated & set up shop somewhere else, hopefully as something other than a postal worker."

"I guess that makes sense, handlers have to be in one place for decades & it wouldn't work well if they never aged."

"Exactly. So, is everything still green?"

"All six indicators."

"Excellent. Only a little over three months to go now. So far, the time & location are unchanged."

"Good, I like it when things go according to plan."

Alex looked over to Abigail. He knew that she wasn't sleeping as well as she should due to her nightmares. He intended to bring it up in a minute.

"So how's work Abigail."

"We're going into tax season, how do you think work is, it's exhausting & it's only going to get worse over the next month."

"Alright, how are your friends?"

"Exhausted, but unstoppable. I'm actually meeting them for drinks tonight. I was actually worried about Molly for a bit after the robbery, but she seems to be doing well."

"That's good to hear, how about Lola? Still playing the role of the Spanish inquisition?"

Abigail lowered her head & sighed.

"The Spanish inquisition could learn a thing or two from that woman. It's like nobody explained the concept of privacy to her. Are you sure that she's not one of ours that's been keeping an eye on me?"

"I'm sure Abigail. She really is just a nosey neighbor."

"A noisy neighbor that can get through the great depression without a job. I wouldn't be surprised if she's extorting someone. Lord knows that she knows how to dig up dirt."

"Stick with it, Abigail, you might be done here by the end of July."

"July…"

"How's Renee?"

"Wonderful. If I knew for sure that I was going to have more time here, I would definitely try to coax her out of her shell a bit."

Alex smiled. He was glad to see that there were things that Abigail wanted in this time. Agents that did nothing but long for the future tended to lose it & break down. Ironically, getting back to the future with your sanity intact meant forming connections to the past. He then asked the question that he knew would lead to more questions from Abigail.

"So, how are you sleeping these days?"

Abigail took a deep breath.

"Better. It's only about once a week that I wake up in a panic. I think that time is all I'll need in the end."

"Are you sure, we have a proper therapist in New York, if you need help, all you have to do is ask."

"You know what would help me Alex, if someone could explain to me how in the hell our intel could have been so wrong."

"We're still working on it."

"Working on it? Alex, there were two more gunmen then there were supposed to be, it went on for hours instead of minutes & there were shots fired. The police showed up & it turned into a hostage situation. This isn't the normal kind of differences where something is a minute off, or someone wears a grey suit instead of a brown suit. This is a major deviation. How the hell did that happen?"

Alex took a deep breath. He then leaned forward a bit & looked forward as he explained the leading theory.

"Chaos theory."

"I'm going to need more than that Alex."

"Chaos theory states that even a small change in initial circumstances can build up to enormous consequences. That was one of the major worries about starting this project in the first place. Just our subtle presence can change things. Take your apartment for instance, the fact that you live there means that the person who was supposed to live there is now living somewhere else. Which means that the person that should have lived there is living somewhere else. When we take up a residence, it displaces a whole bunch of people from where they were supposed to be. Then they take different routes to work, arrive at different times, meet different people."

Alex took a deep breath & then he continued.

"The differences are small at first, but they accumulate over time until after a decade or two, people are working at different jobs, marrying other people, having different kids."

"All this is because of where I live?"

"No, I'm saying that the small, microscopic changes that we make just by being here led to other changes, which led to more changes, which lead to more changes. From what we can see, the man that you referred to as Shotgun 1 was supposed to be in jail that day for getting into a bar fight with his cousin over an issue of twelve dollars."

"So what happened?"

"Apparently, his cousin was able to pay him the money. We can't be sure, but according to the original police report from our time, the cousin was unemployed. We looked into it & somehow, here he has a job. We think that our presence has changed things just enough so that whoever was supposed to get that job was either late or unable to seal the deal. The cousin gets the job, Shotgun 1 doesn't end up in prison, he brings along a friend & things go differently for you."

`Abigail looked like she was about to have a headache.

"Great, so just by being here, our intel on what's supposed to happen is going to become less & less dependable as we go along."

"It's possible Abigail, but you'll be glad to know that command is doubling its efforts to track these anomalies & account for them."

Abigail leaned back on the bench.

"That does make me feel better."

A minute later, Abigail handed Alex the satchel containing all of the files that she had managed to copy since their last meeting. A few minutes after that, they parted ways & headed off.

May 22nd, 1935

Abigail wondered if she was pushing things too far. She had just less than six weeks until her primary mission was complete. Just less than six weeks until she could be transferred to another city at any moment. Yet here she was, letting Renee get closer to her. She already felt guilty for confusing the poor girl, now she was risking confusing her again as she stood outside the movie theater, waiting for Renee to make her way.

Her friendship with Renee had been one of the things that had given her strength over the last few years. Over the last few months, she had come to appreciate that friendship all the more. Yet here she was, taking her confused friend to see Dracula's Daughter, a movie that many noted as being the first major Hollywood lesbian flick. The movie was even said to be based off of the first book to introduce the concept of the lesbian vampire. Abigail was slightly concerned that the movie was only supposed to come out in 1936, but she just chalked that up to another anomaly, like the robbery.

Abigail didn't know why she had invited Renee to come down to Hell's Kitchen to see the movie, she just couldn't stop herself. All that she knew was that Renee had just walked around the corner & was coming up to the theater fast.

Renee was wearing a long red skirt that fluttered in the gentle spring breeze. The bright red contrasted sharply against her white blouse. It took Abigail's breath away for a second as she stood there in a brown pair of pants that looked like they were the common ancestor to bell bottoms & parachute pants, & a beige blouse.

Renee's smile lit up when she saw Abigail standing there. She rushed over & wrapped Abigail up in a hug.

"I'm not late am I Abigail? It feels like it took forever to get down here."

"Not at all, we still have a few minutes before the movie starts."

"Great! I remember seeing Dracula a few years ago & if this is anything like that, it'll be great."

Abigail wanted to say that it wasn't anything like that. But then she would have to explain how she knew so much about a movie that she had supposedly never seen. Not to mention, she would then have to explain what it was like.

The two women made their way into the theater & by the time the curtains were lifting, they were in their seats in a sparsely populated section of the theater as the pre-movie cartoon & ads played.

Renee watched the movie with rapt attention as it started exactly where Dracula had left off five years earlier. As Professor Hellsing was explaining to the police that the man he killed had been dead for five hundred years, Abigail turned her gaze away from the movie. She watched as Renee's chest slowly rose & fell; she watched Renee's unblinking profile as the young French woman watched the movie.

From time to time, she had to remember to watch the movie, but in the same way that countess Zaleska couldn't take her vampiric eyes off of the young model that she had hired to pose, Abigail couldn't take her gaze off of Renee without some effort.

Forcing herself to watch the movie, she watched as the countess kidnapped Janet & brought her to castle Dracula. She laughed with some others in the audience when the townsfolk panicked at the sight of a light on in the castle. She watched as the countess hovered over an unconscious Janet, slowly giving into her desire to give the captured woman her vampiric kiss.

Feeling overly warm herself at the scene, she snuck one more glance at Renee only to see her glancing back. Renee, realizing that she had been caught, snapped her head forward to watch the movie as if nothing had happened. Despite this, Abigail could swear she saw the faintest hint of a blush on Renee's cheek in the dim light reflecting off of the screen.

Abigail stared at Renee for a little while longer, just long enough to see Renee glance back in her direction for a moment. Abigail smiled & managed to watch the rest of the short movie. When it ended & the credits began to roll, the lights in the theater started to slowly come back on. Making their way through the crowd leaving the theater, they found themselves standing outside, each of them a little too shy to say anything. After a minute of awkwardness, Abigail broke the silence between them.

"That was a pretty good movie."

"It really was. Thank you for inviting me to see it, Abigail."

"I'm glad that you came out to see it."

"Me too, but it's starting to get a little bit late. I should probably start on my way home soon."

Renee stood there for a second, almost as if she were inviting Abigail to ask her to stay a while longer. An invitation that Abigail accepted.

"You know Renee, my apartment is only a few blocks from here & the bus stops right on the corner. You could come over for a drink or a late supper & then you could catch the bus home without needing to walk down any dark streets."

Renee seemed to consider it for a moment.

"Alright. A drink sounds nice."

They both smiled for a moment as Abigail led the way. Along the short walk back to Abigail's apartment, she pointed out a few spots around the neighborhood. Renee hung on every word & Abigail was grateful that she had something to distract her from the fact that this whole two friends seeing a movie was turning into something that more closely resembled a date.

The last thing that Abigail pointed out was the bus stop. It felt like she was pointing out the emergency exit in case Renee freaked out again. The next thing that she knew, Renee was walking through the front door of her apartment building, past an older Irish couple that was going to see the movie that they had just come from, & right into Lola.

Lola, naturally, had an excuse to be out of her apartment & observing her neighbors. This time it was the garbage bag in her hand that looked like it had a few paper towels in it.

"Oh Abigail, fancy running into you. I was just taking out the trash before the garbage men come by."

"Alright, but they only come on Monday, so there isn't really much of a rush."

Lola froze for a second, realizing the flaw in her excuse. She then carried on as if nothing had been pointed out.

"Who's your friend? New roommate maybe?"

"No, she's just my friend, Renee. Renee, this is my neighbor, Lola."

Renee gave a small awkward wave.

"It's nice to meet you."

"It's lovely to meet you deary. So what are two lovely ladies such as yourselves doing out tonight? Going dancing? Meeting some friends?"

"Actually, we're just coming in for a bit. We just saw a movie & we felt like calming our nerves before I headed home."

"Oh, is that so."

While Lola went on to question Renee about the movie they saw & how they knew each other, Abigail struggled to find the key to her apartment. Fumbling with the lock, she got the door open & tried to separate Lola from her new source of information on Abigail.

"I'd hate to break up your conversation ladies, but I wouldn't want to keep you from your chores Lola."

Abigail indicated the nearly empty garbage bag that Lola was holding. Lola glared daggers at her for a moment.

"It's no bother Abigail, like you said, the garbage men only come on Monday. It's no bother for me."

"Yes, but Renee can't stay long if she plans to get home at a sensible hour."

Lola picked up on the fact that her intrusion was very quickly becoming very unwelcome. She then apologized & let the girls go. Abigail was certain that she would be waiting by her door for Renee to leave so that she could corner the poor French girl & pump her for the information that she's always wanted about Abigail. Once inside, Abigail breathed a sigh of relief, hopeful that her nosy neighbor wasn't jumping to any conclusions.

"Sorry about that Renee, Lola can be a little bit nosy."

"I figured as much when you said that garbage day is on Monday. I hope that I didn't tell her anything that you didn't want her to know."

"No, I think that I'm safe. Have a seat, I'll get us something to drink from the kitchen."

Abigail then made her way to the kitchen. She grabbed two glasses & a cheap bottle of wine from her fridge. While she was popping the cork, she imagined Lola going around to her neighbors, telling everyone that the girl who lives alone & hasn't had a boyfriend in the five & a half years that she had been living here had brought home a beautiful French girl.

Abigail shook her head. Renee would probably be leaving in half an hour & of course, Lola would see that & she would go around telling everyone that the boring lonely girl has a friend. She then headed to the living room & handed Renee a glass.

"I'm afraid that all I have is a cheap red wine."

"C'est pas problème. Sorry, it's no problem."

"Cheers."

They both clinked their glasses & sipped the surprisingly good wine.

"So, Renee, you liked the movie?"

"Oh yes, although the countess wasn't the scariest part."

"What was?"

"It was her… terrifiant… terrifiant… creepy, it was her creepy manservant."

"Yeah, he was a total creep. I mean, how desperate was that girl he grabbed on the bridge that she would go with him."

"Yes, he was all; *The river is cold & dark, & I know a place that is warm with food & money.* Any smart girl would think that he was out looking for a prostitute to murder."

Abigail burst out laughing. For the next little while, the wine flowed as they dissected the movie, talking about how Von Hellsing confessed to murder & didn't find himself in a jailcell, how the doctor just happened to have a machine that could hypnotize people, & how the doctor seemed to have no issue with a beautiful female patient that could only see him at night.

Soon they were sitting next to each other on the couch, laughing & talking about the movie. Eventually, the topic turned towards one of the movie's most famous moments. Renee finished her glass of wine before bringing it up.

"Did you see, Abigail, the countess when she had Janet lying there unconscious?"

"Yes, & she was standing over her, about to bite her."

"Bite her, it looked like she was going to kiss her!"

"I don't know Renee, it looked like she was hungry. Like she was going to eat poor little Janet."

Abigail then did her best impression of the countess's stare & slowly leaned into the Renee.

"Does this look like someone coming in for a kiss?"

Renee laughed & did her best impression, moving towards Abigail until they were an inch apart & staring at each other with deeply hungry looks in their eyes. When they were only a few inches apart, they stopped & laughed, neither one backing up again.

Abigail's heart was hammering like a jackhammer in her chest. Her mind was racing, telling her all of the reasons that she should back up, that she was far too close to crossing a line that she shouldn't be crossing. That Renee would just freak out again & that she might only be here for a few more weeks. Every fiber of reason & logic & duty to her mission told her to pull back, that it wasn't fair to Renee to be doing this when she might be leaving so soon.

As much as Abigail knew that she had a hundred good reasons not to do this, she could barely hear them over the sound of her heart beating like a drum in her chest. A drumbeat of desire that drowned out all reason with the simple fact that she wanted Renee, right here, right now, more than she had ever wanted anything before.

She wanted to calm her heavy breathing. She wanted to look at anything other than Renee's lips, or her green eyes, or the lock of dirty blonde hair that was hanging over her cheek, or her lips. As Abigail sat there, paralyzed by indecision, Renee must have come to a decision of her own as she leaned forward & closed the gap between their lips.

Abigail could taste the wine that they had been sharing on Renee's lips. Renee's warm, hungry lips, devouring hers. Every objection that had once had a voice in Abigail's mind was silenced & forgotten. Time froze. Time stretched on for ages. The time traveler lost all sense of time. The only thing that made sense was Renee's lips pressed against hers.

Eventually, the endless, frozen moment came to an end as their lips parted. They sat there, face to face, their hearts beating furiously. Neither of them backed away. Neither of them said anything for a moment. They stared into each other's eyes until Abigail's last lingering shred of sensibility made its last stand.

"Renee… we shouldn't."

"I disagree."

Renee started leaning in again.

"Renee…"

"I won't run away tonight, Abigail."

That was the end of Abigail's resistance. Their lips met. They barely managed to put their wine glasses down on the table before moving beyond just kissing. Abigail's hand was soon buried in Renee's dirty blonde locks as Renee's hand vanished into Abigail's raven hair.

Abigail's free arm wrapped itself around Renee's side, her hand pressing against the French girl's back as Renee did the same, the two women pulling each other closer together, until their bodies were pressed against each other like their lips.

Their kisses were long & sensual, only broken from time to time so that they could draw in fresh breath before tasting each other again. Abigail wanted to throw Renee down & ravage her on the couch. To rip her clothes off & hear the sweet sounds of her moans of pleasure. But she held back, she went slow, desperately hoping that she didn't scare Renee off despite her promise from mere moments ago.

After a few minutes of passionate, sensual kissing, Renee didn't resist when Abigail started leaning forwards, slowly pushing her down to the couch until she was lying back with Abigail's body pressing down on top of hers. Abigail's nervousness vanished when she felt Renee's hand leave her back & slide down to rest on her firm ass. Sliding her own hand out from under Renee, Abigail's hand slid between them, between their breasts. Renee shuddered as she felt Abigail's hand squeezing her breast.

Their kiss broke. They lay there for a moment, breathing heavily, staring into each other's eyes. The only thing keeping

Abigail from rushing forward was an incessant voice coming from… somewhere… that forced her to give Renee one more chance to turn back before they became much more than friends.

"Renee…"

"Yes…"

"My bedroom… is just… through that door…"

Renee looked to the door, understanding the implication. She knew in her heart that if she went into Abigail's bedroom, into her bed, she wouldn't say no to what she wanted to do. She looked to the front door for a moment, knowing that Abigail wouldn't stop her from leaving. She thought for a moment before turning her head to face Abigail.

"If your bed is in there… … … why... are we… still… … here…"

Abigail smiled & lifted herself off of Renee. Standing up. She offered Renee her hand. Renee, whose heart was pounding while her mind was racing, took Abigail's hand & followed as the raven-haired girl led her to her bed.

Once across the threshold of the bedroom, Abigail turned to close her door. In that moment, Renee looked to the bed, the narrow bed, barely big enough for a person, with a heavy blanket thrown over it despite summer being just around the corner. Just as she thought that her heart couldn't possibly beat any faster, she felt Abigail's arms wrap around her.

Renee moaned as one of Abigail's hands found her breast, her fingers gently squeezing as Abigail's other hand made for Renee's long red skirt. As Abigail began gently kissing Renee's neck & shoulder from behind, Renee reached over her shoulder with a hand & held Abigail against her neck. She felt in this moment like a willing victim to Dracula's daughter as Abigail's surprisingly capable hands made quick work of the slide fastener on Renee's skirt.

Renee felt a slight chill on her legs as her skirt crumpled to the floor. She let out a gasp as Abigail's now free hand caressed her bare thigh. Her mind flashed back to the night in the bakery when Abigail's hand had sought a place even more intimate. That night, Renee had been afraid. Tonight, after a year of dreaming of that moment, she was eager.

Abigail pulled her hand back for a moment, drawing confusion from Renee for a moment before Abigail turned her around. Face to face, Abigail pulled Renee in for a long, sensual kiss. Renee found herself lost in the sensations of being kissed by Abigail. For a moment, it didn't seem fair that she should know so much about how to affect Renee's body when Renee hadn't even been aware that she could be affected like this.

When their kiss broke, Renee was surprised to find that Abigail had nimbly managed to undo several of the buttons on her blouse. Renee stood there smiling as Abigail's hands went back to work.

Abigail kept working at the buttons, eager to finally see the treasures that lay beneath Renee's white blouse. She then watched as Renee hesitantly reached forward & began working on the buttons to her own blouse. Abigail's hand raced up the length of Renee's blouse while Renee was making slow work of the first of Abigail's six buttons.

Renee could sense how desperate Abigail was to rip the blouse from her body. She could see it like a hunger in Abigail's eyes. Yet Abigail waited, with the unbuttoned shirt giving her just the faintest peek of the white bra beneath. Renee worked her way up slowly as she undressed another woman for the first time in her life.

After what felt like an eternity to both of them, Renee finally slipped the last of Abigail's buttons. She only now noticed that at some point they had gotten closer to the bed so that it was right behind her now. The two women looked each other in the eye for a moment before looking down as they opened each other's blouses.

Renee had believed that she would be nervous & shy, standing there in only her bra & underwear in front of the woman that hungered for her. Instead, she was stunned as she realized that Abigail was now standing there bare breasted, no bra in sight.

"Mon Dieu."

Abigail smiled as Renee took in the sight of Abigail's large, full, pale, freckled breasts. Each feint freckle was like a feint star on two heavenly globes that were capped with a pair of pale pink nipples that were hard as diamond. Renee was mesmerized by the heavenly sight before her. She offered no resistance when Abigail took her hands & brought them to her breasts.

As Renee clumsily fumbled & groped Abigail's breasts, Abigail reached around Renee & began working at the French woman's clasps. Not used to taking 1930s bras off of another woman, it took Abigail a minute to unlock the garment. Pulling it free from Renee's chest so that it might join her blouse on the floor, Abigail took in the sight of Renee's fair, perky breasts & their small light brown nipples.

Standing there in just their underwear, Renee again offered no resistance as Abigail stepped forward to bring her in for a kiss. Renee's mind was on sensory overload as her lips met Abigail's & Abigail's breasts pressed against her own. Her own hardening nipples flooding her mind with overwhelming pleasure as the dug into Abigail's breasts & made contact with Abigail's nipples, causing both women to gasp & moan.

Abigail's hands felt like heavenly warmth as they moved across Renee's back. Renee had no idea what was going on until Abigail pulled back a bit, revealing that they were now on Abigail's bed. Renee looked up at the nearly naked woman above her. Not knowing what she should do next, she was grateful when Abigail took the lead & kissed her neck.

Before Renee knew what was happening, Abigail was trailing a line of kisses down Renee's neck, down her chest, along her breast & nipple. Renee gasped & writhed as the trail of kisses continued down her stomach towards the last piece of clothing separating her from Abigail's desire.

Abigail slipped the silk underwear down, revealing a dirty blonde bush that was damp with arousal & desire. As Abigail's lips & tongue found the French girl's slick opening, Renee's world turned into a world of pleasure.

There were moans & cries. Renee's hand was buried in Abigail's raven hair. Legs trembled & strings of French obscenities that could put a sailor to shame filled the room. When Renee finally shuddered & convulsed with climatic bliss, she lay back as Abigail trailed a new path of wet kisses up the length of Renee's body, leaving a warm trail along Renee's skin.

While Abigail planted a wet kiss on Renee's cheek, she took Renee's trembling hand & brought it to her own moist opening. Soon, as the two women held each other close on the narrow bed,

Abigail was bucking from pleasure as Renee's fingers probed her depths.

That night, the two women shared climax after climax until they were finally exhausted so late in the night that most would say it was early the next morning. They fell asleep in each other's arms, their bodies pressed against each other, their legs entwined together as they drifted off to sleep in each other's warm embrace.

Chapter 7
June 30th, 1935

The last forty days had been a whirlwind of emotions for Abigail. From waking up entangled with Renee, to their awkward interactions in the bakery over the next few days, things were rocky at first. After about a week, Renee was able to come to terms with the new state of their relationship. The two of them then started meeting up every chance that they could get.

They'd go out to movies, get dinner with some of Abigail's coworkers, get drinks at a bar. Then they would inevitably end up at Abigail's apartment where after dodging around Lola, they would find themselves in Abigail's small bed again.

As they got closer, Renee started to notice one or two minor oddities that she had either ignored or not been close enough to notice before. Small, strange things like how Abigail's teeth seemed a little too white up close, or how her skin seemed to be a little too youthful for someone in her thirties. Judging by all of Abigail's quick grabs & pinches, it was as if she had never learned to be afraid of someone finding out that she was intimate with another woman. Then there was her accent.

From time to time, usually when Abigail was distracted or a little drunk, or being intimate, her English accent would suddenly sound more American. But what really seemed odd to Renee was Abigail's lack of a past. She had no photos, no letters, nothing from home. She never talked about her time before coming over from England. It almost seemed as if she just came into being in 1930. She couldn't even remember the name of the boat that she had come over on.

While Renee was secretly noticing all of these little things, Abigail was always silently kicking herself. Once the beacon was lit, she could be transferred at any time. It could be in ten years, in could be in ten hours. She knew that she was risking breaking Renee's heart, but she couldn't stop herself. She was in love. That was the only word for it & just like every other time, it felt like the first time.

Now, the day was here. She had just gotten back from a Sunday morning visit to the bakery. She ordered a great big loaf of bread &

some croissants & while nobody was looking, she had planted a quick kiss on Renee's lips.

Abigail loved kissing Renee in the bakery. She always tasted like flour & she always blushed. The look on her face was always priceless. She lingered for a moment before leaving the shop. She wanted to take in every detail of the place & her new love just in case there were reassignment orders waiting for her when she got home & this was the last time that she would see Renee.

Walking through the front door of the apartment building, she checked her mailbox & found a postcard from London. This was it. Her final coded message for her primary mission had arrived. She slipped into her apartment, ate one of the croissants, & proceeded to decode the message.

PRIMARY MISSION IS GO. CHECK BEACON BEFORE DEPARTURE & BEFORE USE. ANY ISSUES TO BE REPORTED TO OMEGA CONTACT IMMEDIATELY!!! PRIMARY MISSION SITE IS GREEN. GOOD LUCK CANDY SKULL.

It had been over five years since anyone had called her Candy Skull. She missed being able to use her username. She spent the next hour triple checking the message. She then burned it & got to work.

She closed her curtains & took the beacon out from its hiding place for the last time. Taking it to her kitchen table, she performed a system check. She almost expected the indicators to turn red tonight. After a minute, they all turned green. There were no problems. She would deploy the beacon, suffer a small temporal distortion & be on her way.

Abigail then put the beacon in her satchel & spent the next hour preparing for the moment. With a revolver in her pocket, she waited until ten o'clock that night before leaving the apartment. Grateful that Lola wasn't out tonight, she slipped out of the apartment & started walking.

A few blocks away from her home, she slipped into an arched doorway where she was hidden from view. She then reached into her satchel, pulled out her blonde wig, slipped it on with expert skill & headed off.

At the next intersection, she looked left, the direction that she should go to get to Central Park. Figuring that she had plenty of time, she turned right instead. Half an hour later, she was standing outside the bakery again.

The whole way there, she had felt like there had been a voice in her head telling her to turn her ass around & get to Central Park. She couldn't be a single minute late. Still, she had to see the bakery one more time. She never approached it. When she got to it, she stood across the street & stared at it for a moment. She spent about three minutes just standing there, imagining. She imagined finishing tonight's mission & resigning. Telling Alex that she had done her job & that she wanted to stay here with Renee.

She imagined getting a job at the bakery. Working side by side with Renee. Sneaking kisses while nobody was looking & when Renee's father died in 1939, she would find a way to keep Renee from going back to France & disappearing in World War II.

Putting her dreams aside, she checked the small discreet watch that she had been given for the mission & turned on her heels to get to Central Park with plenty of time to spare.

Inside the bakery, Renee had just finished doing a quick inventory & making sure that everything would be set to go tomorrow morning. She was about to head upstairs to relax with a copy of one of her favorite science fiction pulp magazines when she saw something through the front window.

Noticing a blonde woman just standing there across the street, she was partly glad that the lights were off. It was a bit creepy. Staring back at the woman, it took Renee a moment to realize that it was Abigail. Abigail in a wig, standing across the street.

Confused, Renee ran upstairs to tell her father that she was going out for a bit. Taking a minute to reassure him that she would just be going over to see Abigail, her father raised his eyebrows. For a terrifying second, she was worried that he had just figured something out. Still, she headed back downstairs & made her way out the door, only to see a blonde woman walking away rather quickly.

Concerned about why her secret lover would be standing across the street from the bakery at quarter to eleven at night in a blonde wig, she followed behind her. Thinking that Abigail might be hiding from something, she didn't shout out or run after her. She stayed a short distance away, partly out of concern & partly to observe this latest strange behavior.

When Abigail didn't turn to head home, Renee started getting concerned. Abigail seemed to be almost in a rush. She had a death grip on her satchel & one hand buried in her pocket. Several times, Renee was tempted to run up to Abigail & ask her what was going on. Instead, she continued to keep a distance.

Was Abigail running from an old boyfriend that had caught up to her? Was she running from someone that she owed money to? Did the police want her for something? All kinds of thoughts ran through Renee's mind as she secretly followed behind her love.

Things only became more confusing when Abigail ducked into Central Park. Renee saw a police officer stop Abigail & talk to her for a moment. Renee watched as the officer took his hat off & looked around to see if anyone was watching them. Renee headed for one of the benches in order to not arouse suspicion.

Abigail almost had a heart attack when the policeman approached her. Remembering that she had been expecting him, she waited for him to look around before they started talking. When he took his hat off, Abigail knew that it was safe to talk as he addressed her.

"Agent Oldman, you're cutting it a little close."

"It's not that close."

"You're supposed to activate in twelve minutes."

"Shit, I lost track of time."

"Is this going to be a problem? I can call in an emergency."

"No problem. It's just around the corner & I only need a minute to set it up. Sorry if I worried you."

"It's not my ass on the line if that thing lights up late. There shouldn't be anyone around. I tossed out a few vagrants & sent them back to the tent town. I've got a few officers patrolling the area for other tent folk, but Turtle Pond should be clear. Only person I see is some woman on the bench behind you."

"Do you think that she's a threat?"

"No, probably just a prostitute trying to get through the depression & taking a break."

"Alright. I'm off. Again, sorry that I'm running late."

"Good luck Agent Oldman, I'm going to do another lap of the area, see if I turn up anything that poses a threat."

The officer then put his cap back on & headed off, leaving Abigail to make her way to Turtle Pond.

Renee was completely confused. Was Abigail in trouble with the police? Was she working with them? For a moment, Renee was worried that she was sleeping with an undercover cop that had been sent to root out homosexuals & other undesirables. She shook her head of such thoughts. The police wouldn't hire a woman for over five years to do undercover work.

As the police officer wandered off, Renee watched Abigail head further into the park. Renee waited a minute to avoid arousing suspicion. She then got up & slowly followed Abigail, all the while wondering what was going on, & what in the hell she was even doing out here. When Renee caught up to Abigail, she saw Abigail sitting by the shore of the pond with what looked like a thermos in front of her. A thermos with a glowing rod sticking out of it.

Abigail was keeping an eye on her watch as the armed beacon went through one more last-minute system check. With the check finished & showing six green indicators, she pressed the second button & listened to the strange, metallic hum as it powered up. As the last minute counted down, she watched as the central component, now extended from the rest of the device, began to emit a blue glow. With seconds left before midnight, she took a deep breath & reached for the button, activating the beacon.

Renee took a few tentative steps towards the sight before her. The strange noise had freaked her out & the glowing object in front of Abigail was reminding her of some of the stories that she read in her pulp science fiction magazines. She was about to call out to Abigail when at the stroke of midnight, there was a blinding flash of pale blue light.

Renee felt like she had been sent flying in a direction that she had not known existed. She lost all sense of direction. The next thing that she knew, she was standing at the pond again, only now, there was a man in a dark green suit with a heavy, grown out mullet.

Another push that knocked the wind out of her, & she was staring at a woman in front of the pond. A woman with a pompadour under a large hat & an ankle length dress that narrowed quite a bit at the waist. A few more flashes & she saw half a dozen more people wearing strange clothes & with strange hair standing in front of a device like Abigail had had.

As she saw a man that looked like a police officer with some sort of black vest & a strange glowing rectangle in his hand that was showing him the time, she was suddenly knocked to the side by a push & a flash that was stronger than all the others so far combined.

She was lying in a bunk with three other women. The bunk was in a cabin that was crowded & hot. Looking down at her body, she was wearing a black & white stripped uniform over her emaciated form. She was ravenously hungry & every muscle in her body hurt. There was a strange downward pointing black triangle sewn onto her shirt over her chest.

She was about to ask where she was when a wooden door burst open, waking the dozens of half-starved women in the room with her. Three men in black uniforms walked in. Two of them had machine guns. They started talking in German.

Suddenly, she found herself being hurled in some unknown direction once again, struggling to breathe until she was standing in front of the pond again. This time it was noon & there were dozens of people standing in a semicircle around a woman who was talking to them.

Some of the people looked like the people that she had seen standing at the pond in strange clothes. Now all of them wore strange clothes & unbelievable hair. Standing among them was Abigail, but something was wrong. Half her hair was shaved down to peach fuzz & the other half was dyed nine different colors from her roots to the top of her shoulder.

Around the park, there were buildings that seemed to climb up into the heavens. They looked like they shouldn't be able to stay standing upright as messages made of light were displayed in the air around them.

She suddenly felt like she had been hit by a train as another flash had her slowly standing up in a forest. Looking around, she saw a man & woman with dark, sun-tanned skin & what looked like hide clothing having a little get together in the privacy of the forest. Just as the woman's dress started to come up her legs, she again felt like she was being hit by a train.

She found herself standing in the bakery in the middle of the night. Abigail was standing in front of her, crying. As Abigail wiped away her tears, she only said three words.

"I'm sorry Renee."

The back & front doors both burst open as men dressed as police officers & wielding shotguns & revolvers came in with a black bag to put over her head. As they were leveling their guns at her, she felt another push, as if she had just fallen to the side.

Once again, she was in the bakery, only now it was morning. Customers were looking around at some of the items that they had on display while Renee was handing Abigail her Monday morning bagels. Their fingers touched over the bag of three sesame & poppy seed bagels & it almost felt like static, as if one of them had an almost electric charge to them. They looked each other in the eyes & smiled. Abigail then moved with lightning speed & planted a small kiss on Renee's lips. A quick little peck on the lips while nobody was watching.

Renee blushed while giving Abigail a glaring look. Abigail smiled, winked & walked out as Renee looked around to see if they had been noticed.

As Abigail walked out of the door, Renee suddenly felt like she had been shot out of a cannon. Once again, she found herself in a forest. This time, there was a herd of what looked like furry elephants. They were standing around, grazing on the grass & the leaves from the trees with their long trunks. Just as Renee was wondering about why these elephants had thick fur, she suddenly felt like she had been shot through another cannon.

Blinking in the light of the noon sun, she looked around the car that she was driving in. Looking in the mirror, she saw her reflection. She looked to be about a decade older as her hair blew in the wind. Looking to her side, she saw a slightly older Abigail grinning as she drove the blue convertible down the highway. Abigail then pointed ahead & shouted.

"There it is babe!"

Renee looked to the sign that Abigail was pointing at & read Welcome to San Francisco.

One more time feeling the wind get knocked out of her & just as she felt like she'd never be able to breathe, Renee found herself standing by the pond.

Since she was alone this time, she sat down in the grass. To the east, the sun was just rising over the horizon. She sat there for about ten minutes, watching the sunrise & catching her breath. She was fairly certain that whatever the hell that had been, it was now over. Seeing that nobody was around, Renee didn't bother keeping her thoughts to herself as she started talking to herself in French.

"What the hell was that? Have I lost my mind? I was following Abigail. She had a glowing… something… in front of her. Then I saw… What did I see?"

Renee rubbed her temples, trying to make sense of everything that she saw. It didn't help. Who were all of those people? Where was the cabin with all of the hungry people? Why was she being stormed by police in her bakery & why was she driving to San Francisco with Abigail? It didn't make any sense to her at all. She was older in some of the visions, were those images of her future?

Renee was determined to confront Abigail about it, but then she remembered the vision of Abigail crying & apologizing as police stormed the bakery. Maybe a confrontation wasn't a good idea. As the sun rose above the horizon, Renee decided to head home & try to figure things out before she did anything.

Picking herself up, she started walking on legs that were unsteady for a few steps. Once her legs remembered how to walk, she put one foot in front of the other & headed home slowly. Almost two hours later, she walked into the bakery to find her father both furious & concerned.

"Renee! Where the hell were you!"

The one customer that was in the room was startled by the sudden sound of a panicked father screaming in French.

"Sorry Papa, I… lost track… of time…"

"Don't. Papa. Me. You said that you were going to be gone for a bit. I figured that you'd be back in an hour at most. You were gone all night. It's 7:30 in the morning."

Renee wondered how it could be so late. The flashes had only lasted a few minutes.

"What happened to you Renee!? I was worried sick!"

Renee then did her best to make up an excuse on the spot.

"I… I went… I went to see Abigail. We were supposed to meet up yesterday… but I couldn't, because of… … the hours… that I had to spend working here."

Maurice lowered his shoulders.

"You should have told me that you had plans with your friend. I wouldn't have made you work so hard."

"It's okay Papa. I know that times are tough. So does Abigail. I went over to apologize. We… had a drink… or five… & I slept on her… couch."

"Well next time, your apology can wait until morning. I was up all damn night."

"Sorry."

"As long as you're alright. Can you mind the store for a bit? I need to take a nap before I get a start on the next batch of bread. We should have plenty of everything. I was up all-night baking to avoid thinking about you being mugged or attacked in an alleyway."

"I can handle it."

Maurice shook his head & headed upstairs to rest his weary head for a bit. Renee put on her apron, helped the one customer that had watched the shouting match & took a look at how much her father had baked the night before.

Nearly an hour later, a clearly exhausted Abigail walked into the bakery. Renee's heart froze in her chest. She had no idea if Abigail had seen her during those missing hours or if something equally strange was about to happen. As Abigail approached, Renee tried to keep calm.

"Good morning, Renee."

"Abigail, you're here a little later than usual. Is something wrong?"

Renee's heart was beating like a drum in fear.

"No, I just overslept, although I'm still tired. I had some weird nightmares last night."

"Yes, me too."

Abigail smiled.

"I guess that we're starting to dream alike."

Abigail leaned in & whispered so that the other customers wouldn't hear her.

"I hear that that happens to couples sometimes."

Renee then tried to quietly shush Abigail. Abigail laughed.

"So what was your nightmare about Renee?"

"Oh… uh… I don't… remember…"

"Don't you hate it when that happens?"

"Yes. What was… your nightmare… about…"

"My nightmare. I dreamed that I didn't have you anymore."

Renee blushed. Abigail stepped aside as an older man in a threadbare suit bought a muffin. She then stepped back to her spot at the counter by the cash register.

"So Renee. Can I have… three bagels, with sesame seeds, or poppy seeds, whichever you have today."

Renee reached behind the counter & produced three bagels that had both sesame & poppy seeds on them. Abigail's face lit up. It was hard to believe that this was the same woman that had been stalking around Central Park at midnight in a blonde wig. Then again, a lot of what Renee had seen was hard to believe. Maybe it really had just been a nightmare.

That was the thought that comforted Renee. She had actually just followed some random blonde woman to the park, fallen asleep, had a weird dream from reading too much science fiction & that was that. She smiled at the thought & handed Abigail the small bag of bagels.

Their fingers touched over the bag of three sesame & poppy seed bagels & it almost felt like static, as if one of them had an almost electric charge to them. They looked each other in the eyes & smiled. Abigail then moved with lightning speed & planted a small kiss on Renee's lips. A quick little peck on the lips while nobody was watching.

Renee blushed while giving Abigail a glaring look. Abigail smiled, winked & walked out as Renee looked around to see if they had been noticed.

It took Renee a moment to realize that that kiss had just played out exactly like the kiss in one of her visions. Right down to the three sesame & poppy seed bagels. A shiver ran up her spine as she told herself that it had to be a coincidence.

Chapter 8
July 2nd, 1935

It was strange waking up & not having the importance of her primary mission on her mind. No impulse to check on the beacon. No more mentally going over the route to Central Park. It felt like a weight had been lifted. Now all that was left of her primary mission was to meet up with her handler & see if she was going to be relocated right away, or if she would have some time here in New York. Time with Renee.

Slipping past Lola, she made her way out into the city & headed off to work like any normal Tuesday. Along the way, as she usually did, she stopped by the Rodin bakery to get her morning bagel & hopefully, a morning kiss from Renee.

When she first walked in, Renee seemed oddly surprised for a moment before she smiled at the sight of Abigail. Abigail walked up to the counter, leaned forward & grinned, waiting for the other morning customers to turn away.

"Good morning, Renee."

"Hello Abigail. You seem happier this morning."

"I'm just in a good mood."

"Oh? Why is that?"

"Because a beautiful baker is about to hand me a warm bagel. Why wouldn't I be happy."

Renee blushed a bit.

"Abigail, you can't keep talking like that."

"Why not?"

"Someone will overhear you. The last thing that I want is for one of us to end up in an asylum for confused women. Now what kind of bagel do you want?"

Abigail smiled. She liked it when Renee worried about her.

"Something out of the ordinary. Something special."

Renee shook her head as Abigail winked & turned to pick something that Abigail wouldn't normally order. Abigail did a quick look around to see that nobody was looking & quickly unbuttoned the top two buttons of her blouse, revealing just the topmost hint of her cleavage. When Renee turned around with a pumpernickel bagel in her hand, she smiled before her face turned stern.

"What did I just say Abigail?"

"You told me to watch what I say."

"Mon dieu. What am I going to do with you?"

"I can't wait to find out next time you come over."

As Renee turned beet red, Abigail paid for the bagel, took it from Renee's hand & headed off to work. Along the way, she enjoyed her bagel & quickly did up her blouse again. She then spent her morning playing the role of a simple secretary as she had been doing for the last several years. When lunch time rolled around, she went to see her boss.

"Mr. Parker, can I ask you something?"

"Sure Abigail, what's up?"

"I was wondering if I could take an extended lunch today. There's something that I need to take care of."

"Is everything alright?"

"I just have a personal thing that I need to take care of & I'm going to need more than the usual time that I take for lunch."

"What kind of personal thing?"

Abigail had to resist smiling as she thought about how he was about to regret asking that.

"A… womanly… personal matter…"

His face was the definition of a blank expression. So Abigail pushed a little further.

"A womanly personal matter… the kind that only comes around… once a month… … …"

His eyes lit up with recognition & disgust.

"Sure, take as much time as you need to… deal with… all of that… I'll see you later."

"Thank you, Mr. Parker."

Abigail almost felt ashamed using that excuse. Still, if the men of most centuries were going to be babies about it, that was on them. Abigail headed out to lunch, leaving no personal belongings at her desk, just in case her handler handed her a bus ticket & told her that she was leaving that afternoon.

She made her way to a diner down the street, slipped into their bathroom & locked herself in a stall to change into her favorite red wig. Slipping on a pair of fake glasses, she then left the diner & made her way further down the road to the café where Alex was waiting for her. It only took her a second to spot him in his grey wig with some red highlights weaved into it. He had already ordered her a small sandwich.

"Hello Abigail, how are you doing?"

Abigail sat down across from him while eyeing the BLT that he had ordered for her.

"I'm doing alright. Just can't wait to find out what happens next."

"We'll get to that. How was your mission? Any problems or issues that I should know about?"

"No problems. Everything went by the book."

Abigail took a bite out of her sandwich while he eyed her & stirred whatever it was that he was drinking in place of coffee.

"Are you sure about that Abigail. There's nothing that you want to report about your mission?"

"What are you getting at Alex?"

"Well, most beacon carriers show up at least an hour before the appointed moment, giving them time to deal with any technical issues. But according to the support staff that was there, you only showed up twelve minutes before the deadline. Is there any particular reason that you cut it so damn close?"

"No particular reason, I just… lost track of time."

Alex stopped stirring his drink & took a sip of it before continuing.

"You're only supposed to lose track of time when the beacon is lit & it causes that brief timeslip. How did you get distracted before?"

"I… may have… taken a… … detour."

Abigail bit into her sandwich to keep her face from betraying her in front of her handler. She honestly felt bad for causing Alex another potential issue.

"Detoured. Why?"

"Well, I may have stopped at…. … well…"

"You went to the bakery."

"Yeah… Sorry Alex. I wanted to see it one more time. You're not mad, are you?"

"No, it's natural to want to see the people & places that are important to you when you don't know if you're going to be around much longer. But twelve minutes is a little too close for comfort for some of the higher ups."

"Am I in trouble?"

"No. There weren't any problems in the end. You did your job." Abigail felt a weight leave her shoulders.

"So everything was good Alex? There weren't any issues?"

"No issues. The beacon did exactly as it was supposed to, exactly when it was supposed to. The localized timeslip is established in this timeline & I've got a report from the top brass that our arrival accuracy is now down to 52 hours. Which means that incoming agents will arrive within two days of their target."

"So my mission?"

"It was a complete success, Abigail. Well done, a little close for comfort, but well done."

Abigail felt like if any more weight was lifted off of her shoulders, she might float away. After taking a moment to collect herself, she asked her burning question.

"So. What's next for me? Am I being shipped out to another location?"

Alex smiled.

"Not for a while. The financial data that you have access to is incredibly valuable. You're probably going to be here until the start of the war, at least."

Abigail was certain that she would be floating away any moment now. The Start of the war was six years away. That meant that she would have at least six years with Renee. Six years together. She'd be able to convince Renee to not go back to France. Alex must have quickly figured out what the look of relief was about.

"Yes, you're going to get at least half a decade with her. I'll admit, I was nervous when you told me that you two were a thing five weeks ago. It seems that it might just work out for the two of you in the end."

"You have no idea how happy I am. So am I just gathering information now?"

"Not entirely, your apartment is going to be reclassified as a tertiary safe house. You probably won't see any action, but you're going to have to maintain alert readiness. Over the next few weeks, you'll receive a series of 'care packages' from your older brother in London. In reality, they'll be first aid, basic firearms & false identification papers. Make sure that Renee doesn't see any of it."

"You know, it would probably make it easier for me to operate an emergency safe house if I didn't live next to the gossip queen of Hell's Kitchen."

"Sorry Abigail, I've put in an official request, but for a tertiary safe house that will only be manned when you're not busy with work or Renee, the brass doesn't see it as being an issue if your neighbor is a bit nosey."

The two of them then finished lunch together & parted ways. After a little while, Abigail was back at her desk, her handful of personal belongings back where they ought to be. Her boss discreetly asked if everything was alright & she happily told him that there weren't any problems.

When the day was over, Abigail walked along the path home with a new skip in her step. When Abigail walked into the bakery, Maurice & Renee both noticed that she seemed to be in a rather uplifted mood. After Maurice went back to start working on the last batch of things that he was baking for the day, Abigail leaned over the counter to talk to Renee.

"You're not mad about this morning?"

"You mean when you started undressing, no, I'm not mad. Although I do wish that you would exercise a greater degree of caution."

"I'll think about it. In the meantime, would you like to come over on Friday? I was hoping to cook you a big, delicious supper."

"I ah… ah… yeah… I can come over."

Abigail noticed the nervousness in Renee, but she chalked it up to Renee always being nervous when they were close & customers were around. She had no idea that Renee was trying to sort out the visions that she had seen in the timeslip & that she was worried about some of the things that she saw.

Sep 14th, 1935

The empty desk to Abigail's left was a stark reminder of why she had come into work on Saturday morning. If ever there was a time to look like a diligent, hardworking employee who's willing to go the extra few miles, it was now. Unemployment was climbing again & after the troubles of the last few years; the board of directors had told every department to make cuts.

Since Abigail's access to bank information was the main reason that she wasn't being transferred in the next few years, Abigail got to work. Every Saturday morning for the last month, Abigail had been at her desk, furiously typing away. If she could convince the bosses not to fire her, she could continue to spend the rest of the week copying information for her handler. If she could do that, she could stay in New York with Renee.

When lunch time rolled around, her boss, Mr. Parker, came over to her desk to take the latest batch of typed files. With nothing else to give her, he stared as her fingers danced across the keys of the typewriter.

"I don't know how you do it. I've never seen anyone else type that fast without making a hundred mistakes per page."

"Just talent & practice. Do you have anything else for me?"

"Nope."

Abigail stopped typing & looked at him weirdly.

"Sorry Abigail, but I've got nothing more for you. Once you finish that pile, we'll be up to date on our work. If you keep this up, I'll have to start asking some of the other accountants if you can work on their backlogs."

He smiled. None of the others were anywhere close to having their workload finished. Most were several days, if not a few weeks behind.

"Do you want me to finish this pile up before I head home?"

"No, leave yourself something to do on Monday morning. Go & enjoy your weekend."

"If you're sure Mr. Parker."

"I'm sure."

Abigail then finished up the last few lines of the page that she was on & packed herself up. She then headed home while enjoying the crisp autumn breeze that blew down the street.

As she walked past several shops that were clearly struggling & a few that were already closed, she walked up to a clothing store & saw some of their winter wears in the window. Seeing the mannequins dressed up reminded her of Renee's older clothes. As she stood there thinking about it, she thought about Renee who was probably going to be wearing the same winter clothes that she had been using since before they met. Abigail remembered how threadbare some of those clothes were getting.

Seeing that she didn't want Renee to freeze, she walked into the store. The moment that she walked in, the store owner, a little old man, walked right up to her. Looking around, she quickly saw that she was the only customer.

"Well hello miss, how I can help you today?"

Abigail was tempted to ask to see his jackets, but she stopped herself. Remembering that people would not take to kindly to women who were too close in this century, she decided that gifting Renee a full winter jacket would be a bit weird.

"I was thinking of getting a little something for a friend of mine who could use a new scarf or gloves."

"Well you've come to the right place. Let me show you what I have in store."

Half an hour later, Abigail was walking out of the store with a bold red scarf tucked away in a paper bag. She then headed home to make herself some lunch. After running into Lola, who was strangely suspicious of the scarf, Abigail made her way into her apartment & got a start on lunch.

As she started warming up her leftovers, her mind started drifting off to a thought that had been bothering her for weeks. Eventually, she was going to get a new mission. Even if she stayed in New York, she was going to be rejuvenated. Even if she was just rejuvenated, she would still have to break things off with Renee.

These thoughts led Abigail to the question that had been plaguing her for weeks. When the time came, would she be able to break it off for the sake of the mission? Could she break both of their hearts, or would she give up her mission? Could she look her handler in the eye & tell him that she was resigning?

As she ate, she wondered if she would be able to come up with an answer before the time came for her to decide. She tried to put it out of her mind, but the thought would always be there. The knowledge that one day, she was going to have to choose between the mission & Renee.

After lunch, Abigail started checking on the small cache of weapons that she now had to keep in her apartment. Since this was now technically a safe house, she had to keep all kinds of new equipment in working order. She kept it all behind a false panel in her closet so that Renee would never accidentally stumble on to any of it. So where she once had to perform beacon tests on Saturdays, she now how to clean guns, check first aid kits & look over a stash of fake passports & emergency currency.

As Abigail disassembled & cleaned one of the period accurate revolvers that was now being kept in her emergency cache, she imagined saving Renee. She pictured the scene in her mind. It would be 1939, she would be rushing through a crowd of people in a port & grabbing Renee just before she got on the boat to France. She would pull Renee out of the crowd, saving her from a France destined to surrender to evil. They would then live their lives in New York city, over the bakery, making bread during the day & making love at night.

As she started reassembling the revolver, she grinned, not caring at all that saving Renee would violate severe protocols & that she would be in a world of trouble.

Once she was finished with her new Saturday morning routine, Abigail decided to pay Renee a visit, so she got dressed again & headed back out. Soon enough, she was walking up to the bakery, bag in hand & grinning as she walked into the always wonderful smell of freshly baked bread.

When the surge of customers that had been crowding the bakery finally filed out, Renee came out from behind the counter & surprised Abigail with a long hug.

"I whisper small flirtations with you & you panic, but now you're hugging me out in the open?"

"Nobody is watching us, Abigail."

"Except for that guy in the window."

Renee went white as a ghost as she separated from Abigail.

"Where? Which window?"

"Just kidding Renee."

"Enfer sanglant."

"Do I want to know what that means Renee?"

"It means bloody hell. You scared me, Abigail."

"I'm sorry Renee. Would it make it up to you if I told you that I got you a present?"

Abigail held up the bag that she had brought in. Renee's eyes went wide for a moment before she looked around to see if there was anyone around. The only person nearby was her father in the kitchen.

"Don't worry Renee, it's not like I got you a diamond ring or lingerie, it's safe to open it."

"Sometimes Abigail, I think you don't realize how much trouble we could get into for being… you know."

"Lovers?"

Renee went beet red & looked around again. She then gave Abigail that age old look that meant she should be more careful before opening the bag & pulling out the long red scarf.

"I was walking past a store for winter clothes & I remembered how chilly you got last year. I hope you like it."

Renee wrapped it around her neck, imagining it over her threadbare coat.

"I love it. C'est merveilleux. It's like a hug from you that'll keep me warm all winter."

Renee blushed as Abigail smiled.

"Well since you like it, why don't we go for a stroll & see how much it keeps you warm? We can go for a walk tonight after you close the shop."

"Hold that thought Abigail."

Renee then went back to where her father was baking more bagels & talked with him for a moment. A minute later, she was walking out with her coat on & a smile on her lips.

"Father says that since it's slowed down, he can handle the shop by himself. I'm all yours."

For a minute, Abigail's grin turned wicked. A minute later, they were out in the cool September afternoon, walking down the street.

Abigail wished that she could wrap her arm around Renee as they walked. Sadly, it would be more than half a century before they could walk down the streets of New York as an obvious couple, so instead they maintained the appearance of two friends enjoying an afternoon stroll as the world was falling apart around them.

"Thank you for the scarf, Abigail. It really is beautiful."

"You're welcome, Renee. I figured that since I can't keep you warm by wrapping my arms around you, this would be the next best thing."

They walked past an older couple that were with their young grandson & continued walking.

"Can I tell you something Renee?"

"Sure."

"When I was in the store, I was tempted to get you the coat that went with that scarf. Then I figured that that would be a bit too obvious."

"Yes, it would have been. Not to mention the fact that you probably couldn't afford it anyway."

"What do you mean?"

Renee stopped for a second & looked at Abigail before they continued on their gentle walk.

"Abigail, how do you afford so much? I know that you work in a bank, but after these last few years, no woman can afford to live on her own."

"My brother in London helps me out, you know that."

"Still, between living on your own & always taking me out, you must be having a hard time."

"I'll admit Renee, it can be tight at times, but if it means that you'll be thinking of me when you wear that scarf, it was worth every penny."

Renee blushed a bit. She would be thinking about Abigail every time that she put that scarf on. When they turned into Central Park, Abigail could swear that Renee suddenly looked a little more nervous than usual. She could almost swear that Renee looked like she wanted to ask something. When it got to the point that Abigail was about to ask what was wrong, Renee, her cheeks turning rosy from more than just the autumn chill, stood a little closer to Abigail.

"How about we go back to your apartment so that I can thank you for being so wonderful properly."

A while later, when time no longer meant anything to Abigail, she was sitting on her living room sofa, her legs spread wide & her hand over her own mouth desperately trying to cover up her cries of pleasure.

Renee was on her knees. Her red scarf was sitting on top of the rest of her clothes in a pile on the floor next to Abigail's. As Renee reached up the length of Abigail's body to fondle her large breasts with one hand, her face was buried in the moist triangle between Abigail's thighs. As Abigail cried into her hand & trembled on the couch, Renee was tasting a woman for the first time in her life & discovering that she loved it.

As Renee's inexperienced lips kissed every sensitive fold, Abigail was gasping for breath. As Renee's tongue brushed against Abigail's hard clitoris, Abigail shook with pleasure. When Renee plunged her tongue into Abigail's slick entrance, flooded with arousal & desire, something inside of her own body felt right for the first time.

Renee didn't care about Abigail's strange quirks or whatever she thought that she saw in the park that night back in June. All that mattered was that she was in love & for the first time since they had started making love, it was Abigail who was writhing in pleasure, desperately trying to muffle her ecstasy.

Dec 24th, 1935

The red knit gloves were incredibly soft & warm. Renee held them up over the paper wrapping that she had just opened & smiled. The gloves would go perfectly with the scarf that Abigail had gotten for her a few months ago.

"Thank you, Abigail, they're perfect."

"I'm glad that you like them."

"I'm sorry that I didn't get you anything."

"That's alright Renee, seeing you happy is more than enough of a gift for me."

Renee blushed. She was glad that she had brought Abigail up into the apartment over the bakery. Since there was nobody around, she felt more than comfortable enough to pull Abigail into a deep kiss. It felt strange to her, kissing Abigail in her home. Almost taboo. As if this was something that was only safe to do in Abigail's home. As Renee felt a hand sliding down her back to rest on her rear, she broke the kiss.

"Now that… sorry… now that, was better than any present that you could have gotten me in return."

Renee scrunched up her face for a second. There it was again, in the first two words that Abigail had just spoken. That strange, almost American accent that she heard from time to time when she caught Abigail off guard. Renee let it go, probably just her imagination again.

"I wish that I could take you back to my room, but my father is going to be up in a few minutes so we can have our Christmas supper."

"That's alright Renee. I know that you have plans tonight. I just wanted to drop this off."

"You're not going to be alone, are you?"

"No. I'm going out with a few friends from work. We're going to a fancy restaurant together to celebrate having a few days off of work."

"Alright, as long as you're not alone tonight. I would have invited you to have supper with us tonight, but I don't know if papa would have thought it strange."

"I'm sure he would have been alright with it if you told him that I was alone. Your papa seems like a nice guy."

"I'm sorry Abigail."

"Don't be sorry. Just be at my place the day after tomorrow so that we can celebrate the holidays together. Alone."

Renee blushed & nodded her head. The two of them kissed one more time before Abigail turned to head home. Maurice came up just as Abigail was walking out. He offered to let Abigail join them, but she told him that she had plans. They hugged each other & wished each other a merry Christmas before Abigail left to find her way to the restaurant.

"It's too bad that she doesn't have any family in town. You know you can invite her over for supper sometime if you'd like."

"Thank you, Papa."

"Come, let's eat. I have a nice bottle of wine from your aunt, she sent it to us to remember the family back home in France."

"She sent a bottle of wine?"

"Yes, along with some letters from her & your cousins & a few pictures of the family. We can look at them after supper."

"Sounds wonderful Papa."

The two of them sat down to a small roast beef supper. They enjoyed the wine & each other's company as the night progressed. After supper, they opened the letters & read them out, discovering what their family back home had been up to in the last few months. Renee marveled at the photos of her aunt & cousins, some of the only pictures of them that she had. The two of them then got started on the letters that they would write back home while wishing that they had had time to write them months ago so that they might get to France before the holidays.

Later on, after another glass or two of wine, they wished each other goodnight & headed off to their beds. Normally, after a big meal & half a bottle of wine, Renee would have been out like a light. Instead, she was tossing & turning.

Every time that she closed her eyes, visions of being in that prison camp with the German guards plagued her. While she was lying there awake, she kept hearing Abigail saying 'Now that' in that strange accent. Abigail had lost count of how many times she had heard it.

It seemed that Renee had finally reached the point where she could no longer just ignore all of these strange things. Getting up, she pulled a small notebook out of her dresser drawers & managed to find a pencil. Lighting a candle, she sat down at her desk, intent on writing down some of the things that she had seen & heard so that she could try & make sense of them.

Maybe it was the wine, or maybe it was the season. She didn't know, but once she started writing it all down, it just kept coming. She described every time that Abigail's English accent seemed to disappear for a few words. She wrote down about the time she came to the bakery after the robbery & started talking nonsense. She wrote about how Abigail seemed to have no understanding of how dangerous it was to be seen together. Then, there was the night in the park.

She wrote about seeing Abigail in a wig, following her to the park, seeing her talk to the cop & finally, her visions. She wrote down each vision in as much detail as she could remember half a year later. From the bad visions of armed police storming the bakery, to the good visions of them driving to San Francisco in a rather strange looking car. When she was finally finished writing it all down, she sat back, took a breath, & started looking over it.

Right off the bat, she crossed off the day of the robbery. Abigail had clearly been in shock; anyone would be talking nonsense. That still left a number of strange things.

Focusing on Abigail's accent, she tried to come up with a number of reasons for it. Maybe she had tried to learn how to talk like an American a few years ago & it didn't work. That could explain why sometimes her accent slipped. Then again, maybe she was in danger & her normal English accent was to throw someone off of her trail. Renee pictured a husband that wasn't too happy that Abigail preferred the company of women. If he was mean enough, it would make sense that Abigail would run away, change her name & even adopt a new accent in case anyone came looking. It would also explain why she didn't really talk about anything before 1930.

But a crazy husband wouldn't explain the night in the park. Remembering seeing her in that wig & the way that she talked to that cop got Renee's mind racing. Maybe she & the cop were part of some military project & they were testing a new weapon. Renee quickly put a big X next to that possibility. The military wouldn't be testing new weapons a few hundred feet away from the thousands of people living in Central Park. They'd test it in the dessert or the forest, not to mention that they probably wouldn't use women.

Maybe Abigail was a spy. Maybe some foreign country had sent her here to investigate something. It would explain her lack of a past, how she could afford to live on her own & why she worked so hard at the bank. There was probably a lot of useful information there for foreign governments. But that still wouldn't explain the visions.

Thinking about the visions, Renee was tempted once again to just pretend that they were a dream. She wanted to tell herself that she had just passed out in Central Park, hit her head & had a bunch of strange dreams. But it was getting harder to pretend that was the case.

Abigail wouldn't have just left her there alone. Someone would have come across her over the hours that she couldn't remember. Not to mention the fact that one of her visions had come true. That almost electric kiss that they had shared that morning was exactly like she had seen in the vision.

Renee decided to start from the vision & figure out what could explain all of that. She was fairly sure that Abigail wasn't a mad scientist testing something. She was also fairly sure that nobody had anything that small that could glow like that, make you see a bunch of things that might come true & make you skip a few hours of time. That was some sort of science fiction nonsense. Surely, Abigail wasn't some sort of space woman from Mars or Andromeda.

Although that would explain a lot. The science fiction vision flash; alien technology. The cop; a fellow alien. The accent; aliens struggling with human languages. The boldness of her affection; maybe her race is accepting of women being together.

Renee shook her head. Cleary, she was reading too much science fiction. She wanted to put a great big X next to that explanation, but she couldn't. Since it was the only thing that explained everything, she put a question mark next to it.

Shaking her head again, she hid the notebook in her drawer. She felt that she clearly needed to sleep if the only explanation that she could come up with for her lover's strangeness was that she was from another world.

Feb 12th, 1936

The blistering cold winds & the foot of snow on the ground couldn't do anything to deter Abigail or to dampen her mood. Valentine's day was two days away & Renee would be coming over for a late supper after the bakery closed on the day. Nothing could ruin her mood. After a quick stop at a farmer's market & the butchers for some fresh ingredients, Abigail had stopped by the florist to pick up some lavender.

The man behind the counter gave her a knowing wink as he bragged about having the best lavender stalks in the city. Abigail remembered from her briefings on twentieth century subcultures that queer couples would often exchange lavender instead of roses to avoid arousing suspicion. That was why she was here now. She wanted to give Abigail flowers & buying another woman a bouquet of roses would be the same as wearing a neon sign.

Was the florist trying to tell her that he knew & that this was a safe place to buy her lavender in the future? Abigail had smiled & paid him in cash before walking out of the store with fresh lavender in her bag. She had made her way back to her apartment in Hell's Kitchen & bounded up the stairs after checking her mail. Everything was going perfectly until Lola opened her door.

A great number of swear words from the next century ran through Abigail's head, but she didn't let any of it show or get her down. She simply nodded her head & headed towards her door in the desperate hope that somehow, for once, Lola actually had to be somewhere. No such luck.

"Well look at you, grinning like the cat that caught the canary."

Nothing to do but to bare through it.

"Hi Lola, I guess I'm just in a good mood."

"Yes, I've been seeing a lot of that lately. You seem to be incredibly happy these last few months."

"I suppose I have been."

"So what's got you in such a good mood lately?"

Abigail braced herself for Lola's fishing expedition. Sometimes, Abigail could swear that her neighbor was another agent, sent to see if she's about to break.

"What's not to be happy about? I've still got my job despite the economy & management laying people off. I've got good friends; I've got my health & I just feel… good."

"I see. Do I smell flowers?"

More obscenities ran through Abigail's mind. What was she thinking, trying to sneak flowers past Lola this close to Valentine's Day? She could sense Lola's curiosity as if it were a trap that she had just run into.

"Yeah… yes… I got myself some flowers to… spruce up the apartment. Nothing chases away the winter blues like some fresh flowers."

Lola was not impressed.

"I suppose you're right. Flowers are good at chasing away February, especially if they're from a good-looking young man, just two days before Valentine's Day."

"Wouldn't that be nice. Sadly, I have to pick my own flowers once again this year."

"I don't recall you getting yourself flowers on any other year."

"I'm certain that I did."

Again, Lola was not impressed.

"So if you're not going to be entertaining a nice young man, I suppose that you're going to be doing something with your good friends. Perhaps Renee."

Abigail was suspicious of the possible way out that Lola was giving her, it had to be a trap. Still, what other way was there?

"Some of us are thinking about it. Possibly Renee, why do you ask?"

"Well I figured that if you're doing something with your good friends, she'll be there. The two of you are rather close, I see her here all the time, sometimes staying the night."

Abigail had a vision of needing to explain to her handler why she needed a clean-up crew in her neighbor's apartment. She did her best to keep her cool.

"Renee doesn't exactly live next door… Sure her home isn't that far, but at night… especially after a few drinks… That's a long walk for a young woman to go on alone."

Lola nodded her head. She couldn't deny the truth of that. Lord knew that she had spent a night or two on a friend's couch rather than walk home alone at night.

"Good on you Abigail, letting your friend sleep on your couch instead of sending her out among the men that prowl the night. If more people were that thoughtful, this would be a much better world."

"Thank you, Lola, that's kind of you to say."

"Alright, well, I'll let you get to your night."

"Thanks Lola. Goodnight."

Abigail fumbled with her keys & unlocked her door. Slipping in, she took her groceries & flowers to her kitchen & cursed. She was worried about what would happen if Lola saw Renee & only Renee come over on Valentine's Day & not leave until the next day. With any luck, tonight's excuse would hold. She'd just tell Lola that all of her other friends got dates.

To cheer herself up, she went into her bedroom & took a look at the lingerie that she bought a few days ago. The light blue satin gown would show off mountains of her cleavage. The slit that ran all the way up to her hip would expose her leg & damn near everything else with each step. The material was so sheer that it left almost nothing to the imagination.

Abigail imagined the look on Renee face when she walked into the apartment in two days. Abigail would stay behind her door so that no neighbor could see her. Only when Renee was safely inside would she see Abigail.

She imagined Renee's adorable blush as she took her coat. She imagined the poor French girl mumbling & swearing in French as they ate dinner with Abigail on full display the entire time. She pictured Renee almost shaking with anticipation as they danced together, slowly in her living room, until Abigail led her here, to the bed. Renee would move the thin little shoulder straps to the sides, the sheer gown would drop to the floor & ….

Chapter 9
May 11th, 1936

Abigail walked into her apartment. Despite how easy her day had been, she still felt exhausted. She put her fresh loaf of bread down on the kitchen table & decided that what she really needed was a nice, long, hot shower. That would be just the thing for her. Heading into the bathroom, she got the water running nice & hot. Once it was exactly right, she slipped out of her clothes. Taking a second to look over her body in the bathroom mirror, she compared herself to how she used to look before her mission started.

Her body had clearly put on a few more years than the calendar had. Even though she was only 32, she would swear that she looked like she was closer to 37. She didn't know if it was the stress from her mission, life in the great depression, or just the lack of anti-ageing meds. All that she knew was that something was taking a toll. Somethings were too tight; some were just a little looser than she remembered & some things were just starting to lose ground in the fight against gravity.

As Abigail once again thought about the fateful day in her future when she would have to choose between rejuvenation & growing old with Renee, she stepped into the shower. Just as she was about to switch to the shower head, she heard the phone ringing in the kitchen.

"Of Course. When I'm wet & Naked, that's when it rings."

Stepping out of the shower, she quickly turned the water off & dried her feet. She then ran into the kitchen, still naked, & picked up the phone while being grateful that her apartment was high up enough that nobody could see into her windows.

"Hello?"

"Abigail, thank goodness your home, we have an emergency."

"Alex, what's wrong?"

"One of our secondary safe houses in Harlem has been compromised. We need a place for one of our agents to lay low for a day or two."

"You're telling me that there are no tertiary safe houses closer to Harlem than Hell's Kitchen?"

"None that are available. Agent goes by the name of Ornell Page; he'll be there in twenty minutes by means of the bus. He'll need medical assistance."

"Understood."

Abigail hung up the phone & ran to her bedroom. Opening her closet, she slid the false panel out of its place & grabbed the emergency medical kits. She was putting them on her kitchen table, next to the fresh loaf of bread before she remembered that she was still naked. Running back to her bedroom, she threw on some clothes & got back to work.

Throwing on her work shoes, which were still a little warm from being worn all day, she ran outside into the warm Monday afternoon & stood by the door to her apartment building where she waited for the bus to arrive. When one of her neighbors walked out of the building, she said hi & gave the excuse that she was thinking about going for a walk. He bid her a good evening & went on his way.

A few minutes later, the bus pulled up & a tall, handsome, dark-skinned man limped off of the bus. As the appearance of a Black man getting off of the bus drew the attention of a number of people, Abigail mentally cursed whoever had sent him here. A limping Black man with a bloody bandage around his left leg getting off the bus in a predominantly Irish neighborhood in the late afternoon was going to draw attention.

The only way that he blended in was that he was dressed like most of the men that lived in the neighborhood. He wore simple jeans & a simple work shirt. He stood there looking around until he spotted Abigail waiving him over. He quickly limped towards her.

"This the place?"

"Yes, I'm guessing that you're Ornell Page."

"That I am."

"Do you need help up the stairs?"

"I would appreciate that."

Once they were inside the lobby, Abigail put his arm over her shoulder & helped him up the flights of stairs to her apartment. He tried to muffle his grunts as they went up the steps, but a few slipped out by the time they were in front of Abigail's door. As Abigail was opening her door, she heard something familiar behind her. Rushing him into her apartment, she closed the door, concealing him from view as Lola opened the door.

"Hi Lola."

"Hello Abigail. What are you doing in the hallway?"

"Forgot to check my mail when I got home. Went back down."

"I should probably get around to checking mine."

As Lola reached into her apartment to grab her mailbox key, Lola slipped into her apartment to find Ornell leaning against the wall.

"Sorry, nosey neighbor. I've been requesting a more private place for years, but sadly, I've always been deemed a low priority."

"No problem. My leg on the other hand…"

"Shit, sorry, I'm set up in the kitchen. This way."

"That's alright, if it were really serious, I'd be dead by now. Spent an hour waiting by a payphone for instructions, slowly bleeding into a filthy rag & they send me to one of the whitest neighborhoods in New York."

"I guess they figured that nobody would ever look for you here."

"I guess."

Abigail then helped him out of his jeans so she could tend to the injury on his thigh. It looked like it was just a nasty graze, which was good because she basically only had a few first aid kits on hand. She wasn't trained or set up to go digging a bullet out of someone.

"It's a good thing that you're not on the ground floor. I'm guessing that the last thing that you need is for a neighbor to look in & seeing you kneeling before a Black man with his trousers around his ankles."

"Actually, that would probably distract my gossip queen of a neighbor from the girl that regularly spends the night here. This is going to sting a bit."

Ornell winced as Abigail disinfected the wound.

"Alright Ornell, why don't you tell me what the hell happened while I fix you up."

"My partner & I were watching over the main secondary safehouse for Harlem. He was out paying some bills when it all went down. The police showed up & started raiding the building. I'm fairly certain that they were looking for the guys downstairs, they're always dealing reefer. Didn't stop them from busting in everyone's doors."

"Let me guess, 20th century police probably figured that every Black man in the building was buying or selling."

"Just about. Anyway, we can't have the cops searching a secondary safe house. We've got enough firearms, fake idents & currency to draw down the attention of federal investigators. So I followed the scorched Earth protocol & torched the place. Thermite charge should have melted the guns & whatnot down to slag, hopefully."

"There weren't a lot of people living in the building, were there?"

"Not too many. The blaze was in the middle of the afternoon, so most of the people weren't home from work. We were also on the top floor, so it would have taken ages for the flames to climb down the building."

"That's good at least. How did you get shot?"

"I was trying to sneak out when one of them pointed his gun at me. The smoke from the fire distracted him for a moment & I bolted. He emptied his revolver where I had been standing & one of the shots grazed my thigh. Barely made it out of there."

"Well the good news is that you'll be fine. Just keep the wound clean & you should be good. I think I have a pair of pants in my cache that will more or less fit you."

"Thanks. Sorry to just drop in on you like this."

"It's literally why I'm here."

Abigail then went to her closet cache of equipment & got one of the few pairs of pants. She brought them into the kitchen for Ornell to try on over his bandaged leg. While Ornell was fumbling with his pants, Abigail picked up the phone & called her handler.

"Abigail, what's the situation?"

"Ornell is here. His injuries were minor, no indication that he was followed here."

"That's good."

"What do we do next?"

"You're going to need to hold up for a day or two while we sort this all out. Meet me at the Central Park location tomorrow for further instructions."

"Alright Alex, I'll see you tomorrow."

Abigail hung up the phone & turned to her guest.

"Looks like you're staying here for a day or two while they figure some things out."

"I don't suppose that you have a spare bed in here?"

"Sorry Ornell, just the sofa."

"Lumpy?"

"Only a bit."

May 12th, 1936

The next morning, Abigail woke up & started on her normal morning routine for a few minutes before she remembered that Ornell was sleeping on her couch & that she had an emergency meeting with her handler. After taking a minute to practice her sick voice while Ornell woke up, Abigail picked up her kitchen phone & called her boss.

While Ornell got a start on making some tea, Abigail coughed & wheezed convincingly enough to make Ornell think that she was actually sick for a minute. She hung up the phone after promising that she would be back at work in a day or two. As the water for the tea slowly boiled, she turned to Ornell.

"How's your leg doing?"

"It's doing alright. A little sore but in otherwise good condition."

"That's good. Was the couch alright last night?"

"I've slept on worse. I'm sorry if I'm getting you into trouble with your boss."

"Not a problem. I'm the only one that's not behind on my work & this is the first sick day that I've taken since I arrived six years ago."

"Star employee. Where do you work?"

"A bank in Soho. Secretarial work & typing mostly."

Ornell was impressed as he continued preparing the tea.

"Bank in Soho. Nice gig."

"Where did they have you?"

"They had me working construction the last few months. Mostly it just paid the bills, but sometimes it's useful to have access to building plans. Would you like some tea?"

"Please."

The two of them sat down for a bit & chatted about this & that for a bit. Seeing the time on the kitchen clock, Abigail got up so that she could get ready for her meeting.

Half an hour later, she was out the door & on her way. A quick pit stop in a local library & she was wearing glasses & a blonde wig with graying hair. Walking into the Park, it only took her a minute to find Alex sitting on a bench, reading a newspaper. As Abigail sat down next to Alex, she was able to read the headline about the chiefs of police conferring on gambling before Alex folded it up.

"How's Ornell doing?"

"He's alright. He only suffered a graze to his leg."

"Good. I can't stay long, so I'll be brief. You're going to need to keep him at your place for a few days, possibly a week."

"Why so long?"

"The police identified him as a person of interest in an open arson & drug case. He can't go back to Harlem. Hell, he can't stay in New York. We're working to relocate him & in the meantime, we think that it would be best if he stayed as low as possible, which means not moving from safe house to safe house."

"Alright, but I can't just disappear from work all week. I told them that I'd be sick for a day or two."

"It shouldn't be a problem. Ornell is used to watching over a safe house. I'm sure he'll be fine alone for a few hours on Thursday & Friday."

"Guess that means that I'm cancelling on Renee."

"Sorry Abigail. Here, this is for you."

Abigail took the envelope that Alex handed her.

"What is this?"

"Money for food for your new roommate & his handler's phone number."

"Thanks Alex."

"No problem. Now if you have a problem in the next few days, you call me. If you can't reach me, try the Delta number. If that's a bust, you can try Ornell's handler."

"You, Delta, Ornell's handler. Got it."

"Good. Now I've got to get a move on. I've got to get back to work while my friend is still covering for me."

They wished each other luck before they both got up & headed in opposite directions. Abigail slipped the envelope into her satchel & headed off in the direction of the bakery. Figuring that it wasn't too much later than when she normally visited, she figured that she could just say that she slept in if anyone got suspicious.

Waking into the bakery, Renee lit up as usual. Grabbing a pair of muffins, she waited in line behind the last customers from the early morning rush. When she reached the counter, she put the muffins down & smiled.

"You're here a little late Abigail. Is everything alright?"

Abigail faked a bit of a yawn.

"Yeah, I just had trouble sleeping last night."

"Well make sure to get your rest, I can't wait to go dancing on Friday. It's been a while since I've torn up a dance floor."

Abigail's heart sank a bit.

"I'm sorry Renee, but I'm probably not going to be able to make it."

Renee's brows furrowed.

"Why not?"

"Work is going to be insane this week. I didn't want to mention it last night, but there are going to be a lot of bankruptcies & foreclosures this week. So I'm going to have to pull some serious overtime."

"Oh no. That's terrible. Maybe we can go out on Saturday?"

"Maybe, if I'm not dead."

Renee pouted a bit.

"If I can't go Saturday, I'll make it up to you on Monday or Tuesday. On my knees if I have too."

Renee turned lobster red as she looked around to see if there was anyone that had overheard. Abigail then blew her a kiss & paid before she headed out the door with her muffins.

Nothing could lift Abigail's spirits more than seeing Renee blush. She knew that she should be more careful, but it was just so damn cute. Abigail bounded up the stairs to her apartment's floor & almost walked right into Lola.

"Oh, Abigail, I didn't expect to see you here. Shouldn't you be at work?"

"Oh, yeah, I was, but they sent me home since I was feeling sick."

"You don't look sick."

"Must have been the fresh air, I am feeling a bit better. Don't tell my boss though."

Lola grinned in an almost conspiratorial way. She didn't even bother to ask about the muffins before Abigail slipped into her apartment. Once inside, she went to the kitchen where Ornell was sketching something on some paper to pass the time.

"Abigail, did you get any orders for me?"

"Lay low for now."

"That's it?"

"For now. Apparently, the police identified you as the person who lived in that apartment & so now, you're a person of interest in their drug & arson case."

"Well, shit."

"Yeah, it's not good. Apparently, you're going to be reassigned out of state. In the meantime, they want you to lay low here & to not risk having you moving around."

"Did he say how long?"

"He said a few days, maybe a week."

"Well, it sucks, but at least I didn't end up in a depression era jail cell. That might not have ended well for me."

"Probably not, at least not from what I heard about in the briefings for this era."

May 13th, 1936

Not going to work in the middle of the week was messing Abigail up. When she had first started training to show up for a job five or six days a week, she had never thought that she was going to get used to it. Now, she was so used to it that not going to work five days in a row had left her feeling a little disoriented.

Heading downstairs to check her mail, she was grateful to find a postcard showing a scene from London. Taking it upstairs, she decoded the message from her handler telling her to meet him at a café near the post office for another meeting.

Ornell was optimistic that he was going to be getting new orders & that he might not have to stay much longer. He set about reading an old newspaper that Abigail had lying around in order to pass his time. Abigail then left & headed to a supermarket.

Having seen that the pantry was starting to look a little bare for a Wednesday morning, Abigail quickly picked up a few groceries before making her way over to the café. Nobody seemed to notice that she had walked into the supermarket a brunette & walked out a dirty blonde.

Abigail then made it to the café with time to spare. She found a nice & somewhat secluded place so that nobody from the lunch crowd would overhear what she & Alex were going to say. By the time that Alex showed up, Abigail had already finished a sandwich & was nursing the screaming hot cup of coffee that she had gotten.

"Hello Alex, you look… like you haven't slept since yesterday."

Alex indeed looked exhausted. His eyes were barely open & the bags under his eyes almost made him look like a raccoon. He slumped into his chair with his own hot cup of coffee & left a paper bag on the chair next to him.

"Morning Abigail."

"Are you alright Alex, when did you start drinking coffee again?"

"I figured that the last few days qualifies as an exception to my doctor's orders."

"Careful, they serve it hotter than the sun here."

"Yeah, I found that out on my first sip. Who needs taste buds?"

Abigail laughed for a moment.

"So, two meetings in as many days, what's up? Have you all finally figured out what's happening with Ornell?"

"As a matter of fact, we have. He's being relocated to a new secondary safe house in Georgia."

"Georgia?"

"Yes, Georgia. The specifics of his new assignment are here."

Alex slid another envelope across the table.

"He'll be leaving on Sunday. On Saturday, we'll have a standard meeting where I'll give you the bus tickets. Sadly, this means that you won't be able to bring Renee over on Friday."

"I figured that would happen, that's why I broke off our date yesterday."

"How did she take it?"

"She wasn't thrilled, but I promised to make it up to her. That seemed to perk her up."

"I bet it did."

Alex sipped his coffee again before turning in his seat & picking up the paper bag.

"Oh, before I forget, this is for Ornell. It's some fresh clothes to get him through the next few days & a few newspapers."

"Thanks Alex, this'll help the situation."

"Not a problem."

"Is there any word on the police investigation?"

"They're canvasing Harlem, by this point, they've probably realized that there's something strange about his identity. At the rate that they're going, he'll be halfway to Georgia before they think to look outside of Harlem."

"That's good. Is there anything else?"

"Ahh… nope, that's everything. Sorry, the coffee hasn't hit my brain yet, I'm still not firing on all cylinders. To make matters worse, I have to get back to work in a few minutes. There's a lot of mail shifting around this close to the election."

"Six months away. Roosevelt 36. We haven't messed that up in any way, have we, like the robbery or the movies?"

"No, the robbery was an anomaly, & the movies were actually intentional, just to see if we had that kind of influence."

After another minute spent nursing his coffee, Abigail wished him luck with his work. A few minutes later, she picked up her bags & walked out of the café. After a quick wig change near the café, she carried the groceries & the clothes home to her apartment where Lola was waiting at the front door.

"Well hello Abigail."

"Hello Lola, lovely day today."

"It sure is. I guess you're feeling better."

"Better enough to do some food shopping. I imagine that I'll be off to work tomorrow."

"That's good to hear. I've got to say Abigail, that's a lot of food for a single person that just went food shopping on the weekend."

Abigail suddenly felt incredibly nervous. If Lola somehow got a look in the wrong bag, she would have to come up with an explanation for why she had a bag full of men's clothes.

"Yeah, well, there were some good deals this morning, so I stalked up on a few things that I haven't been able to get in a while."

"Smart cookie. Did you get anything good?"

"I…"

Before Abigail could continue, Lola's attention was caught by another one of their neighbors getting off the bus with a look of complete bewilderment on his face. Abigail capitalized on the distraction & nipped inside.

Once inside, she saw that Ornell hadn't moved since she'd left two hours earlier. The only difference was that he was near the end of the newspaper. Looking up, he got up to help Abigail with the bags as soon as the door closed behind her.

"How did it go?"

"It went great. These two bags have food in them. If you could just take them to the kitchen for me."

"Sure."

"Thanks. This bag here is from my handler. It has some fresh clothes for you. I imagine that the shirt you're wearing is starting to get a bit ripe."

"Just a bit."

Ornell took the groceries into the kitchen & then he took the bag with the clothes in it to the living room. Pulling out a fresh shirt, he grinned before taking off the shirt that he had been wearing. Abigail looked over his lean body for a moment.

"Nice. I don't usually go for men, but if I were in a dry spell…"

Ornell grinned as he slid the clean shirt on.

"Any orders for me?"

Abigail reached into her satchel & took out the envelope.

"New marching orders. Apparently, you're leaving on Sunday for a safe house somewhere in Georgia."

"Guess I'd better work on my Southern accent."

May 14th, 1936

Abigail looked over her appearance in her mirror. Hair was done up properly, her outfit was acceptable for work, she was ready to go. Walking into her kitchen, she saw Ornell sitting at the kitchen table, sipping tea while preparing a cleaning kit to clean the handful of guns that Abigail had in her apartment safehouse.

"Are you sure that you'll be alright here alone Ornell? I feel bad leaving you alone while you're on the run."

"I'm good Abigail, you have to maintain your cover, go to work. I'll be fine. I've got guns to clean, stuff to read, paper to sketch on. I'll be fine for a bit."

"Alright. I'll be back later."

Abigail then left the apartment in order to get back to her normal routine. Normal, except that she had a fellow agent & fugitive holed up in her apartment. Abigail made her way out into the surprisingly chilly May morning & headed over to the bakery before going to work. Walking into the bakery, she was greeted by a warm smile from Renee as a customer was walking out the door. Abigail walked up to the counter, smiling herself.

"Hello Renee."

"Well hello there. How is it that the customers always seem to clear out a bit when you show up?"

"Maybe we're just lucky."

Renee smiled.

"Is Friday still not going to happen?"

"Sorry my love. Friday just isn't going to be an option."

Renee pouted as she got a fresh bagel for Abigail.

"Well, in that case, I have something for you."

Before Abigail could possibly ask her what it was, Renee leaned forward & planted a quick kiss on her lips. It was quick & gentle. As if a butterfly had landed on her lips for a second.

"Renee… is there anyone else around?"

"Not at the moment."

Abigail then grabbed the front of Renee's apron & pulled her forward for a deeper kiss. Renee's lips were heavenly. Soft, warm & tasting like freshly baked bread & flour. Abigail could feel her heart beating in her chest. When the little bell over the door rang, they pulled apart from each other as quick as they could.

"Have a good day at work Abigail."

"Work… right, work… ruining my Friday night… I'll be back later though…"

"I'm looking forward to it."

Abigail then headed out so that she could get to work. When she arrived, she found a small pile of work waiting for her. Mr. Parker was thrilled to have her back & was kind enough to check in on her a few times throughout the day. The mountain of work for her to type up was useful to distract her from the situation at home & thinking about how she was going to sneak Ornell out.

Eventually, the day came to an end & Abigail headed back home. She stopped by the bakery again, but this time, she had to wait. The place was packed with customers. Abigail milled around for what felt like ages as the crowd slowly thinned out. When there was just a few people left, Abigail selected a fresh baguette & walked up to the counter where a tired Renee was wiping some flour off of her forehead.

"How are you holding up Renee?"

"Mon Dieu. I'm exhausted. Half of Manhattan must have come in here today. I had to take over the ovens for a bit so that Papa could get some fresh air."

"Wow. That explains why you're coated in a lot more flour than usual."

"I'm sorry."

"Don't be sorry. You look cute like that."

Renee turned red, blushing through the flour as she looked around to see if anyone overheard. Confident that nobody noticed, she turned to Abigail & talked in a whisper.

"Abigail! It's one thing when we're alone, but there are people here. What if they had heard?"

Abigail grinned, puckered her lips, & paid for the baguette before leaving an embarrassed Renee to deal with her next customer. Along the way home, Abigail stopped at a newspaper stand & got the thickest one that they had so that Ornell would have something to do other than to clean the guns the next day.

Walking into her apartment, she found Ornell rereading an old paper in the living room. He put it down & took the things that Abigail had bought into the kitchen for her.

"Thanks Ornell."

"No problem. Thanks for the paper."

"You're welcome."

"I take it that you stopped by the bakery."

"Yeah, it's always the high point of my day when I see Renee."

"I know the feeling."

"I made her blush again."

"Do you do that often?"

"Almost every day. I say something that she doesn't want anyone to overhear & she turns lobster red as she whisper yells at me to stop."

"You should be careful. You could get into a lot of trouble for loving certain people in this era. There was one lady I knew in 33, we were mad for each other, but a man as dark as me & an upper-class woman as pale as her, we were taking a risk every time that we looked at each other. It was incredible."

"Yeah, tell me about her."

"I was working as a bartender at the time. Her name was Martha, she would come in every now & then for a glass or two of gin. She would tell me about her problems & I would hang on every word hoping for a tip. Then one day, she brushed back those blonde curls & our eyes met. Twenty minutes later, we were in the back room, violating health codes that don't exist yet."

"Sounds hot."

"You have no idea. For the better part of a year, she would come in two or three times a week. We'd sneak into the back room while my buddy covered for me. I would watch her slowly take off her clothes, like a proper lady undressing at the end of the day."

Abigail listened, completely intrigued.

"I swear, every inch of her was paler than the last. She would take for fucking ever to get Naked. Empires rose & fell in the time that she undressed in front of me. Eventually though, my Norwegian goddess would be standing there, buck naked & with the look of a hungry animal in her eyes."

"I'm guessing that she wasn't much of a lady at that point."

"No, she most certainly was not. Sadly, someone who was socially acceptable proposed to her. So one night, she had me come over to her home as a 'handyman' so that she could say goodbye. Good God, she was insatiable. I left that place with a limp."

"Sounds hot."

"It was. It was also dangerous as hell. My buddy at the bar was the only one from this century that I trusted to cover for me. If anyone else had found out that an upper-class white woman was climbing on top of me & riding me to a toe-curling orgasm two or three times a week. It would not have ended well for me at all."

"Yeah, if anyone finds out about me & Renee, one of us is liable to end up in a… what did she call it… Asylum for confused women."

"Yeah, you do need to be careful Abigail, last thing that you need is a psychiatrist from this era thinking that you're sexually confused. We've only just started managing to get agents into asylums, so they're still not the kind of places that you want to end up in."

May 15th, 1936

It would seem that the fates were indeed cruel. Abigail had told Renee that she was going to be busy Friday night & as it turned out, she was. A bunch of last-minute reports had left Abigail typing until her fingers were sore. Walking into her apartment, she collapsed onto the couch.

"Hard day Abigail?"

"Long day. Can you cook supper tonight? My fingers feel like they're about to fall off."

"Sure thing Abigail."

As Ornell was getting up, there was a knock on the door. Ornell picked up his emergency orders & hid in the pantry before Abigail opened the door. She was surprised to see Renee standing there. She felt one panic subsiding as another one began to build.

"Renee, what are you doing here?"

"Can I come in?"

She nodded her head in the direction of Lola's door. Abigail stood out of the way & let her in. With the door closed behind her, she wrapped her arms around Abigail.

"I know that we don't have anything planned for tonight, but I wanted to see you for a minute. See if you were alright after a hectic week."

Abigail smiled. Her panic being pushed aside by a warm feeling from her little French angel.

"That's sweet of you Renee."

Renee then pulled Abigail into a deep kiss. For a wonderful minute, the only thing that mattered was Renee's lips pressed against her own. The stress from her job, from protecting her cover, from hiding Ornell, it all slipped away. When they eventually parted, Renee grinned.

"Are you sure that you're too tired to spend some time together tonight?"

It took every ounce of Abigail's resolve to keep from inviting Renee to stay for the weekend.

"Sorry Renee, but I'm dead on my feet. I'll make it up to you, I promise."

"Alright. I'll leave you to get some rest."

They then hugged each other tightly before Renee turned to leave. As she was reaching for the door handle, they both heard the sound of creaking wood coming from the kitchen. It was undeniably the sound of someone stepping on an old floorboard. Renee turned back to Abigail.

"Is there someone else here?"

Abigail calmly panicked.

"No, no, it's just the two of us."

Renee looked suspicious for a moment. It had been a while since she had heard it, but there it was, the undeniable sound of Abigail's accent faltering. Renee shook her head. It was probably just an old building & after all of these months, her growing love for Abigail was more important than Abigail's more minor quirks.

It didn't help that after all of these months, her best explanation for the strange things that she had seen was that Abigail was a space woman from another world.

"I guess that it's probably just an old building. I'll see you soon Abigail."

"Yes, you will."

Renee then headed out. A minute later, when Abigail saw her waiting at the bus stop, she went back to the kitchen & opened the pantry to find Ornell standing there.

"It's safe to come out. She's gone."

Ornell stepped out of the pantry.

"Sorry about the floorboard, I just shifted my weight onto my left foot & it creaked."

"It's fine, everything is under control."

"Is it?"

"What do you mean Ornell."

"Your accent slipped. The first time you said no, there was no English accent."

"Yeah, I think that I've done that once or twice around her over the years. I don't think that she's noticed anything. At least she hasn't mentioned it."

May 16th, 1936

Abigail's satchel hung from her shoulder as she sat in the park. She watched from a bit of a distance as an old man played checkers with an old woman. The two were happy & enjoying a Saturday in spring. Although judging by their wedding bands, they were most definitely not married to each other.

While Abigail was wondering if they were just friends, or both widows, or if one of them was a widow & one was cheating, or if they were both cheating, Alex took a seat next to her.

"Those two sure look sweet together."

"Yeah, but they're not married to each other."

"Well that makes them more interesting."

Abigail smiled & reached into her satchel. She pulled out a small box that was wrapped in newspaper to look like a gift.

"Here you go Alex, this is for you."

"Is it my birthday?"

"It'll feel like it is. It's the typewriter tape for the file that I was copying in work this morning. I put a fresh cartridge into the writer when I started, so the file is the only thing on this tape."

"Sounds important, what's on it?"

"All of the account history & information for Thomas C. Desmond, the New York state senator representing the 27th district of New York."

"How in the hell did you get this?"

"There was some… weird… water damage in the records room. A box of records containing the state senator's file had to be transcribed onto paper that wasn't damaged. Thankfully, none of the records were damaged."

"Weird water damage."

"It's the darndest thing."

"Who found it?"

"I did. I saw it & brought it to my boss, he told me to start copying the records onto good paper."

"Well done, Abigail. I also have a little something for you."

Alex then reached into his suitcase & pulled out an envelope. He then handed it to Abigail.

"This is Mr. Ornell Page's bus ticket & directions to his new safe house in Georgia. Bus leaves tomorrow night."

"He'll be happy to hear that he won't have to be sleeping on my couch for very much longer."

Alex laughed. The two of them then sat there for a few more minutes discussing the normal topics that they usually covered in these meetings. Abigail's work, her friends, Renee, Lola. Abigail then stood up & walked past the game of checkers. She smiled at the two old timers who were themselves, grinning like young idiots.

Along the way home, Abigail naturally stopped by the bakery to see Renee. Walking in as another customer walked out, Abigail walked in to see Renee at the counter rearranging the muffin display. Abigail crept over to the counter as sneakily as she could.

"Hi Renee."

Renee visibly jumped.

"Abigail. Where did you come from?"

"The front door."

"So, what brings you by?"

"Two questions. First, would you like to go dancing with me on Monday after work?"

Renee smiled.

"Always. What's your second question?"

"Can you go on break & meet me in the alley for a few minutes?"

Renee's eyes lit up. The alley might not be perfectly private, but the odds of being caught there were relatively slim. Great place for a few kisses.

"I'll be there in a minute."

"Hurry Renee, I don't intend to wait."

Abigail then slipped the top button of her blouse open as she turned around & headed for the side door that was propped open to let some fresh air in. Renee quickly dealt with another customer that had just walked in & then she told her father that she needed to step out for a minute to get some fresh air. When he asked why, she told him that she was getting a headache & needed to step outside. He told her that he would man the store for a few minutes & she headed out to the alley.

Rushing out into the alley, she was surprised to find it empty.

"Abigail?"

Renee then heard the side door close behind her. She turned around to see that Abigail had completely unbuttoned her blouse & pulled the two sides of her shirt open enough to reveal an inch-wide part. Renee could see where the pale cups of Abigail's bra met, she could see Abigail's navel & every inch of the English girl's enormous cleavage.

"Doux Dieu, tu es putain de fou."

"Does that mean that you like what you see?"

"You're crazy Abigail, what if someone sees us?"

"That would be a problem, you'd better get your hands on me before I take off anything else."

As if to emphasize her threat, Abigail reached down to the buttons at the top of her pants. Renee charged forward, grabbed Abigail by the shoulders & pushed her against the brick wall. Standing over the crazy English girl, Renee went in & pressed her lips against Abigail's.

It was stupid. Abigail was insane. Anyone could walk through the alley at any point & see her going at it with a half-naked English girl. She should stop… but it was so good. The danger, the thrill, the madness of it all. It was incredible.

As their lips & tongues tangoed, Renee felt her hands parting Abigail's shirt even more, exposing more of her familiar body to Renee's eager hands. Soon Renee was cupping Abigail's large breasts, the fabric of the bra cup the only thing keeping Abigail's hard Nipple from digging into the palms of Renee's hands as her finger sunk into the soft flesh of Abigail's breasts.

Abigail moaned into the kiss. She knew that she was crossing a line. She knew that this was one of the most dangerous things that she had ever done. She knew she shouldn't be doing this, but goddamn. Abigail slid her hands between their bodies & started hiking up the front of Renee's skirt. Her mind flashed back to that night in the bakery a few years ago as she lifted the skirt up to Renee's navel & then proceeded to slip her hand into Renee's underwear.

Renee gasped & broke the kiss. She was panting for breath as she stood over Abigail, squeezing the English girl's breasts in her hands as Abigail's fingers tickled & teased a rather wet entrance.

"Baise moi déjà."

Abigail grinned. She was certain that she knew what Renee had just said, but she was in a mood to be evil today.

"What was that? You know that I don't speak French."

Renee looked her in the eyes with a fiery hunger.

"Fuck me already."

"Out here, in an alley when anyone might walk up on us?"

"You wicked little… Dieu!"

Halfway through her sentence, Abigail complied & slid her fingers into Renee's slick entrance. The sudden sensation of being fingered, outside, where they could be caught. She had to bite down on Abigail's shoulder to keep from screaming. Abigail reveled in being bitten, she knew that it meant that Renee couldn't hold it in & couldn't take her hands off of Abigail.

Abigail began sliding & curling her fingers inside of Renee, causing the poor French girls to cry & bite down harder. Abigail was certain that there would be a bite mark on her shoulder through her blouse, but she didn't care. She didn't care that Renee's fingers were digging into her breasts with enough force that they might leave marks. Renee was trembling in her hand & it was heaven.

After a minute of this paradise, their passion was interrupted when they heard Maurice calling out for Renee. At the sound of his voice, Renee shook as Abigail felt her hand get soaked. Abigail used her free hand to help balance Renee.

"Renee, I need you in here, I need to get back to the ovens & there are customers coming in!"

Somehow, Renee gathered enough calm & stability to call back to him.

"Just a minute Papa."

Abigail then slid her hand from Renee's underwear & began licking away the ambrosia like wetness while Renee quickly regained her composure & adjusted her dress.

"Abigail, you must be insane. I have to get back to work."

Abigail grinned & pulled open her blouse.

"You realize that you probably just bruised my tits & left a bite mark on my shoulder?"

"I'm sorry Abigail."

"I'm not."

Renee looked at the crazed English woman that was flashing her bra. Renee shook her head, blushed a bit & headed back inside. Abigail dressed herself back up & headed home to give Ornell his bus ticket.

May 17th, 1936

Abigail knew that her mailbox was empty. She wasn't checking on it to see if she had any mail. She was here in order to make sure of one thing & one thing only. She wanted to make sure that Lola wasn't around. Running into Lola was going to be the very last thing that she wanted to have happen when they made their move. Just as the coast seemed clear, Abigail turned to head back up into her apartment & almost ran right into Lola, standing there in her Sunday best.

"Oh, hello Lola. Where are you off to dressed up all nice?"

"It's Sunday deary, I'm off to God's house."

"Right, put in a good word for us heathens that can't make it."

"I always do."

"Thank you, Lola. You're a saint."

"I do what I can."

Lola then continued out the door & down the street on her way to morning mass. Abigail waited for a few minutes until she was certain that all of the church goers were well on their way. Once she was confident that the coast was well & truly clear, she made her way back up to her apartment. Slipping inside, she saw Ornell standing there in a Sunday suit as if he were heading off to church with a briefcase in his hand.

"The coast is clear. Everyone has either left for church or they're still sleeping."

Ornell wrapped his arms around Abigail.

"Thanks for everything Abigail."

"No problem. Best of luck in Georgia."

"Thanks. Best of luck with Renee."

"Thanks. You have your instructions."

"Memorized them & burnt them."

"Perfect."

Ornell did one last check to make sure that he had everything: shoes, briefcase, hat. He then tipped his hat to Abigail & for the first time in a week, he left the apartment & walked outside to catch the bus. Abigail watched from her window as Ornell climbed onto the bus that would take him to the station where he would catch the long bus ride down to Georgia.

Chapter 10
June 4th, 1936

Abigail was tired after a long Thursday. Typing up reports & records about foreclosures & loan defaults all day was exhausting in more ways than one. But Abigail wasn't going to let it get her down. Today was Renee's birthday & she was taking Renee to the movies as part of her celebration. That was why despite the exhaustion, she practically had a skip in her step.

Abigail walked into the bakery to find that business was slow tonight. Maurice was standing behind the counter with a look of happy exhaustion on his tired face.

"Hello Abigail, Renee is upstairs getting ready. She'll be down in a minute."

"Great, thanks again for manning the bakery alone tonight."

"It's no problem, Renee deserves to have some fun with her friend on her birthday."

Before Abigail could respond, they heard the sound of footsteps as Renee emerged from the kitchen in a red blouse that showed off her slender figure & a black skirt that billowed around her legs. Abigail felt a little underdressed in the white buttoned blouse & grey pants that she had worn to work.

"Ready to go Renee?"

"Yes, in just a second."

Renee then kissed her father on both cheeks.

"Are you sure that you'll be alright alone Papa?"

"Oui, oui mon petit, I will be fine. Go & have some fun with your friend. After all, it's not every day that you turn…'"

Renee held her hand up to silence her father before he could speak her age aloud. Maurice grinned as he held up three fingers to indicate that she was 30.

"Come on Renee, there's no rule saying that a pair of old spinsters like us can't go & see a movie."

As Maurice laughed, Abigail & Renee left the bakery & headed for the theater. As they walked over, they enjoyed the gentle summer breeze as the sun slowly made its way down towards the horizon.

"So which movie are you taking me to see Abigail?"

"It's a surprise."

Renee pouted as they kept walking towards the theater. When they got there, Renee asked again, & again, Abigail kept it a secret. It was only after they had waited in line for a while & they reached the front of the line that Renee found out what she was going to be seeing. The young man in the ticket booth asked them the same question that Renee had been asking of Abigail.

"What would you two ladies like to see tonight?"

"Two tickets for Flash Gordon."

"That'll be 90 cents for the two of you."

"90 cents?"

"It's a very long movie mam, we've had to put in two intermissions for the audience."

"Makes sense I guess."

Abigail handed over a dollar as Renee smiled. She had been reading the Flash Gordon serials in her science fiction pulp magazines for over a year. As Abigail got her change & the two of them proceeded into the theater, Renee's mind flashed back for a moment to her attempts to make sense of the night in Central Park.

It had been nearly a year since she had seen those strange visions. So far, the only one that had come to pass was the kiss the next day. Renee still had no explanation for it. After a year of thinking about it & months of trying to piece it all together, her best possible explanations sounded like the kind of science fiction that she was about to watch.

Shaking the idea of Abigail coming to Earth in a rocket ship from her mind, she followed Abigail into the theater where they found a nice little nook that was sparsely populated.

"Abigail, how long is this movie that it needs two intermissions?"

"It's a little over four hours without any breaks. So we're going to be here for a while."

A few minutes later, when the last of the stragglers had walked in & taken their seats, the curtains parted & the movie began with the usual cartoon. Soon enough, the proper movie began & the two of them were watching as Flash Gordon, Dr. Zarkov & miss Dale Arden climbed into a rocket. A rocket that Zarkov built & tested with monkeys that weren't supposed to come back.

Abigail laughed hysterically as the rocket ship took off towards the planet that was approaching Earth. Renee couldn't help but imagine Abigail in a rocket ship of her own, coming towards the Earth. Was that why she was laughing so hard? because she knew what real rocket ships were like.

Together, they sat there for ages, watching the movie & sneaking the occasional glance at each other. After spending a minute staring at Abigail, Renee turned her attention back to the movie as the wedding scene played out. Renee imagined herself as Dale, trying to resist the evil emperor as Abigail stormed in as Flash to save her.

After the first intermission, a number of people left the movie as it dawned on them just how long this was going to be. After the second intermission, the Thursday crowd thinned out even more, leaving the two women essentially alone in their little corner of the theater. Renee was expecting Abigail to try something outrageous. Instead, Abigail interlaced their fingers together so that they could hold hands together.

As the movie reached its end, Renee watched as Flash, Dale & Zarkov climbed back into the rocket & a part of her wondered if Abigail was going to take her away on a rocket ship. Shaking the ridiculous notion from her mind yet again, she watched the end of the movie with Abigail still holding her hand. The two of them got up, stood there for a moment as sensation returned to their legs, & headed out into the slowly cooling June night.

The darkness of night brought home to Renee just how long they had been in the theater. Stretching her arms a bit, she turned to Abigail who was rubbing one of her legs.

"I think that was the longest movie ever made."

Abigail gave her leg a good smack, drawing the attention of a passing pedestrian.

"If it isn't, it's damn close."

"Thank you, Abigail. Tonight was a wonderful present. I've loved Flash Gordon since he started appearing in the pulps."

"You're very welcome, Renee, but the night isn't over."

"It's not?"

"No, Flash Gordon was only the first part of your present."

Renee stood there curious.

"Five hours watching science fiction together was only the first part. What could possibly be next? Do you have a rocket ship that you want to show me?"

"A rocket ship, no. But I do have something for you to see."

"What is it?"

"I'm not going to tell you Renee. That would ruin the surprise. You have to come back to my apartment to see it."

Renee smiled. Once again, she found herself momentarily not caring about all of the strange things about Abigail. Going back to Abigail's apartment usually meant waking up the next morning in Abigail's arms.

The two of them then started walking towards Abigail's apartment. For half an hour, the anticipation grew with every step. When they got to the apartment, they were both glad to see that Lola was out. Renee didn't like the idea of some old gossip keeping track of how much time she was spending in Abigail's apartment. When they got to Abigail's door, Abigail quickly unlocked it & turned around before opening the door.

"Alright Renee, close your eyes."

"What?"

"Close your eyes, it'll be worth it. Trust me."

Trust her. Renee had so many questions. Why did Abigail's accent sometimes slip? Why does she act so brazenly & bravely? Why does she sometimes not remember things or know things that everyone knows? Renee had spent the last eleven months trying to work up the nerve to ask Abigail about all of this. Yet with those two words, Renee closed her eyes & let Abigail lead her into the apartment.

Walking though the apartment with her eyes closed was strange. Every creak of every floorboard brought back memories of so many nights together. The sound of wood scraping against wood as Abigail pulled out a kitchen chair for Renee to sit in brought back images of half-dressed breakfasts together at this very table. The smell of day-old sour dough reminded Renee of all of their secret kisses in the bakery. The smell of Abigail's sweat as she moved around the kitchen brought back images of Abigail writing on top of her. The sound of cloth rustling brought to mind every night that Abigail tortured Renee by making her watch as she slowly stripped.

Then there was an oily smell. It was faint, barely there at all. It reminded her of the time back home in France, when she was a child, & her grandfather had been cleaning his shotgun before going out to hunt a turkey for thanksgiving. It was the smell of gun oil.

Renee had no idea why she was smelling gun oil in Abigail's apartment, but it soon faded from her mind as she heard something being put down on the table in front of her. It smelled like vanilla.

"Open your eyes, Renee."

Renee opened her eyes to see Abigail sitting across from her, Naked. Renee knew every single inch of Abigail's pale skin & every curve of her body so well that she could draw it in her sleep. Still, she could stare at Abigail's nude form all day long & stay lost in its beauty from dawn to dusk, or from dusk to dawn as was usually the case.

"What do you think Renee?"

"You're beautiful."

"I meant the cake silly."

Looking to the table, Renee saw a small white cake sitting on a plate with the number 30 in smeared light blue frosting. It wasn't from the Rodin bakery, or any other bakery for that matter. This was the work of someone who had never baked a cake in her life.

"Did you, did you bake a cake… for me?"

"Surprise."

"C'est merveilleux. J'adore ça."

Abigail smiled. She then stood up & took the long knife that was next to the cake & cut out a small slice of it & put it on a single small plate. Abigail then stepped forward & with some maneuvering; she was soon straddling Renee's thighs. Abigail then brought the small plate forward, holding it between them, just below her breasts.

Using the small fork, she cut off a small bit of the cake & brought it to Renee's lips. Renee opened her mouth & let Abigail feed her the cake. The cake was a little bit dry & the frosting had not been made with the skill of a baker. Still, it was the most delicious cake that Renee had ever tasted.

Whenever Renee reached forward, Abigail would smack her hands with the fork, forcing Renee to sit there with Abigail naked, on her thighs & feeding her cake. It was torture. It was incredible. When they finally finished a slice of cake, Renee looked down at Abigail's naked body for a moment before looking her in the eyes.

"Now what?"

Abigail smiled.

"Now, birthday girl, I need you to stand up for a moment."

Abigail backed off of Renee's legs & stood there before Renee. Renee smiled & stood up. She reached forward only to have Abigail smack her hands away.

"You just stand right there."

Renee pouted until Abigail stepped forward & reached for the bottom of Renee's red blouse. Abigail slowly lifted Renee's blouse up & over her head. Renee knew that Abigail was going to take her sweet, tortuous, wonderful time. Building the anticipation by forcing Renee to stand there as she was slowly undressed.

Her black skirt rustled a bit as Abigail slowly unfasted it while standing in front of Renee, the tips of their noses separated by a hair's width as Abigail's hands worked blindly.

When Renee's skirt crumpled to the ground, leaving her standing there in nothing but her black underwear, Abigail moved in. Grabbing Renee's hands & holding them at Renee's side, Abigail kissed the birthday girl's lips ever so softly. She then trailed a line of gentle kisses down Renee's body, each one as gentle as if she were kissing a butterfly's wing.

Soon, Abigail was on her knees, planting a gentle kiss on each of Renee's thighs. She then trailed her way back up, leaving kisses that weren't as tender anymore until she was pressing her lips against Renee's.

Renee's heart started beating harder in her chest as Abigail stepped forward, pressing their breasts together as she reached around Renee to begin unfastening the thin black bra that was the only thing between their chests. A minute later, Abigail broke the kiss & stepped back, bringing the undergarment with her to be dropped onto the pile of clothes gathering at Renee's feet. She then stepped forward once more, pressing their bare chests together as their lips were reunited once again.

Abigail's hands roamed over & explored Renee's body, only stopping to smack away Renee's hands when she tried to do the same. When their lips finally parted, Abigail once again began slowly trailing a line of kisses down Renee's body. A kiss on the check, a line of kisses down her neck. A kiss on her shoulder & several running down her chest. Renee gasped as Abigail planted a gentle kiss on each of her hardening nipples. Abigail then continued trailing kisses down Renee's stomach, down past her navel until her lips met the top of Renee's underwear.

"Well now these won't do at all my love."

Abigail then slid her fingers down Renee's body & slipped them into the waist of her underwear. She then slid the black garment down Renee's legs to the top of the pile of discarded clothing that the French woman was standing in.

As Renee stood there, wearing nothing but her red lipstick, Abigail leaned in on her knees to breathe in the heavenly smell of Renee's arousal.

"Hmm, you're going to want to sit down my love."

Renee sat back down in the chair where Abigail had been feeding her cake. It felt like days had passed as Renee had waited, not being allowed to touch, or caress or fondle. As Renee sat down, she spread her legs wide & looked down to see Abigail with a look of pure animal hunger in her eyes.

"Happy birthday Renee."

Before she could respond, Abigail moved in, bringing her lips & her breath & her expert tongue to the sensitive & moist folds of Renee's aroused entrance. Renee grabbed the chair that she was sitting on with one hand & buried her other hand in Abigail's raven-colored locks as the mysterious English woman went to work.

As Abigail kissed Renee's sensitive little button of pleasure with electric lips & ran her tongue over & into Renee's intimate desire, Renee moaned & gasped for breath. She didn't care if Abigail was an undercover cop, a mad scientist or even a warrior space queen from the sapphic gardens of Venus. Everything else in the world was fading away until Renee's world consisted of nothing but the chair that she was desperately clinging too, & the woman kneeling before her. The woman bringing her to the highest heights of heaven's ecstasy as her tongue wriggled, whirled & writhed inside of her.

"Putain d'enfer, christ sur la croix, putain de, Tire la langue… "

Renee's talking soon broke down into an incoherent mess of French insults & pleading. When she felt Abigail's devilishly angelic tongue move away to be replaced by fingers, she could barely hold onto the chair. When Abigail's lips & tongue started caressing her teasing her sensitive little clitoris, Renee's world went blank as she cried out.

The next thing that Renee knew, she was being gently laid down in Abigail's bed. Abigail was the first thing to come into focus as she climbed over the still trembling French woman.

"Don't pass out on me now Renee."

Renee felt one of Abigail's fingers slide into her wet entrance.

"I've only just started with you, my love."

August 29th, 1936

The skies were grey over the waterfront park. Despite the promise of rain, the park was full of young couples enjoying the last Saturday in August. A part of Abigail wished that she could bring Renee out so that they could lounge in the summer sun like these people had been intending to do. Instead, she was sitting on a park bench, in an auburn wig, waiting for Alex to show up.

Just as she was about to go & find a payphone to call an emergency number to try & find out what was going on, Alex showed up with a bandage on his left hand.

"Hello Abigail."

"Alex, what happened to your hand?"

Alex sat down next to her & took his hat off.

"I was handling a pot of boiling water when the phone rang. I got distracted & spilled some of the water on my hand."

"Are you alright?"

"Yeah, I'm fine. Mostly first-degree burns. I spent a bit of time tending to it before I put some petroleum jelly on it & wrapped it up. That's why I'm so late."

"Petroleum jelly?"

"Antibiotic ointments are still about twenty years away."

"Are you sure that it's alright Alex?"

"No idea. After our meeting, I'm going to see one of our field medics about it. I'll find out then."

"Alright Alex, I hope it's nothing serious."

"I'll be fine."

Abigail sighed & opened her purse, having left her Saturday satchel at home. She pulled out a small box that was just big enough to hold a typewriter ribbon.

"This is all that I could get you this week, it's not much I'm afraid."

"Is something wrong at work?"

"I wouldn't say wrong. We've got some new employees at work & I've been assigned to help one of the new secretaries out for a week or two."

"So between your job & training a new girl, I imagine it must be difficult to also acquire information."

"Exactly. Instead of staying late to copy files, I'm staying late to proofread her work."

"How's that going?"

"She's a nice enough girl, but clearly, she only just finished some sort of basic typing class. Here's a typewriter, there's some paper, type."

Alex chuckled.

"So how's the home life going Abigail?"

"Going well enough, although it would be a bit easier for me if…"

"If we moved you to a place that wasn't next to the gossip queen of Hell's Kitchen. I'll make a note of it, like I do every week."

"Does anyone actually read those notes Alex?"

"Yes, & she's as tired of hearing about it as I am. She says that if something becomes available & it would fit in your cover story as being able to afford it, we'll move you."

"You've been saying that for six years."

"How's Renee doing?"

Abigail eyed him suspiciously.

"I know that you're just trying to change the topic."

"Yes, but I still would like to know, how are the two of you doing?"

"We're doing rather good. I wish that we didn't have to hide from everyone else, but that's life in these parts."

"How's she handling the secret relationship?"

"She's doing alright, although, it's probably nothing."

"If it was nothing, you wouldn't have mentioned it, what's up?"

"Sometimes, I catch her staring at me when she thinks that I'm not looking."

"Are you sure that she isn't just fantasizing?"

"Maybe, I don't know, for a while now, something has felt a little… I don't know… off… I think."

Alex frowned. Domestic issues could become mission issues if they weren't addressed.

"The two of you have been together for over a year now, is it possible that this is just the two of you settling into a long-term secret relationship?"

"Maybe, I mean, I wasn't expecting to fall for any natives."

"Or it could be something else, the market is supposed to crash again in May, maybe the bakery is already feeling the pinch."

"Right, the recession of 37. I don't know, maybe I've just been imagining it because I've been thinking about the future."

"The future as in back home, or the future as in the next few years?"

"The next few years, here in the depression, with Renee."

Alex leaned forward, he always paid close attention to what his agents said when they started talking about their personnel futures.

"Something on your mind Abigail?"

"I know that you said that I shouldn't be getting a new primary mission for a few years, but I'm starting to worry about being reassigned. I don't know if I could just leave Renee. I keep picturing her going back to France just before… just before 1940."

"I see."

"I'm becoming a problem again, aren't I? I'm getting to involved with the locals. Protocol 4 violations all over again."

"No, Abigail, after so many years, no one can fault you for forming deep bonds. Hell, I didn't exactly stop you from pursuing this if you remember."

"I don't know what I'm going to do. Even if I stay here in New York, eventually I'll have to be rejuvenated. I think that she'll notice if I suddenly start getting younger again, she has a very intimate knowledge of the state of my body."

Alex put his hand on Abigail's shoulder, almost in the way that a father would in order to comfort a distressed child.

"We'll figure something out Abigail. For now, I'll put a note in your file to keep you in your current cover, that way you don't get reassigned anytime soon."

"Thanks Alex."

"No problem, Abigail."

When Abigail headed home a little while later, Alex took out his notebook & wrote in code that Abigail was not to be relocated & that she may have relationship issues in 1940.

October 7th, 1936

The oddly cold wind cut through Abigail's jacket. It was a bitter cold, especially for early October. Everyone had been bundling up as they travelled outside in autumn coats despite the preview of winter that had descended down on them. As Abigail stepped into the lobby of her apartment building, shivering, she rubbed her arms to try & get warm. Cursing under her breath, she missed the days of weather forecasts.

Not expecting anything other than bills, Abigail checked her mail once she had warmed up a bit. Opening the mailbox & clenching her teeth at the high-pitched metallic squeak that its hinges made, Abigail was surprised to find a letter. There was no return address, instead, all that she saw was a large letter B. Looking at the handwriting, it took a second for her to realize whose handwriting it was.

Eager to read the letter from Bess, Abigail hurried up the stairs & made it to her front door just as Lola was opening hers. The thought occurred to Abigail that Lola must be able to hear the squeaking mailbox & therefore know that there was someone outside that wasn't in too much of a rush.

"Hello there Abigail. I was about to head out for a little stroll."

Abigail doubted that very much. As she contemplated a stop at the nearest hardware store for some oil for the mailbox, she smiled & turned away from her door.

"Hello Lola, you might want to bundle up if you plan on heading outside."

"Oh? Is it a bit chilly outside?"

"Chilly is putting it mildly. Its freezing bloody cold out there. It's like February decided to pay us an early visit."

"Oh my. Perhaps I'll get myself a heavier coat then. Say, what's that you got there?"

Lola pointed to the envelope. Abigail wasn't surprised that it took less than ten seconds for the conversation to veer off in that direction.

"Just a letter from an old friend that I haven't seen in… a little over… three years now."

"Oh how lovely. I hope your friend is doing well."

"As do I."

"Very well, I won't keep you from your correspondence, I ought to get that heavier coat for my stroll."

Abigail bid Lola goodbye & walked into her apartment. After kicking off her shoes & changing into some clothes that were significantly more comfortable, Abigail sat down in her living room & opened the letter.

Dearest Abigail,

I know that it has been a number of years since that day when you helped me to escape a rather horrible situation. Words cannot begin to convey how grateful I am & will always be for your help. I will not ask where you managed to get such a gift, but by whatever means that you came across it, I am eternally grateful & I never told a soul about it.

I wanted you to know that I did not let your precious gift go to waste. As soon as I got home that day, we began packing. First, we stayed with a distant cousin who was willing to take us in for a few days while I found a new place for us to live. We managed to find a cramped little place where my sister & I could find part time work & take care of our mother.

Shortly after we were settled in, I began taking night classes to become a nurse. It was not by any means easy to accomplish this. A home to provide for, a mother to care for & a child on the way. I often believed that I wouldn't be able to succeed. But as your gift to me was slowly depleted, I found a strength to carry on that I did not know that I had. I do not know what risk you took or what trouble you got into to help me, but I was not going to let it go to waste.

I gave my fellow nursing students the fright of their lives when I went into labor shortly after finishing one of my exams. Across the road we went & in the wee hours of the night, my beautiful daughter came crying into the world. A few days later, when I had regained some strength, I named her Abigail. Most of my class expected me to drop out, but I carried on.

The next two years were not in any way at all easy. My mother's condition worsened, & I have had to balance caring for her with work, school & raising a young child of my own. If my sister hadn't been there to help, I do not think that I would have been able to do it.

As I am writing you this letter, I am looking at my freshly minted & signed diploma, certifying me as a nurse. Tomorrow is my first day of work at a local clinic. The hours will be terrible & the work will be hard, but I am grateful for it.

Without your intervention, I dare not think about how my life would have turned out. I forever owe you a debt that I can never repay.

Thank you, Abigail. You saved my life.
Your friend.
Bess.

Abigail wiped away a tear. She had spent the last three years wondering what had happened to Bess. Abigail searched through the envelope & the letter for a return address but couldn't find one. This letter had been a one-time event, to let Abigail know that her efforts weren't in vain. She decided not to tell her handler about it; just in case he could track Bess down from it.

Abigail hid the letter where she was certain that Renee would never find it. That night, her supper tasted delicious & she went to bed with a smile, knowing that somewhere out there, Bess's story was going to turn out much better than it would have otherwise.

December 24th, 1936

The snow on the sidewalk was getting deeper & harder to walk through as the snow continued to fall. The sun had set over an hour ago & the only other people out on the streets were the police & people trying to get to their own Christmas celebrations. Arriving at the bakery half an hour late, Abigail knocked on the locked door under the Rodin sign.

Almost as soon as she knocked on the door, she heard the door unlock. Renee pushed the door open & ushered Abigail into the empty bakery.

"Abigail, are you alright? I was about to go out looking for you."

"I'm alright Renee, just got slowed down a bit by the snow. Here, take these while I warm up a bit."

Abigail handed the two boxes wrapped up in newspaper to Renee before rubbing her hands together to generate some warmth in her cold fingers. Renee locked the front door & put the gifts down on the counter. She then returned to Abigail & helped her out of her coat.

"Abigail, you're freezing."

"Just a bit. Wasn't expecting it to get that cold all of a sudden."

"Here, let me help you out."

Renee then wrapped her arms around Abigail & rubbed her arms against Abigail's back to generate some warmth.

"Feeling warmer Abigail?"

"If I say no, will you keep holding me?"

Renee chuckled. She then pulled back to see that Abigail wasn't shivering anymore. The two women than leaned in close & shared a quick kiss with one another. The sharp sensation of Abigail's cool lips against her own left Renee feeling warm with desire. After a minute, they pulled apart so that they could head upstairs before Maurice came down looking for them.

Abigail picked up her gifts where Renee had put them down & followed Renee up the stairs. Abigail was almost hypnotized by the sight of Renee's behind swaying ever so slightly as she climbed the stairs to the apartment above the bakery.

Walking into the apartment, Abigail felt her spirits lifting a little bit higher as music filled the air from an old gramophone sitting on the living room mantle. As some sort of jazz or swing music filled the apartment, Maurice came out of the kitchen, bringing the smell of roast beef with him.

Abigail, entrez et réchauffez-vous, il gelé là-bas."

He took the gifts that Abigail had brought & handed them to Renee who put them next to a small little Christmas tree that was sitting on the dining room table. The little tree, no more than a foot tall, was decorated with a few small ornaments & some paper decorations that looked like they had been used a few years in a row. Maurice then wrapped Abigail up in a great big bear hug as he remembered that she didn't speak French.

"Come on inside Abigail, it must be freezing out there."

"It sure is. Thank you for having me over."

"Of course, no friend of Renee should have to spend Christmas alone. You're more than welcome to join us."

Maurice took Abigail's coat & hung it up before following her into the apartment. Instead of the one electric lamp, the room was lit by a bunch of candles, filling the apartment with warmth & dancing shadows as the candle flames flickered.

"You are right on time Abigail, supper will be ready in a few minutes, I just need to go & check on it."

Maurice then headed back into the kitchen to tend to the feast that he was cooking up, leaving Abigail alone with Renee. Renee was in front of the gramophone, slowly dancing to the upbeat music. Abigail walked up to her & started dancing with her. For a minute or two, they just enjoyed dancing with each other. When Maurice called out that supper would be served momentarily, Abigail took what might be her last opportunity for the night to grab Renee & pull her forward.

Before Renee knew what was going on, Abigail was planting a quick little kiss on her lips. It only lasted a second before Abigail pushed Renee back a bit, just in time for the stunned girl to see her father come out of the kitchen with a tray of roast beef & vegetables that smelled like heaven served up on a platter.

"All right ladies, supper is served."

Abigail made her way over to the table while Renee took a second to get her wits about her. She planned on having words with Abigail if they had some time alone.

The roast was pink & juicy, the vegetables were steaming, the bread smelled as if it had just come out of an oven. The gravy was waiting to be poured & Maurice was cracking open a bottle of wine. Abigail hadn't seen a home cooked feast like this since she left 2088 to begin her mission. She had to resist to urge to dig into it, knowing from Renee that Maurice would want to say grace or maybe a quick prayer.

Being a guest in his home & not wanting to put a damper on the incredible job that he had done to prepare this evening, Abigail clasped her hands together & bowed her head as Maurice gave thanks. Before they could eat, Maurice also offered up a prayer for his family back home in France to be watched over & kept safe.

Abigail felt a pang of guilt. She alone knew that in three & a half years, there would be no safety in France. She wished that she could tell them that a boat ticket out of Europe was the only way to protect them, but she couldn't. After everything that she had already done, a major disruption like that would have her removed & sent to an isolated little town in the middle of nowhere to wait out the next century & a half.

Abigail did her best to put it out of her mind as Maurice finished up the Christmas prayer & reached for the carving knife. Soon, he was piling heaps of food onto everyone's plates. The food was delicious. It was quite simply the best thing that Abigail had eaten since she'd arrived in New York. A fact that she shared with Maurice & that he took as a point of pride.

Here, in the middle of the great depression, Abigail found herself experiencing a perfect night. Great food, great company, endless laughs, stories from Maurice & playing footsies with Renee under the table.

Abigail tried to be as vague as possible when questions about her life before New York came up, but she still had to fabricate a number of things. All that she could do was hope that she remembered it all the next morning & that she wasn't making any contradictions that Maurice or Renee would remember. The wine wasn't helping.

When Abigail felt like she was about to burst, Maurice got up & started taking the plates away. Abigail offered to help, but he waved her off by saying that it would be rude to make his guest do the dishes. As he was leaving, Renee dropped a small fork that ended up under the table. She went to get it as Maurice was heading into the kitchen. A few seconds later, Abigail was surprised when she felt Renee's hand running up her calf, lifting her pant leg up.

Looking down, she saw Renee looking back up at her. Renee winked & planted a quick kiss on the exposed leg before coming back up from under the table with the fork. As Abigail grinned & readjusted her pant leg, Renee took the fork into the kitchen. The three of them then sat down & spent a few minutes talking while nursing their overstuffed bellies.

When Maurice felt like he could stand back up, he picked himself up & got the gifts. Since he had cooked & cleaned, Abigail & Renee insisted that he open his gifts first. Maurice agreed & reached for his gifts. The long underwear from his daughter & the simple smoking pipe from Abigail made him smile. He thanked them both & handed Abigail her gifts.

Abigail was surprised to get a gift from Maurice as well as from Renee & she opened them eagerly. She grinned at the bottle of French wine that she got from Maurice & she smiled when she unwrapped the scarf from Renee. Wrapping it around her ncck, she was reminded of the scarf that she had bought for Renee. She hugged Renee & thanked her for it before handing Renee her gifts.

Opening the one from her father, she was delighted to find a few pairs of thick, soft socks. She thanked her father & turned to the gift that Abigail had brought. Opening the box, Renee was confused by the fur until she managed to slip it all out of the surprisingly small box. Sitting in her hands was a small, fur lined muff that was just big enough for her hands.

"Abigail, thank you, but how can you possibly afford to get me a fur lined muff?"

"I robbed the bank that I work at."

Maurice almost chocked on his drink as he started laughing. Abigail grinned & continued.

"Don't worry about it a bit Renee, just enjoy your muff."

Abigail had to resist the urge to laugh at what she had just said since she wouldn't be able to explain to them that muff was slang for something else in the future.

"I will Abigail, thank you. I'll think of you every time that I'm keeping my fingers warm in my furry muff."

Abigail practically had to bite her tongue to keep from laughing at the innocent expression of gratitude from Renee. The three of them then cleaned up the small mess that they had made & Maurice put a new record on the gramophone. As one of Lewis Armstrong's singles started playing, Maurice broke out a deck of cards & the three of them spent the rest of the night playing cards, playing games, chatting & laughing well into the night.

As midnight drew close, Abigail looked outside at the snow that was gently falling & she realized that she would have to get home at some point.

"Oh… god, it's getting very late."

Renee looked at the clock & realized that it was way too late & dangerous for a half drunk & exhausted woman to walk home, alone, in the snow.

"You can't go out tonight, it's far too late."

"What else can I do?"

"You can spend the night here, right Papa?"

"Of course Abigail, you can stay here for the night."

"Are you sure that it's not a problem?"

"Bien sûr! It's far too late & the snow is far too terrible for someone to be walking home alone."

"You don't mind if I sleep on your couch?"

Before Maurice could answer, Renee waved the suggestion off.

"Your back will feel like it's been beaten if you sleep on this lumpy old thing, you can sleep on my bed. It'll be a bit tight, but we should fit."

Maurice raised his glass.

"It's settled, you'll spend the night."

Abigail & Renee both smiled as Maurice finished his drink & bid them both goodnight before heading off to his own bed. Once he closed his door, Abigail turned to Renee with a wicked grin.

"Looks like after all these years, you're finally going to get me in your bed."

Renee grinned. She then told Abigail to meet her in her room while she got some water. Abigail yawned & headed off to Renee's room while Renee headed to the kitchen. Once alone in the kitchen, she got a scrap of paper & quickly tried to jot down all of the things that Abigail had said about her past.

It had been subtle, but Renee had noticed one or two points that didn't seem right. She couldn't tell at the moment if it was because Abigail had been lying or if it was simply because she didn't know much about growing up just outside of London, but she wanted to remember it. She wrote a few quick points & hid the note in her pocket.

Heading into her room, she was expecting to find a naked Abigail waiting for her. Instead, she found that Abigail had gotten down to her underwear & was lying back on the bed, sleeping like a log. Careful not to make too much noise, she slid her dresser open & slipped the note into her notebook where she kept track of all of her ideas to explain the woman sleeping in her bed.

Abigail was an endless mystery to her. She loved her, but she knew that there was something that this remarkable woman was keeping from her. Hiding the notebook back in its place at the back of her drawer, Renee stripped down & slipped on a nightdress before climbing into bed.

December 25th, 1936

Abigail woke up to the sensation of someone getting out of bed. It was an all too familiar sensation from all the nights that Renee had slept over, but as her eyes slowly opened, she realized that she was in Renee's bed.

In her half-awake state, she realized that she could hear Renee & Maurice talking outside in the apartment. She didn't understand a word since they were talking in French. A minute later, she heard the front door open & close before Renee came back into the room & slipped out of her nightdress.

"Now that's what I like to see in the morning."

Renee jumped when she realized that Abigail was awake. Standing there naked, she turned away from her dresser.

"Seeing you next to me is how I like to start my mornings, it's just too bad that you fell asleep before I even made it to bed last night."

"Sorry Renee. You finally got me in your bed & I just passed out."

"It's alright."

Abigail then pulled her clothes back on & headed out of the room to the bathroom. Remembering that the bakery would still be open on Christmas day, Abigail figured that Renee probably had to get to work soon. A few minutes later, she was walking back into the apartment to ask Renee if she had time for breakfast before she & her father opened the bakery. That was when she saw Renee standing against her bedroom door, still naked.

"Renee?"

"Papa is downstairs, getting a start on the first batch of fresh bread for the day. Normally, we'd be serving customers by now, but we open late today. While Papa is busy baking, I don't need to head down for about another hour."

"I see, & what were you planning on doing for the next hour." Renee grinned.

"Well nothing that involve those clothes that you put back on."

Renee then turned around & headed back into her room. Abigail grinned & followed her as she started taking her own clothes off. Abigail walked into Renee's room & dumped her clothes on the floor. Standing there naked, she saw Renee lying on her bed. Abigail closed the bedroom door behind her as Renee patted the spot on the bed next to her.

Abigail climbed into the bed & before her head could reach the pillow, their lips were locked together as their legs entwined & their hands began exploring the familiar terrain of each other's bodies. As thighs rubbed against intimate areas & hardening nipples pressed into soft breasts, the two women were soon moaning & in pleasure.

Renee brought one of her hands to Abigail's large breast. There was little more in life that she loved more than to hold & fondle & kiss those pale, heavenly orbs. Yet, her hold on Abigail's chest was short lived as Abigail grabbed her hand.

Staring into Renee's eyes with a hunger in her own, Abigail pulled Renee's hand down between their bodies. They were so close together that She had to let go of Renee's hand as both of their hands wouldn't fit between them.

As Renee's fingers found their way to Abigail's moist entrance, Abigail reached around Renee. Expecting to feel Abigail's hand on her rear, Renee was surprised when she felt Abigail reaching further, reaching all the way around until she felt Abigail's fingers prodding at her wanting moistness from behind.

"Merry Christmas Renee."

Both women then gasped & moaned as their fingers slid into each other's bodies. They kissed each other passionately as their fingers probed, teased & caressed while their bodies writhed as they made love in Renee's bed for the first time.

Chapter 11
April 22nd, 1937

The line at the post office had been endless. Even though she was standing in the line for international deliveries, it was a hell of a long wait. Renee felt like she had been standing in line for ages, eternity seemed to be slowly crawling by. But at long last, she had reached the end of it & had paid for her postage so that she could send her father's package back home to France. It was mostly postcards & letters & a few bars of dark chocolate along with a bit of money that they could spare for their relatives back home.

The package was on its merry way & Renee was heading towards the door when she saw it. She couldn't believe her eyes. There was Abigail, waiting in line, in that same blonde wig as that night in the park. There she was, just walking up to the counter. She was dressed a lot more conservatively than normal, the way she sometimes showed up on Sundays, as if she had just come from church.

She wasn't at the counter long, & when she turned around, Renee turned around to avoid being seen. As visions of that night almost two years ago flashed in her mind, Renee felt her curiosity burning in her. She wanted some answers. She needed some answers. Seeing Abigail walk out the door, Renee followed behind, keeping a bit of distance between them.

It was tricky for Renee to follow Abigail. More than once, Renee almost lost her in the crowd. At one intersection in particular, Renee completely lost sight of her until by chance, she looked down an alleyway to see a flash of blonde hair turning a corner.

Renee wrestled with her resolve for a moment. She didn't like the idea of walking down a strange alleyway. Then again, she didn't want to miss this chance. Taking a deep breath, she jogged through the alley & around the corner. Seeing a distant flash of blonde again, she kept going until she came out onto a street. She was confused about where she was for a moment until she looked out across the street to see an entrance to Central Park.

There was Abigail, buying a newspaper & heading into the park with the paper & her purse under her arm. As Abigail walked into the park, Renee's mind flashed back to some of her visions. She steadied her nerves, took a deep breath & walked forwards towards the park.

She followed Abigail from a distance until Abigail sat down on a bench. Renee saw another bench nearby that was slightly around a corner & facing a different direction. Carefully keeping a distance & hoping that she wasn't seen, she made her way to the other bench & sat down, not quite knowing what to expect. Bravely sneaking the occasional glance, she saw that Abigail wasn't looking in her direction as an older man took a seat opposite Abigail.

They seemed to know each other quite well, Abigail & this olive-skinned man with the greying hair. It didn't seem likely that they were related, unless Abigail's mother was ridiculously pale. Closing her eyes & listening carefully, Renee could just make out a handful of words over the sounds of people passing by & the tent city a little ways off.

She heard the man ask about something urgent or what was urgent. Renee couldn't tell which. She heard Abigail mention something about an account.

Renee wondered if this was something to do with Abigail's job at the bank. Was she involved with some sort of stock market scheme? There had been a number of stories lately about that sort of thing. It had been in the newspapers, something about corporate criminals risking another depression before the first one had been recovered from.

Renee lost track of what they were saying for a moment as a young couple walked by. After that, all that she could hear was Abigail mentioning something about a man named Thomas, a senator, the 27th... something. Renee then watched as Abigail reached into her purse & pulled out some folded papers.

Abigail then handed the papers to the older man who seemed amazed as he whistled. He opened up his briefcase & put the papers in. Renee couldn't tell if she was looking at some sort of insider trading, extortion, or some sort of spying.

As she listened closely, the handful of words that she could pick up seemed less formal & more friendly. He heard them throw around words like friends & feelings & stress. Renee couldn't be sure, but it seemed like they were just chatting. That was, until she heard the two words from the older man that unnerved her. She heard him say the words girlfriend, & Renee.

Renee panicked. This man, this unknown man seemed to have some knowledge about her secret relationship with Abigail. Did Abigail tell him? Did other people know? Was she going to wind up being shunned by her neighbors? By her papa?

Renee did her best to put such thoughts out of her mind. Clearly, these two have known each other for a while. That means that this man might have known about the two of them for years & hadn't done anything about it. This left Renee wondering what kind of a group or organization they could be in that they could openly discuss a romantic relationship between two women & be perfectly fine with it. It didn't seem possible. Renee couldn't think of a single group that would be fine discussing queer women.

Her train of thought was interrupted when Abigail hugged the older man. Whatever this meeting was, it was coming to an end. Renee turned away so that Abigail wouldn't recognize her. A minute later, she heard footsteps walking away from her & realized that Abigail was heading away from her, back towards the park's entrance. Carefully getting up, she saw that the man was still sitting there, writing something down in a notebook.

Carefully walking past the man as to not get his attention, Renee just barely managed to keep her eyes on Abigail as she left the park. Following Abigail was a lot easier than it had been when she was making her way to the park. It was still a challenge to follow her without being noticed, but it was significantly easier with Abigail apparently not being as cautious. Renee almost lost her at an intersection, but just managed to see Abigail duck into a bar.

It took Renee a minute or two to reach the bar & make her own way inside. Once inside, she couldn't find any trace of Abigail. She wasn't sitting at a table or the bar. Renee tried the bathroom, but that was empty as well. Wondering where Abigail could have gone, it dawned on her that if Abigail had gone to the bathroom & taken off the wig, she would look completely different & might have been able to slip out unseen.

Renee quickly gave up & left. Even if Abigail simply headed home, Renee had no idea what she would have said. Taking a moment to figure out where she was, she then made her way back to the bakery, hoping that her father wasn't going to ask why it had taken her so long to get back.

When she got there, there was only a single customer, so she headed upstairs & quickly wrote down everything that had happened in her notebook while it was still fresh in her mind. She then went downstairs & got back to work, all the while wondering what the hell Abigail was involved in & what it had to do with those strange visions almost two years ago.

April 23rd, 1937

Renee was wondering where the morning rush was. Friday morning, the bakery should have been packed tightly with people who were too tired to make themselves breakfast & would rather exchange a few nickels for some freshly baked bagels. Instead, there was only a handful of customers. Renee had heard that some people were having trouble & that the economy was slipping again, but surely, there couldn't be this many people who were having financial troubles again. As a middle-aged man called her sweetheart & winked at her, Abigail walked into the bakery as she did almost every morning before heading off to work.

As she usually did, Abigail spent a little bit of time browsing around, hoping that the crowd would thin out enough to give her a few minutes to talk to Renee.

Renee's mind went back to the night before, pouring over everything in her notebook to try & figure it all out. Once again, she had come to the same conclusion. Either Abigail was some sort of a spy or informant, which didn't explain that night in Central Park, or Abigail & possibly that older man, were space people with weird space powers that could make people see things.

When the last of the customers had made her way out, Abigail walked up to the counter, a poppyseed bagel in hand. Renee took a deep breath. She loved Abigail. That much she was sure about. But she needed to understand. She needed to know about the things that she had seen that night were & she needed to know why Abigail was meeting men in the park in disguise to talk to them for a few minutes & hand them some papers.

"Good morning, Renee. Not that busy today, is it?"

"Not really. There's been a real slowdown these last few weeks."

"Are you alright Renee? You seem a little… worn out."

"Honestly, I had a bit of trouble sleeping last night."

"Are you alright? You're not feeling sick, are you?"

"No, it's just… can we meet up at your place tonight, Abigail. I need to talk to you about something."

"You can always come over Renee, but now you have me worried. Is everything alright?"

Renee was tempted to say no, but she didn't want to overly worry Abigail. So she brushed a strand of hair away from her face as she took a deep breath.

"Nothing's wrong Abigail, I just… I want to see you tonight, say around 8?"

"Of course, I'll be waiting for you."

"Great. I'll see you tonight then."

Abigail then blew her a quick kiss before heading out to go to work.

///

Later that night, after the bakery finally closed for the night, Renee had told her father that she was going to go out on the town with Abigail. He wished her well & soon she was on a bus heading for Abigail's apartment. As Renee was getting off the bus, Lola gave her a quick hello as she was climbing on the bus. While Renee wasn't thrilled that Lola knew she had arrived at Abigail's, she was glad that their encounter was just a quick greeting as Lola was getting on the bus for parts unknown.

Standing in front of Abigail's door, she took a deep breath to calm her nerves. She had no idea what to expect. She didn't know if this was a good idea or if she might be about to ruin the greatest relationship of her life. She knocked on the door & hoped to God that she was doing the right thing.

Abigail opened the door & welcomed Renee in with a hug once the front door was closed again.

"Is everything alright Renee? You had me worried this morning."

"I'm sorry about that Abigail, I really am, but I need to ask you something & I need you to tell me the truth."

Abigail sat down on her living room couch. Renee sat down next to her, turned a bit so that their knees were touching. As memories of everything that they had ever done on that couch came back to her, Renee felt more nervous than she had ever felt before.

"What's up Renee?"

"Abigail… who are you?"

There it was. The question that had been bothering Renee for nearly two years since that night in the park.

"What are you talking about Renee? You know who I am."

"No… I don't. For almost all of our relationship, if not longer, there's been something that you haven't been telling me."

Abigail seemed visibly shaken for a moment.

"What… what do you mean Renee?"

"I didn't notice it at first. Just the little oddities that never seemed like much, like how you almost never mention your family, or how your accent slips when we're… together…"

"My accent slips… because of the things that we do to each other. Sometimes when you're crying out, you sound funny as well."

"Then there was Christmas."

"What about Christmas?"

"The few things that you told us about your life before coming to New York, a lot of them didn't make sense & some of the things that you said contradicted the other things."

"So I mixed a few things up while I was a bit drunk, it has been seven years since I've seen my family, I think that I'm aloud to mix up a detail or two after that much wine."

"Then there was that night in Central Park two years ago."

Abigail fell silent. Clearly, she had not been expecting to hear that. Renee had been right in thinking that that would be the thing that stumped her.

"I saw you that night Abigail. I saw you standing outside the bakery in a wig while I was locking up. I guess that you didn't see me because I had already turned out the lights. I saw you, & I followed you. I was scared for you, so I followed you to see if you were alright. I followed you to Central Park where I saw you talk to a policeman. Then I followed you to the shore of that pond, I saw you working with something that was glowing like an electric lamp, then… … I don't know what I saw after that."

Renee leaned back in the sofa as a stunned Abigail listened to Renee describe that night.

"It felt like I was being pulled every which way, seeing things & places. I saw all kinds of strange people standing at that very shore. I saw you standing there with half your head shaved & the other like some kind of a rainbow. I was in some kind of German prison, crammed into a room with a lot of French women. I saw an Indian couple getting intimate in the woods. I saw men what looked like police storming the bakery. I saw us driving to San Francisco, & I saw us kissing in the bakery. Then the next morning, you kissed me, exactly how I saw it, & since then, I've been wondering if those other things are going to happen."

"Renee… I… I…"

"Then yesterday, I was sending a package back to my family in France, & I saw you in that same wig. So I followed you again. I almost had a heart attack when you went back to the park, but this time, there was no… magic… vision explosion. Instead, I saw you talking to some old man & handing him papers like you were a spy or something."

Renee fell silent as Abigail sat there in her stunned silence at the realization that Renee had seen everything & knew nothing.

"Please Abigail. I need to know what the hell is happening. I won't tell anyone, but please, I can't go on not knowing. I'm afraid that some of the other things that I saw will happen & it's too damn much. I don't know if you're in danger, or if I'm in danger. I don't know what's happening or what the woman that I love is doing… C'est juste trop pour moi."

Renee slumped back in the sofa. It felt like she had just dumped half the weight of the world off of her chest & just that felt like a relief. Now she just needed for Abigail to tell her the truth.

Abigail sat there, stunned & silent for a minute. She was clearly shocked by everything that Renee had just said. She took a breath & looked away from Renee.

"Renee… I… I don't know… what you think that you saw…"

"No… No Abigail, please don't say that. Anything but that."

"Well what do you want me to say Renee? Half of what you just said sounds like it came right out of a pulp magazine. How am I supposed to make any of that make sense? It all sounds kind of…"

"Crazy. I know how it sounds Abigail, but that doesn't change the fact that I saw you that night in the park & I saw you yesterday."

Renee tried to take a few deep breaths to calm down. It didn't help much.

"Please Abigail. I can't go on only knowing these bit & pieces that I've managed to witness. Please, tell me what's happening."

"Renee… I don't know what to tell you, I mean, are you sure that you didn't… follow someone else into the park &… I don't know… maybe you slipped & hit your head?"

"It wasn't some dream, Abigail. Please. Just tell me. Please."

"Renee… I don't know what you're… Renee!"

Renee stood up & started walking towards the door.

"No Abigail, I won't be lied too. I'm tired of wondering if I'm losing my mind & not knowing if you're lying to me or what's going on. I can't do that anymore. God knows that I love you, but I can't be with someone, especially another woman, if you won't tell me the truth. So either you start making all of these things make sense to me, or I'm leaving & we'll be done."

"Renee… I… I…"

"Goodbye Abigail."

Renee turned around & walked towards the door. As Abigail saw Renee about to walk out of her life, she knew that she should let it happen. She knew that that the right thing to do was to let Renee walk out & to immediately call her handler & tell him that she was compromised. That protocol had been drilled into her head since she had started training. That was what she was supposed to do.

"Renee, wait."

Renee stopped with her hand on the doorknob. Abigail's English accent was gone. In its place was something that Renee couldn't quite place. It was clearly some sort of an American accent, but Abigail had never heard anything quite like it.

"I'm not supposed to tell anyone anything, we could both get into a world of trouble like nothing that you could imagine. I need to know that I can trust you, that I can trust you absolutely."

Renee was almost in a state of pure shock. She turned around to see Abigail, still sitting on the couch, barely able to make eye contact with her.

"Abigail… you could tell me that you're from Mars & I would keep your secret, I just can't keep telling Papa & pretending to the world that we're just good friends if you can't be honest with me."

"So I can trust you. Completely. Absolutely. I can trust that you would never, ever, even under torture, repeat what I tell you."

Renee was taken aback at the mention of torture. The vision of the police storming the bakery & the German prison flashed before her eyes for a second.

"Yes. You can trust me, absolutely & completely."

"Then sit back down & give me a minute."

Renee approached the sofa & sat back down next to Abigail. Abigail was silently reeling in her mind. Five years of training & seven years of experience were screaming at her to stop, but there was a feeling in her chest screaming louder, telling her that whatever kept Renee here tonight was the right thing to do.

Renee sat there silently for a minute, her heart pounding in her chest as her lover of the last two years tried to figure out how to reveal something that she had been hiding for ages.

"I don't even really know where to begin."

Renee took a deep breath.

"Are you from Mars?"

"No Renee, I'm not from Mars."

"Venus then… or Pluto… or the Andromeda nebula or…"

"Renee!"

"Yes…"

"I'm not from Mars, or Venus, or Pluto, or the Andromeda galaxy, or from space at all. I'm from Seattle."

"Is that what people sound like in Seattle?"

"It will be… in about a hundred & fifty years."

"What?"

"Renee… I'm from… the future."

"The… future… like… H.G. Wells the Time Machine or Mark Twain's A Connecticut Yankee in King Arthur's Court?"

"Yes, sort of. It's complicated. If you want, I can make us some tea & I can start at the beginning. Well, my beginning, in the future."

"Please."

Abigail stood up & walked over to the kitchen, her heart beating like a jackhammer in her chest. She was breaking the biggest rules that her organization had. Don't tell the natives about time travel. She hoped that the time that it would take to brew the tea would calm her down. The beautiful thing about brewing tea in stressful times is that it forced you to slow down, calm down, & focus. By the time that it was ready, Renee seemed slightly less on edge & her own pulse was slowing down to something less than an imminent heart attack.

She brought the slowly cooling tea into the living room where she & Renee both sipped at it for a minute before continuing.

"Do you want me to switch back to my English accent?"

"Somehow, I think that would be even stranger."

Renee put her tea down & turned to face Abigail.

"Didn't you say that you would start from the beginning. I assume that's future Seattle."

"Yes. Let me know if you need me to stop at any point."

Renee nodded her head.

"Alright. The beginning, I was born in Seattle in 2062. I had a fairly normal life growing up. School sims, friends, games, girlfriends, teenage rebellion, protested overpriced brain implants. The usual stuff."

"If that's all usual in the future."

"Yeah, anyways, when I was about 14, scientists figured out how to open up passages into the past, sort of."

"Sort of?"

"Well, they're not passages into our past. Every time a passage is opened up, it creates a new timeline that branches off from the original history."

"What?"

"Sorry, the multiverse is complicated. When we open up a passage to the past, it… it makes a new world that runs parallel to ours in the fourth dimension."

"You've lost me."

"Sorry, basically, it all means that there are multiple versions of the world, each with the same original history up until the moment the passage was created. So we can come here & change the past without changing our own history."

"Okay…"

"Over the next few years, they figured out to stabilize these passages & how to send things & people through to specific places & times. Once we got a hold on that, & figured out how it all works, a bunch of organizations started creating passages into their own timelines for all kinds of purposes."

"Like what?"

"Some wanted to reshape worlds based on political ideologies, some wanted to become world rulers, some wanted access to resources from other worlds, some people just wanted to live in simpler times."

"You just… change the histories of entire worlds… to suit your own desires?"

"Some people do. When I was 19, I signed up with the organization that opened the passage to this timeline."

"I see. What exactly is your organization… intending to do here?"

"We want to bring about the freedoms & equalities that we enjoy in the future while avoiding the hardships that occurred in our timeline like the climate wars or neo-nationalism."

"This all sounds… I thought that I was crazy for thinking that you were an alien warrior woman."

Abigail smiled.

"Do you need a minute, Renee."

Renee just reached for her tea & sipped it. Abigail waited patiently until Renee had enough time to process & put her tea down on the table.

"So, you say that you're here to bring us freedoms & equalities & to create a better world. But you've been here for a while & the world doesn't appear that much better."

"We're still setting everything up. We're gathering information that could be useful about this time, that's what I was doing yesterday, I was handing my handler useful financial information about a state senator. We still haven't even fixed the navigation issue."

"Navigation?"

"Sending someone from 2088 of the original timeline to 1930 of this timeline is tricky. Often times, our agents land days, or weeks before or after their supposed to. That's why I was in Central Park that night. That flash of light was a beacon, marking out the first of July 1935. Like a lighthouse in the timeline, making it easier to send our people to specific points in history."

"A beacon. But, what about what I saw?"

"When the beacon went off, it created a disruption in the timeline, allowing people caught in it to move between & experience parts of the original timeline & parts of potential futures for this timeline."

"So when I saw us kiss, & then it happened just how I saw it?"

"You saw a potential future that thankfully happened."

Renee thought for a moment about the things that she saw.

"In one vision, we were driving off to San Francisco in a strange car. Is that going to happen?"

"I hope so. San Francisco is where a lot of the fights for queer rights were won. After a bit of chaos & madness, it's going to be one of the first safe place where a couple of women can be together openly."

"No… that'll never happen. Now I know you're pulling a fast one."

"No Renee. Even without interference from us, the world is going to change a lot over the next century. Hopefully, we can speed that up & make the changes more far reaching & less painful."

"So queer women could just be together… like a normal couple. Get married, own a house, the picket fence & all that."

"By 2062, two queer women can even have children together. That's how my mothers had me."

Renee reached for her tea again. She clearly needed another minute to process more information than she had not been ready to handle.

"Abigail… I also saw a vision… of myself, in what looked like a German prison. Is that going to happen?"

Abigail went a bit pail.

"That's part of the original timeline & I am going to do everything that I can to make sure that that never happens here."

"I take it that I don't survive that."

"No."

"When's it supposed to happen."

"I'm not exactly sure, things get a little bit… chaotic… by that point, reliable records can be hard to find. But it's somewhere between 1941 & 1944. I'm going to do everything that I can to stop that from becoming a reality."

Renee reached for her tea again. She seemed shaken & a little scared.

"I don't know what to say. I want to believe that you're telling me the truth. But… I mean… Time travel. That's a bit much to swallow Abigail. How do I know that you're not trying to trick me & make me sound crazy if I talk to anyone?"

Abigail thought about it for a minute.

"What if I told you about a few things that are about to happen that I couldn't possibly know if I were lying? Then you could just read the news & know that I'm being honest."

"Okay. What's going to happen?"

"Let's see, today's the 26th, have you been following the news about King Edward the 8th?"

"The English king that abdicated last year over an affair, yes, everyone has."

"Right, well tomorrow, Wallis Simpson's divorce will be finalized & on the next Tuesday, the two will get engaged."

"Okay, anything else that I should know about?"

"On Friday, women in the Philippines will win the right to vote & next Thursday, assuming we haven't changed things too much yet, a German zeppelin called the Hindenburg will catch fire & crash in New Jersey. The crash will be caught on film as a radio journalist named… Herb… I think… he'll immortalize the words 'oh the humanity'."

Renee's eyes opened wide. It sounded like the next two weeks would be filled with scandal & chaos that would shake the world.

"I… I'm sorry Abigail… I need some time to think."

"Don't apologize Renee. It's a lot that I just dropped on you. Just… please don't tell anyone."

"That you're a time travelling spy here to bring about a queer utopia. Who would believe me?"

"The people that I work with. They would believe you & they wouldn't be happy."

May 7th, 1937

Renee had left Abigail's apartment shaken to her core. Of all of the things that she had expected to her Abigail say, confessing to being a time traveler sent back to set the world on a better path had not been one of them. Lying in bed that night, she looked over the list of her visions in her notebook before updating it with the future events that Abigail had described. What Abigail said would sort of make sense, but Renee just couldn't completely bring herself to believe it. That was, until the following day.

As a dismally thin Saturday crowd came & went, she eventually saw someone with a freshly printed newspaper. As he bought himself a loaf of rye bread, she looked around to make sure that nobody was listening to them & asked him the question that was on her mind.

"Is there by any chance, a story about the King of England in there, the one that abdicated six months ago."

"Yeah. How did you know?"

"Oh, just something that a friend heard over the radio. I didn't get all the details. What exactly happened?"

"Well, it turns out that the old King's mistress divorced her husband. So she's now free & clear to be with the abdicated King."

Renee couldn't believe her ears. It happened exactly as Abigail said it would. An hour later when Abigail walked in as she did every day, Renee was genuinely surprised to hear Abigail talking in her normal English accent.

Over the next several days, Abigail kept coming in as usual, but there was something different about her. Renee could almost swear that she seemed nervous. Renee tried to tell her as subtly as she could that she hadn't told anyone, which seemed to help a bit.

As the days went by, one by one, Abigail's predictions came true. As Renee read newspapers & listened to news over the radio, she heard about Wallis & the former King getting engaged to marry, & women in the Philippines getting the right to vote.

It was now finally the 7th of May & when Renee went into the back of the bakery; she saw the newspaper that her father was reading as he took a quick break. Seeing the newspaper's front page, Renee was shocked to see a picture of a German zeppelin crashing to the ground in a ball of flames.

Taking the front page from her father, she read the article. Just as Abigail had predicted, in a field in New Jersey, the Hindenburg had erupted into a fireball. The story even quoted the news reporters famous words in bold, oh the humanity.

Renee couldn't imagine how anyone could possibly have made that up. It finally sunk in for Renee, Abigail really was from the future.

Later that night, Renee made her way to Abigail's apartment. Practically pounding on Abigail's door, Abigail opened up & let her in, closing the door behind her just as she could hear Lola approaching her door. Seeing that Renee was freaking out a bit, Abigail kept her English accent in the hopes that it would calm Renee down & because after all these years, hearing her own voice was a little weird.

"Renee, what's wrong, you look like you're about to have a full-blown panic attack."

"I don't even know what that is! Although it sounds about right!"

"Hear, calm down, have a seat on the sofa, I'll get you some tea before like last time."

"That would be nice."

"Okay, in the meantime, just breath. In & out, nice & slowly."

Renee did her best to stay calm as Abigail prepared some tea as quickly as she could. A few minutes later, Renee was sipping the steaming hot tea. Abigail sat there next to the woman she loved, calmly waiting as she collected herself & tried to calm down a bit.

"You're really from the future."

"Yes."

"All of these things. They happened just like you said they would."

"Yes, well, the Hindenburg showed up seven minutes late, although that just might have been some bad time keeping in the original timeline."

"Everything you said is real."

"That it is."

"That's not your real voice."

"No, no it isn't. Do you want me to switch?"

"No. No. I… Je ne sais pas vraiment ce que je veux."

"You lost me there Renee."

"I don't know what I want."

Renee remembered the warning that Abigail had given her before she left two weeks earlier.

"Abigail… am I… in trouble… with your… I don't know what to call them. Your team?"

"No. They have no idea that you know anything. As far as they know, you're just my beautiful French girlfriend."

Renee's eyes opened wide as Abigail caught up to the fact that Renee wasn't used to the idea of people knowing about them.

"Renee, Renee, it's okay. My people have no problem with two women being lovers. It's okay."

Renee sipped some more tea to calm down.

"How are you doing Renee?"

"I'm scared."

"It's alright Renee, it'll all be alright. Here, have some more tea."

"This tea is awful."

"Sorry Renee, I was so nervous when I was making it that I'm fairly certain I missed a step or two. I'm not even sure if I actually boiled the water."

Renee suddenly started laughing. Abigail wasn't quite sure what was so funny, but her girlfriend laughing hysterically for a minute was better than her freaking out & having a proper panic attack. Eventually, Renee calmed down enough to take one more sip of the awful tea before asking the burning question that was on her mind.

"So… what happens now?"

"I… I don't know Renee. Telling you the truth like that & telling you about future events was a major breach of protocol. I should have followed the procedure. There is a right way to tell people the truth, but when you were leaving, I guess that I panicked."

"There's a procedure for this?"

"Yes. I would have had to ask for permission from my handler, he & his boss would have had to be sure that you were trustworthy, there would be investigations into your background."

"Is that what we're going to do?"

"I don't know. I guess that it would be the safest way."

"Wouldn't it be safer if they don't know that I know?"

"Only until 1940. After that, I would have to explain to them why you aren't going back to France."

"Could we just tell them that I've gone back home?"

"No, since we've been together for years, they'll check to make sure that you're on that boat. At some point, we need them to trust you with the truth. But that can wait, we still have time."

Renee sipped her tea, at a complete loss for words. After a minute, she turned to face Abigail.

"Now what?"

"Now… since I'm being honest… do you have any questions?"

"Oui…, yes… about a thousand."

"What would you like to know first?"

Renee was at a loss for a moment.

"I don't… I guess… is your name really Abigail Oldman?"

"No. Abigail was the name of my favorite virtual teacher & Oldman… it just seemed funny."

"So what is your real name."

"It won't make sense."

"Abigail… Please."

Abigail sighed.

"My real name is Candy62Skull. All one word."

Renee looked at her as if she had just started dancing while talking in Spanish.

"What kind of a name is that?"

"My Moms were hardcore gamers & like most gamers in the 2060s, they gave their kid a name that was based off of their gamer tags with the year of my birth thrown in the middle."

"I… you were right. It doesn't make sense."

"My friends would call me Candy for short. Or Candy62 if we were in a deep dive, which probably doesn't make sense to you either."

"No. It doesn't. But thank you for being honest with me Abi… Candy."

"It's so weird hearing you say that. These days, it's so weird hearing anyone say that."

The two women just sat there for a minute, looking at each other in a new light.

"Renee… do you… do you still love me?"

As an answer, Renee put her tea down, looked at Abigail, or Candy, smiled & leaned in to kiss her. The kiss was strange for both of them. It felt like the thousands of kisses that they had shared together, yet it somehow felt like their first kiss all over again.

June 13th, 1937

The last few weeks since Renee had learned & accepted the truth had been strenuous on Abigail. Taking off the light brown wig, she hid it in her satchel & looked herself over in the café's bathroom mirror. Once again, she was telling herself that she wasn't exactly lying to her handler. After all, she did intend to tell him the truth just as soon as she figured out how to tell him & worked up the nerve.

Between temporarily delaying the truth with her handler & giving Renee the time that she needed to process, Abigail was feeling a little overwhelmed. She had gotten so used to meals & movies & wonderous nights with Renee that she was wondering how she had lived without Renee for so many years.

When another woman walked into the bathroom, Abigail took a deep breath, shifted a thin lock of her raven hair out of her eyes & headed out of the bathroom & the café. The summer sun was pleasant & the gentle summer breeze was just wonderful, especially as she approached the bakery. As the air filled with the scent of freshly baked bread, Abigail rounded the corner & walked into the bakery just as the only customer was walking out. She walked up to the counter & leaned over it as she & Renee both smiled.

"Hello Renee."

"Hello Candy."

Abigail's eyes opened wide.

"Renee! You can't call me that when there are other people around. What if your father overheard?"

"Papa isn't working today. He's not doing too well."

"So it's just you down here?"

"You & me. Candy."

Abigail shook her head as Renee grinned.

"Sorry Renee. I know that you wouldn't risk something like that. I just got back from my weekly meeting with my handler, so I'm a little extra jumpy."

"Were you in disguise again?"

"Every week."

"That blonde wig?"

"No, I change it every week. Today was light brunette that was done up in a bun."

"I'd really like to see that sometime."

Abigail smiled. It had been a little while since Renee had even remotely flirted. She took it as a sign that Renee was finally getting comfortable.

"So does your handler know that I know?"

"Not yet Renee. I know that I should tell him, but every time that I try, my mind just goes to the worst-case scenario, even though I know that the odds of that are slim to nil."

Renee reached out & put her hand on Abigail's.

"I trust that you'll know when the time is right."

Not wanting her mind to go to a dark place, Abigail quickly changed the topic.

"I see that it's a little slow in here again."

"Yes. It's the economy. Everything was getting better & then all of a sudden, it started getting worse again, almost overnight. It hasn't been this slow on a Sunday afternoon in years."

"That sounds about right. Mid 1937, everything slows down again."

"I don't suppose that you can tell me when it'll pick up again?"

"For any one business, no. Overall, it takes about thirteen months for the economy to start recovering, but it won't fully recover until sometime in late 1941."

"Jésus Christ. Comment allons-nous survive à ça."

"I lost you after Christ."

"Is that the reason that I'm supposed to go back to France in 1940? Because the bakery fails?"

Abigail stopped herself from just blurting out too many answers. She looked around as if she was worried about being overheard to buy herself a moment to think about her answer.

"I don't know if the bakery fails or if you just think that it doesn't have a future, but I'm fairly sure that economics are a factor."

Renee shook her head for a moment.

"Are you alright Renee?"

"Yes… No… I don't know. It's a lot to handle. All the work that Papa & I have put into this bakery. Eleven years of working together to get this place off the ground & it feels like it's all for nothing."

"I'm sorry Renee. I wish that I had better news for you. I know that my lying to you for so many years didn't help matters."

"No. It didn't. For years, you kept me in the dark. It hurt, but I understand why you did it."

"I'm sorry Renee."

"I know Abigail. The truth is, I'm not even angry anymore. I just… I miss you."

"I miss you too Renee."

They just stood there on opposite sides of the counter for a minute, Renee's hand still on Abigail's.

"Renee… would you like to come over tomorrow night?"

"Perhaps… if you'd be willing to show me that brunette wig done up in a bun."

"I'll model all my wigs & disguises for you if you want. Hell, I'll even show you a few future bedroom moves."

Renee blushed a bit. Even though Abigail was the source of so many feelings of confusion & future dread, all that Renee wanted to do was to fall into Abigail's arms & wake up next to her.

"It sounds like a date… Candy."

Abigail grinned wickedly as she imagined Renee calling out her real name in bed.

Chapter 12
February 12th, 1938

Shock. That was all that Alex could feel as he sat across from Abigail in the small café. When she had sent a message requesting an emergency Saturday meeting, he had been worried that she might be in trouble. Now he knew for a fact that she was in trouble because as the shock slowly faded away, he felt like he might ring her neck in his rage.

As she sat there across from him, their coffees slowly cooling, he was reeling from her confession. Over the years, a number of agents, including one or two of his own, had gone through the proper procedure & requested that a loved one that they had grown attached to be brought into the loop. But none of them had ever done anything like this.

It wasn't just the fact that Abigail had told Renee without permission or even adhering to the protocol. There had even been a case or two of that over the years. It was the fact that she had done it back in April, almost ten months ago.

As he felt his imminent future becoming more complicated, he took off his fake glasses, folded them up & placed them in his pocket. He then looked Abigail in the eye for a moment before asking the burning question that was on his mind.

"What the hell were you thinking?"

"I'm sorry."

"Sorry. Abigail. Help me to understand. Please."

"She had just confessed that she had seen me light the beacon…"

Alex's eyes went wide & his heart skipped a beat as he heard Abigail tell him that a native to the timeline had been observing her for years. He sat there with his mouth open as Abigail continued.

"She told me that she had noticed a few discrepancies in my back story & that she had followed me to a meeting where I gave you information about our state senator friend…"

"Christ Abigail."

"She just dropped all of that on me & demanded an answer. I couldn't think of anything on the spot that could explain it all away. I tried a blanket denial."

"Well at least you tried something. Christ."

"It didn't work. She turned around & started walking out of my door. I know that I should have let her leave & then called you, but I couldn't. I just… I… I love her."

"Abigail, I… That much I understand. More than one of our agents has blurted out the truth like an idiot. But they called their handlers within an hour. You waited ten months. Ten months Abigail."

"I know, I just… I don't know what I was thinking."

Alex sat back in his chair. In his mind, he remembered her report from just after the beacon was lit. Showing up with mere minutes to spare after stopping by the bakery. He remembered thinking then & there that it might be a good idea to transfer her to another post. It should have been obvious that she was getting too attached to her life. He had even figured that she would request that Renee be trusted with the truth in the next few years. But this.

"Alex."

"Yes Abigail?"

"I know that this isn't the way that we normally do things, but I would like to register Renee as an Alpha Trust."

The balls on this woman. Alex sat there absolutely dumbfounded for a minute as he tried to process what his next move was going to be.

"Alex?"

"This… is what's going to happen. You are going to bring Renee to secondary safe house Delta, tomorrow, at noon. Not at 11:59, not at 12:01. Noon. Decisions will then be made."

Alex then stood up, left a tip for the waitress & walked away, leaving Abigail sitting there nervously. Abigail sat at the small table for a few minutes, collecting herself. The meeting had not gone as bad as she had feared. She wasn't being reassigned; she wasn't being told to break off contact with Renee. Still, bringing Renee to a secondary safe house, that probably meant that they were going to be questioning her to see if she could be trusted.

Getting up, Abigail walked out of the café & headed over to the bakery, barely remembering to duck into an alley & change out of her red wig. Reaching the bakery, Abigail was surprised to find a small crowd of customers. Then she remembered that Monday was going to be Valentine's Day. Realizing that the bakery was going to get a surge in Sunday business as people prepared a Sunday night Valentine's feast at home for their loved ones, she wondered how Renee would be able to get out of working.

Abigail waived at Renee. When she got her girlfriend's attention, she signaled to her to meet her out back in the alley where they could talk. When Renee nodded her head, Abigail headed out & waited for Renee to show up. It was almost half an hour before Renee came out.

"Abigail. I'm so sorry for making you wait. We've had more business today than we have had all week."

"That's great. Listen, I talked to Alex today, I told him that you know the truth."

Renee pulled up a small crate & sat on it. She had been hoping that Abigail had just wanted to sneak a quick kiss before Valentine's Day. She then took a deep breath before turning back to Abigail.

"How did he take it?"

"He was less than happy. If we hadn't been in public, he probably would have thrown a fit, or a haymaker."

"That doesn't sound good. So what do we do now?"

"Now, he's given me orders to have you at one of our secondary safe houses tomorrow at noon."

"Étais-vous fou? Abigail, I can't leave the bakery tomorrow, it's the Sunday the day before Valentine's Day, it's one of our busiest days of the year."

"Renee!"

Abigail had slipped out of her English accent, something that she only did when she was deathly serious.

"Renee. He said that we had to show up, precisely at noon because decisions would be made."

"What kind of decisions?"

"He didn't say. He just made sure to make it clear that we were to be on time."

"Well... how long will it take?"

Abigail slipped back into her accent effortlessly.

"I have no idea. Might be half an hour, might be the rest of the day. There really isn't a protocol for an idiot agent that blurts out the truth to the woman she loves & doesn't tell her handler for ten months. I imagine that it'll be similar to the protocol for just blurting the truth out, but I don't know what that protocol is."

Renee thought about it for a minute.

"Well, I suppose that I can tell Papa that I'm feeling too sick to work, then I could pretend that I called you & asked you to take me to the clinic."

"That's good thinking. I'm sorry Renee. I really am. I know that tomorrow is not a day that you want to miss at work."

"That's alright Abigail, but you're going to have to make it up to me on Monday night. I'm thinking a movie, a good long night walk & then you showing me one of those future techniques when we get back to your apartment."

Abigail smiled.

"You can count on it."

February 13th, 1938

The secondary safehouse looked like a simple brick & mortar warehouse, like the hundreds of others that were spread throughout New York. The guards that seemed to be acting as security seemed a little bulkier than other men, but other than that, it was completely unremarkable. Renee wondered if this place could really be a safe house for a team of secret agents from the future trying to set the world on a better path.

What really worried Renee was how nervous Abigail seemed to be. The same woman that seemed to have no problem kissing her in places where they could easily be seen was clearly nervous. As the two of them walked up to the front gate of the three-story tall warehouse, Abigail walked up to the man at the gate.

"Agent Oldman. We have an appointment set by agent Xenas."

The tall, nondescript man looked at them. He then made some hand signal to another guard who slid the gate open.

"Director Porter is waiting inside. Through the main entrance."

"Thanks. Come on Renee."

Renee followed Abigail towards the main door. As they passed a number of security guards, Renee noticed that they all looked alike, like twins, but half a dozen of them.

"Abigail, why do all of the guards look the same?"

"Because they are the same. They're genetically engineered clones. Sorry, they were all grown from an altered human template."

"Grown? Altered how?"

"Well, they could probably rip a bus apart with their bare hands & anything less than a machine gun will just annoy them. We started using them at certain vital sites about a year ago."

Renee felt thoroughly terrified by these guys. Hoping that they weren't in any real trouble, she followed Abigail into the warehouse. The interior looked more like a large office, a large office with tiny little lights that could turn night into day. Renee didn't ask about the lighting; she would save those questions for later. Inside, a secretary was sitting at a desk. She handed each of them a card with a clip. Abigail's identified her as an agent. Renee's identified her as a visitor. At Abigail's directions, she clipped the visitor pass to the lapel of her blouse.

The secretary then pointed down a corridor that led deeper into the warehouse. Abigail led the way & Renee followed close behind. As they approached an intersection, Renee could hear the sounds of typewriters & people talking to each other. Except for the strange lights, it seemed to look exactly like an office. They stopped at the intersection & waited for a minute. When Renee was about to ask what they were waiting for, she heard a voice coming from behind her.

"I'm Director Porter & you must be my noon appointment."

Renee turned around at the sound of the woman's voice & was shocked by what she saw. The tall woman that stood before her was wearing a white blouse & a red pencil skirt, but her clothes seemed to be made out of some sort of shiny, skin-tight, almost rubber like material that seemed to dramatically overemphasize her already substantial curves. Hanging off of her belt was an id badge that identified her as the director. Her dark red hair was done up in a tight bun. In her arm, she was holding a thick file folder.

While Renee stood there with her jaw dropped, Abigail stood before the latex clad woman & tried her best to smile naturally.

"Director, I'm agent Oldman, this is Renee. I'm sorry for springing this situation on you."

"I'm sure you are Abigail, please go upstairs & wait in apartment 32, someone will come get you when we're done here."

"Yes ma'am."

Abigail then turned to Renee, offered up a hopeful look, & headed to the staircase leading up to the third floor. As Renee stood there with the site director, she took a deep breath as she turned to the woman in the weird clothing.

"Follow me to my office Renee."

"Y… Yes Ma'am."

Renee then followed the weirdly attractive woman into an office that was on the opposite side of the building from the front door. Renee felt like it had been designed like this to make visitors feel like there was a fortress of future security between them & the exit.

Inside the director's office, the room looked like a dream that Renee had once had. The walls were covered in paintings & prints of naked women in rather intimate embraces. On her bookshelves, her bookends were made to look like busty women pleasuring themselves. There was even a small statue on the woman's desk that looked like a curvy woman caressing herself. Renee found it hard to focus on any one thing.

"Have a seat. Please."

Renee quickly sat down in the velvet chair opposite the director. The director then dropped the folder that she had been carrying onto her desk.

"Renee Rodin. Born in 1906 in France. Your mother worked as a nurse in Paris until her death in 1919. You emigrated to the United States in 1926 with your father, Maurice Rodin. The two of you quickly opened up a bakery & have been working there tirelessly for the last twelve years."

"Yes… that… basically sums up my life."

"It doesn't scratch the surface of your life Renee. This file is everything that either we have uncovered, or that agent Oldman has reported about you since she first mentioned you to her handler in October of 1932. If you don't mind, I'd like to ask you a few questions about yourself."

Renee was curious about what they could have. She didn't think that her life was so important to warrant a two-inch-thick folder. It was the only thing in the room that she could focus on that didn't leave her feeling pleasantly uncomfortable.

"Sure, ask away."

"Thank you miss Rodin. Is it true that you have three light brown freckles on your inner left thigh?"

Renee's eyes widened in surprise. She had not been expecting that to be her first question, or any question.

"I'm sorry, freckles?"

"Yes, in one of her meeting with her handler, agent Oldman let slip that you have three light brown freckles on inner left thigh. Is this information accurate."

"Ye… Yes. It is."

"Excellent. Now tell me, do you prefer when agent old man wears the blonde wig to bed, or the red wig?"

The questions continued on in this fashion for a few minutes, getting more & more intimate & explicit until Renee was turning red & was visibly shaken from answering an endless barrage of questions about her sex life with Abigail. Once the director was confident that Renee was completely uncomfortable & unable to form any sort of lies or mistruths, she began the endless barrage of real questions.

The director questioned her about her father, her mother, her cousins & extended family. She asked about customers that frequented the bakery. She asked about brushes with the law. She asked about the suspicious details that she had picked up from Abigail over the years. She asked for detailed descriptions of her visions when the beacon was activated & she hounded Renee for any information that Abigail might have revealed about the future with an endless series of confusing & intricate questions.

Over the hours, while this interrogation was going on, the director also sprinkled in more questions designed to keep Renee from getting comfortable. Questions like when she first noticed an attraction to women, when she first felt attracted to Abigail, her favorite sexual position with Abigail so far. Renee answered honestly like Abigail had instructed her too on the way over. Of course, she was fairly certain that she couldn't lie anyway since she was stunned by the questions themselves.

As the director asked her endless array of questions, she was slowly flipping through the files in the folder. When she neared the end, she closed the file.

"Final question for this interrogation. Has agent Oldman revealed any information to you concerning your death?"

Renee took a deep breath to try & steady her frayed nerves.

"A little bit. After I mentioned my vision of the German prison camp, she told me that in 1940, I go back to France & that afterwards, I end up in that situation. But she hasn't revealed how I end up in a German prison camp."

The director seemed to consider things for a moment. She then pressed a button on a small box on her desk before she stood up & walked towards one of her bookshelves for a minute, confident that Renee's eyes were on her.

"I won't go into any details about major historical events that are about to occur, but suffice to say, you go to work in France in another bakery that will end up being held in German controlled territory. They then begin… a program of rounding up individuals that they consider… undesirable. These people are taken to… work camps, if their lucky. In 1942, a German officer spots you kissing another woman. You get accused of being a lesbisch, the German word for lesbian & you get rounded up & taken to one of these work camps. After that, the records get… spotty. Since there's no record of you after the camps are closed, we assume that you were worked & starved to death sometime between 1942 & 1944."

Renee was shocked. Not only did she now know that at least part of France would be controlled by Germany in the near future, but she also knew how she ended up in the German work camp. Worked to death in hellish conditions because she was caught kissing another woman. The beautiful future that Abigail had described seemed even more impossible now than it ever had before.

"Why… why are you telling me this?"

"Because if we're going to trust you, then we have to start trusting you. The thing is this trust has to go two ways."

"What do you mean?"

"Well, we're trusting you with future information about yourself, we're trusting you to remain in the intimate company of one of our deep cover agents & we're trusting you with the location of my safe house. That's a lot of trust we're giving you. I'm asking if you would be willing to trust us with something?"

"I suppose that would be fair."

The director then smiled & picked up a box from her bookshelf.

"Good. Roll your sleeve up to your shoulder."

Not sure about what was going on, Renee rolled the long sleeve of her blouse up to her shoulder. Director Porter then walked over to Renee & sat down on Renee's lap, straddling her legs. Renee could feel her heartrate jumping. The only other person to sit on her lap like this was Abigail & only when they were being intimate.

The woman opened her box & pulled out a cylindrical device that fit easily into the pam of her hand. She then tossed the box onto her desk & turned her attention back onto Renee. Director Porter then wrapped one arm around Renee's shoulders & leaned in, giving Renee an up-close view of her rather well-endowed chest constrained by the rubber like material.

"Like what you see?"

"Yes… uhm… sorry… what?"

"The latex. It's a special variety that was developed in the 2030s. Slides on effortlessly, doesn't squeak when you move & unlike the earlier versions that were rather delicate, this latex could stop bullets & blades. So, do you like what you see?"

"Uhm… Ow!"

Renee felt a slight pinch in her exposed upper arm. Director Porter then stood up & swayed her hips as she walked towards her office door.

"We're done here Renee."

"We're done?"

"For now. We'll be bringing you in again at a later date when we've made some assessments, but for now, we're done. Abigail should be waiting for you with the receptionist at the front. I trust that you can find your way."

Renee then stood up & bid the director farewell. She was then surprised when the director pulled her into a tight hug, pressing their bodies together tightly.

"It feels good to trust one another, doesn't it Renee."

"Uhm… yes, I suppose it does."

The director then broke their embrace & allowed Renee to quickly walk towards reception where an impatient Abigail was waiting for her. After a quick & awkward hug, Abigail escorted Renee out of the safe house & back to her apartment a few blocks away. Once Renee was sitting down on Abigail's old, familiar couch, she finally started talking.

"Jésus Christ, qu'est-ce que c'était? C'était absolument fou."

Abigail was in the kitchen putting a kettle on to boil to make some tea for Renee.

"Renee, I promise you that I'm going to start learning French one day, but I only got about three words of what you just said, so please, I need you to stick with English."

"That was insane. That woman, that office. Christ."

"Yeah, the latex pencil skirt was a bit much. I'm guessing that her office was like walking into pornography."

"To put it mildly. Abigail, everywhere that I looked, it was… it was… it was tits & women pleasuring each other. Is that what the future is like? Just pornography everywhere you look?"

"There are some places like that, but I think that all of that; the office, the outfit, I think that all of it was designed to throw you off of your game. To keep you from being able to think clearly."

"Well it worked. I've never felt so… so… so…"

"Terrified & aroused at the same time?"

"Yes."

As the kettle started to boil, Abigail quickly got up & prepared Renee's tea for her. Renee took the steaming beverage & quickly took a sip before continuing."

"I know that you had told them that we were intimate, but she opened up with a barrage of questions about our… our… sex life."

"Yeah, that's not an uncommon tactic."

"The things that she knew, I mean, did you give them a roadmap of my body? The director was wearing a skin-tight suit that revealed everything & yet, somehow, I'm the one that was naked."

"Sorry Renee, I didn't realize that I had said so many things to my handler."

"Did you know that they were going to try & make the experience so… so… erotic?"

"I figured that they would do something like that. They needed you to be uncomfortable & I guess that their analysis of your file told them that being asked about your sex life while in a room devoted to lesbian erotica would be the most effective way to do that. I would have told you, but they would have noticed if I had prepared you & they would have held it against you. I'm sorry."

"I forgive you Abigail, but what the heck did that woman do to my arm? It's still a bit sore."

"What do you mean?"

Renee then unbuttoned her blouse & moved it out of the way enough so that Abigail could see the mark on her upper arm. While Abigail looked at the all too familiar bruise pattern, Renee continued with her story.

"Then she told me how I was going to die, vaguely, that I was going to be caught kissing another girl by a German soldier & that I would be labeled a lesbisch & that I would then be worked & starved to death in a German work camp. She then asked me if I would be willing to do something that would allow them to trust me after all the things that I had found out about them."

"What happened next?"

"That woman sat on my lap, with her massive tits in my face. She then asked if I liked what I saw, started talking about the virtues of future latex & suddenly I felt a pinch in my arm where she had asked me to roll up my sleeve."

"Makes sense, I've seen these bruises before. Got one on my neck before I came to this timeline. You know that tiny little soft bump that you sometimes feel on the back of my neck."

"Yes."

"It's a tracking chip. They use it to keep track of my exact location when I'm within range of a scanner. There's probably one in your arm now so that they can find you if they have to."

"They can just follow me & know where I am?"

"Only if you're within a hundred meters of a scanner. There's one near here, so they'll know when you're here. They're probably also going to assign one or two people to keep an eye on you until your next meeting, whenever that is."

"Is that… normal?"

"Oh yeah, everyone in the future is tracked by devices & implants like these. We're all tagged at birth & with the satellites overhead, the authorities always know where we are."

"Is that a good thing?"

"Well a lot of people were nervous about it in the beginning, but it actually got a lot more people out of trouble than into it because it allowed people to prove where they really were when crimes were committed. A lot fewer people were convicted of crimes they didn't commit & it became a lot easier to catch actual criminals."

"I don't like the idea that someone can know exactly where I am every minute of every day."

"Yeah, it takes a little getting used to when you first realize that they know where you are all the time."

Renee sipped her tea a bit more to calm down before Abigail continued.

"She also probably took a blood sample to test for any drugs that I might have given you to help you out. They probably also ran a genetic analysis."

"Genetic. That is that thing you told me about where they can read the blueprint of your body & know where your ancestors came from & if you're vulnerable to certain diseases & conditions."

"Yeah, you'll probably get a full genetic health report when you're registered as trustworthy."

"So they'll know more about me than I do. Is that normal in the future? Do you get tested at birth?"

"Yes. Everyone does. At first it was voluntary, a way to check for childhood diseases, but eventually all parents were doing it & they overwhelmingly voted yes on government propositions to make it a legal requirement for everyone born in the country."

Renee sipped some more tea.

"Does this mean that they trust me now?"

"It means that they are willing to go through the process of learning to trust you. Which is good."

That seemed to relax Renee a great deal. It seemed that she felt that these violations to her privacy would be worth it, which would probably be the first question that Alex asked her at their next meeting. Abigail didn't bother mentioning what would have most likely happened if the director had determined that Renee couldn't be trusted.

May 13th, 1938

The pitiful excuse for a lunchtime crowd had been served. As the last customer in the bakery walked out the door, Renee grabbed a sign from the behind the counter & hung it up in the door. As the sign informed customers that she would be back in ten minutes, Renee locked the door & headed upstairs to the apartment that she shared with her father.

Walking in, she heard coughing coming from the small balcony in the back. She walked over to the kitchen where the back door was open & her father was standing on the balcony with a hot cup of tea in his hand.

"What are you doing out here Papa? You're supposed to be resting & taking it easy."

"The weather is beautiful today & some fresh air will really help with this cold."

"It's not that beautiful outside Papa, come inside before you catch your death."

He bent over & coughed more deeply than Renee had ever remembered hearing him cough before.

"Papa, please, come in & rest now, it sounds like you just tried to cough up a bar stool."

He nodded his head in agreement, sipped his tea & followed his daughter into their home. He sat down at the kitchen table & just seemed to slump down a bit, like the weight of the world was on his shoulders.

"Papa, are you sure that you shouldn't go see a doctor?"

"I'm fine. It's just a bad cold."

"Yes, but you never used to get sick & I've never heard you cough like that before."

"It's alright Renee, I'm just getting a bit older. This is what happens. You get sick more often & it hits you harder than when you were young."

"You're not that old Papa."

"I'm not that young either. A lot of the men that are my age are grandfathers."

"Is that your subtle way of trying to tell me something Papa?"

Maurice laughed.

"I'm not trying to pressure you Renee, I know that these last few years have not been an easy time to find a spouse."

"Finding a husband has been… challenging."

"Well don't you worry. If you intend to give me grandchildren, you have plenty of time. The men in our family usually live well into their sixties & I won't be the exception."

Renee smiled.

"I'm glad to hear that you're going to be here for a while longer."

"Still, it would be nice to hold my grandchild before I get too old."

"As soon as I find the right man Papa."

"I'm just glad that you've become friends with Abigail, I used to worry about how you didn't seem to have any friends."

"I'm glad that I met her too Papa."

Renee then quickly prepared some soup for her father & made him promise to lay down & rest while she worked the bakery. Several hours later, Abigail had finished for the day & was walking in to find an exhausted Renee covered in flour & standing at the counter.

"Damn, as cute as you look, you look exhausted."

Abigail noticed that Renee was too tired to even look around the bakery to see if anybody had overheard her.

"Hello Abigail. Sorry, I've had to run the bakery alone today."

Abigail walked up to the counter where Renee was leaning.

"No need to apologize, I guess your father isn't feeling better from this morning?"

"Not much. He'll probably be alright tomorrow, at least I hope he is. It's hard to man the ovens & the counter & to stack the shelves at the same time."

"I bet. How's he holding up?"

"All of this time not working today seems to be giving him more time to talk to me about finding a husband & having a child before he dies."

Abigail froze for just a second at the mention of Maurice's death. She knew that she should tell Renee that she only had about two more years with him, but she could never bring herself to tell Renee that truth. Renee didn't seem to notice as she continued.

"I told him that I was waiting to find the right man. I'm glad that he understands that helping him run the bakery these last several years has made it a challenge to meet new people."

"One of the few good things about hard times, it's easier for women like us to get away with not having a husband."

Renee considered that for a moment & felt a little guilty that a small part of her life was being made easier by everyone's suffering of the last few years. With so many men & women needing to devote everything to work & making enough money to get by, it was easier for her to explain away being unmarried despite coming up on her 32nd birthday.

"Do you really think that your father will be up on his feet tomorrow, Renee?"

"I hope so. The truth is, I'm a bit worried about him. His cough a few hours ago was rather bad & he's been getting sick more often lately. Up until a year or so ago, I don't ever remember him taking a day off for being sick. Now it's the third time in as many months."

"I'm sure it's nothing Renee, I mean, he is getting older. People do tend to get sicker as they age."

"I suppose that I just have to accept that my father is becoming an old man. I'm sure he'll be fine."

Abigail resisted the urge to blurt out that her father only had about two years left. She didn't want to tell Renee right now when her father was sick & she really didn't know how to tell her that she had known about this since they first met & that his death was the reason that she gave up on their bakery & went home to meet her fate.

September 16th, 1938

The first chills of autumn were in the air. The evening breeze was just sharp enough to make Renee shiver a bit as she climbed off of the bus in front of Abigail's apartment. Business at the bakery had finally started to pick up again this week & it wasn't a moment too soon. Their belts had been getting a bit tight. After a long week of getting just enough customers to stay ahead of the bills for a little while longer, Renee was finally going to get to enjoy herself.

This was one of her favorite moments of going on a date with Abigail, the moment when she didn't quite know what she should be expecting. Sure, Abigail had just invited her over for supper, but with Abigail, that could be anything from a simple meal to an erotic adventure worthy of any good romance novel.

Walking along the sidewalk with a spring in her step, Renee noticed some sort of a van or truck parked behind a familiar looking car. Renee couldn't prove that it was the same black Cadillac that she had been seeing around the bakery for the last few weeks, but she was sure that it was the one. It had to be the people that Abigail worked for, keeping an ever-present eye on her.

Renee was sometimes a bit disturbed by their presence, especially when they weren't being obvious. It was difficult to associate this kind of behavior with a group that sought to bring freedoms & equalities to the world. Then again, Abigail had waited ten months before telling them that she had spilled the beans. Some mistrust was to be expected.

Looking up, she saw Lola staring out her window at the Cadillac & the van. The one good thing about the not-so-subtle observation was that Lola wouldn't notice Renee coming over. Renee entered the apartment, bounded up the stairs & knocked on the door with the gentle knock that she had perfected to avoid rousing Lola's attention. From inside, she heard Abigail call out to her.

"It's open Renee."

Renee opened the door, stepped in, not sure what to anticipate, & closed the door behind her.

"I'm in the kitchen."

Renee heard the sound of a knife chopping something on a cutting board & followed it. When Renee walked into the kitchen, she turned to see Abigail standing at the counter & her jaw almost dropped open. Abigail was standing there in a little red half apron & nothing else.

Renee's eyes were instantly drawn to Abigail's pale, firm rear, covered by nothing but the knot of the apron. As Abigail chopped away at something, Renee's eyes went further down to take in the sight of Abigail's long legs, before looking up to take in the sight of her bare back. Abigail finished chopping whatever it was that was on her cutting board & turned around.

The little red half apron was the smallest apron that Renee had ever seen. It only covered from Abigail's waist to just below the wonderful place where her legs met. Renee was sure that it was a very pretty apron, but she couldn't focus on it at all as her eyes ran over Abigail's lean stomach & paused for a good long while on her large, round breasts. The sight of Abigail's porcelain colored bust never failed to stir passions in Renee's heart that were once long hidden from her.

Eventually, her eyes managed to keep moving up Abigail's body until she took in the sight of her lover's smile. This wasn't the first time that Abigail had started off their night together nearly naked, but Renee never imagined that she could become accustomed to walking in on such a breath-taking sight.

Renee could only stand there motionless as Abigail sauntered over to her, swaying her hips hypnotically with each step. Without saying a word, Abigail walked right up to Renee until her nude body was barely a hair's breadth away from Renee. She then cupped Renee's cheeks in her hands & pulled her in for a long, sensual kiss. Renee lost all track of time for a moment, or perhaps for a month, she couldn't tell. When their lips parted, Renee didn't much care how much time had passed. She only knew that she was feeling weak in the knees.

"You're a bit early Renee, I've only just started putting everything together. But you can have a seat & watch if you like."

"Okay."

Abigail smiled. It was good to know that just the sight of her body still left Renee speechless after so many years. Renee turned around, a little stunned & disoriented & made her way to the familiar kitchen table. Pulling a chair out & taking a seat, her eyes focused on Abigail who got a glass out of her cupboard.

"Would you like a drink while you watch me prepare supper?"

"Yes, please."

Abigail then started putting together some sort of a drink that was a lot more complicated than pouring some peach schnapps into a glass. A minute later, Abigail turned around & walked towards the table with the large glass in hand. As Renee stared at the peach-colored drink that Abigail held just in front of her breasts that bounced ever so slightly with each step, Renee wondered just what the hell Abigail had prepared for her.

"Here you go."

"It looks… what is it?"

"It's a cocktail that will be invented in the mid-1980s, it's called a sex on the beach."

"Seriously?"

"Seriously. Go on, try it."

Renee brought the fruity drink to her lips & tried it. Peachy, tart & citrusy, it actually made her feel like it was summer again for a minute.

"Hmm, that's good. That's really good."

"I'm glad that you like it. I also need to say that I'm sorry."

Renee scrunched her eyebrows in confusion.

"Sorry for what?"

"I'm sorry for what's about to happen, I promise you, I will make it up to you."

Before Renee could ask what was going on, she suddenly felt dizzy & drowsy. Leaning back in her chair, she saw Abigail walking up to her as her eyes slowly closed.

///

Renee remembered feeling a few odd jostling sensations. Maybe hearing the occasional incomprehensible sound. When her senses finally started coming back to her, she found herself looking up at an office ceiling, & two large, shiny, white, round lumps.

"Hmm… Abigail?"

"Not quite I'm afraid."

The voice brought her mind into focus. As her mind suddenly cleared, she realized that she was lying on a red velvet couch, with her head in someone's lap. She was looking up at the ceiling & Director Porter's latex clad breasts. Renee bolted upright, brushing against the Director's large chest as she sat up. Looking around, she found herself back in the Director's office, surrounded by almost obscene displays of sapphic love. The statues of lone women pleasuring themselves & couples pleasuring each other. The paintings on the wall depicting sensuous orgies & positions that ought to be impossible for anyone with a spine.

Director Porter was still sitting in her original position, reading from some papers that Renee had not noticed earlier. She seemed completely unsurprised by Renee's actions.

"Sorry about that Renee. We know that you had a date planned with Abigail, but we need to continue our interview to make sure that you are trustworthy."

"I… I'm… I'm…"

"Here, have some water, there's more on the desk if this isn't enough to sate your thirst."

Renee only cared for a moment that the glass that the Director handed her was shaped like the torso of a naked woman. She was thirsty. She drank down the water a little too quickly & sat back down next to the Director when she started feeling a little dizzy. After giving Renee another minute, the Director, in the same white latex blouse & red latex pencil skirt as last time, closed her file & turned to Renee.

"First of all, I'd like to apologize for having Abigail drug you like that. It's not normally something that we like to do. You've been unconscious for about three hours & rest assured, nobody tried anything… funny."

"Why… why are you drugging me at all?"

"It was partly to make sure that Abigail was still willing to do what has to be done for the mission. She doesn't know where we brought you or what's happening. The second reason was to see how you would respond to ending up in strange circumstances with no warning. You mostly kept calm & you seem to be holding together despite the environment & what may very well be feelings of betrayal & violation."

What Renee found most disturbing about that reasoning was the fact that Abigail had no idea where she was. It sent a chill down her spine that unnerved her far more than the décor that was designed to make it hard for her to concentrate. The Director adjusted the tight bun that her red hair was done up in before continuing.

"So Renee, how's your father doing?"

Renee was thrown off by the question, still, she figured that she should be honest, especially if Abigail had no idea where she was.

"He's doing well. A little tired from working so hard, but that's normal for a man his age."

"Abigail reported that he's getting sick every now & then. Have you noticed the same thing?"

"I suppose, he says that he's just getting older."

The Director nodded her head before shimming closer to Renee on the couch.

"What was Abigail wearing when you came over?"

Renee swallowed while wondering just how personal this conversation was going to get.

"A half apron."

"A half apron & what?"

"Nothing… just a half apron."

Renee blushed as the Director grinned. Renee then started getting really nervous as the Director leaned in close.

"Sounds like you were expecting one of the best nights of your life. Did she promise to make it up to you?"

"Y… Yes, just before I passed out."

Renee's heart was pounding as the Director grinned & carried on.

"How far would you go for Abigail? What would you do for her?"

Renee couldn't help but recall some of the stories that she had heard of women submitting themselves to their bosses for jobs or raises or for favors. A part of her told her that something remarkably similar was about to happen.

"I'd… I'd do anything."

The Director leaned in close enough that Renee could feel the woman's heavy breasts against her arm.

"Good."

The Director then leaned back & reached for a cup of tea that had been sitting on the table next to the couch. As she sipped her tea, Renee sat there, breathing heavily.

"For the record, I think that you're trustworthy Renee. I honestly believe that you would have gone down on me if I had told you to. All for Abigail. Understand, I take no pleasure from making you think that you were going to have to do that. We've gone through an intense screening process to ensure that none of our agents would ever try that with anyone."

"Mon Dieu, je pense que mon cœur s'est presque arrêté pendant une minute. You had me convinced. I was expecting to not be able to look Abigail in the eye tomorrow. I understand that this is all top secret, but how much more do I have to go through before you all stop playing these games with me?"

"Sorry about making you think that your heart was going to stop for a minute. You're very nearly done. I just have a few more questions for you & if you answer correctly, our superiors will trust you."

"Ask away."

"Abigail's mission will most certainly involve her eventually moving to a new location & assuming a new identity. Would you be comfortable going along with her & changing your name?"

"Yes. Yes, I would."

Renee only realized in that moment that she would have no problem at all with following Abigail to the ends of the Earth & even changing her own name in order to be with her.

"Very good. You understand that from time to time, Abigail may be called upon to do dangerous things. Even in data acquisition, there can be risks."

"I know."

"Do you understand that if anything happens to Abigail, you may have to continue living out your fake identity, especially if you're given anti-ageing medications. We can't have you coming back here in forty or fifty or a hundred years & picking up your old life while looking like you've barely aged a day."

"I… I understand. If that's the price that I have to pay to spend time with Abigail after she's done here, so be it."

"True love. I take it that Abigail has shared with you what our values & ideals are. Do you agree with them?"

"You mean these seemingly impossible dreams of equality for women & queers like us?"

"Among other things."

"I agree with them, I just don't see how you're going to achieve them even with time travel."

"The work towards equality for the genders, races, orientations & all things will begin on their own in a few years, we're simply going to help the natural process along while helping to thwart a few problems along the way."

"Well if you can make it happen, I would welcome it. I don't quite yet understand everything that Abigail has talked about in her descriptions of equality, but from what I gather, I would like to live in such a world."

Director Porter smiled.

"Very good Renee. I do believe that will suffice."

"Are we finished here?"

"Just about. Assuming the higher authorities are happy, you'll need to get a full medical evaluation in a few weeks & then you'll be granted clearance as an alpha trust."

"Then I'll be able to stay with Abigail?"

"Yes."

Renee reached forward & hugged the Director for a second.

"Thank you, Director Porter."

"You're very welcome. Abigail is waiting for you in the lobby, I'll take you to her."

"But I thought that you said that she didn't know where I was."

"Yes, again, I must apologize. We needed to see your reactions when you thought that you were most vulnerable."

"I... forgive you Director."

"Thank you, Renee. Out of curiosity, may I ask you a personal question? Just between us."

"I suppose."

"Abigail's reports don't mention your reaction to something important. I was wondering how you took it when she told you that your father is due to... pass away... next year."

Renee suddenly felt as if she had been hit by truck carrying bricks & that it had turned around & dumped the bricks on her.

"Papa... next year... what do you... qu'est-ce que tu veux dire l'année prochaine!"

"Didn't Abigail tell you? I'm sorry Renee, I thought that she would have told you by now."

"When... how..."

"Middle of next year. July, I believe. As for how, we're not entirely sure. The records simply say natural causes."

"Papa… that's… that's why I leave for France in 1940. Without Papa…"

"Yes, in the original timeline, without Abigail, the combination of the slowly recovering economy & the difficulty of running the bakery alone & the loneliness caused you to go home to your aunt."

"Christ. Is there anything that you can do for my father?"

The Director took her reading glasses off & placed them on the table before turning back to Renee.

"I'm sorry Renee. Even if it's something that we could fix, we would need direct orders from our superiors & they have never authorized such an intervention. I'm afraid that there won't be anything that we can do."

"Papa…"

The Director put her hand on Renee's shoulder.

"Listen Renee, I know that I just dropped a bombshell on your world, & I understand that it's probably very insensitive for me to ask this right now, but even knowing that Abigail kept this from you for so long, would you still do anything for her?"

Renee sat there for a moment, trying to process what had just been said to her. Director Porter waited patiently.

"Yes. I would."

"Even after she didn't tell you about your father?"

"I might punch her, but I still love her. I still want to be with her."

Director Porter then reached behind Renee's ear & puled something off of Renee's skin. She then explained that it was a device to monitor her vitals & brain activity while being interviewed. She then escorted Renee through the familiar safe house to the front lobby where Abigail was waiting patiently in some simple pants & a coat.

As Abigail walked up to Renee, Renee slapped Abigail with lightning speed, producing a sound that echoed throughout the building, drawing the attention of half a dozen agents.

"Renee?"

"That was for not telling me about Papa."

"Renee… I…"

Renee then wrapped her arms around Abigail.

"Please, take me back to our home. If I see papa tonight, I don't know what I'll say or do."

Abigail then flipped off the Director & escorted the woman that she loved home.

The night was dark & chilly. Still, they walked the long way back to Abigail's apartment. For a while, there was silence as Renee began processing everything that she had learned. When they were only a few blocks away from the apartment, Renee finally asked the burning question on her mind.

"Why, why didn't you tell me about my Papa?"

"I… I didn't know how. With everything that you were already going through, finding out about me, trying to earn my boss's trust, I didn't know how to pile that onto you. Then as time went by, I just started coming up with excuses for why I hadn't told you yet. I'm… I'm sorry Renee."

"He's just going to keep getting sicker, isn't he?"

"I honestly don't know Renee. The only record that we could find was his death certificate & it simply said natural causes."

"He's the only family that I have on this continent. I can't even go back until after this war. When does this war end?"

"1945."

They continued on in silence for a little while until the apartment building was in sight. Once inside, Renee sat on the couch, still a little shocked by what she had learned. Abigail did the only thing that she could think of to help. She made a cup of tea & sat down next to Renee.

"Renee, I'm sorry for not telling you. Can you forgive me?"

Renee wrapped her arms around Abigail.

"I forgive you. But you can't keep important things like this from me again. After everything that's happened since I saw that beacon go off, I need you to be honest with me."

"I promise Renee. No more secrets"

Chapter 13
July 17th, 1939

Renee couldn't remember a word that the priest had said. She could barely make sense of what he was saying now. She knew that she was crying. She knew that Abigail was there, by her side, having called in sick so that she could be here on a Monday. She knew that the eight or nine people gathered in the small chapel were here for her father's funeral. But her mind just couldn't stay in this moment.

When she should have been saying goodbye to her dear Papa, she was going back to a cold day in November. The day that she had gotten into a car with Abigail & her handler so that they could spend an hour driving out of the city.

Despite multiple reassurances from both of them, Renee had been partly certain that they were taking her way out into the woods to dispose of her. When they arrived at the log cabin with the smoke rising from the chimney, she had been relieved.

Once inside the cabin, she was introduced to a doctor, a trauma surgeon & some nurses from the future. After changing into a hospital gown, the nurses began wrapping strange bands around her arm & taking blood samples with some sort of painless needles while the doctors stared at screens displaying all kinds of information about her vitals & asking her a series of questions. Renee had watched with fascination as they filled in the answers that she gave on similar screens that they held in their hands.

Then came the machines. As she had laid down on a table, a number of machines & devices were passed over her body from head to toe. With each pass, large screens on the walls suddenly filled with images of the inner workings of her body. As she watched images of her heart beating & her lungs breathing, the screens pointed out a few minor anomalies. Each one was like an alarm in her mind, but the doctors reassured her that most of them were typical bodily anomalies that would resolve themselves. They pointed to one in her left kidney & decided it could use some long-term monitoring, but that it was probably another nothing.

After the machines had created a complete image of her body from head to heel, the doctor spent the next few hours going over her bloodwork & her genetic analysis with her. As the doctor listed off conditions that she was a carrier for or things that she might be predisposed to, she had asked the question that had been burning in her mind. Did any of these results explain what was happening to her father?

The doctor had shaken her head. Renee's report revealed nothing that might be afflicting her father. Whatever was making him sicker was not something that Renee had inherited or been exposed to.

Renee tried to remember what the doctor had told her next about how she should try to change her diet as she was given a small number of vaccinations, but she couldn't. The reality of the moment came rushing back to her as the priest put his hand on her shoulder.

"My child, would you care to say a few words?"

Renee tried to say something to him, but all she could manage was one word.

"Papa…"

Renee broke down into tears. As Abigail wrapped her arm around Renee so that she could cry into her shoulder, the priest nodded his head & moved onto Maurice's friends. As two of his older friends stood up & said kind things about her father, Renee sobbed as she wished that it were a dream that she could wake up from. She wished that she could just curl up into a ball & let Abigail take her away from here. Instead, she leaned on her lover for support as Abigail resisted the urge to wrap her arms around the love of her life in front of the priest & Maurice's friends.

As Abigail sat there, being the shoulder for Renee to cry on, she remembered the previous Christmas. She had been thrilled to be invited over again. With gifts in hand, she made her way to the bakery. But when she entered the apartment, the first thing that she heard was Maurice coughing. Abigail had refused to let Renee send her home. She had stayed the night & helped her take care of Maurice. She had even stayed over the next day & helped to take care of Maurice while Renee manned the store.

As memories of the night played in her mind, Abigail felt yet another pang of guilt at having not told Renee about her father earlier. Now all that she could do was to help her as best as she could to get through this day & the next few months.

As one of Maurice's friends talked about how stubborn he could be at times, Renee remembered the day near the end of February when she had asked Abigail to come over. Maurice had been sick for three straight days but wouldn't go to see a doctor. Renee watched as Abigail made up a story on the spot about her non-existent brother in London that worked as a doctor. She watched her father slowly be convinced as Abigail told him about how her brother was always dealing with cases where it was too late to save someone because they had been too stubborn to go to the doctor when they could still be saved.

The doctors had only been able to diagnose the pneumonia that was plaguing him at the moment. They couldn't find any reason for his chronic ailments or any explanation for why he was getting worse. She remembered Abigail hugging her afterwards & whispering an apology into her ear. Renee knew that Abigail was apologizing for not being able to use her advanced future doctors to help Maurice.

The funeral procession almost seemed like a dream to Renee as the last words were said. Maurice's friends then gathered together to carry his casket out to the cemetery behind the church. As Renee stood there, silently crying, she watched as the casket was lowered in & the first shovelfuls of dirt were thrown in.

In that moment, she wondered how long it would take for her letter to the rest of her family to get to that small town in France. How many weeks would it be before they found out that they would never see or hear from Maurice again. The sudden realization that they didn't know yet brought Renee to tears as she realized that she would never see any of them again.

She wasn't sure why this upset her. Aside from a handful of photos & one phone call with horrible noise on the line, she hadn't seen or heard any of them since she was 19. Still, the thought that she was probably never going to see them again hurt her dearly.

Eventually, after what felt like both a moment & an eternity, the funeral was over. Maurice's friends offered Renee their condolences & any help that they could offer her in this dark time. Then it was just her & Abigail, standing over a rectangular patch of dirt with a small sign acting as a temporary head stone. Abigail did nothing to rush Renee. She never said that it was time to go. She just stood there by Renee's side until she was finally ready to leave. As they waited at the bus stop, Abigail sat dangerously close to Renee.

"Renee, if you don't want to be alone tonight, I can stay over if you want. I can even call in sick to work again tomorrow if you need me to."

"Thank you, Abigail. I was actually wondering if I could spend the night at your place. I'm not ready to go back to the bakery tonight."

"Of course Renee. You can stay as long you like."

The trip back to Abigail's apartment was mostly silent. When they finally got back, they ran into Lola on their way up. Instead of questioning them on what they were both doing here at three in the afternoon, she offered Renee her condolences. Renee figured that Abigail must have run into Lola before leaving & had been questioned on why she was dressed like she was going to a funeral.

Once they were inside Abigail's apartment, Abigail helped Renee to her couch where she helped Renee out of her shoes. Not entirely sure what to do, Abigail resorted to an age-old tactic.

"Would you like me to get you a cup of tea?"

"Tea sounds good."

"Alright, I'll just be a minute."

Abigail then went & put the kettle on to boil. She went to her room & quickly slipped out of her black dress & into something a little less depressing. She then went to sit by Renee while the water for the tea slowly boiled.

"How are you doing Renee? I'm here if you need to talk."

Renee then saw Abigail's hand on top of her own.

"How… how could I have gotten through today… without you?"

"What do you mean Renee? I'm right here."

"Yes, but you said that your past is a different… a different…"

"A different timeline."

"That's it. That means that there was a me that never met you. A me that was alone today. How did she get through today alone? I had you by my side all day & I could barely hold together. How did she do it alone?"

"I don't know Renee. Maybe you're stronger than you realize?"

"Maybe, but I had almost a year to brace for it. She… the other me… she wouldn't have had that. Her Papa would have gotten sicker & sicker & then she would have had to go through all of that alone. How did she get through today? How did she go back to her bakery alone? How did she open it after a day or two & start serving customers alone?"

Abigail threw her arms around Renee.

"I don't know Renee. I don't know how she did it alone, but you won't have to. I'm right here for you."

They kept hugging for a minute until the kettle started to whistle. Abigail then got up & prepared tea for both of them. When Abigail came back with the steaming hot teacups, they sat together for a minute, quietly sipping their tea & enjoying each other's company. Eventually, Renee asked the question that was burning in her mind.

"How long is it going to be until I'm… until I'm supposed to… sell the bakery?"

"Sometime in December."

"Six months? How am I supposed to run the bakery alone for six months? I could barely handle doing it for a few days when papa was sick. Six months. It's forever."

"I'm not sure. Maybe you started trying to sell in November or October even. After all, the records only say that you sold the bakery in December. It doesn't say when you gave up."

"That's still several months of working alone. How am I supposed to do that?"

"Maybe it seems more overwhelming right now because you're not ready to go back yet. Maybe when you've had some time to process, it won't seem as impossible."

"Maybe."

"Besides, you're not alone Renee. I'll be there every day. Every morning to wish you well, & every evening to congratulate you, & rub your shoulders, & to have a drink with you."

"That does sound nice."

"Not to mention, you can come over any night you want. If it's ever too much to be alone, you can come over & spend a night or two here."

"Can I spend every night here?"

"Each & every night if you want."

Abigail kissed Renee gently on the lips. They then sat together & continued to sip their tea for a good long while, talking about Maurice & the next few months.

December 9th, 1939

Renee was surprised by how few boxes she needed to pack up her life. Even if they just carried the boxes on the bus one or two at a time, it would only take a handful of trips to get them to Abigail's apartment. The hardest thing to move would be the couch & the record player. The rest of the furniture would stay in the apartment, now the property of the new owner who would be moving in next week.

As Renee sat on her couch, she looked over to her father's favorite chair & for a moment, she felt guilty that she was selling it. Looking around & seeing most of her possessions in boxes, she was grateful that Abigail had given up one more Saturday to help her here. Abigail had given up a lot of her Saturdays to help Renee over the last several months.

Renee tried to imagine a world where Abigail hadn't been there & she couldn't see any possible way that she could have made it this long on her own. The first few weeks had been the worst. The endless hours, never being able to afford to hire someone to help, working the ovens & the front of the store at the same time & keeping track of all of the bills & payments. It was endless, exhausting work.

Renee had lost track of the number of days where she felt like she was going to collapse by the end. So many times, Abigail had stayed at the bakery after work, for hours sometimes, helping Renee out at the end of the day & heading upstairs with her to make supper for a tired baker. Renee would then sit down after supper & Abigail would rub her shoulders, or on some days, her aching feet.

As the months had worn on, Renee had spent many evenings lying in bed, complaining about the bills that just kept coming in, demanding money that she didn't have. She would lament that there was no way that she would be able to keep the bakery open until December as Abigail would wrap her pale arms around Renee, their bodies separated only by Renee's nightdress, if that. Abigail would hold her close, often times without a stitch of clothing on her since that was her preferred way to sleep & they would talk about their future together in the decade to come. They would lay there & make grandiose plans that would probably never come to pass until Abigail could not stay any longer or until Renee fell asleep in the arms of her angel from the future.

Renee pulled herself up from the couch & made her way to her small kitchen. As she went to get a glass of water, she saw the receipt for the bakery on the counter. It had just been a week ago that Abigail had brought her the news from her handler that it was now okay to sell the bakery. Any changes to the timeline would be minimal. At the end of the day, Renee had put up the closed sign for the very last time.

The next day, she had gone with Abigail to an agent from the future that was in charge of acquiring properties & businesses. He took care of everything, from getting Renee her own bank account to selling the business & the bakery. Renee was amazed at how quickly it had all gone. Now she just had to finish packing her life.

As Renee drank her water & thought back to the last few days when she had not needed to open the bakery, Abigail came out of her bedroom with a box under her arm.

"Renee, I was packing your socks & underwear when I came across this. Thought that it might be a journal."

Renee looked at the book in Abigail's hand & laughed. Abigail looked at the small notebook she was holding & wondered what was so damn funny that it had Renee in stiches.

"Did I miss the joke?"

"Sorry Abigail, that was the notebook that I wrote all of my observation & ideas in when I was trying to figure out what was going on with you."

"Really. What exactly did you write in here?"

"Nothing interesting."

Renee reached for the notebook, but Abigail snatched it away. Putting the box down, she cracked open the book to a random page to get a peek at what might be written inside.

"Let's see, let's see. She must be a witch, if she isn't from another planet, she can only be a witch or a demon, some beautiful creature sent from the devil to seduce me with her goddess-like body…"

Renee stood there, blushing until her whole face was red as Abigail looked up from the passage.

"You thought that I was a witch or a demon?"

"I was looking for ideas that didn't involve aliens."

"You know that witches don't actually worship the devil, that's just propaganda from the church."

"I didn't know that."

"The body of a goddess."

Renee's blush deepened as Abigail continued.

"I have to say, some of my girlfriends have called me beautiful, gorgeous, hot & worthy of simping over, but nobody has ever called me a goddess."

"Yes… well, I don't know what simping is, but you're the most beautiful person that I've ever seen."

Abigail smiled & almost teared up as she wrapped Renee in a hug & kissed her.

"Renee, that's so sweet. Do you gush over me like this in the rest of this book?"

"In some places."

"We're definitely reading this tonight. I want to read about all of the beautiful things that you thought I was."

"Maybe. I suppose it might help me to get my mind off of how much I'll miss this place. It's been my home… almost since we arrived in this country."

She looked around at the home that she had known for so many years & drank in the fact that it wasn't hers anymore.

"Just this last week, this week of not waking up early enough to be ready for the morning commuters. This week of not needing to spend all day slaving away over the ovens & keeping the store stocked & taking care of the customers. Just this last week has been so strange. I can't believe that after tomorrow, this will never be my home again."

Abigail held Renee tight.

"Trust me, I know how weird it can be to move to a new place."

Renee laughed as she imagined what it must have been like for Abigail to cross the continent & a century & a half to come here.

"I suppose your last move was a little more dramatic."

"Not more dramatic, just a bit further. This has been your home for a rather long part of your life. It makes sense that you're going to miss it. Truth is that when the day comes that we have to leave my apartment, I'll miss that little place, next door to the gossip queen of Hell's Kitchen."

Renee laughed a bit as Abigail continued.

"Just remember to look on the bright side."

"Hmm… remind me what the bright side is Abigail."

"Well, from now on, we're going to wake up in the same bed every single morning. No more coming up with excuses to spend the night, you just get to wake up next to your goddess every morning."

"That does sound heavenly. What else is on this bright side?"

"Well, you won't need to wake up at the crack of dawn & work yourself into an early grave. You'll be able to sleep in, relax, get to enjoy your days. On top of that, we'll never need to have an excuse for why you're always over at my place, because it'll be your place as well."

"My home, where I get to wake up next to you each morning, see you off when you go to work, find something to do until you come home & tell me about your day. It'll be like I'm your kept woman."

After a quick chuckle, Abigail backed up a bit so that there was some space between them as she rested her hands on Renee's hips.

"There's also another benefit to you living under my roof."

"What's that Abigail?"

"There will be absolutely nothing to stop us from being together every single night."

"Every night?"

"Every night, & twice on Sundays. Soon, you'll sleep naked, just like I do, because there won't be any point in getting dressed for bed since I'll be ripping your clothes off every night."

Renee grinned as she leaned in & kissed Abigail. As she imagined what it would be like, to be able to wake up next to her every morning, to kiss her every day, to go to bed with her every night, their kiss got deeper & more passionate. After a minute, Abigail broke the kiss & looked Renee in the eye.

"The new owner is only coming tomorrow, right?"

"Right."

"Good. Have a seat then."

By the time that Renee was sitting in the one chair that was in the kitchen, Abigail was already on her knees, reaching for the bottom of Renee's skirt. Before Renee could ask what Abigail was doing, the hem of her skirt had been hiked up past her knees as Abigail began kissing her way up Renee's legs.

As Renee spread her legs apart in order to give her lover easier access, Abigail ducked underneath Renee's skirt, disappearing beneath it. Renee felt a flurry of kisses along her thighs as Abigail's hands slid up her legs. Without even needing to be asked, Renee lifted herself up at just the right moment so that Abigail could slide her underwear down her legs, leaving her naked beneath her skirt & exposed to Abigail's hunger.

As Abigail's lips tenderly kissed, & her tongue probed & her breath tickled, Renee closed her eyes & leaned back. As she started to gasp, she envisioned all of the countless encounters that she was soon going to have with Abigail once they were living under the same roof. As Abigail continued to pleasure her tenderly & mercilessly with her wondrous skill, Renee said goodbye to her home as she sank deeper & deeper into the pleasures that Abigail was bringing her.

June 26th, 1940

A month & a half of working late every night & going into work on more than a few Saturdays had left Abigail exhausted. As she placed the latest batch of copied documents into her satchel, she stretched her arms, & finally looked at how late it was. She had known that she was going to be working well into the night along with most of her coworkers. That was just what happened at a bank with a lot of international clients when a major country was conquered.

With a mountain of information for her handler & the certain feeling that carpal tunnel syndrome was setting in from pounding away at her typewriter all day, Abigail got up & wished her exhausted boss a good night. He barely said a word as she walked by him & made her way to the exit along with some of her coworkers that had also been burning the midnight oil.

The night was dark as sin as Abigail made her way home in the dead of the night. New York might be the city that never slept, but Abigail needed to rest. The way home felt longer than usual as she fought to stay awake.

Eventually she made it back to the apartment building that she called home. Seeing the light on in her apartment, she smiled knowing that Renee was still up. Ever since Renee had moved in, the apartment felt more like home than it ever had in the ten years that she had been calling it her home. Walking past the mailbox & up the stairs, she was about to walk into her home when Lola's door opened. As the words 'you've got to be kidding me' flew through her mind, Abigail turned around to see Lola there in a nightrobe.

"Abigail? It's the middle of the night, what on God's green Earth are doing only getting home now, it's just past eleven."

"Sorry if I disturbed you Lola, work has been chaotic these last few weeks. Apparently, we have, or had, a lot of clients with assets & accounts in France. So now that France is Germany, everyone is moving their stuff out of France while they still can."

"Of course, those poor people. How is your roommate handling the news about France surrendering?"

Abigail was certain that she could hear something in Lola's voice when she called Renee her roommate.

"Renee is handling it well. Her family lives in a small town that nobody really cares about, so they're probably not being harassed too much."

"The poor dear, first her father's passing, now her family is trapped behind enemy lines. You let Renee know that she'll be in my prayers tonight."

"Sure thing Lola."

Lola then turned away & headed back inside, apparently satisfied that there was no real gossip here. Just a very tired neighbor.

Abigail opened the door & walked into her apartment. As she did, Renee looked up from the old newspaper that she was reading. Abigail didn't know if Renee said anything, she simply walked over to the sofa & collapsed on it. As she sat on the sofa, fighting the urge to just fall asleep then & there, Renee walked up to her.

"Abigail? You look exhausted."

"A fourteen-hour day will do that. I feel like my fingers are going to fall off. I didn't realize that the bank had this many investments & assets in France."

"I'm guessing that a fair bit of tonight wasn't for the bank."

"You're not wrong. How are you doing? You weren't reading the newspapers all day, were you?"

"No. Well, not all day. It's just, I know you told me that it would be quick, but how did France fall in seven weeks?"

"I have no idea; European history isn't my specialty. All I know is that the few records that survive show your family making it through."

Abigail then opened up her satchel so that she could put away the small pile of information that she had collected. As she fumbled with the latch in her exhausted state, Renee took the satchel from her.

"Here, let me take care of that, you just rest up. Jesus, what do you have in here, bricks?"

"Thank you, Renee, just put it with the rest."

Renee then took the pages of documents & the typewriter tape out of Abigail's satchel & took it to the closet in the bedroom with the false back. She then stacked it all up on top of the other information that Abigail had brought home since her last meeting with her handler. Renee wondered how in the hell she was going to lug all of that to her next meeting with Alex.

When Renee came back to the living room, she took a deep breath & sat next to Abigail. Ever since she sold the bakery, & especially since she was supposed to leave for France on that boat, she had had a burning question on her mind that she had never asked. She hadn't asked it all these months because she was afraid of the answer. But now that France had fallen, she needed to know, so she took another deep breath before turning to her exhausted lover.

"Abigail, can I ask you something?"

"Sure, but if I fall asleep before I answer, ask me in the morning."

"You remember the boat that I was supposed to be on, the one that was supposed to take me to France?"

"I'll never forget that boat. I can't tell you how long I was afraid that it was going to take you away from me."

"I know, but what I want to know is… did someone else take my place on it. Because those companies wouldn't leave an empty berth, so did someone else end up going to France in my place? Is there someone else that's now in danger over there because I stayed behind?"

"Yes. Some of our agents are being transferred to Europe to gather intel & to begin laying the groundwork for future missions. One of them took the vacancy that you left so that there would be less disruptions from you staying behind."

"Another agent, not someone else heading home to France that would have avoided the war if I had gone?"

"Exactly. No need to worry, Renee. The only suffering caused by your absence is that one of our agents now has to sail on a packed boat instead of the private boat that we lined up for the rest of his team."

Renee was thrilled. She had been dreading the idea that someone else was going to end up in German occupied France, or one of those camps, simply because she hadn't gone.

"Are you alright, Renee?"

"Yes. Thank you. I'm going to go & get supper."

Renee went to the kitchen where she had turned the stove top back on when Abigail had come home so their food could warm up. She then got two large bowls & using towels to keep from burning herself, she carried the hot bowls back to the living room.

"Supper is ready."

"I can get to the kitchen."

"It's alright Abigail, we can eat here. Hope that you're in the mood for a hearty bowl of Navy Bean soup."

"I sure am. Wait, so we can eat? Didn't you eat already?"

"No. I wanted to wait for you."

"But I told you this morning that I wouldn't be home before ten. You really waited all this time so that we could eat together?"

"Bien oui. Of course I waited. Don't people in the future wait for the woman that they love to get home from work before having supper?"

"Not when I told you that I would be working this late. You must be ravenous; you didn't have to wait."

"I wanted to wait."

Abigail smiled as Renee put the towels & the steaming hot bowls of soup down on the living room table. She then helped Abigail sit up so that they could eat together. Before they could start, Abigail pulled Renee in for a long, gentle, loving kiss.

"You're wonderful Renee."

"You're worth being wonderful for."

They then kissed again before getting a start on their meals & talking about their days.

March 15th, 1941

Renee was lying on their bed next to the dresses that Abigail was going to choose from for her special meeting with her handler. While Abigail was brushing her teeth & filing her nails in the bathroom, Renee had turned on the radio & was listening to the latest news about the war in Europe.

"… Fascist forces of Italy managed to successfully sink the English cargo ship known as the Western Chief. The ship was once part of the American Navy & helped to repel & defeat the Kaiser's forces in World War 1. The ship was carrying…"

Abigail turned off the radio as she walked in. Wearing nothing but her underwear, she walked over to her dresser & pulled a pair of nylon stockings out of her underwear drawer.

"Sorry Renee, but I need to concentrate on being ready for this meeting."

"That's alright, I'd prefer to pay attention to you right now anyways."

Tossing the Nylons onto the small pile of dresses, Abigail went into her closet. From behind the hidden panel, she pulled out one of her wig caps. More of a net than a cap, she managed to fit it over her hair as Renee watched from the bed.

"Have you decided between blonde or brunette yet?"

"The Blonde, I've got it styled as a pageboy cut & I just think that it's the right way to go."

Abigail then focused on herself in the mirror while she tried to adjust the wig net so that she could be sure none of her own dark hair would be poking out from under the wig & that it would be comfortable while she went out & about. Renee picked up the postcard that Abigail had received her orders on. It showed an English soldier standing resolute in front of a lighthouse.

"Abigail, I know that I've asked you a few times already, but are you sure that this postcard doesn't mention anything about what your new orders are going to be?"

"Nope, they could be anything. They might tell me to stay put & carry on, they might tell me to move to Canada. All I know is that the new agent with my orders will be waiting for me with Alex. He's going to give me my new orders, maybe some new supplies, & then after he's dished out a whole bunch of orders for various other agents in New York, he'll be heading off to Houston Texas."

"You don't know what your orders are, but you know what his are?"

"According to Alex, he's part of a group that's heading to Houston to set up a safe house & to prepare for important work in the 60s."

"What's going to happen in Houston Texas in the 60s?"

"Not much, it's just where they're going to build the launch pads for NASA & the Apollo program."

"Right, the space program."

Abigail turned around to face Renee.

"What, you don't believe me when I tell you that America is going to the Moon?"

"No, I believe that part. It's the part about how they go to the moon half a dozen times over three years & then just stop until… when was it?"

"2027, when Artemis 3 takes the first woman to the moon."

"Yeah, why would they go a few times & then not go back for fifty-four years? It does not sound plausible to me."

"Well that's what happened. Originally the Americans weren't even going to dream of going to the moon until the 80s, but they wanted to one up the Soviets. When the Soviets gave up after losing the race, America lost its drive to keep going."

"America lost its drive to go to the Moon. The country that used to be the new world lost its drive to reach for a new world. I'll believe it when I see it."

"Well you might not see it. At least not as it originally happened. From what I hear, we might try to get agents into NASA that'll find the water in Shackleton crater during the Apollo program, instead of in 2008."

"That's where Artemis 3 landed, right Abigail?"

"That's right. It became the foundation for Artemis base."

With her wig net in place, Abigail got up & started looking over her dresses to determine which one wouldn't draw too much attention without making it look like she was trying to hide in plain sight. While she did that, Renee got up & walked over to the dresser where Abigail had taken out her wigs. Taking the curly red wig, she slipped it on over her hair, struggling to get most of her dirty blonde hair underneath the wig.

"What are you doing Renee?"

Renee turned to Abigail, grinned wickedly, & laid on an even thicker French accent than she normally spoke with.

"My name is agent Rodin, & I happen to have a few questions for you miss Oldman, if that is your real name."

Abigail laughed. She always found it funny when Renee put on one of the wigs & pretended to be the secret agent that need to interrogate her. It had become one of their favorite games. Since Abigail had started getting ready early, she figured that she had some time to play.

Still standing there in her underwear, Abigail grabbed the blonde wig that she was going to be wearing to the meeting later on & slipped it on. Abigail than ditched her all too familiar English accent & started talking in her actual voice.

"Please agent Rodin, I promise that I don't know anything about anything. I swear."

Renee walked up to Abigail until Abigail backed up to the wall, as if she was a scared housewife.

"That's not what I hear miss Oldman. From what I hear, you know a lot about the Artemis base. I'm going to need for you to tell me everything that you know."

"I'll never tell you anything."

Renee grinned.

"You will, I have ways of making you talk."

Renee stepped right up to Abigail. When there was scarcely a hair's breadth between them, Renee leaned forward & planted her lips on Abigail's. Abigail wasn't sure when Renee had started taking the lead in some of their fun time, but she definitely liked it. Figuring that it must be something to do with being in the privacy of their own home, with no chance that anyone would catch them, Renee was finally able to relax & have some fun.

Abigail wrapped her arms around Renee's waist as Renee's hands started roaming over Abigail's exposed body, slowly caressing their way closer to Abigail's undergarments. When their kiss broke, Renee pulled back until the tips of their noses were just about to touch.

"Are you going to tell me what I want to know miss Oldman?"

"It's going to take a lot more than that, miss agent woman, if you want me to sing like a canary."

Renee grinned & slid her fingers down the front of Abigail's underwear. Abigail gasped as Renee's fingers, once clumsy amateurs, quickly began teasing Abigail's quickly moistening entrance.

"Fuck… it's going to take… more than a bit of… hmm… pleasant torture…. To break me…"

Renee leaned in until their lips were just brushing against each other's.

"I was hoping that you would say that miss Oldman."

Abigail's moans of sensual bliss were swallowed by Renee's kiss.

Two hours later, Abigail was nearly running late. She had planned on having plenty of time to get to the bar where they were meeting, but Renee's little game had her running late. Grateful that Lola had gone to do her Saturday groceries, she was able to walk out the front door in her full wig unnoticed. Something that she rarely did.

Grateful that the buses were running on time, she made it to the meeting place with nothing more than a minute to spare. Walking in, she saw Alex in a light brown wig sitting across from someone in the nearly empty bar. Walking over to the table, she found a tall glass of beer & a surprisingly friendly face waiting for her.

"Imp62? Is that you?"

The agent that was sitting opposite Alex turned around & smiled. He sat there in a grey three-piece suit with his once pink hair now a dark blonde. His angular face was just as she remembered it though.

"I'm fairly certain that one of the first rules is to not use our real names here, especially if they're gamer tags, Candy."

"Sorry, I just wasn't expecting to see you until after the Apollo program. I guess we're not exactly on the original plan anymore."

Abigail sat down next to Alex & opposite her old friend. She took a sip from the beer that they had ordered for her & got down to business. The first thing that she did, after checking to make sure that there was no waiter coming up on them, was to pull the folders with this week's financial information out of her satchel & to hand it to Alex. He quickly placed it in his briefcase. He asked her the usual questions about her work life & her home life & she answered as she normally did.

With the usual weekly stuff out of the way, Abigail turned to her friend, who had been sitting there quietly, looking a little exhausted.

"So, what do I call you now?"

"You can call me Cameron McHugh. Sorry that I look so tired, I've been running around New York city almost nonstop for the last three days."

"That's alright, Cameron, I'm sure I look a little different to."

"Just a bit. Actually, it's a bit weird seeing you a decade later when for me, we just parted ways a few months ago. But hey, for someone who just lived through the Great Depression, you're still looking pretty damn good."

"Thanks, I think. So what's up? I'm fairly sure that you're supposed to have new orders for me."

"Right. Well as I was telling your handler, Alex, we're abandoning the Alpha-3 plan & protocols. The minute changes that we've made are rippling out further than we thought they would."

"You don't have to tell me. I was in what was supposed to be a quick crash & grab bank robbery that turned out to be a prolonged hostage situation. Still not entirely sure what happened because of the blow to my head that I took that wasn't supposed to happen."

"Yeah, exactly like that. Now, fortunately, we're still in the Alpha plans, but as of right now, we're in the Alpha-7 plans. Specifically, we're starting Alpha-7-4."

"Damn, I figured that we would be moving down the list, but we're skipping straight to 7-4. I guess that means I'm being relocated."

"That you are Abigail, though not right away."

"Just to make sure, Renee is going to be able to come with me, right?"

"Yes. She can go with you."

"Alright, so where am I going?"

"For the duration of World War 2, you are to stay in your current position. Shortly after Germany surrenders in 45, you'll be relocating to Detroit."

"Detroit? I don't have any training or knowledge for Detroit."

"Not a problem. We've got a supply package for you & it includes a complete primer for Detroit post WW2. You have four years to memorize it."

"Great. Am I still going to be in data acquisition?"

"Yes & No. You'll be working as a file clerk, allowing you to help us set up fake ids & records. You'll be stationed there for at least ten years, probably closer to twenty, so be prepared to move sometime in the early sixties."

He then reached into his briefcase & pulled out a small box made to look like a postal package from London. He slid it to her over the table.

"Inside the box, you'll find your mission primer & a pair of vaccine doses. They should immunize you & Renee against all of the outbreaks that are supposed to occur in New York for the next decade. Don't mix them up, they're personalized to you two."

"Understood."

"You'll both also receive age reversing treatments before you leave, they'll bring you back to your early twenties."

"Great. Any information on my next identity?"

"We see no reason to change your identity or backstory. You'll be moving two states & a great lake over, the odds of recognition are slim. We'll simply give you two new background information for Abigail Oldman & Renee Rodin. As long as nobody does a background check for you in New York, you should be fine & if someone does, just tell them that Oldman is a popular name in England."

"Sounds like it would be popular there."
Abigail then put the package on top of her Satchel.
"Anything else that I need to know about, Cameron?"
"For the mission, not so much."
They then raised their glasses together & drank from their beers before catching up with each other about the last few months for him & the last eleven years for her.

Chapter 14
January 28th, 1942

The flame was white hot as the edges of the two steel lengths glowed red hot & began fusing together. Dialing the flame down until it was just red hot, Renee raised her visor up so that she could look at her work. Seeing no immediate problems, she turned off the torch, set it aside & began inspecting her latest weld. The connection wasn't like the professional welds that her teacher had demonstrated, but it was her best butt weld to date.

She spent the next little while carefully polishing it as the teacher wandered around the room, checking on his students. When he stopped by Renee's station, he examined the weld for a minute as if he wanted there to be something wrong. After looking it over for a minute, he was forced to concede that it was well done.

"Impressive miss Rodin. Another month, & I might actually trust you to build something."

"Thank you, sir."

"Remember to stay after class for a few minutes along with some of the other students."

"Wouldn't miss it sir."

Renee then reached for two more steel plates to begin her next weld. Later on, after class ended, Renee was up at the front of the classroom with five other students. Once again, the six students gathered together for an after-class talk were the six female students. The teacher then sat down & looked up at the women standing around him.

"The six of you have done surprisingly well since you began in October. I'll admit that I wasn't expecting much when a bunch of housewives, waitresses & bakers joined my class. That being said, you all seem to be making excellent progress. Don't let this go to your heads though, you still have months of training ahead of you & you can't afford to let your work slip. You can all head on home now."

As the six of them then filed out of the classroom, welding handbooks in hand, one of the women, a woman in her fifties with a number of grey hairs in her long brunette locks walked up behind Renee & tapped her on the shoulder.

"I see that you actually managed to impress him today."

"Hi Willa, yes, he actually said that one day, he might trust me to build something."

"Wow, look at you. That's higher praise than any other woman in this class has ever gotten. You would think that nobody told him that men are in short supply these days."

"He's probably just making sure that we're getting the practice we need."

"Then how come it's always the six of us that he's overly scrutinizing? Alex who works next to me, he damn near set himself on fire last week, but who does the teacher keep picking at, the old housewife, that's who."

"I suppose he does tend to hover a bit."

"He hovers around you most of all. In his eyes, I at least did my womanly job & got married & had kids. I don't think he's too fond of the unmarried French baker in his class. Must grind his gears that you're his best student."

Renee grinned.

"How are your boys?"

"One is still a lazy fool like his father, the other is actually making me proud to call him my boy. Takes after his grandfather, the colonel."

The two women walked together for a bit, huddling up in the wintery cold. It felt good for Renee to be working & doing something again, it felt even better since unlike in the bakery, she was actually making friends. When they reached Willa's bus stop, they hugged each other goodbye as Willa reminded her that she was having the girls over for lunch on Saturday. Renee smiled, looking forward to the weekend all the way home.

Slipping past Lola's questions, Renee walked into the apartment that she called home & turned on the radio as she got to work cooking supper for her & Abigail. As she listened to the news of the first American forces landing in Northern Ireland to join the allied forces in the war, Abigail walked in the door, looking a little tired as she normally did.

"Hello, Renee?"

"I'm in the kitchen, supper should be ready in a minute."

Abigail then made her way to the kitchen where she wrapped her arms around Renee's waist & kissed the back of her neck.

"That smells good."

"Go get changed, it'll be ready in a minute."

Abigail then started unbuttoning her blouse, making it down to her naval before heading to their bedroom to change. When she got back, Renee was putting supper on the table. Abigail kissed Renee once more before sitting down to eat.

"How was your day, Renee? One day closer to becoming Wendy the welder?"

"Wendy who?"

"It's like Rosie the riveter, their inspirational posters that'll start showing up in a few months to encourage woman to get industrial jobs so the men folk can go off & fight."

"Ah, I see. Yes, I'm one day closer to becoming Wendy the welder. A lot of women are. I know that you said the change would be quick, but in the last few months, I've seen women walking into & out of factories to work all over the city."

"You haven't seen anything yet. As the years go on & more men keep getting sent overseas, more & more women will start showing up to work. In the decades that follow, the stories & pictures of working women will add fuel to all kinds of feminist movements. When the Rosie the riveter poster starts showing up, get used to them. She won't be going away after the war."

Renee smiled. Four months ago, when she said that she wanted to work again & Abigail had suggested that she get some sort of mechanical or industrial training, she had thought that it was a joke. Even after years of listening to Abigail talk about how much things were going to change; she didn't think that a woman who had worked as a baker would ever be able to just become a riveter, a welder, or a builder. Yet here she was, taking fire to steel five days a week.

I'm guessing that I'm not going to be able to keep this job after the war ends & the men come home."

"Not likely, of course, when the war ends, we're off to Detroit, the motor city. Maybe you'll be able to get work as a welder there."

"That would be nice."

"So I take it that you like welding."

"I really do. There's just something so incredible about being able to cut through steel with fire, or to join two pieces together. It's incredible."

"I'm glad that you like it, Renee."

Renee smiled.

"It's also good to have friends. Before I met you, it was always just me & Papa. Now, I actually have friends that I'm studying with, & I'm going to have friends that I'll be working with. It's wonderful."

Abigail smiled. It warmed her heart to see Renee so happy. After how hard she had been working all of her life & everything that she had to go through. Abigail believed that Renee should get to spend the rest of her life smiling.

"Abigail, you're hardly eating."

"I Love you, Renee."

"I love you too, now eat."

March 9th, 1942

Knocking on her boss' door, Abigail walked in with a thick folder in her arms. Placing it on Mr. Parker's desk, she stood there for a moment while he finished the sentence that he was writing.

"The Cavendish file, up to date & typed out from the written records that he brought over from England."

Taking the folder from its spot, he opened it up & looked over it.

"Fastest fingers in the West. Some of the people in this office have been typing since they invented typewriters, or near enough, but not one of them can match you. Quick as a shot & I think that I've only seen a half a dozen spelling mistakes from you in the last decade."

"Thank you, sir. Since this is the only task that was urgent today & since you have a meeting to attend, would you mind if I took an extended lunch break?"

"You seem to be taking a lot of those lately miss Oldman, nothing's wrong I hope."

"Nothing at all Mr. Parker."

"Going to meet someone then, maybe a handsome fellow."

"Not exactly."

"Alright then, enjoy your lunch, Miss Oldman."

"Thank you, Mr. Parker."

Half an hour later, when her boss left for his meeting, Abigail took her lunch break, slipped on her coat & headed for the door. In what seemed like no time at all, she found herself approaching the school where Renee was learning to weld. She only had to wait a few minutes before she saw the class breaking for lunch.

As the students filed out for lunch, many of them men that would be shipped out after graduating, Abigail saw Renee rounding the corner, talking to her new friend Willa. They were both still wearing the heavy overalls that welders have to wear. When Renee saw Abigail waiting for her by the entrance, she turned to Willa with a new smile on her lips.

"Would you mind telling the girls that I can't make it too lunch today, I just remembered that I already had plans."

Willa noticed Renee's smile & looked towards Abigail for a moment. This wasn't the first time that Abigail had just randomly stopped by to have lunch with Renee. For a moment, Willa thought that it was a bit odd for two roommates to be spending that much time together outside of their home.

Shaking off the feeling, she agreed to let the girls know that Renee couldn't make it to lunch. They shared a quick hug before Renee went to see Abigail.

"Well this is a pleasant surprise. Did you get another extended lunch?"

"Yes, I did. My boss is starting to suspect that I'm meeting up with a handsome young man that's trying to romance me."

Renee laughed as they walked down the road towards the dinner that was quickly becoming their usual lunch place. Renee was getting more than a few strange looks in her overalls as most Americans weren't yet used to the idea of women in the workforce. Once inside, they sat down at one of their preferred booths & ordered lunch from the waitress that smiled as she recognized two of her favorite customers. Once the waitress left with their orders, Abigail smiled from across the table.

"How's your training going today, Renee? You said that you were starting a new section of your course this morning."

"It's getting pretty tough. Only about half of the class has made it this far, the other half have failed the tests."

"Wow, how many women are left?"

"Including myself, five of the original six."

"I imagine that losing ten men & one woman might be causing your teacher to rethink a few things."

Renee smiled.

"I hope so, the next class that started this week has twice as many women as ours did. It's incredible. I actually saw some of those propaganda posters that you mentioned about Rosie the Riveter."

"Now is about the time that they're starting to show up since the government is realizing how many men will have to go overseas & how many jobs will need to be filled here at home."

"It's not just the government."

Renee reached into one of the large pockets in her overalls & pulled out a newspaper clipping. She then handed the clipping to Abigail as their food arrived. It was an ad from the classifieds section looking for workers, men, or women, in a manufacturing plant.

"Willa gave me that. She said that she never thought that she'd live to see job ads like that for women."

Abigail smiled & reached under the table to give Renee's thigh a gentle squeeze.

"Think, in a few more months, you'll be applying to one of those jobs. Welding metal together, maybe for the war, that beautiful long blonde hair of yours tied back behind a welding mask."

"That's assuming that I don't cut it short."

"Give me some warning if you plan to do that."

They both laughed as they made a start on their lunch. For the next few minutes, they talked about a variety of things from news about the war to what they might like to have for supper. Time was quickly running short for both of them as Abigail had a long walk to get back to work & Renee's afternoon class would be starting soon.

After they finished their meals & paid, they hugged each other outside the dinner for as long as they could & still have it be socially acceptable. Ten minutes later, Renee was back in class, next to Willa, seeing what she was going to have to spend her afternoon welding.

"I hate welding on a curve."

Renee turned to Willa who was clearly dreading welding the vertical pipes to the steel plate.

"It doesn't look to hard Willa, the pipes are vertical this time, that should be easier."

"True but take a look at the pipes. One of them is copper."

Abigail looked at the small chunks of pipe that she had been given to weld to the steel plate. One of them was indeed made of copper.

"Merde! Cuivre et acier, pourquoi nous feraient-ils ça?"

"Sorry Renee, but some of us don't speak angry French woman."

"Sorry Willa. I was asking why they would do this to us."

"Because they think that we won't be able to talk people out of welding steel & copper together when we have jobs."

As the two of them started cleaning the ends of the pipes & the plates that they were going to be welding them to, Willa took a step closer to Renee.

"How was lunch with your roommate?"

"It was good. We went to that dinner down the road again."

"Your roommate, Abigail, doesn't she work in a bank in… Soho, I think you said."

"That's right. What's up Willa?"

"Nothing's up, I'm simply curious. Soho to here is a long way to go for lunch, two or three times a week."

Renee could immediately sense that Willa was hinting at something. Someone becoming suspicious of her & Abigail had been something that she had been afraid of for years. Now she could swear that Willa was probing for information. Living next to Lola for the last two years had made it easier for her to tell when someone was looking for information.

"We've been friends for over ten years. She's just checking up on me. Making sure that I'm not in over my head."

Willa looked at Renee for a second & decided to let up on the questioning. Thinking about the look on Abigail's face when she saw Renee, she was certain that she had spotted something. Not sure if Renee was simply naïve or if they really were just really good friends. She didn't want to push the subject. Renee was a good friend

& she didn't want to risk alienating her just because she gave off a hint or two of being like her.

Willa then turned her attention to the young woman in front of them, the one that had been engaged for three years before her boyfriend went to war.

May 22nd, 1942

The candles were lit. The champagne was chilled. The knots were tight. Abigail was ready to celebrate as soon as Renee walked in the door.

Renee was tired from a long week. She had exams coming up & she was spending as much time as she could practicing at the school. At the end of the day, she had put her welding gear away, splashed some water in her face & made her way back home, wondering if Abigail had done something to celebrate the date. It was the anniversary of the day that they had become more than friends, the day that they had first made love & it was their favorite day of the year.

Riding the bus home in the overalls that she had been wearing all day, she ignored the strange looks from the other passengers. She could tell that a lot of them weren't happy to see a woman in pants, let alone in working clothes, but there was a war on. Everyone had to do their part & that included not bothering women who were contributing to the war effort by picking up the industrial slack at home while the men went to war.

Once she reached her stop, she got off the bus & headed for the apartment building. The lights in their apartment window were on, but they seemed different. They seemed to flicker, as if there were candles lit instead of an electric lamp. Sensing that there was a romantic evening ahead of her, she dashed up the stairs, no longer so tired from a long week.

Standing at their door for a moment, she took a deep breath, hoped that she wouldn't fall asleep halfway through, & opened the door, expecting to find an elaborate supper waiting for her.

Instead, she was greeted by the sight of Abigail, standing in their candlelit living room, pouring a glass of champagne while wearing nothing but a dark blue corset. Renee was absolutely stunned. As she stood stare in silent awe, Abigail finished pouring the champaign.

"Welcome home Renee, please close the door."

Renee closed the door behind her & locked it. She then watched Abigail turn around to put down the bottle. She could see that the back of the corset had seven pairs of silken strings tied in seven knots holding it tight against Abigail's body.

"Seven knots for seven years together. What do you think Renee?"

"Je t'aime. I love it."

"Good."

Abigail walked over to Renee & handed her a glass of champagne.

"Happy anniversary Renee."

They then clinked their glasses together & took a long sip of their drinks. Abigail then took the glasses to the kitchen & returned to the living room where Renee was just starting to get her mind working again. Abigail then turned her back to Renee.

"Well, aren't you going to unwrap your present?"

Before charging towards Abigail, Renee took a moment to untie her own hair that she had kept tied back while training at school. Once her own hair was free, she walked up to Abigail & set her tired fingers to work on the first knot.

Judging by how well she had tied them behind her, & by how easily she was wearing it, Renee figured that this wasn't the first time that Abigail had slipped into a corset. She didn't know if it was how tired she was or if it some sort of special future knot, but she struggled with it. Just as she was about to get a knife & cut Abigail out of her corset, the first knot finally slipped.

She could hear Abigail breathe a little more deeply as the restrictive garment loosened a bit. Looking over Abigail's shoulder, she could see that her lover's pale breasts weren't pushed up as much as they had been when she first walked in. She then got to work on the second knot.

The whole time that she was manipulating the knots, Abigail never said a word. She just stood there as Renee worked tirelessly to free her lover from the dark blue corset. When the second knot finally gave, Abigail gasped once more.

When Renee reached for the next knot, Abigail stepped away. She turned around to face Renee. With her Breasts no longer being squeezed so tightly, they jiggled just a bit with each step, just enough to keep Renee's eyes focused on them.

"Come with me to the kitchen Renee."

Without saying a word, Renee followed Abigail to the kitchen where she saw a delicious looking chocolate cake sitting on the table with the number seven written in pink frosting.

"Have a seat my love."

Renee took her seat in front of the cake. Abigail then got a plate, a fork & a knife. Walking back to the table, swaying her hips with each step, she stood on the opposite side of the table. She then leaned over the table, her cleavage practically spilling out of the top of her corset as she sliced the cake.

"Do you want the seven, or should we save that for later?"

"Huh… ah… the seven… please."

Abigail laughed, causing her breasts to bounce a bit. Renee was transfixed. She watched as Abigail heaped the slice onto the plate & put it in front of Renee. When Renee reached for the fork, Abigail slapped her hand away.

"Not yet…"

Abigail then walked around the table. Without even letting Renee slide her chair out, Abigail maneuvered her bare leg over Renee's legs & took a seat, straddling her French girlfriend. Remembering this exact seen happening more than once over the last few years, Renee looked up at Abigail.

"This seems familiar."

"Shh… there'll be time for talking later."

Abigail then took Renee's hands & brought them up to her chest. Leaving Renee's hands there, she reached behind & got the plate & fork. She then fed Renee a delicious piece of dark chocolate cake. It was the greatest piece of cake that Renee had ever tasted. It was almost enough for her to close her eyes. Renee imagined that if she ever made it to heaven, this is what it would be like. Sitting on her kitchen chair, her hands on a nearly naked Abigail as she was hand fed this cake. It was sublime.

For what seemed like a sweet eternity, Abigail would feed Renee a piece of cake before having a piece herself. Every time that Abigail had a bite, Renee watched as Abigail's expression become seraphic, right before it became devilish again as she fed Renee her next piece.

Eventually, the last piece of Abigail's heavenly slice of cake was finished. Abigail put the plate & the fork back on the table. Turning her attention back to Renee, she leaned forward until Renee's hands were pressed between their chests & kissed her deeply. As their lips & tongues entangled, they could each taste the chocolate once more on each other's lips.

When their kiss finally broke, Abigail leaned in close to Renee & whispered in her ear without her familiar English accent. Her voice deeper & more sensual, her breath tickled Renee's ears.

"Don't you think that it's time to get back to unwrapping your present?"

Finally prying her hand away from Abigail's chest, she slid her hands around her lover to begin attacking the knots that separated her from Abigail's naked body. With her mind full of dark chocolate cake, sensual kisses, the feel of silk against her palms & the feel of Abigail's bare breasts against her fingertips, it was hard for Renee to focus.

Trying to keep her mind trained on what her fingers were doing behind Abigail's back was hard enough. Doing it while Abigail's hands were wandering over the rough fabric of her overalls was harder. Doing it with her face almost buried in Abigail's cleavage was nearly impossible. With a herculean effort, she managed to slip the third knot. As she began on the fourth knot, Abigail leaned in again & whispered in her ear in her real voice.

"If you hurry up, I might let you call me Candy tonight my love."

Renee almost tied her own fingers into a new knot. As Abigail laughed her evil little giggle, Renee focused as best as she could & got to work on the knot in her fingers. Eventually, the fourth knot came loose, leaving two more silk strings dangling down Abigail's back as the corset loosened on her body.

Before Renee's fingers could get to work on the next knot, Abigail kissed her forehead & got up from where she had been straddling Renee's lap. Abigail then walked towards the bedroom door, swaying her hips in an exaggerated fashion.

"If you want the rest of your gift, you'll have to join me in the bedroom."

As Abigail slipped into their room, Renee bolted out of the chair & followed. When she walked into their room, she saw Abigail sitting on their bed amidst the rose petals that she had scattered. As Renee took a step into their bedroom, Abigail pointed at her.

"Stop."

Renee stopped dead in her tracks, almost eager to hear about what sensuous torture now stood between her & her love.

"Tonight, there are no clothes allowed in here, you can enter, but those clothes of yours will have to stay out there."

"You're still wearing clothes."

"Well then, you're going to have to get in here & fix that, once you've gotten undressed."

Renee grinned. Compared to the knots in Abigail's corset, the zippers & buttons of her overalls were child's play. In a moment, she was standing in her underwear as she stepped out of the pile of her clothes. As Abigail watched, licking her lips in hungry anticipation, Renee quickly tossed her bra aside & slid down her underwear. Standing there naked, her little brownish nipples hard as diamond & her sex practically dripping with arousal, she walked towards the bed.

Abigail then turned over until she was lying face down, the offending knots on full display to Renee's hungry eyes. Renee then climbed onto the bed, disturbing the lovingly placed rose petals as she moved into position & straddled Abigail's thighs. While Abigail lay there face down, eagerly waiting for Renee to untie the last few knots, she had to fight her own desire to just reach into the night table & grab the pair of scissors.

Knot by knot & strand by strand, Renee made her way through the final obstacles until at long last, all seven knots were undone. Pulling the two sides of the corset away from each other, Renee quickly exposed Abigail's back.

Climbing off of Abigail, Renee lay down next to Abigail as Abigail lifted herself up. Renee lay there watching as Abigail sat up, having left the corset behind on the bed. Abigail then ran her hands along her naked body as Renee grabbed the offending corset & tossed it over to lie with her clothes. Renee then drank in the site of Abigail's body as Abigail climbed on top of Renee.

"Happy anniversary my love, are you ready for your present?" Renee grinned.

"I've been ready for half an hour."

"Then I won't make you wait for another second."

Abigail leaned in & planted her lips on Renee's. A heartbeat later, Renee could feel Abigail's body pressing against hers as Abigail's fingers began wandering, caressing & probing.

Soon their bodies were entwined & entangled as they kissed, gasped, moaned & pleasured each other in celebration of their seven years as lovers.

July 6th, 1942

Renee had gotten used to watching Abigail running around to get ready. Wishing her well, kissing her goodbye as she was about to walk out the door. She was glad that she still got to do that, even if she was rushing herself. Today was the first day of Renee's new job & she honestly had no idea how she had landed it. She was certain that Abigail, or one of the people that Abigail worked for must have pulled some strings. How else could she have gotten hired at the Brooklyn Navy Yard three days after she graduated from her welding course.

With the ink on her diploma barely even dry, she accepted the job & proceeded to interrogate Abigail to see if she knew anything about it. Either Abigail didn't know, or she was taking that secret to her grave.

As Abigail slung on her satchel, she double checked to make sure that she had everything, the way that she did every morning. She then walked up to Renee who was sitting on the bed in her underwear, putting her socks on. Renee looked up just in time for Abigail to bend down & plant a deep kiss on her lips. Renee sat there, frozen in the process of putting her socks on as Abigail's lips caressed her own.

"Good luck on your first day Renee, I can't wait to hear about it tonight."

Another quick peck on the lips & Abigail was out the door like a shot to make her way to SoHo. Renee quickly finished getting dressed & made her way out to head to Brooklyn.

Once she reached the Navy Yard, she was directed to a small crowd of new hires where she met Willa, who had also been hired days after graduating.

"Morning Renee. It looks like it's just you & me. Guess that means we can have our pick of the boys."

Renee laughed as some of the eight men that were starting that day chuckled with her. A few minutes later, when everyone had shown up, including two men that were making a mad dash to the group to avoid being late, a man with a clipboard showed up.

"Good morning recruits. You ten fine lads… sorry ladies… you eight fine lads & you two fine gals are now employed by the US Navy. Follow me & I'll take you to your departments."

The eleven of them then walked into the base. The first stop that they made was at Slipway 1 where four of the men were told that they would be working on the USS Missouri that was under construction before them. When Renee saw the unfinished hulk in front of her, she remembered what Abigail had told her the night before. That the Missouri was one of only four Iowa class ships that would see service & that in three years' time, it would be the site of the surrender of the Empire of Japan.

What they were building was the place where World War 2 would one day come to an end. As Renee stood there, watching the men at work on the boat, she felt like she was watching history happening in front of her. While she wondered if that was what Abigail felt every day, the group continued on. Renee had known that she wasn't going to get to work on the Missouri, she wouldn't get to help build it. Still, maybe she was going to get to do something important. A few minute later, they were standing in front of a slipway with a burned-out wreck of a boat in it.

"Willa Bell, Renee Rodin, John Graves, you'll be working here in the salvage department."

Their supervisor in the salvage department, a gruff man who looked like he was going to be retiring before Japan surrendered walked out to meet them.

"Which of these pieces of meat are for me?"

The man with the clipboard pointed to the three people he had named before & they raised their hands.

"You've got to be fucking shitting me. It was bad enough when you gave me one broad to work in my department, now you're giving me two more. What did I do to deserve this shit?"

"As I recall, the first woman welder that we gave you is actually turning out to be one of the best employees that we've ever had work salvage."

The gruff supervisor waved him off & signaled for his three new hires to follow him. He led them into a small office that was cluttered with papers, tools, components, a collection of used large caliber bullets & a plaque on the wall for 20 years' service.

"Alright, listen up. I'm in charge of salvage operations here. Take a good look at my office. Unless you manage to get promoted to the point where you would regularly have to report to me, the only time you'll be in here is when I'm about to rip you a new one. Now, while the real men are out there building the ships of war, the three of you will be here, carving up the ones that barely came back for useful materials & parts. These boats are already barely above the waterline, so try not to sink them while you're working."

He sat back in his chair & looked out the window at the former boat being held up by salvage pontoons that they were in the middle of carving up.

"John, you're an electrician, right?"

"Yes sir."

"The salvage crew are going to be bringing electrical equipment like radios, telegraphs, fuse boxes & whatnot to your department. Your job is to try & get some of it into serviceable condition. Ladies, you two will be using those welding skills that you supposedly have to carve steel off of the boat. Teaching women to weld, what's fucking next in this fucking country?"

He then stood up & led them out of his office. He took John to the electrical recovery department. He then took Willa & Renee to where a team was cutting large chunks of steel off of the boat. He left them in the care of the only other woman in the department. She then took her welding mask off & grinned at the gruff man, knowing that he couldn't fire her because she was the best cutter in the yard.

"Welcome to the floating scrap heap ladies. Either of you ever work your torches on a boat before?"

September 17th, 1942

Abigail was dumbfounded. The papers in her hand clearly showed that the man in charge of Renee's salvage department was embezzling from the Navy. It was all right there in black & white. Money that was supposed to be going to buying equipment & acetylene from one company was instead being used at another company that was giving him a discount. He was then pocketing the money that he didn't have to spend.

Overall, the theft was small, about a thousand dollars, not enough for anyone to really care about, but enough to get him into trouble if anyone reported it. This was exactly the kind of thing that Abigail had spent the last twelve years looking for. Money ending up in bank accounts that it wasn't supposed to be in.

Abigail looked up at Renee who was sitting on the couch next to her, still wearing her overalls from work. Abigail had been concerned when Renee came home looking nervous. When she had sat down next to her on the couch, she had been surprised when Renee reached into one of the deep pockets in her overalls & produced the financial documents.

"Renee… how… how did you get this? How did you even know to look for this?"

Renee slumped back on the sofa, exhausted. After taking a minute, she started recounting how it happened.

"It started this morning. I was waiting for one of the pontoons that keep the wrecks above water to be repositioned. That was when I heard, or when I overheard my supervisor talking to my boss. He was pissed because my boss has been buying cheaper equipment from a new supplier."

"Yeah, I saw that in the records, about two months ago, the supplier being listed changed & the price went down a bit."

"Exactly. My boss told my supervisor that the new supplier was cheaper, which meant more money for other things. I then overheard my supervisor complaining to himself that the only other thing getting more money was a certain bank account."

"So then what? You decided to go all James Bond?"

"Who?"

"He's a famous fictional spy, never mind Renee, continue."

"Right, well, I knew that he was going to his weekly meeting with a bunch of the section heads at the naval yard, so he would be gone for a few hours. So while I was on break, I may have snuck into his office."

"Why would you do that?"

"I don't know. It just seemed like a good idea at the time."

"Okay, so you MacGyver your way into his office, he's a famous TV spy, then what?"

"I closed his blinds & just started looking around. Truth is that at that moment, I realized that I didn't really know what I was doing or what I was even looking for. When I saw his safe, the only thing that I could think of was that you could probably get into it a bunch of different ways."

"Not really, the only way that I know how to get into a safe is with the combination."

Renee was a bit surprised. She figured that Abigail could break into or out of anything. She was a spy from the future after all.

"Anyway, I was about to give up when I got the idea to check his pockets. That was when I found his bank statement in an open envelope. I had to read it a few times to figure out that three of the payments to his account were for small random amounts from the Navy salvage supply fund. Looking through the rest of his pockets, I found the key to his filing cabinet & that was where I found the purchase records."

Abigail looked at the purchase records in her hand. The difference in the amounts that he used to be spending on supplies compared to what he was now spending on supplies perfectly matched what was being deposited in his bank account. Abigail figured that the Navy was too busy to pay attention to where every single dollar & penny they spent was going.

"That's impressive Renee, but what happens when he eventually realizes that his bank statement & purchase records are missing?"

Renee smiled like the cat that caught the canary.

"They aren't missing. They're still in his office & in his jacket."

It took a second for it to click in Abigail's mind.

"You copied the documents. That's good, but how did you copy them?"

"I found a mimeograph machine in his office, underneath the clutter. It took me a few minutes to figure out how to make it work, but once I did, I copied the documents & put the originals back."

Abigail was impressed. Renee had successfully infiltrated his office & stolen intel without getting caught. Abigail didn't want to admit that she was a little turned on by the idea of Renee as a secret agent. Still, Renee wasn't trained for this. If anyone had caught her…"

"Renee, I'm grateful for the intel. It's really impressive, but please, please don't do this again. You don't know how much danger you put yourself in today. You spied on the American military in a time of war. What if you had been caught? You could have been held, tried, maybe even executed as a German spy."

"Je doute qu'il pensent qu'une Français venue ici il y a seize ans puisse être une espionne allemande."

"I don't know most of what you just said, but I get it Renee, they would be hard pressed to think that a French woman that's been in this country for sixteen years could be a German spy. That doesn't mean they would go easy on you. You committed espionage against the military. Please, promise me that you'll never do that again."

"I promise Abigail."

Abigail then pulled Renee into a hug. Her mind was racing. What had Renee been thinking? How could she be so reckless? What would her handler think when she gave him Navy intel that included embezzlement that Renee had acquired?

Chapter 15
May 15th, 1943

Alex was enjoying the cloudy day in mid-May. The cool spring air, the people enjoying Central Park, the peaceful time before Abigail showed up. Truthfully, she hadn't caused too much trouble in the last few years. He was glad for that. At the age of sixty-three, he was feeling a bit too tired to be putting out her fires. As he dreamed of the day about 2 years in the future when he could be made young again, that was when Abigail showed up on the trail.

She was wearing a familiar blonde wig that was done up in a long ponytail. Judging by her smile, she wasn't bearing any bad news for him. She sat down next to him, putting her satchel down on the bench next to her with an audible thud.

"Good morning, Abigail. You look like you're in a good mood."

"I am in a good mood. Tax season is just about over, just a few stragglers left, mostly military files that arrived late because it's hard to file taxes from Northern Africa. It's a nice enough day out here, Lola went on vacation to visit her sister in Chicago for a few days & Renee is back home baking something. Life is good."

"I'm glad to hear that all is well. So the extended tax season is probably why your bag sounds so heavy then."

"You have no idea. So much money is moving around these days, it's insane. I'm not even sure that anyone is keeping track of it all. I think that the government's position is first we'll win the war, then we'll sort out all the minor money details."

"Sounds like it's going to be a lot of overtime for the boys that have to file & sort all of this."

"Definitely. It you hadn't spent the last few decades hauling mail, I'd feel upset about making you carry all of this at your age."

Abigail opened her satchel & pulled out a bag that was designed to make it look like a dutiful daughter had gotten some small things from the store for her ageing father that liked to spend his days in the park. As Alex slipped them into his briefcase, he could imagine the people in the data processing department cursing him out & wishing that they could transfer out to another department.

Turning back to Abigail, he took a second to wave back to the toddler being carried by his father through the park before getting back to her.

"So how's Renee doing these days?"

"She's absolutely thriving. I don't think that I've ever seen her so happy. Despite how much she complains about her department head, she loves her work. She's made a bunch of new friends, she's always smiling & I swear that when she comes home from spending some time with the girls, she has an actual spring in her step."

"That's wonderful to hear."

"I'm hoping that when we get to Detroit, she'll be able to find more work as a welder. It's going to suck that the Navy isn't going to keep any female welders. Sucks that all of those women are going to lose their jobs because the men come home."

"That it does."

They sat there for a moment as the sun peaked out from behind the clouds for a moment.

"I've got some news for you from upper management Abigail."

"I swear I haven't done anything."

Alex laughed.

"No… no… This is good news, about our mission."

"What's happening Alex?"

"Once Japan surrenders, we're officially entering phase 2. Technological acceleration."

"You mean that we're going to start changing things?"

"Yes. Orders & plans are being sent out all over for agents to start setting up companies that will "invent" technology years ahead of schedule. Our goal for the moment is to have a fully commercialized internet by 1980 & the first gigahertz processors on the market by 1985. That would put this world's technology 15 years ahead of schedule."

"So when can I start blaring my fav elf metal bands?"

Alex laughed.

"It'll still be a while. But if our estimates are accurate, accelerating technology should help to accelerate social progress, so you might get your elf metal in the 2010s instead of the 2030s."

"Sweet. So how long until I can propose to Renee?"

"Well… Society always evolves a little slower than technology, so our preliminary estimates tell us that gay marriage should be legal across the US by 2010 instead of 2015. Of course, if we have a full-blown internet by 1980, we might be able to combat the stigmas of the Reagan era. So maybe it'll be earlier than we estimate."

Abigail smiled. She imagined exchanging vows with Renee & getting to go out in public with her before the end of the century.

December 18th, 1943

The trip had seemed endless. Nine long hours on a cramped bus, driving out to Rochester during a snowstorm. Abigail & Renee had both been surprised by how many people had been on the bus. It hadn't been full by any means, but there were a lot more people than they had expected to see.

The whole way there, the bus had either been freezing cold when they had the windows open a crack, or a sweat box when they closed the windows up. Abigail had preferred it when the windows were open. It gave her an excuse to cuddle up with Renee without anyone asking questions.

The best parts had been when the person sitting near them took a nap & Abigail could slide her hand between Renee's shivering legs to give her thighs a playful squeeze & receive a small slap on her hand from Renee.

Nine hours, three stops, 4 dull conversations with strangers & half a dozen small slaps from Renee later, they finally arrived at their destination. They were picked up by an agent who was driving a great big red Cadillac. Half an hour later, they had pulled up to their destination just as the snowstorm was finally starting to lighten up. Once in the countryside house, their overnight bags were taken upstairs & they were ushered into an exam room to begin their physicals.

They had changed into medical gowns before the doctor started poking & prodding them & taking various samples for testing. Renee had been reminded of when Abigail's people had found out that she knew & had started examining her. Now, as they waited for their test results, they were sitting in the living room, watching a movie.

Renee was mesmerized by the holographic display in front of her. She had heard Abigail describe 3d holograms, but it was another thing to see them for herself. As she watched the holographic screen, the movie unfolding before her eyes had her captivated. When Abigail had described the classic 2040s movie about a closeted lesbian couple in Georgia that struggled to hide who they were until gay marriage was legalized across the country, Renee hadn't believed it.

It was one thing when Abigail told her that women could marry, but she hadn't believed that Hollywood would make a movie where two women ended up living happily ever after. Yet here it was. She watched as the two women stood before the altar, one in a beautiful white dress, the other in a white suit. She watched as they exchanged vows in front of the small fraction of their families & friends that hadn't turned their backs on them. She could feel herself beginning to tear up when they were pronounced woman & wife & they kissed to cheers & applause.

As the scene faded to the credits, the doctor walked into the room with a thin tablet in his hand.

"Love Set Free. A classic. I'm guessing that you enjoyed it."

Renee wiped away her tears.

"Yes, it was incredible."

"I'm glad that you liked it. Movies like that help a lot of our agents to remember the kind of world that we're working to bring about. Anyway, I have both of your results if you're ready."

They both nodded that they were ready.

"Alright, Abigail, everything seems to be perfectly normal with you. Despite the stresses of mid-20th century life, you appear to be in fairly good health. Your body doesn't appear too much older than a calendar would say that you are. Everything seems to be functioning exactly as you would expect from a 39-year-old woman in this era."

"Did you have to remind me that I'm 39?"

"Sorry Abigail. But like I said, everything seems to be good. I would just recommend that you cut back on your caffeine intake a bit."

"I would love to, but my boss would frown on me taking naps in the middle of the day."

The doctor laughed before swiping to the next set of test results on his tablet & turning to Renee.

"Alright Miss Rodin, you also seem to mostly be doing well, although your kidneys do give me a bit of concern."

"That does not sound too good."

"I don't see any immediate issues, but it almost looks like you have the kidneys of a 50-year-old woman. Have you stuck to the diet that was prescribed for you back in November of thirty-eight?"

"For the most part."

"That's even more concerning."

"Should I be worried?"

"Hmm, no. As far as we can see, it looks as if your kidneys were simply over stressed all of your life, leading to the damage. A few more years of this would be problematic, but you're scheduled to be rejuvenated in about a year & a half, so you should be fine."

"Thank goodness."

"Your rejuvenation treatment should reverse the damage, but just to be on the safe side, I'm going to order a slight modification to it so that it will have a more targeted effect on the damage to your renal system. You'll also need to check in with the medical staff near Detroit from time to time to monitor all of this, just as a precaution."

"I understand."

"In the meantime, stick to the diet that was prescribed to you back in thirty-eight."

"I will try."

"Excellent. If the two of you would like, we've prepared a room for you upstairs, your bags are up there waiting for you. When you get dressed, you can come back down for supper which should be in about half an hour."

They both thanked the doctor & proceeded to head upstairs as the movie player shut down after finishing the credits. Inside the room, Renee saw everything that she assumed Abigail would call a modern amenity. Lying back on the bed, she was surprised by just how intensely comfortable it was. As the advanced memory foam contoured to fit her body, it felt like she was lying down on a cloud. The wall opposite the bed seemed like the same setup downstairs, a movie player that they could watch. Next to the bed was something that Abigail called a gaming station.

As Renee slowly managed to pull herself up into a sitting position, she watched as Abigail untied her medical gown & let it slip to the floor. Even after all the years that they had spent together, she was still mesmerized by the sight of Abigail's naked body. Sure, her pale skin looked slightly tighter in some places & slightly looser in others. Sure, her large breasts hung just ever so slightly lower than they used to & sure, the freckles on her face & chest were a little bit paler than she remembered. But that stuff didn't matter. Renee's heart started racing just as it always had at the sight of Abigail, standing there in nothing but a tight pair of grey boxers.

"Are you going to get dressed for supper or are you just going to sit there all-night staring at my tits?"

"I'll stare."

Abigail laughed as she reached into her bag & pulled out a pair of slacks & a sleeveless button-up blouse. Slipping her well-toned legs into the comfortable slacks, she made sure that she was facing Renee as she pulled on the blouse without a bra & proceeded to only secure one of the buttons. As the blouse threatened to pop open, she turned to Renee & grinned.

"I'm going to head down to supper in a minute, are you going to get dressed & come with me?"

"I'll always come with you."

Abigail grinned as she watched Renee stand up & untie her own medical gown. Just like with herself, Renee was starting to show a few signs of being thirty-seven, not that it mattered to Abigail. Abigail's eyes still wondered all over Renee's pale, naked body. From her thin legs to her toned arms & shoulders, to her little light brown nipples. As Abigail's stomach hungered for food, she felt something else hungering for Renee.

Still being more modest than Abigail, Renee wasted no time in digging slacks & a blouse out of her bag. In what seemed like the blink of an eye, Abigail watched as Renee buttoned up her blouse & pulled on her slacks over the grey boxers that she had changed into earlier.

"Are you going to come with me to supper Abigail, or are you just going to stand there staring at me?"

"I think that I'll stare."

They both laughed. Abigail then walked up to Renee & wrapped her arms around her.

"I love you, Renee."

"Even after seeing me naked now that I'm becoming an old woman?"

"You're younger than I am Renee."

"Tell that to my little old lady kidneys."

Abigail laughed.

"I still love you, even the parts that are in their fifties."

"I love you too Abigail."

"What do you say that we go downstairs, eat as fast as we can, then say that we're tired & come back here to watch a movie?"

"I like that. What kind of movies can we watch?"

"Anything that's in the database, which is nearly everything. Dramas, science fiction, comedies, action, mystery, suspense, lesbian porn…"

Renee suddenly went beet red.

"What was that last one? They have… pornography… on these things… with just… women?"

"Oh yes. We can also listen on ear pods so that we don't disturb anyone else in the house. So if we were interested in watching a loving scene of passionate romance, or a twenty-woman orgy, nobody would be any wiser to it."

Renee's blush intensified for a moment.

"That… that could be… wow…"

"Come on Renee, let's go have supper. Then we can come back here & I can show you some wonders."

"Okay."

July 11th, 1944

Abigail & Renee had enjoyed a wonderful supper together after a long day for both of them. Abigail had told Renee about the new secretary that was always buzzing around & making it hard for her to copy information. Renee had talked about how she hated knowing that she & all of her female friends at the naval yard would be fired in about a year when the war came to an end.

Despite both of them being exhausted, they were now standing side by side, washing the dishes. Despite the fact that they were both working at the chore, they were taking a good long while to clean the dishes as they enjoyed each other's company & listened to the music on the radio.

They were so wrapped up in each other's presence that they hadn't noticed when the music had turned to the evening news. They simply kept washing & swaying together as the broadcaster talked about the allied victory in the French city of Caen. As he talked about British & Canadian troops liberating the city North of the Orne River, Abigail handed the last bowl to be cleaned to Renee.

"You know Renee, until you moved in, I couldn't wait for the 1970s to roll around, just so that I could get a dishwasher. But now, I don't think that I mind waiting."

"C'est si doux de dire mon amour."

Abigail leaned in closer to Renee, smiling.

"I love you when you slip a little French in Renee."

"Well maybe later I'll slip a little more in."

Renee winked at Abigail. Renee could almost swear that she saw Abigail blush a bit before they came together for a sweet little kiss. As their slightly pruney fingers intertwined, Abigail suddenly noticed the new story that was on the radio. She then reached over to the radio & turned it up as Renee noticed & listened carefully to the story.

"Future Dynamics, a new company that has grabbed a bit of attention with its innovations, announced today the creation of the first practical solar cell in their lab. This cell made of silicon can convert sunlight into electrical energy with no moving parts. While solar powered devices have existed since the last century, this device marks a serious leap forward from simple oddities to a practical device that could one day, with some more innovation & refinement, eliminate the use of coal & oil in producing electricity…"

Abigail smiled as the story played.

"Now we're making some progress."

Renee looked at her for a moment, a little confused.

"What do you mean?"

"That solar cell my love, that little chunk of silicon that's only 6% efficient at turning sunlight into electricity, that was us, changing the future."

"Future Dynamics is one of the companies that your network set up to help change the future."

"Yes. That little solar cell wasn't supposed to be invented for another ten years. Now when people finally realize that burning all of that coal & oil is going to cause a lot of long-term problems, solar power will be a much more effective alternative. No more decades of politicians & oil executives calling it a pipe dream that isn't ready to replace fossil fuels."

As Abigail's eyes seemed to light up from the story about the solar cell, Renee recalled some of the stories that Abigail had told her about the climate disasters. Stories about cities abandoned to a rising sea. Entire states being plunged into anarchy & lawlessness. Global migrations of tens of millions of people setting off conflicts & humanitarian crisis all over the world.

A lot of it had sounded like some sort of science fiction horror story. A part of her couldn't believe some of what she was hearing. Yet as Abigail stood there with a tear of joy in her eye, Renee felt a shiver run up her spine at the realization that those horror stories were all true & would all happen if her lover's network of future spies failed in their mission to improve the future of this timeline.

Chapter 16
June 21st, 1945

Running his hand through his grey streaked hair, Adam Parker looked up from his desk to accept a file from Abigail Oldman for the last time. He had been upset when Abigail gave her two weeks' notice, but there was nothing that he could do about it. After 15 years, his best secretary was moving on. He took the folder from her & forced a sad smile.

"Thank you, Abigail. I imagine that it's as perfect as everything else that you've done here."

"Thank you, Mr. Parker."

"So I guess that this is it. End of your last day, I guess you'll be heading back to England over the weekend."

"That's the plan governor."

Abigail put on an extra thick English accent for governor, causing her boss to chuckle.

"We're going to miss having you around here. All of these years & we still haven't met anyone who can keep up with you without making any mistakes. Not to mention that you always know how to keep Reginald in line."

"He's a teddy bear, you just need to look him in the eye until he backs down."

"I'll keep that in mind."

Abigail smiled.

"It's been a pleasure working here sir."

Adam stood up & extended his hand over his desk.

"It's been a pleasure having you here."

Abigail ignored the outstretched hand, walked around the desk & wrapped her arms around him in a big hug.

"Thank you for not being like some of the other bosses. I hope my next boss is as well behaved as you."

Adam slowly returned the surprise hug.

"Best of luck to you Abigail."

After a few seconds, they broke their hug & parted ways. Abigail went to her desk & looked it over one last time to make sure that she hadn't missed anything in her last seven inspections. She then picked up the small box with all of her things in it. As she made her way out, she stopped to say goodbye to all of her old friends that had been working with her for years & were still there. Grace & Jasmin were both sad to see her go.

As several people walked out the door to start their weekends, Abigail stood in the main lobby for a moment & looked back. For 15 years, this had just been the entrance to her job, the place where she worked tirelessly & copied information for her fellow future agents to use. Now, as she was walking out the door for the last time, it suddenly struck her how weird it was going to be now that she would never need to come back here again. Feeling a bit bittersweet for a moment, she turned around & headed out the door to her future with Renee in the motor city.

A few miles away, Renee was clocking out from the Brooklyn Naval Yard. She had packed up the last of her few personal possessions from her locker & was heading out with her welding gear in tow. Outside the main gate, she found Willa, the remaining girls from her team, & a bunch of the guys waiting for her.

Underneath a sign that said Bon Voyage in big blue, white & red letters made to look like the French flag, they all shared one last beer with her. Compared to the party that they had had the night before, the six of them were just a small little gathering. As they drank & reminisced, one of the soldiers raised his beer & shouted out.

"Here's to Renee the Riveter Rodin, first she helped us fight Heinie, now she's heading back home to France to help rebuild, Viva la France."

"For the thousandth time, I'm a welder!"

Everyone laughed. She couldn't remember when they all started calling her Renee the Riveter, but for as long as they had been calling her that, she would always follow it up with a proclamation that she was a welder. After a few more tearful goodbyes from her first group of work friends, she picked up her welding gear, hugged Willa one last time, & made her way home with a picture in her purse from the night before of her & the whole gang partying.

By the time that Abigail made it back to the apartment, Renee had been back for some time. When Abigail walked in, she had been tempted to put her keys down where she normally did but remembered that they were leaving in a few minutes. Renee walked in from the kitchen with a nostalgic look in her eyes.

"It's strange, this place has been my home for years, since before I moved in really."

"I know what you mean Renee. I spent years hating this place because I felt like I was trapped in the dark ages. Then you started coming over & this little apartment became home. You know, last night, I was cleaning out the secret cache in the bedroom closet & I found these."

Abigail pulled out a pair of ticket stubs. Renee took them & read the faded paper.

"Dracula's Daughter. That was one of the first movies that we saw together, back when I was still afraid of my feelings for you."

"You weren't afraid after the movie. That was the first night that we made love."

"Mon Dieu, I was so nervous that night."

"So was I. After the times that you had freaked out, I was worried that I was pushing too far."

"Then a month later, I saw you light the beacon & I started wondering if you were even human."

"That's right, you thought that I was a sexy space alien."

The two of them laughed. Taking a moment to make sure that they hadn't missed anything else, they then picked up the last of their boxes & headed out to make their way to the truck parked outside that Alex had arranged for them so that they could move. The two of them then opened the door & walked out of the apartment, just as Lola was walking out of hers.

"Oh, hello ladies, I didn't realize that you were still here."

They both resisted the urge to roll their eyes as Abigail responded.

"We're actually on our way out. We were just taking a moment to reminisce about this place."

"Ah, yes, I see. Still heading off to France?"

"That we are. It'll be nice to be close to family after all these years, for both of us."

"Isn't your family in England?"

"Yes, but England is a lot closer to France than it is to New York. Just a drive, a ferry & a drive & I can visit my family whenever I want."

"Ah, yes. I suppose that would be much easier than spending weeks on a boat to cross the Atlantic."

Abigail simply nodded her head as Renee cut in.

"Also, now that the war is over & France & England need to rebuild, there will be work for woman that can weld. All the women here are being laid off now that the men are coming home from Europe."

"Yes, I imagine that rebuilding a country would require all hands-on deck. Well, since the two of you are off, I'll wish you both bon voyage."

They both thanked Lola for her well wishes & didn't bother to question it when she turned around & walked back into her apartment. They both figured that since they were leaving, she probably felt she didn't need an excuse to come out & question them.

Heading down to the street where the truck was parked, they found Alex waiting for them, leaning against the truck.

"Ready to go ladies?"

They both nodded & climbed into the truck with Alex. As Alex drove, the two of them squeezed together in the passenger seat. As the truck pulled away from the apartment building, they both stared out the window at the place that had become their home. Once it was out of sight, Abigail turned her attention to Renee.

"You know, when Lola came out for one last chance to snoop on us, I was kind of tempted to give her something to gossip about."

"What would you have done? Told her that we're lovers?"

"I was thinking that I would have pinned you against the wall & kissed you in front of her."

"That… that would have been incredible…"

"Can you imagine the look on her face?"

Renee & Abigail laughed as they left their old life behind. The better part of an hour later, the truck pulled up to the same safe house that Renee had come to when she was being interrogated by Director Porter. Renee couldn't tell if the cloned guards were the same cloned guards that she saw last time. All that she knew was that they were as massive as gorillas & that they look menacing.

The three of them were quickly escorted into the Director's office where to Renee's delight, almost all of the sexual artworks had been removed. The three of them stood around waiting for a moment until she walked in the door.

"Ah, there are my favorite protocol violations. Here to bring an end to their time in my domain."

Walking into her office, she hugged Alex for a moment before standing there in her red buttoned, short sleeved blouse & her black mini shorts. Despite the paleness of her skin & the sharpness of her canines, she looked more like a sexy librarian than a vampire dominatrix.

"A room has been set up for the two of you upstairs so that we can monitor you after you receive your injections. You'll be able to head out in the morning for Detroit."

Abigail stepped forward.

"I trust that our new identities & lives have been set up."

"Of course. Your new contact in Detroit will be Agent Ash Bailey. He operates out of a pawn shop at this address."

Director Porter took a folded map off of her clipboard with a business card attached to it.

"This is a map of Detroit with Agent Bailey's location highlighted. He'll provide you with all of the information regarding your new lives, new home, new jobs, etc."

"Thank you, Director Porter. I can't wait to meet him."

"He is looking forward to it as well, please try to be less troublesome for him & Director Strand."

Abigail rolled her eyes as an assistant appeared to escort the two women to the doctor. Alex stayed behind to chat with Director Porter about his own reassignment in a few months' time.

A moment later, they were both sitting on patient beds while the doctor, a lean man with lustrous, thick black hair, pulled a pair of small packages out of refrigerated storage.

"Alright ladies, here we have your anti-ageing treatments. You'll feel the first effects of these treatments tomorrow morning when you wake up, but it'll take a few weeks to fully revert you back to your twenties. The two of you will also have to wear vital monitors overnight so that the system can keep an eye on you. Any questions?"

They both nodded their heads no. With that, he then proceeded to give them both their injections. Renee found it hard to believe that something as simple as a single injection could shave the last twenty years off of her life. Abigail, having seen so many people take these treatments, couldn't wait to be able to wake up without anything being sore like she used to do before coming back in time to help build a better alternate timeline.

The doctor wrapped a vital monitoring band around each of their upper arms & kept them there for about half an hour. After seeing no immediate problems, he released them so that they could head to their rooms & reminded them not to take the monitors off for any reason, even if they got frisky. Renee blushed at the thought that some computer would record her vitals as she was being intimate.

Injected & cleared, they made their way out of the medical room & towards their room for the night. Outside the room that was prepared for them, they found Alex waiting for them.

"Everything go alright with your treatments?"

Abigail smiled & threw her arms around him in a great big hug.

"Everything is fine. Thanks for coming to check on us."

"I didn't want our goodbye to be an assistant escorting you out of the boss's room. I wanted to say it properly."

"That's so nice of you. I'm sorry that I caused you so much trouble."

"Don't worry about it. I'm going to miss the two of you."

Renee walked up to them & wrapped her arms around both of them before asking the question that was on her mind.

"What's going to happen to you?"

"Well, in a few months, I'll retire from the post office, then I'll get my own rejuvenation treatment, along with a very well-earned vacation. Then in forty-seven, I'm heading to Nevada to help build up our presence in Vegas. Apparently, after dealing with this one, they feel that I can handle sin city itself."

Abigail gave him a good poke in the side. They all laughed about it for a moment until they broke their hug. Alex then wished them both well & headed out as they made their way into their room.

Peter Evan Fatouros

August 14th, 1945

The trip to Detroit hadn't exactly turned out like a fairy tale. Waking up early in the morning & getting yet another confirmation that they weren't having any adverse effects to the injections, they hit the road. Renee had been a bit disappointed when she looked into the mirror that morning. She knew that it would take several weeks for the effects of the injections to work, but she had still expected to see some change.

To make matters worse, the trip took the entire Saturday. Leaving just after dawn, they only made it to their destination shortly after sunset.

To make matters worse, they couldn't move into their new home yet. Even spread over weeks, their neighbors would notice if they were actually getting younger. As a result, they had to spend several weeks in a motel in a small town just outside of Detroit. A motel where nobody asked questions & privacy was respected.

When they first saw the small room, they were not impressed. With one lamp, one small bed & a refrigerator that looked like it was thirty years old, which was impressive since they had only been invented eighteen years ago, it didn't look like much. Yet despite the shoddy accommodations, it actually turned out to be quite nice.

Once they figured out which neighbors to avoid, they met a number of rather interesting people. From truckers on long hauls across the continent, to a starving writer trying to create the next great American novel, to a number of gay & lesbian couples that were retreating from the real world & their spouses for a few days on fake business trips & vacations.

Of course nobody ever actually admitted to what they were doing at this roadside motel twenty miles past civilization. Everyone just understood what was going on. The sounds of muffled cries & headboards slamming against walls at night made it very clear why people were actually here. On more than one occasion, the two of them reveled in adding their own moans & cries to the symphony of secret scissors & sodomy.

Almost nobody at the motel was there long enough to realize that they were getting younger. The few that were didn't ask, chalking it up to them being free from having to hide who they are.

Eventually June turned to July, which turned to August & the transformation was complete. When they looked in the mirror, they appeared to be no more than twenty-years-old. After two months, they packed up their things & spent one last brunch with the elderly lesbian couple that were "visiting relatives" in the room next door. They then got in the truck that another pair of agents had dropped off for them the day before on their way from Detroit to New York & they set off.

Less than an hour later, they were driving down the roads of Detroit's East English Village. As Abigail focused on finding the right address, Renee marveled at the homes.

"Are you sure that this is the right neighborhood? This all looks rather upper-middle class."

"The documents that Director Porter gave us say East English Village, I think that this is our street."

Abigail slowly turned onto the street & drove slowly as she checked the addresses for the one that had been bought for them.

"Remind me again how we're supposed to be able to afford this place Abigail."

"Do you remember my cover brother that doesn't exist?"

"Yeah… Gary Oldman, the doctor that lives… North of London."

"Very good. Officially, he owns the house. He bought it when he was going to come to America, but those plans fell through, so instead of selling it, he's letting me live here rent free with my best friend."

"Right, the doctor that's so well off in war torn London that he could buy a house like this & just hand it over to his sister. What if somebody asks how he was able to afford this?"

"The story is that I haven't seen him since I moved here in 1930, no, sorry, in 1930, I'm supposed to have been five. I haven't seen him since I came here with my father in 1940, just after the first German attacks."

"Right, & my story is the same, except that I came over here with Papa in 1926 as a baby, not a twenty-year-old."

"Right. I start as a file clerk at the new bank on Monday & we are going to meet my new contact in September."

"While I get to open another bakery."

"I can't wait. As incredible as it's been having a steel welding girlfriend, I miss the days when you always smelt like fresh bread."

"You miss the days when you could steal a kiss & grab a feel in an empty bakery."

"I can miss more than one thing."

"You're about to miss our house."

Abigail slammed on the brakes just as she was about to drive past the new house. The two of them laughed for a moment before getting out of the truck to see their new home. The red brick house was smaller than the houses on either side. Its black shingled dormer roof stood in contrast to the mint green painted wood around the windows & door. The small stone steps that led up to the front door were flanked on either side by a small flower garden. A brick walkway that was riddled with weeds led up to the front door. The house looked like it hadn't been lived in in a few years.

"That's another thing Renee, Gary Oldman bought this house almost a year ago, it's been vacant since the last owners moved out."

"It just needs to be cleaned up a bit. It looks like home sweet home."

"It sure does."

September 9th, 1945

Abigail was nervous. She had been nervous about meeting her new handler & hoping that his first impression of her would be more impressive than her disciplinary file. Now she was incredibly nervous because she had gotten word just two days ago that he wanted to meet with Renee as well.

After packing up the first file that she had copied from the bank's records, the two of them had left their new home & made their way to the meeting place. Along the way, they had carefully stepped into a hardware store owned by another agent where they could use the bathroom to put on wigs & fake glasses.

With their long ,burgundy red wigs, they became rather noticeable. A trick often employed by some agents. Nobody would suspect somebody that obvious of being a spy & if the wigs were the defining characteristic of their descriptions, simply throwing them away would render them unrecognizable.

In their pale blue, floral, 2-piece dresses & bright wigs, they made their way to the café where their new handler was waiting. He was waiting in a private little booth where the miniscule Sunday morning crowd wouldn't bother them. From the entrance of the café, they could see his red, slicked back hair over the newspaper that he was reading. The front page was dominated by a photo of Mamoru Shigemitsu signing the instrument of surrender on the deck of the USS Missouri.

Renee remembered seeing that ship under construction when she had started working for the Brooklyn Naval Shipyard. She wished now, as she had back then, that she could have worked on it. The two of them sat down across from him as he folded up his newspaper.

"You know, I always found it funny that somehow, just signing a big piece of paper meant that a world war was over & that an empire was dissolved. Yet here we are, a week into a post war world & in a few months, the boom of babies to be born will reshape the world even more dramatically than the war & not always for the better."

The two of them just sat there for a moment, not knowing what to say to that until the waitress came by & they each ordered a coffee. The waitress was bemused by their accents & went to get their orders.

"Ladies, I'm Ash Bailey, authentication, Valentina Tereshkova."

Recognizing the name of the first woman to fly in space & the only woman to ever fly a solo mission in the 20th century, Abigail relaxed a bit.

"It's a pleasure to meet you, I'm Abigail Oldman, authentication Edge of Tomorrow."

"Yes, & I am Renee Rodin, authentication Primer."

Recognizing the names of the two famous time travel movies that wouldn't be made for another sixty or seventy years, he sipped his coffee & relaxed.

"Thank you for the authentication protocols. Abigail, this is for you."

He then handed her a business card.

"That is the pawn shop that I own & operate. We'll continue to meet on Sunday mornings, but from now on, it'll be at this address unless you're otherwise notified."

"Understood."

"Excellent. So how are you two settling into your new home?"

Before Abigail could say anything, Renee smiled & answered.

"It's lovely. It's a beautiful home in a beautiful neighbourhood. We've been there for weeks & I still cannot believe that I get to wake up there every morning & that I'm going to get to wake up there every morning for the next ten or twenty years."

Ash smiled.

"I'm glad that you like it. How are you getting along with the neighbours? Have they given you any trouble?"

"Not at all. Some of them were curious about two young women living together & being able to afford a house in that neighbourhood. But they all seem to believe the cover story that you gave us about Abigail's brother & my just being her best friend."

"That's good to hear. You're not going to have any trouble with pretending that you're just friends in front of them?"

"It might get difficult, but maybe every now & then you can send a male agent to take one of us on a 'date' so that nobody gets suspicious."

Abigail was surprised by the suggestion. Renee hadn't mentioned it to her earlier & it sounded like a good idea to her.

"That's a good idea Renee. A number of the higher ups have suggested that agents having a hard time finding or maintaining romantic connections could help each other out by going on pretend dates to throw off rumors. Particularly in this coming two decades. If we can get some sort of a program up & running, would you be interested in participating?"

"If Abigail is alright with it."

"No, it's a good idea. It was easy enough to hide when we were a pair of depression era girls struggling to scrape together a living. But now that we're living it up in an upper middle-class area, it'll be a good idea to have a way to thwart the rumors that are bound to start circulating."

"I'll add your names to the list. How are the jobs going? Abigail?"

"I'd say it's going well. As per usual, they're impressed with my typing skills. I've already established myself as someone who is willing to work long hours & I'm already being asked to make duplicates of files & create new files. I've actually got a copy of a new corporate expense account information here for you."

Abigail pulled the envelope out of her purse & handed it to her new handler who then slipped it into his briefcase.

"Well done. There are a number of important people that do their banking at this institution, many of them in this very branch. While it may take you some time to get full access to the upper-level files, Information like this is priceless."

"Hopefully, they'll be trusting me with important files soon enough."

"Here's hoping. How's the bakery going?"

Renee lit up.

"Rodin Bakery will soon be up & running. The electrician is coming next week to hook up the ovens to the fuse box & shortly after that, we'll be able to open our doors."

"Is your new employee giving you any trouble?"

"Not at all. Martha is wonderful. She's a bit mousy, but she seems to get along with everyone. She used to work as a bus driver during the war, but then the men came home. Sadly, her husband didn't come back. I have her personal information here if you want to look into her."

Renee then pulled a slip of paper out of her pocket & handed it to Ash who took it & slipped it into his pocket.

"Thank you, Renee. She's probably nothing to worry about, but it's good to be sure. Have you had any issues with your cover around her?"

"No. My cover story is true enough. My father owned the first Rodin bakery in New York until he died. I moved in with a friend & started training to become a welder so I could get a job. Then the war ended & we came out here to her brother's house. The only hard part was that on her first day, I almost forgot that she thinks I'm a decade younger than her instead of a decade older."

"Well make sure that you maintain that cover, this Martha sounds like a lovely young woman, we don't want any consequences coming her way."

"I understand."

"Good, this brings up a point that I wanted to make today. The two of you are famous among the upper ranks of our program. While we're all glad that your situation seems to have worked out, do remember that you need to keep a low profile. You live in a decent neighbourhood & both the great depression & the war are over. We're entering into an era of paranoia & suspicion. McCarthyism, the house un-American activities committee, the red scare, the lavender scare. As leftist, lesbian spies, you're basically the embodiment of what a lot of people will be afraid of. You need to be careful. I want you two to report any indication of suspicion against you to the second phone number on the business card that I gave you."

Abigail could almost feel the weight of the card in her pocket. "We understand."

"Good. In that case, I have one thing left for you."

Ash then reached into his briefcase & pulled out what looked like a large box of chocolates.

"In here is a set of dossiers on all of the major local historical events that'll occur in Detroit in the next decade. A set describing the original version of history, another describing what we hope the next ten years will look like, & useful information about our organization. Obviously, this is all written in New Valerian, to make sure that nobody from this century can read it. I trust that your fictional language skills are still good enough to read it."

"It's been a while since I've needed it, but I've kept my skills sharp with practice, & by listening to the one music player that I'm allowed to have. My favorite bad has an entire album sung in New Valerian."

"Good, because you're going to get a dossier like that every few years. We plan to have you posted here through the fifties & into the sixties. Last thing that we need is an info leak. It's happened before that an agent was mugged & almost lost their files, which is why we started writing future dossiers in New Valerian, a language that won't exist until 2042."

"Understood. Low profile, informational security set to maximum."

"Exactly."

Chapter 17
January 20th, 1946

The files from the bank were neatly folded & safely stored in Abigail's oversized satchel. Checking her dress & her coat in the mirror one last time, she decided that it looked good enough & headed out. The Sunday morning air was clear, crisp & just a degree above freezing. As the morning chill caused her to shiver a bit, she walked over to her neighbor's freshly shoveled driveway where he was under the front of his Cadillac Fleetwood & Renee was under the hood, holding a flashlight in place.

"Shouldn't you be doing car maintenance like that inside, where it's warmer?"

Brian, their neighbor, chuckled from under the engine of his Fleetwood as he tried to loosen a particularly stubborn screw.

"Normally I would, but if I spill anymore oil on the garage floor, she's threatened to beat me to death with a wooden spoon."

Abigail & Renee both laughed. Renee took her attention away from the engine for a moment to talk to Abigail.

"Are you heading out then?"

"Yes, I'll be back from lunch in an hour or two."

"Alright, have fun with the girls."

Abigail waved goodbye to Renee as she headed to meet her handler. When their neighbors had started asking about where she went every Sunday, she said that it was to have lunch, & sometimes drinks, with some of the girls from work. As she walked to the bus stop at the end of the street, Renee turned her attention back to the engine.

"How is it coming with that screw?"

"It's stubborn, but I think that I'm starting to loosen it."

A heartbeat later, there was a metal clang as the screw gave way, followed by a quick curse as Brian hit his hand against part of the car & reddish-brown transmission fluid started draining into the pan that he had put in place. Climbing out from under the car, he grabbed the rag that Renee handed him & started wiping the fluid off of his hands.

"Do you ever go to spend time with that girl that works for you?"

"Not really. We spend a good fifty to sixty hours a week together, I think that's enough for her."

"Sounds like long hours, which makes sense, you do leave early & get back late. How's the bakery doing?"

"It's doing very well, despite the fact that the fuse box is trying to kill me. I don't know what that *foutu crétin* that hooked everything up did, but we go through about ten fuses a week. Pardon my French."

Brian chuckled for a second. It wasn't every day that somebody actually spoke French before asking that it be pardoned.

"You should get that checked out."

"I've got a guy coming next week, hopefully it's a small thing. I don't want to have to shut down for a few weeks while he rewires the building. I'd be alright, but my employees might start looking for work elsewhere."

"I thought that you only had one employee, Marcy, Mathilda, May? The one that used to drive a bus."

"Martha. It was just the two of us, but I hired another girl a few weeks ago. Sandra."

"Another girl? Wouldn't you be more comfortable hiring a young man in case some troublemaker comes along?"

Renee laughed.

"Sandra used to be a WASP."

"A WASP? Not sure that I've heard that one before."

"Women Airforce Service Pilots. They flew military planes between bases & tested new aircraft before they were sent to the frontlines."

"Wow. I didn't know they had lady pilots in the war."

"It was mostly too free up the men pilots for the frontline."

"Ah, makes sense."

"Between my military girl & my former bus driver, I think that the three of us are plenty safe. Besides, the bakery is in a very nice area."

"Well alright then. A bus driver & an air force girl. Sounds like any miscreant that tries anything will come to regret it."

They both chuckled & got back to draining & replacing the car's various fluids."

Later that afternoon, when the car was safely back in the garage & Renee had gone back home, Brian was in his living room, reading his Sunday newspaper when his wife came in.

"Is everything all right with the car?"

"Yes hon, everything is fine. Just needed to change some of the fluids & it's good as new."

"That's good. I saw you talking to the French girl next door for a while. What did she want?"

"Oh she offered to help me with the car. Apparently, she used to help her father with mechanical things at his bakery in New York, so when she saw me working on the car, she offered her services. I let her hold the flashlight."

"That's nice, assuming that it's the car that she's interested in."

"What do you mean?"

"Pretty young thing, that little French girl."

"What are you implying honey?"

"Just wondering if I should be worried about the cute girl that's younger than our children & likes working on cars with my husband?"

Brian chuckled.

"While I'm flattered that you think I can still turn a young girl's head with my thinning hairline & my thickening waistline, you have nothing to worry about. I'm not going to risk thirty-one years of marriage for some French girl that's probably more interested in my Cadillac's engine than in the man behind the wheel."

As he finished his sentence, a strange feeling came over him, almost like a chill in his spine. His wife laughed.

"I suppose that she was just trying to be neighborly. Those two are very friendly. Just yesterday, Abigail helped me bring the groceries in. She even taught me a trick for telling if eggs have gone bad. If they float in cold water, they've probably spoiled."

"That's useful to know. I'm sure she'll make a lucky young man a great wife one day."

"I'm certain of it, Brian."

"Of course, she would have to find a man first. I don't suppose that you've heard anything about that for either of them?"

"Nope. It seems that they're both single & that they've been that way since they moved in, at least that's what the girls around the neighbourhood say."

"A little strange, two young women, somewhat attractive, no sign of a man."

"I'm sure that it's nothing strange. Don't forget, they moved here from New York, so they probably don't know many people or where to go to find good men."

"True."

"Plus those two are always working. I bet that by the time the weekend rolls around, they're exhausted."

"You're probably right hon. They'll both probably find someone once they've sorted out a few things."

February 14th, 1947

"Abigail, hurry up, your date will be here soon!"

Renee was lying back on the couch, resting her feet after a long day. As much as she enjoyed working in a bakery again, she was glad for the help she had since Valentine's Day was always horrible.

She lay there reading the February issue of Thrilling Wonder, a sci-fi pulp magazine with an image of a woman in a red bathing suit & a glass diving helmet speeding through an underwater scene on the cover. As she turned to a story called Trouble on Titan, Abigail came down the stairs in a pale blue, knee-length dress with two white lines just above the hem & at the ends of her short sleeves.

"How do I look Renee?"

"Based on the last time that I was twenty, like a harlot, showing off that much leg. These days, you look respectable, but available. Are those heart shaped buttons?"

"Yes."

"I know this guy is another agent, but are you sure it's alright to be that revealing on a date? That is a lot of leg Abigail."

"If you think that showing off this much leg is a lot, wait until miniskirts come along in the sixties. They stop mid-thigh."

"Mon Dieu."

"Then there's the stuff in the next century. Some of it is actually just a square inch of fabric & two nylon strings."

Renee made a motion as if she was clutching her chest while having a heart attack. At that moment, they heard a car pull up. Abigail looked out the window & saw the agent getting out of his car.

"It's him. How's my hair?"

"You look good. Everyone will think that you're actually trying."

"Great. It takes a lot of effort to look like you've put in a lot of effort."

The agent walked up to the front door & rang the doorbell. Abigail walked over to the front door & opened it to see him standing there in his greyish blue suit with a red & black checkerboard tie. He looked to be only a few years older than Abigail, with a narrow frame & a sharp jawline.

"Hello there miss Oldman, I'm John Roland."

"Nice to meet you John, & please call me Abigail, we're supposed to be on a nice vanilla date."

"Right, sorry, are you ready to go?"

"Just need a minute to get my shoes."

Abigail quickly slipped on a pair of black high heels & made her way into the living room to kiss Renee.

"Don't stay up to late, miss back in my day."

Renee smiled.

"Don't stay out to late, miss hemline at the knees."

Abigail smiled & headed out. She slipped her arm in John's & they walked to his car. She climbed in just as one of her neighbors was getting home, an event that was perfectly timed so that he would talk to his neighbors about the good-looking guy that Abigail was going out with on Valentine's Day. Once inside, Abigail checked out the interior of the car as John started it up.

"So where are we going?"

"I made reservations at an Italian place downtown. I hope that's all right for you."

"It's fine."

Twenty minutes later, they were walking into an Italian restaurant that was jam packed with young couples that looked exactly like them. As the waiter led them to their table for two, he was sweeping the room for his colleague that was bringing his wife to the same restaurant.

Yet another engineered coincidence. This way, when his co-workers at the FBI were gossiping about each other's love lives, the rumors that swirled around the single men wouldn't reach him.

When he spotted his coworker, he gave a quick wave. The coworker took a look, nodded his head & gave him a thumbs up when he saw Abigail.

"Well, I guess that my coworker over there approves of you. He just gave me a thumbs up."

"A thumbs up? What is he, a child?"

"Pretty much. His wife takes care of him like one."

Abigail laughed as they sat down. A few minutes later, the waiter took their order & made off with the menus.

"So, John, how's 1947 treating you?"

"It's getting rough. While the war was going on, everybody was too obsessed with finding spies to care about some junior agent's lack of a love life. These days, you go too long without a date & they start looking into you."

"They actually investigate you?"

"Not officially, a few higher ups might just request a few records to see where I've been & if I've been taking young women out on dates."

"Sounds difficult."

"Not as difficult as it has to be for you. I just don't have the time to date while I'm spying on the spy agency that I work for. Actually living with your girlfriend in post war suburbia. You've got some brass ovaries lady."

"It is harder for two girls to be roommates these days. Back in the depression, we could just say that it was to save money & everyone let it slide because everyone was struggling. These days, if we don't have some handsome young men coming to call every now & then, rumors start to fly."

"The depression. So you've been here long enough to get a treatment then."

"Yes. I've been here since 1930."

"Wow. I just arrived back in forty-two."

"So this is still early days for you."

"That it is. Any advice for a young buck?"

"Yeah. When the time comes to marry in order to maintain your cover, go with another agent. It's hard to hide all of this from a civilian. I had to spend years lying to Renee, it wasn't great. Not to mention that she freaked out when she saw some things that she shouldn't have."

"Yeah, I heard a bit about that. Did she really see you light a beacon & then wait two years before talking to you about it?"

"Oh yeah. I'm just glad that telling her the truth worked out in the end. That night, hell, that month could have gone wrong a thousand different ways."

"That must have been a challenge. I'm glad that it worked out for the two of you. Here comes the waiter."

They stopped the spy talk as the waiter brought them their meals & wished them a wonderful dinner.

After the waiter left, they continued to make small talk as they enjoyed their meal together. Sometimes as John would talk about this or that, Abigail would let her mind drift forward to a time when she could be taking Renee out to a fancy restaurant for Valentine's Day. Realizing that it would be another 30 years at least, she sighed under her breath.

When John asked her if she was alright, she told him about what she had been thinking about. He nodded his head in understanding. While he was glad that she was here to throw off the suspicions of the FBI, he couldn't help but feel sorry for her. Pretending to be happy on a date with a man she just met an hour ago while her girlfriend was waiting at home.

Eventually, long after they had finished their meals & enough time had passed, they got up & left the restaurant arm in arm. On the way out, they passed John's coworker again & he again gave them a thumbs up. They both laughed as they got into John's car.

Once they got to Abigail's house, they lingered in his car for a little while. They nestled up close to each other in an attempt to make it look like they were sharing a few intimate moments. When Abigail spotted one of her neighbors taking his dog out for a late-night walk with his wife, she got an idea.

"John, do you have an hour to kill?"

"Sure. What's up?"

"I want you to get out of the car & follow me into the house. I need you to look like some guy that's about to get lucky."

"Alright."

"Good, really lean into it, get handsy when you get to the door."

Just as her neighbours were coming up on the car, she gave John a quick kiss on the lips before getting out of the car, shaking her ass, giggling & running up the walkway to her front door.

John wasn't far behind. He turned the car off, got out, & quickly followed behind her with an idiot grin. When he got to the front door, they started making out a bit. The neighbours walked at a slower pace for a bit. As the dog's leash pulled tight, John started running his hands all over Abigail while she pretended to fumble with her keys.

After a minute, she opened the door, grabbed John by the lapel, & pulled him into her house. She was confident that any rumors about her & Renee being a little unusual would soon be replaced by rumors that she was less than ladylike in her appetites.

Once inside, they quickly separated & headed into the living room where Renee was sitting on the couch with the curtains closed.

"You two are back a bit early for a Valentine's Day date. Then again, the way that you were going at each other out there, I'd be home early too."

They both laughed as John sat down on the couch.

"That was some of my best spy work."

"I saw that. We thank you for your dedication. It must have been challenging."

Abigail got her shoes off & breathed in a sigh of relief. After a full day at work, she had not been happy about putting on date shoes to go out with a guy.

"What do you think John, would an hour be good to convince the neighbours that you've thoroughly ravaged me?"

"Sure, plenty of time for a good ravaging & 58 minutes of cuddling."

Abigail & Renee both burst out laughing. A moment later, when they regained their composure, Abigail remembered her manners towards her guest.

"Can I get you something to drink, water, beer, lemonade?"

"Water is fine Abigail, thanks."

Abigail went to the kitchen & got his drink for him. The three of them then sat around the living room.

"Interesting place that they choose to set you two up in."

"Yeah, right in the middle of post-war suburbia, perfect place for a pair of lesbians to hide in."

"It must get hard to hide from your neighbors sometimes."

"It's challenging, but as long as we occasionally make them think that we're trying to date men & as long as we don't start groping each other outside, we're fine."

"Really?"

"Yeah, they just think that Renee & I are good friends that lucked into a good house in a good neighbourhood."

Renee then reached for her drink before chiming back into the conversation.

"Do people often grope each other in public in the future?"

"They sure do. Right John?"

"That they do."

Renee took a long sip of water before she turned back to John.

"So how come you have to pretend to be on dates? Nothing about you looks suspicious."

"Thanks Renee. Sadly, even for those of us who are interested in the opposite sex, you have to have some sort of family or love life if you want to work for the FBI. They're so scared that gays might be helping them to fight communism that if you don't brag enough around the water cooler, suspicions get raised."

"Yes, but surely you can just make things up."

"Of course, I do that all the time, but eventually, just hearing me brag about women I've been with isn't enough. They have to see me leaving the bar with one or taking one out to a fancy restaurant on Valentine's Day."

"Ah, I see. So tomorrow at the water cooler, you'll have proof for them because one of them saw you at the restaurant."

"Exactly. Tomorrow when he asks if that was the English girl that I've been talking about for the last two weeks, I can say yes & then he'll tell the others that he saw us together when he was out with his wife."

"They're really that afraid that if they don't see you with a woman, they start getting nervous?"

"That they are, & it's only going to get worse. In a few years, I'm going to have to get married. A bachelor in his 30s, not exactly the kind of thing they like in their agents."

"Really? If you're not married by 30, you're a queer communist?"

"Maybe not by 30, but it helps to have a spouse. All of which is a bit ironic when you take into account the rumors that Hoover was gay himself. Of course, those are just rumors."

For about the next hour, the three of them talked about all manner of things. They talked about life in 1947, some of the things that they had seen that weren't in the original history books, & how hard it was to live a more or less normal life while spying on your coworkers.

Eventually the time came for John to leave, having fulfilled his job of making Abigail look like she craved men from time to time. In order to further sell the illusion, he undid a few buttons on his shirt & made it look like he had gotten redressed in a hurry.

Abigail smeared her makeup a bit & ruffled her clothes a bit, to make it look like they had been pulled off & carelessly put back on. She then stood on the front porch with John & talked for a minute before he leaned in & gave her a quick kiss goodnight.

She then stood there, doing her best impression of a lovestruck young woman as John went off to his car, waved goodnight, blew her another fake kiss & drove off. She then went back inside to Renee, who was waiting for her.

July 24, 1949

Renee stood over the leather gym mat, wearing shorts & a simple tee shirt like Abigail had asked her to. Abigail walked down the stairs in a slightly tighter version of the same outfit. Abigail had set up the basement for training the night before & now that she was back from her weekly meeting with her handler, she intended to teach Renee a few lessons.

"Are you ready Renee?"

"Yes, although I don't know why I need to learn how to fight."

"Really? After what happened at the bakery last week."

"It is not a big deal Abigail."

"Not a big deal! The bakery was robbed! Martha's arm is still in a sling because it was dislocated!"

"It wasn't actually dislocated. It was just wrenched a bit when she fell awkwardly."

"You mean when the robbers threw her down to the ground. Renee, not only should every woman know how to defend herself, a woman in a relationship with a spy should really know how to protect herself."

"Do you really think that I'm in that much danger?"

"Yes Renee! You're dating another woman, who is also a spy, in a conservative area, just months before the lavender scare starts. History recorded a lot of horrible things happening to people for any one of those things. I'd be a lot happier knowing that if someone ever found out about our situation & came after us, that you could defend yourself."

Renee thought about it for a moment. She knew that Abigail was right about most of these things. She also knew that people who were outed as homosexual often had trouble start following them. She also knew that Abigail was freaked out about the bakery being robbed.

"Alright Abigail, I suppose that learning a few futuristic self-defense techniques would be a good thing."

"Good."

Abigail then stood on the leather mat & faced Renee.

"Alright Renee, I want you to come at me as if you were a mugger."

Renee shrugged & took position in front of Abigail & a few feet away. She then took a deep breath & lunged at her lover. Everything was going well, until her foot landed on the leather training mat. The next thing that Renee knew, she was looking forward at the ceiling.

It took Renee a moment to realize that Abigail had grabbed her & somehow, she had managed to turn Renee's momentum against her. She remembered flipping over, almost like a summersault, & then hearing the sound of her body hitting the mat. Looking up, she saw Abigail standing over her, barely ruffled.

"Abigail."

"Yes Renee."

"Fils du pute! I know what just happened, but what just happened?"

Abigail chuckled.

"What happened is that I just showed you what you might be capable of if you learn some self-defense. That way if a mugger or worse ever comes after you & tries to do more than just steal your purse, you'll be able to come out on top."

Abigail then held her hand out so that she could help Renee up. Renee took Abigail's hand & pulled herself up to her feet. Managing to stand upright, Renee looked around for a second, as if to get a bearing on her position. She then turned to Abigail who had a serious look on her face.

"Are you ready to take this seriously Renee?"

"After having my world turned around like that. Yes, you have my attention."

"Good, because I should probably have taught you most of this ten years ago & I'll be damned if you get hurt because I didn't teach you how to protect yourself."

Renee could hear a slight tremble in Abigail's voice. It was in that moment that she realized that Abigail actually was worried for her safety.

"Alright Abigail, let's start."

Renee stepped onto the mat & Abigail began her first lesson. Over the course of the next hour, Abigail began running Renee through some of the basics of Krav Maga, a form of martial arts that most Americans wouldn't know about for at least a few more decades. Renee very quickly lost track of how many times she had ended up on her back or in some sort of a hold.

After a while, they had both started working up a sweat as Renee slowly started to learn the techniques that Abigail was demonstrating. As they were wrapping up their first lesson, Renee got a little bold. Thinking that she could catch Abigail off guard, she tried to make a move that she had seen Abigail demonstrate earlier.

Once again, Renee ended up on her back, the sound of her body hitting the mat echoing in the basement. As she was regaining her sense of what had just happened, Abigail was suddenly straddling her stomach & leaning over her. Abigail then grabbed Renee's wrists &

pinned them over her head as she leaned in until their faces were only an inch apart.

"First rule of any martial art, avoid unnecessary combat. Second rule; don't get cocky. That technique I showed you is an example of what advanced practitioners can do. This is literally your first lesson, which is why you're now under me."

"There could be worse places to be."

Abigail smiled.

"How are you going to get yourself out of this situation Renee?"

"Why would I want to get out of this situation?"

Renee then leaned up as best as she could in her pinned position & kissed Abigail's lips. They lay there together, slowly kissing each other for a minute. Just when the muscles in Renee's arms were starting to burn a bit from the uncomfortable position that she was being held in, Abigail let go.

As Renee rested her arms by her sides for a moment, Abigail's hands moved to Renee, with one hand cupping the French girl's face & the other slowly moving down her shoulder to her chest, to her breast. As Abigail's heart started beating faster, she broke the kiss & looked Renee in the eye.

"Should we take this upstairs?"

"That would involve getting up, I'm kind of enjoying having you on top of me like this."

Renee then grabbed Abigail's hips & blew her a kiss. Abigail responded by leaning in & kissing her. As their lips locked, their hands began to roam over each other's sweaty bodies. As Renee's hands slid from Abigail's hips to her buttocks, Abigail's hands slowly slid up & down Renee's body until they slipped under the hem of Renee's shirt.

As they broke their kiss once more, Abigail slid Renee's shirt up, revealing her stomach, As Renee lifted herself a bit to help her shirt slide under her, Abigail continued sliding the shirt further up, soon exposing Renee's plain white bra.

Once Renee's shirt was bunched up near her shoulders, Abigail bent down & began planning kisses on the exposed skin between Renee's bra & her bunched up shirt. While Renee gently moaned with each kiss, she was tempted to start lifting Abigail's shirt as well, but she couldn't. She simply lay there, hands on Abigail's firm backside as Abigail kissed her chest.

With each kiss, with each moan, Abigail wanted more. After fondling Renee's bra covered breasts for a moment, she reached down & slid her hand underneath Renee's bra, to caress the sensitive skin of her pale breasts. Renee gasped & moaned as her nipple hardened against Abigail's palms. Wanting more, Abigail did her best to unhook Renee's bra before sliding it up, exposing her girlfriend's bare chest as her bra bunched up under her shirt.

Renee was barely exposed for a heartbeat before Abigail's lips attacked her hardening nipples. Renee gasped & moaned as Abigail kissed, sucked, licked & grazed her nipples with her teeth. Renee didn't know how it was that after fourteen years, Abigail could still titillate her like this. Somehow, it was still like the first time that Abigail's lips had made her feel like she was in heaven.

It was almost tortuous when Abigail sat up, separating herself from Renee's body. But Renee was soon rewarded as Abigail grabbed the hem of her shirt, lifted it over her head, & threw the offending garment away. A moment later, Abigail's bra was sailing away through the air as her large breasts made Renee feel warm with desire.

"Now, where were we?"

Abigail then leaned back in & began kissing Renee's lips as their breasts pressed together. Renee wished that she could throw her own clothes away as Abigail had, but she was also content to lay there, her lover's chest against her own as they kissed.

As they kissed, Abigail scooched down Renee's body so that she was straddling Renee's thighs. As Renee's arousal grew, she felt the familiar & welcome sensation of Abigail's hand sliding into her shorts. As Abigail's fingers slid into Renee's underwear, Renee hoped that every training session would end like this.

Abigail's fingers began caressing the moist entrance to Renee's body, causing Renee to gasp & shudder. Abigail broke the kiss & grinned wickedly as she teased Renee's sensitive folds with gentle caresses.

"Abigail... Abigail please..."

Abigail ignored her pleading & continued to slowly build Renee up for what seemed like an eternity. Slowly bringing her closer &

closer to her release with gentle caresses. Renee hated the teasing. She also loved the teasing. As what felt like hours of gentle teasing continued, Renee got closer & closer to her climax until one last caress of her hard clitoris brought forth the tidal wave of pleasure that came crashing over her body.

"Ah… Ah… Ah… Abigail!"

As Renee's orgasm rippled through her, Abigail sunk her fingers into Renee's shuddering body. With every nerve in Renee's body singing in ecstasy, Abigail's fingers plunging in & out of her body were driving her mad. Abigail's fingering was not only enhancing the waves of pleasure rippling across her body, but they also made her feel as if another was building up.

As her whole world became nothing more than waves of orgasmic pleasure, Abigail's fingers driving into her, caressing her inner most depths, brushing & tickling that most sensitive spot inside. Renee cried out as a second climax rippled out before the first one even finished, sending her mind over the edge of madness as she cried out Abigail's name loudly enough that she would later be sure that the neighbors had heard her.

When Renee finally came back down to Earth, she was lying on the mat, her shirt & bra pulled up & her underwear soaked through with her climax. Looking to her side, she saw Abigail lying there next to her, slowly sucking the flood of Renee's bliss off of her fingers. It took a moment for her to regain the ability to speak.

"Je pense… je pense que, I think that you… just fucked… my soul… out of my body."

"Good thing that our neighbours aren't home yet, they would have heard that for sure."

"God… Abigail…"

Abigail turned onto her side & lay there next to Renee, pressing her body against her lover's & slowly caressing her body until Renee was eventually ready & able to stand up again.

Chapter 18
July 4th, 1950

It felt weird to Renee to be home so early on a Tuesday. Walking up to the house, she could smell the smoke coming off of the grill from across the street. The annual Independence Day neighbourhood BBQ was about to get underway & Renee didn't want to miss it. Leaving Sandra in charge of the bakery, Renee had left early so that she could be home at five thirty, just in time for the event.

Once she was home, she rushed to the bedroom to change out of her flour covered clothes when she ran into Abigail who was changing out of her work clothes.

"I should come home early more often, just so I can watch this." Abigail smiled.

"I wouldn't mind having you home more. I'd even put on a show for you every now & then if you wanted."

They both smiled as Renee began undoing the buttons on her work blouse so that she could slip into the 4th of July outfit that she had picked for the BBQ. Once she was down to her underwear, a topless Abigail wrapped her arms around her waist.

"You know, nobody would probably mind if we were a bit late."

"Is that so Abigail?"

"People will be showing up for the next hour, they won't notice if we're not there by six."

"True, but if we go to the BQ first, then we won't have to rush later tonight, when we won't have to be anywhere."

"I suppose."

Abigail then kissed Renee on the cheek & gave her rear a quick grab before turning her attention to her outfit. Soon, the two of them were done up in the outfits that they had specially bought for the Independence Day BBQ that their patriotic neighbor hosted every year.

The matching halter dresses were dark blue & covered with white stars all the way down to their knees where the dresses then changed to bright red & white stripes. Taking a minute to look each other over, they agreed that the neighbours would get a kick out of the dresses. Abigail then took a minute to practice a slightly more Americanized version of her fake English accent. She had learned at their first BBQ that the neighbours hosting the event didn't appreciate a thick English accent on Independence Day.

Stopping by their fridge to pick up the bowl of cowboy salsa that they had prepared the night before, they made their way out to the BBQ. Before they were three steps from their door, they heard their neighbor from two houses down whistle.

"Well, don't you two look like you belong on the cover of Stars & Stripes. Those are some dresses."

They turned to see Delores in a blue dress with red & white buttons running up the front & a fresh apple pie in hand.

"You're not looking too bad yourself there Delores. Hmm, that pie looks & smells delicious."

Delores looked at Abigail funny for a second when she heard the new version of her accent.

"The accent is terrible, isn't it Delores."

"I wouldn't say it was awful, it might need some work before you bust it out. Just try to stick to American English words this year. Don't go calling Derek's truck a lorry again."

The three of them laughed at the memory of every man at last year's BBQ looking at her like she had just spoken in tongues. Once they composed themselves, & Delores's teenaged son reluctantly showed up to accompany his mother, they made their way to the BBQ.

Together, they said hello to the people that had already shown up. They laid their dish out on the table where everyone was putting out what they had brought & as more neighbours showed up, they separated to mingle with their neighbours.

Abigail made her way over to the host of the BBQ & tried to put on an accent of an English person trying to imitate an American accent. While he complemented her dress, Renee moved around from neighbor to neighbor, enjoying a chance to catch up with some of them. After a number of conversations, she found a man that she hadn't met before talking to Delores. Before she knew what was going on, Delores waived her over.

"Renee, this David, he just moved in down the road where Mark used to live."

"Oh, so you're the new neighbor that I've heard about."

"That I am."

"I'd stay to introduce you two, but my husband is giving me the signal to come bail him out of a conversation with Ted."

Renee laughed as Delores rushed off to save her husband.

"So Renee, how long have you lived in the neighbourhood?"

"Oh, I think that it's been about five years now. I'm sorry that I haven't introduced myself yet, I run a bakery in town & sometimes it just seems to take over my whole day."

"It's no problem, I've only been here for about a week, I'm still meeting new people every day. Some of the local gossip has only just started flowing my way."

"Oh, heard anything interesting, I'm always falling behind."

"Well, you probably know this, but apparently there's a pair of young women living together in the neighbourhood. I didn't get the full story, but it stuck out as a bit strange."

Renee panicked for a heartbeat as he mentioned two women living together. But as he went on, she realized that he really didn't know the full cover story, or even the whole story that might be going around the neighbourhood. With Abigail firmly busy trying to impress the more patriotic party goers with her Americanized accent, Renee saw an opportunity to stop him from spreading any rumors.

"I don't think that it is strange."

"Really?"

"Not at all. Of course, I'm a bit biased as I'm one of the two women that are living together."

David paled a bit on the spot.

"It's alright. Everyone thought that we were a bit odd when we moved in. I guess you don't get too many roommates in the suburbs."

"No, no we don't. I didn't mean to offend when I said it was strange."

"It's alright David, there's nothing untoward going on. Abigail, she's the one by the BBQ in the dress that matches mine, we shared an apartment in New York."

"You lived in New York!"

"That I did. I worked with my father at his bakery after we immigrated from France when I was young."

"Wow. The furthest that I've been from Detroit was Cleveland."

"Yes, well, I met Abigail a few years before we came here & we became fast friends. I moved in with her after my father passed. Shortly afterwards, her brother bought a house intending to move to America, but after the war, he was still needed in London."

"Needed for what?"

"Oh, he's a doctor. Apparently, England is still in short supply of nearly everything, so he stayed behind to help out as the country rebuilds & he told Abigail that she could live there until he could come over."

"Abigail just let you come along?"

"She's a true friend. She didn't want to leave me with a bakery that I couldn't manage just after my father passed, so she invited me to come out West with her."

"Wow. She really is a good friend."

"She is. I'm lucky to have her in my life."

David then noticed someone at the Bar-B-Q waiving him over.

"Sorry Renee, but it seems that I'm being called over to meet the host of the party."

"Go, go, we can chat later. It was lovely to meet you."

"You too Renee."

David then started walking over to where a bunch of the men were congregating around the hot-dogs & hamburgers being grilled. As he did, Abigail slowly made her way from where she had been chatting with the host's wife to come talk to Renee.

"Good news Renee. The star-spangled dresses are a hit. Apparently wearing the American flag as a respectable dress to the 4th of July party can make up for having an English accent."

"That's good. This year will be a lot more fun if the host of the party id happy to have us here."

"There's also another benefit."

"What's that?"

"Tonight, you can help me lower the flag."

"Abigail."

Renee blushed a bit as her mind flashed back to all the times that Abigail would flirt with her or steal a kiss when nobody was looking in her father's bakery. Feeling her heart race as she looked around to see if anybody overheard felt like old times.

"Sorry Renee, I can't help that seeing you in that outfit makes me want to get down on my knees & sing the star-spangled banner."

Renee's eyes opened wide as she wanted to silence Abigail while she was simultaneously imaging Abigail on her knees, lifting the hem of her flag dress up.

"I met our new neighbor; his name is David & he had heard a rumor about two women that live together in the neighbourhood."

Abigail's eyes opened wide.

"What did he say?"

"He just heard that there were two young women living together. You should have seen the look on his face when I told him that I was one of them."

"He's not going around telling people that there's something to suspect about us, is he?"

"No, it's alright Abigail, I gave him the story, that we're just good friends & that you didn't want to abandon me in Hell's Kitchen."

"Oh thank goodness. We've still got a few more decades to go before people can find out that we're more than just good friends."

"I still find it hard to believe that such a day will ever come. But I can't wait."

They both smiled, wishing that they could share a kiss as a series of pops started sounding off from the street. Once again, a trio of boys were setting off firecrackers & roman candles while their mothers chased after them.

February 11th, 1951

As Abigail walked in the front door, she couldn't remember for a second if she had taken off her wig. Checking to make sure that it wasn't there, she sighed in relief. It would have been challenging explaining why she had been wearing a blonde wig to any of her neighbors that might have seen her walking into her house.

"Renee, I'm home."

"I'm in the kitchen."

Following the sound of Renee's voice, Abigail found Renee at the kitchen table where she seemed to be writing a lot of things on as few papers as she could.

"The clouds out there are starting to get a bit dark. I'm thinking that we might get snowed in for Valentine's Day. We may have to keep each other warm."

Renee smiled slightly for a moment before returning to the letters that she seemed to be organizing & composing. Abigail stood behind her as she sat at the table & put her hands on Renee's shoulders.

"What are you up to?"

"I'm writing a letter back to my aunt in France."

"Right, the letter we got yesterday. How is the extended family?"

"For the most part, they're doing well. My second cousin is pregnant with her sixth child."

"Dear God, isn't she forty-eight?"

Renee chuckled.

"Forty-seven. She's told her husband that this is the last one, & that if he wants anymore, he'd better find himself a mistress. She's praying that it's not another boy."

Abigail sat in the chair across from Renee & in her limited French, tried to express her feelings as she had a moment ago.

"Mon Dieu"

Renee smiled before Abigail continued in English once more.

"How's your aunt doing? She had that cough last time she wrote."

"It's not gotten better. According to this, the doctors are very concerned about her health. I don't remember from the reports that Director Porter showed me about my family, but I think that the time of my aunt's passing is coming up."

Thinking back to the reports that Alex, her handler in New York had shown her, Abigail knew that Renee was right. Her Aunt wasn't long for the world.

"I am right, aren't I Abigail."

"Yeah. She doesn't have long left."

"That's why I want to fit as much as I can into this letter. It might be the last one that I get to send to her. I almost got the camera out to take a picture of myself, but then I remembered that I don't look anywhere near as old as I am. She knows that I'm forty-five, even if I appear twenty-five."

"It's too bad that I don't have my phone, I could age up a picture of you to make you look older."

Renee starred at Abigail for a second in a moment of utter confusion until she remembered twenty-first century phones could do just about everything but flip pancakes.

"Why would you want to make your picture of yourself look older?"

"It's fun."

"If you say so Abigail. I just want to make sure that I get as much as I can into this letter so that she can know I'll be alright."

Abigail thought about the information in Renee's file. She had memorized just about all of it & even now, almost twenty years later, she could still recall almost every detail of her love's file. Including the important dates of a number of her close relatives.

"Not to rush you Renee, but even though normal mail is probably fine, I would pay for it to be delivered by air mail if I were you."

Renee stopped writing for a second. As the memories of her file came back to her, she realized that she only had a few weeks left. Abigail was right. Regular mail would probably be sufficient, but she didn't want to take that chance. She wrote herself a note reminding herself to request her letter be delivered by air mail before returning to the task at hand.

"Thank you, Abigail. I was do distracted by composing the letter, I almost forgot how long it will take to get there."

"I'm sorry that you can't send a picture to your aunt or go to see her."

"Don't be sorry Abigail. Without you, I wouldn't have had the last six or seven years. At least I'll still have the rest of my cousins & nieces & nephews to write to."

"If you need anything Renee, I'm here for you."

"Je sais, I know. I think that I'll be alright. But this has all made me think that I'm going to be a complete mess in 1965."

"1965?"

"Remember, I'll be 59 years-old."

"Right. The plan, that's when we decided that…"

"I would pretend to get sick & die so that nobody questions how I'm still alive at such an age. I'm still not sure why it has to be when I'm 59."

"Family history & life expectancy. Your mother died young & your father died just past the average lifespan. That means that the odds of you naturally living into old age are slim. You shouldn't make it too far past the average life expectancy & for people born in 1900s France, the average life expectancy was about fifty."

"So if I made it to sixty, it might seem odd."

"Exactly. Plus, that's around the time that we'll probably be reassigned again & we might have to change our cover stories."

"I see. Out of curiosity, our cover stories right now say that we were born in the mid-1920s, what's our… Comment l'as-tu appelé, life expectancy?"

"Closer to sixty."

"I see, & what's the life expectancy of someone born in say… 2062?"

"Without age reversal, we think it'll be about a hundred & twenty, but you & I have age reversal. You're not going to lose me anytime soon."

Renee smiled.

"Très bien."

September 3rd, 1953

"Oh God, I think I might be sick."

"Not in my car you won't kid. Stick your head out the window if you have too."

Detective Rinaldo Porzio was having a miserable night. Some might say that the drunken teenager in his passenger seat was having a worse night, but Rinaldo wouldn't. After fifteen years in the Detroit Police Department, he was getting sick of the nights when he had to be a chauffeur for idiot teenagers.

As this particular fool managed to keep the contents of his stomach within his stomach, Rinaldo caught a strange sight out of the corner of his eye. A good-looking blonde woman in her mid-twenties putting what looked like welding equipment away in her garage. She didn't look like a typical young housewife putting her husband's or her boyfriend's stuff away. From the looks of her, she had just finished using the gear herself for something & was putting it away.

Ignoring it, he pulled up to the house across the street from the strange woman & marched the drunken miscreant up to the door of his house. Rinaldo knocked on the door with his skinny fingers & waited for the kid's parents to open the door. As he was waiting for someone to answer, he looked across the street & saw the blonde woman from before.

Seeing her through the living room window, he watched as she sat down on her couch & curled up next to another woman. Passing it off as just a woman entertaining company & remembering that she had forgotten to put some equipment away, he ignored it. Yet as he heard footsteps approaching him, a feeling nagged in the back of his mind. A strange feeling that he had had before, years ago, but couldn't quite place. As the door opened, a burly man who looked like he was dead tired opened the door.

"Can I help you?"

"Sir, I'm Detective Porzio with the Detroit Police Department. Is this kid yours?"

"Fuck me, what did he do now?"

"It seems that he & some of his acquaintances got their hands on some fresh moonshine."

The kid threw up on the porch.

"God damnit boy, tomorrow I'll make ya choose between a whooping & cleaning that up with your toothbrush. Get in the house."

The youth then stumbled into the house, having already forgotten about the punishment options that were in his near future.

"I'm sorry Detective, I try to raise my boys right, but it ain't easy with some of them."

"That's alright. Since he didn't hurt anyone, or damage any property, I told the officers to let this slide, but you might need to start knocking some sense into him before he does something that can't be overlooked."

"Thank you, Detective. Believe me, I'll get some sense into his head. Is there anything that I can do to thank you?"

As Rinaldo was about to say goodnight, the feeling from before popped up again. Looking back to the living room window across the street, he suddenly got curious.

"Can you tell me about the woman that lives across the street in that house over there?"

"Not much to tell, the two of them are fine neighbors."

"The two of them?"

"Yeah, Abigail Oldman & Renee… Rodin. They moved in a few years ago. Nice ladies."

"Either of them married?"

"No sir. A few men have showed up from time to time to take them out. One or two of them even came back a few times, but I guess they ain't found suitable husbands yet."

"Not often that you see a pair of single ladies living together in East English Village."

"I guess not. From what I hear, Ms. Rodin moved in with Ms. Oldman after her father died. One friend helping another through a tough time. They've lived together ever since."

"You said that they were pleasant neighbors?"

"The best. I was a little weary at first since one is French & the other is English, but they've grown on me."

Rinaldo shook his head.

"Thank you, sir. Sorry, to take up so much of your time gossiping about your neighbors like a mother hen."

"No problem, Detective."

"Goodnight."

As Rinaldo headed back to his car, he noted the address across the street & the names of the two women. When the man mentioned that they were both European, he started wondering if there might be something a little… unamerican about them."

September 5th, 1953

Abigail's boss had not been happy when she told him that she had to leave early. Managing to convince him that she was legitimately feeling sick & that she wasn't just trying to get out of work two hours early on a Friday, she moved fast.

In what felt like a blink of an eye, she was walking into a laundromat. When her handler had sent her an emergency message, he had told her in code to come to this place because it was a business that was owned by the agency to produce revenue for their work. It wasn't a safe house, but it could serve as a useful meeting place if nothing else was closer.

Once she was inside, she saw Ash by a washing machine in the back corner doing a load of laundry. The five machines next to him all had out of order signs on them, probably to give them some measure of privacy.

"Ash, what the hell is going on? What's with the emergency meeting in a laundromat?"

"Do you happen to know a Detective Rinaldo Porzio?"

"Never heard of him."

"Well he works for the Detroit Police Department & it seems that he's trying to open an unamerican investigation into you & Renee."

"What! How? Isn't that the authority of the American House of Representatives?"

"He plans on submitting a file to the House Unamerican Committee to show that the two of you are either communists from Europe or that communists are blackmailing you. As we speak, he's trying to look up information about the two of you."

"Christ."

"Don't worry Abigail, all that he'll find are the records that we created. On top of that, we've already directed our agent in the Police Department to sabotage his efforts."

"That's good at least. Does this mean that we might get an emergency reassignment?"

"Unlikely, but for the time being, we're going to be taking much stricter safety measures."

"Whatever it takes."

"That's what I like to hear Abigail. First off, just in case, you & Renee need to be ready to bug out at a moment's notice. If you get the call, you need to haul ass to the Alpha emergency site."

"Got it."

"Secondly, do you remember the little coffee shop that we met at last week?"

"Yeah, they have good bagels."

"I'm glad that you like it because that's our new weekly meeting place. From now on, our Sunday meetings are there & we'll be wearing the same brunette wigs as last week. We're going to maintain the image of a Father & Daughter getting together once a week."

"That all sounds doable. What I want to know is why is he even investigating us?"

"Apparently, two nights ago, he was dropping off your neighbor's drunk teenage son when he saw you & Renee sitting together on the couch through your living room window. He then found out from your neighbor that your both European & apparently, he had a feeling."

"That's it. A feeling."

"People have been targeted for less. The truly disturbing thing about this is that this isn't the first time that a gut feeling of his has led him to investigate one of our agents."

"It's not?"

"Nope. Back in 43, we had an agent infiltrate the NRA. Detective Porzio got a feeling one day & tried to open an investigation into him. It's probably a coincidence that he's found two agents to investigate in ten years, after all, our operations are far reaching. Still, it's making a lot of people upstairs nervous to know that he's picked out another agent. For now, just be careful."

May 22nd, 1955

As Renee admired the white & pink flowers that her cover date had gotten her the night before, she was also counting the seconds. She could swear that the damn clock was running slow. Renee couldn't wait to find out what Abigail had planned for the night. So far, the only thing that she knew was that Abigail had bought them new dresses & that Renee would be getting a surprise at seven.

Renee had already spent the entire day trying to figure out what Abigail had planned for their twentieth anniversary, but she was no closer to knowing what was coming.

Twenty years to the day since they had gone to that theater. Renee could still remember every line of Dracula's Daughter. She remembered going back to Abigail's apartment, remembered her heart pounding in her chest as Abigail invited her to her bed. She could recall the fear & desire both coursing through her veins as she made her choice between the front door & the bedroom door. Renee thanked God for the strength & courage to choose Abigail's bedroom instead of the life that she had been living until that point.

At six thirty-three, Abigail popped out from the kitchen & reminded Renee she wanted to be gone by seven. Renee had no idea where they were going, but she loved the emerald dresses that Abigail had gotten for them. Renee was slowly getting accustomed to the fashions of the nineteen fifties, the dresses that only went down to just past the knees, the way the dresses flared out instead of hugging the legs like the pencil skirts back in the day, the more hourglass figure. She was even growing fond of the fashion. Still, she was fairly certain that lavender-colored gloves were not part of the trend as Abigail would say.

The short gloves, made of lavender satin, seemed completely out of place. Still, Abigail insisted that she wear them, so she did. Just as she had that night twenty years ago, she was putting her trust in this woman from the future that spoke of mad & wonderful things as she prepared to follow her to destinations unknown.

At exactly two minutes past seven, they made their way to the bus stop. Thankful that none of the neighbours were asking why they were so well dressed as they headed out on a Sunday evening, Renee wondered where they were going as they got off of one bus & onto another.

Renee had asked if it was safe to go out with Detective Rinaldo out there. After nineteen months of him occasionally making inquiries into their lives, Renee didn't want to be overly risky just because it was their twentieth. Abigail had assured her that according to a contact they had in the Detroit PD, Rinaldo was backing off of his side investigations for a while since his boss had given him a stern lecture about wasting department resources & taxpayer dollars chasing gut feelings.

According to the contact, Rinaldo wouldn't be looking into anything for a few weeks, hopefully giving the agent time to derail the investigation all together after all this time.

Eventually they got off at a stop in Walkersville. Not sure why they were there, Renee simply followed at Abigail's side until they reached what looked like a closed bookstore. The store was called Curious Books. It had a heavy blackout curtain closed in the window, covering everything except for an old copy of a trashy looking book with a picture of women changing clothes in a locker room on it. The title read Women's Barracks, which only left Renee even more confused as Abigail walked up to the door.

Despite the fact that the door had a sign on it that said the store was closed for a private event, Abigail knocked on the door. As Renee watched, the door cracked open. The woman that opened the door gave them both a quick once over before opening it for them & hurrying them inside.

Once inside, the confusion didn't let up for Renee. The small store was full of women who like them, were all wearing lavender gloves. As the one that was ushering them in welcomed them, Abigail led the way.

"Have they started yet?"

"Only just, head on in."

As they slowly moved past the entrance, Renee started noticing more about this group of women. Aside from the fact that they were all wearing lavender-colored gloves, the women seemed to have little in common. Some were young, some were old. Some were clearly wealthier than others & a number of different races & religions were present among this small group of twenty or so women in this now crowded bookstore.

In the back corner of the store, there was a small section that was clear of shelves where chairs had been set up around a central area that was clearly meant to be some sort of stage area. Taking a step closer to the stage while Abigail talked to one of the women, Renee saw a young Latina woman sitting on a chair on the stage, facing the crowd of women. She had taken off her gloves & in her golden, caramel & calloused hands, she held a few sheets of paper that she was reading from.

"How many boys had followed her to that back room,
Not one among them her groom,
Calling them to her when her boss was away,
With hips that know just how to sway,

How I dream that she would look in my direction,
Call on me to receive her affection..."

Renee turned when she felt a hand on her shoulder. Seeing Abigail by her side, she followed Abigail back to the bookshelves so that they could talk.

"Abigail, what is going on here?"

"What's going on, is that you & I are guests tonight, invited to attend the weekly gathering of the Lavender Glove Society."

"What is that? What's happening here?"

"It's a group of women who like us, are attracted to more feminine individuals."

In a hushed whisper, Renee leaned in close to Abigail before continuing.

"Abigail, is this some kind of… lesbian… sex club?"

Abigail chuckled.

"No, sadly. It's a lesbian book club. They gather every Sunday night at one of a handful of places for a night of poetry, book readings, pulp fiction readings, & conversations about one central theme. Women loving women. Apparently, some of the things they read are things that they themselves have written."

Renee was stunned. Looking around, she took in the sight around her. For so long, she had felt like an oddity, like the only woman in the world that wasn't interested in men. Then when she met Abigail, she had felt like she had found the only other person like her. Now here she stood, in a room with twenty something more women who according to Abigail, were just like her, even if many of them looked nothing like her. She could hardly believe it, until she started to notice the little displays of affection here & there.

An old woman & a middle aged woman holding hands. An African woman brushing a strand of hair out a white woman's face as they gazed into each other's eyes. Two middle aged women holding each other as they listened to the woman on stage read her poem about wishing that the boss's secretary would invite her for a romp in the back room.

"Is this place real?"

Abigail smiled.

"It's real Renee. They're hard to find in this era, but groups like this have always existed if you could figure out where to look. The woman that I was talking to a minute ago is a fellow agent. Her job is to find groups like this that we didn't know about so that we can help them fight for equality in later decades."

"This is… this is fantastical."

"This is nothing."

Abigail then wrapped her arms around Renee in a hug that had them face to face in a clearly intimate way. As Renee nervously looked around, Abigail cupped her chin, & brought Renee's attention back to her.

"For the last twenty years, I've been promising you that the future holds freedom for us. Parades & the promise of open love. While I still can't give that to you, I can give you this. A taste of what is to come. A place where we don't have to hide. A place where I can kiss you out in the open, in front of everyone."

"Abigail…"

Renee was cut off as Abigail leaned forward & kissed her. Renee panicked for a heartbeat, but Abigail's words left her feeling safe. This wasn't a fiery kiss of imminent passion, nor was it a quick peck on the lips. It was long, sensual, & every second of it was filled with the kind of love that could make the rest of the world stop mattering for what felt like an eternity. When their lips finally parted, Abigail leaned in & whispered so that nobody else could hear them.

"Happy twentieth anniversary my love."

Chapter 19
June 4th, 1956

Abigail believed that there was nothing that could make a Monday better than spending her lunch with her favorite coworkers in a diner on a beautiful day in June. Well actually she would prefer to be spending a long lazy day in bed with Renee, reading, listening to music, chatting, forgetting to get dressed. Sadly, her cover demanded that she work, so here she was, chatting & gossiping with her coworkers.

Just as one of the secretaries was complimenting her incredible typing skills, Abigail was distracted by a song on the radio. The song was eerily similar to a song that she hadn't heard since before she had walked through the gateway to come back in time & start her work in this timeline. Shaking the thought out of her head, she turned her attention back to her friends & that was when she saw him.

Sitting two tables away from her, was Detective Rinaldo Porzio, looking a little bit older than the photos of him that she had been shown & clearly trying to remain unnoticed.

Resisting the urge to panic & get out of there, she breathed deep a few times, repositioned the napkin holder so that she could see if he was moving, & tried to think. She would have been informed by the agency's mole in the Detroit PD if there was an investigation looking into her. That meant that either he was following her when he should have been doing something else, or he just happened to be getting lunch in the same place that she was. Abigail knew which option she wanted to be true. She also knew which one she would bet her money on.

"Did you hear me, Abigail?"

"What, sorry?"

Abigail hadn't noticed that Susan, one of the secretaries, had asked her something.

"Don't you think that we should be getting back? Our lunch hour is almost over."

"Actually…"

A thought had occurred to Abigail, if Rinaldo wasn't supposed to be looking into her, then he could only afford to spend so much of his time tailing her. Sooner or later, he'd have to get back to work. Otherwise he'd have to explain to his bosses why he wasn't looking into his assigned cases. Abigail just had to see when he left & she would know how much trouble she was in. Not wanting to risk losing him in a crowd, she decided that she needed to get the girls to stay here.

"Actually, maybe we should stay a bit longer."

"I don't know Abigail, it's getting late."

"Yeah, but all the bosses & top brass are going to be in meetings all day & it's such a lovely day. I say that we take an extra half hour & order some pie."

Susan was stunned.

"What have you done with Abigail? I've been working with her for four years & she has never broken a rule. Now she wants to play hooky?"

"So is that a no then?"

Susan smiled & reached for the small pamphlet that listed their pies as the others all agreed that an extended lunch & pie was something that they all deserved.

As they all ordered & Abigail half paid attention to conversations about boyfriends, husbands & mid 1950s life in general, she nervously kept an eye on Rinaldo. When the waitress brought him another cup of coffee, Abigail got concerned. He didn't seem to be intending to leave any time soon. If that meant that he was conducting some sort of official investigation, she could be in trouble.

As she worked to appear happy & chatty with her coworkers, she was nervously going over worst-case scenarios in her head. She had visions of him arresting her at work or at home. Dragging her down to a police station, questioning her about her relationship with Renee. She pictured Renee in an interrogation room as he demanded she tell him what she knew about gay clubs in the area. She imagined newspaper headlines outing her & Renee as a couple. She would lose her job, Renee's bakery would probably go out of business, they would probably be pressured to move by their neighbours.

Abigail couldn't ever remember being so afraid of anything in her life. The closest that she had ever felt to this was the night that Renee had demanded to know the truth & was about to walk out.

Taking a bite out of her pie & discovering that it was pecan, she focused on the delicious pie & tried to calm her nerves. Even if she & Renee were outed, the agency would simply move them. If she was arrested, the agency's lawyers would show up to get her out. If that didn't work, they would find a way to bust her out & hide her away.

As she was calming herself down, a man in a very blue suit with a very severe buzzcut came into the diner, looked around & made a beeline for Rinaldo.

"Dammit Rinaldo, what the hell are you doing here?"

Rinaldo seemed annoyed that his partner was blowing his cover. He tried to whisper to avoid being heard.

"I'm busy."

"Busy with what? We can only hold Nelson for about another hour before we have to let him go. You're supposed to be trying to get a confession out of him while I look into his brother. Why the fuck are you here?"

"I'm working on something."

"Well you'd better shift it to the precinct, & hope that the sergeant & the lieutenant haven't noticed that you're not in interrogation. Now!"

To Abigail's immense relief, Rinaldo reluctantly got up & followed his partner out of the diner. Judging by what she heard, it was clear that he wasn't supposed to be investigating her. He was ignoring his duties, something that her handler & the mole they had in the department might be able to use to shut him down for good.

Once the little extended lunch that she had talked them into taking came to an end, Abigail had to resist the urge to run back to her office. Wishing that she had a phone that she could text her handler with, she instead had to wait until she got to the phone in her office. It seemed to take forever.

Walking back into the office, she quickly discovered that a number of employees had taken an extended lunch & that the big meetings were still going on. Glad that she hadn't gotten any of her coworkers in trouble to cover her ass, she made her way to her desk.

Waiting for the rotary phone to spin around as she dialed each number was driving her insane. It didn't help that there were three zeros in her handler's number. It gave her time to remember in her training courses when one of the instructors, a man who had actually been alive in 1956 as a child told them that your popularity in school depended on how many zeros were in your phone number. She understood what he meant as she waited for the rotary dial to make its way around.

When her handler finally picked up, she gave him the secret code that told him she needed to see him after work immediately. He then gave the response to let her know that he would be waiting for her at the bus stop near the bank that she worked at.

When five o'clock finally rolled around, she made her way to the bus stop where Ash Bailey was waiting for her on the bench. As the after-work crowd climbed onto the bus, she sat down on the bench next to him. As the bus pulled away, he lifted his head a bit without looking at her.

"What's up Abigail? You sounded worried on the phone."

"Detective Rinaldo Porzio. That's what's up."

"Again."

"Yes. I was at lunch with the girls from work. A song came on the radio that reminded me of a song from home & when I looked over a bit in the direction of the radio, there he was. Two tables down from me, obviously trying to eavesdrop on me."

"Fuck. Is there any indication that this is an official investigation?"

"I don't think so. After a while, his partner came by & gave him shit for not being back at the precinct where he was supposed to be interrogating someone."

"Double Fuck. If this were an official investigation, we could have agents work to derail it, but it sounds like he's gone rogue."

"Is that bad?"

"It means that he's obsessed."

"What happens now?"

"Now, Abigail, we're upgrading his threat status. I'm going to call up our asset in the Detroit PD & have him reveal that Detective Porzio is conducting off the book investigations during work hours. That'll get him a good long talk with the upper brass which should cause him to pump the breaks for a while."

"Another half measure. If this guy is so obsessed with me, getting fired might not stop him. On top of that, why is he only now becoming a threat? He's been looking into me & Renee off & on for four years now. Shouldn't something have been done about him?"

"Intervention brings unwanted attention. As long as he was just looking at records that revealed nothing & never figuring anything out, the safest course was to do nothing & wait for him to move on."

"Well he isn't moving on. He's stepping up, following me & directly observing me. I'm getting tired of this crap. Like I said, it's been four years. Even if he was just looking at the same old records, something should have been done about him by now."

"You're right Abigail. Last year, when we got word that he was trying to dig up your emigration records, I had some of my people start drawing up plans for ways that we could deal with him. I'm going to present the issue to Director Strand & I'm going to inform her that we need to deal with this."

"Yeah, & what are your plans for dealing with him?"

"Well, if the reprimand from his boss doesn't get him to stop within the next few days, we'll set it up to look like he got drunk & got into a minor car accident. Nobody will be hurt, it'll all be staged, & public. Our agent in the PD will also provide 'proof' that he's been drinking on the job which will hopefully lead to him getting fired. We'll then line up a job as a security guard or something a few cities over."

"That's great, but what if that doesn't stop him?"

"Then he might just have to vanish."

October 6th, 1957

Abigail & Renee were watching the evening news in their living room. The main news story was the same as it had been for the last two days. Sputnik. The small Soviet satellite that was now orbiting the Earth, the first one ever launched. The story had been damn near the only thing that the news had been talking about since it had launched two days earlier.

As the reporters discussed the possibility that it's famous radio beep… beep… beep might be a secret Soviet code or that it might be some sort of a spy satellite, Abigail was watching with fascination.

The first historic moment in the first space race & damn near everyone in the US was freaking out as they imagined Soviet cameras in the sky or Soviet nukes raining down as schoolchildren pointlessly hid under their desks.

Despite Abigail's reassurances that Sputnik was just a one-watt radio transmitter relaying data about the upper atmosphere, it was hard for Renee to remain calm with the collective freakout that the country was going through. Even at work, Renee had needed to turn off the radio because every hour & a half, the music was being interrupted by updates about the satellite as it passed overhead. Sputnik headlines were in every newspaper & it was being mentioned on every channel of the television.

Abigail had once explained to Renee the concept of the 24-hour news cycle & the fear, anxiety & panic it often induced. Over the last two days, Renee felt like she was understanding the concept for the first time. Grabbing the clunky remote control with its two massive buttons, Renee switched off the television set & curled up on the couch next to Abigail. Abigail wrapped her arms around her lover & pulled her close until Renee was practically in her lap.

"What's wrong? Sputnik fever taking hold?"

"It's everywhere. I know that you told me that everything was going to be alright & that Sputnik is harmless but are you absolutely sure that's it alright having that thing up there."

"It's perfectly safe. It doesn't have any cameras or missiles. It's just a tiny little atmospheric probe with a one-watt transmitter. It'll spend a few weeks gathering air samples way up there, then it'll burn up in the atmosphere, harmlessly. The Soviets never rained down nukes or set foot on the Moon. There's nothing to be afraid of. They won't even exist anymore in thirty-five years."

Renee breathed a little more easily.

"The things you've told me are just so… surreal. In twelve years, an American will walk on the moon. They'll do that half a dozen times & then they'll just… stop going? Why would they just stop?"

"Going to the Moon is very expensive. Just the Apollo program, without all the other stuff they had to do first, ended up costing like… twenty-five billion dollars."

"Mon Dieu"

"Yeah. After the Soviets gave up in 1969, it was really hard to convince congress to keep paying two or three percent of the federal budget so that some guys could collect some rock samples. The program was cancelled & nobody went back to the Moon until 2025."

"Is going to the Moon cheaper in 2025?"

"No. not by a long shot. Even after adjusting for inflation, it was crazy expensive. But there was a new space race on. We were up against China that time."

"Yes, because China, China is going to be a superpower to rival America & Russia."

"You laugh Renee, but in two generations, they went from backwater to masters of the Eastern hemisphere. So when they set their eyes on the Moon, the US couldn't just keep coasting on the success of Apollo. They had to get back in the game. In 2025, they managed to beat China to the moon by about a year. That was when the first woman set foot on the Moon. Fifty-six years after the first man."

Renee felt herself calming down. Knowing that nobody apparently seemed to care about building military bases on the moon any time soon was helping to calm her down.

"So there was never any sort of space war?"

"Don't worry Renee. There was never a space war. Well, there was the 2035 incident, but that was a communication & translation issue that resulted in three fatalities near the Shackleton water plant. Things got a bit tense that day. Everyone was just glad that President Cortez had won the election a few months earlier instead of Senator Paul."

Renee took Abigail's word about the last bit as she had no idea who those people were or why it was better that one of them won over the other. Appreciating the fact that space was apparently going to be mostly peaceful, Renee felt a new concern slowly brewing inside of her.

"Is the agency going to change any of that?"

"Well we're not going to start a space war, hopefully, but yeah. A few things will be different."

"Like what?"

"Well I don't know the fine details about all of our space objectives, but I remember hearing something about getting control of lunar satellites to spot water ice just after the fall of the Soviet Union in the early 90s instead of… I think it was 2008 or 2009. Get America interested in going back to the Moon before Russia or China have a chance to get their space programs up & running."

"How is getting to the Moon a few years earlier going to help the human race?"

"I don't know. Something about environmentalism in the second space race. I guess going to the Moon convinced a few more people to take care of this planet. The point is, you don't need to worry about Sputnik or space wars or anything like that."

Abigail hugged Renee tightly before she went on.

"It might seem unlikely at times, but we'll make it through this century. We'll even make it through the next one after that."

It did seem hard to believe, just from what she had already seen. Atomic weapons, satellites, hysteria. With some of the things that Abigail had described about the next half century, it seemed impossible that humanity would get out of it alive. Yet here & now, in her arms, being reassured that everything would be alright, she believed it. She believed that everything might just work out. She then grabbed the large remote again & handed it over to Abigail so that they could turn the news back on.

May 10th, 1959

Even with her hands still coated in flour, Renee lined up the fresh bagels from the oven in the display case while Sandra helped another customer looking for something special. If the last fourteen years of running Rodin bakery & the well over ten years of working for her father's bakery had taught her one thing, it was that Mother's Day was going to be busy.

As the customer accepted his change & left with his fresh sourdough loaf, Sandra walked over to where Renee was stocking the shelf, moved a lock of her own blonde hair out of her eyes & started helping with the warm bagels. As Sandra took over stocking the shelf, Renee stretched her back a bit & cracked her knuckles.

"Thank you again for coming in so early on a Sunday Renee. I was honestly worried that I'd be doing this alone until the afternoon. What are the odds that Martha would go into labor three weeks early & three days before Mother's Day?"

"It's no problem, Sandra. I wasn't going to leave you alone. What did they say in the military, leave nobody behind?"

"That's what they said, back in my days as a WASP before I was told I couldn't fly planes anymore. Before I came here & put on forty pounds."

"Forty pounds gained or not, I was glad that you didn't have to use that combat training of yours to deal with those two customers fighting over that last mint frosting cake this morning."

"Yeah, not exactly what I thought my training would be useful for when they told me that I was going to get to fly fighter planes between bases."

They both chuckled for a second until they heard the sound of the bell over the door ringing. Turning towards the door, they were both happily surprised when instead of another surge of customers, there was a robust, black woman, wearing a curve hugging dress that overemphasized her form.

"Pardon me, I was wondering who I might talk to about the help wanted sign?"

Renee stepped forward.

"That would be me. Please follow me."

Sandra then prepared herself for another customer that was coming into the bakery as Renee led her new applicant to the small office next to the kitchen where she did a lot of the bakery's paperwork. The small office was a tight fit for two people, but they managed.

"Thank you for coming in. I'm Renee, I own & run this bakery."

"I'm Ruby. Thank you for giving me an interview, it's not always easy to find someone that'll give you the time of day."

"Their loss & potentially my gain."

Ruby smiled as Renee moved some papers around so that there wasn't a stack between the two of them.

"I've got to say Ruby, your timing is perfect. We were a bit short handed before my other employee went on maternity leave this week."

"Oh my, so you don't employ any men here?"

"Not currently. It is just us girls here at the moment."

"That's probably for the best. Any man you hired wouldn't be able to focus when you were around."

Renee was thrown off for a moment. Aside from Abigail, she wasn't used to the idea of another woman telling her that she was attractive. Looking over Ruby for a moment, Renee told herself that the tight dress & the compliments were probably because Ruby had been planning on being interviewed by a man & she was just flirting like she had thought that she would have to.

"So, Ruby, what kind of experience do you have with customers?"

Ruby looked to the door for a second before she leaned in close & in almost a whisper, replied in an unexpected way.

"Zdes' bezopasno govorit'?"

"I'm sorry, I didn't quite catch that."

Ruby looked around again & repeated herself. Renee had no idea what the woman was saying. She only knew that it wasn't in English or French.

Renee suddenly started remembering some of the things that Abigail had taught her about avoiding trouble & protecting herself. A random good-looking person walking into your life & flirting with you. Getting you to feel pity or sympathy for their hardships. Attempting to trip you up by saying something weird. If it had just been the flirting & the tight clothes, Renee would have left it alone. The strange language, that was sounding an alarm bell.

"I'm sorry Ruby, but being Mother's Day, we're incredibly rushed today. Could you leave me a phone number to reach you at & I'll call you to set up an appointment to come back in in a day or two."

"Sure, it's no problem."

Ruby then wrote down her name & number on the paper that Renee handed her & promptly stood up.

"I'm sorry to take up your time on such a busy day."

"It's no problem, hopefully we can set up a proper interview soon."

Renee then escorted Ruby out & spent the rest of the very long day helping Sandra with customers & the bakery until it was finally time for them to close up & head home. After wishing Sandra a good night, Renee took the bus home while worrying about how Abigail would react to the news of the strange woman.

When Renee walked into their home, she had been expecting to see Abigail waiting to tell her about her weekly meeting with her handler & getting ready for another week of work. Instead, she walked into the house & found Abigail in the kitchen, yelling at someone over the phone in her natural voice without the English accent that was so familiar.

"It's been years Ash! Seven years of this shit! It's kind of hard to maintain protocol 3 when I've got an obsessed fucking cop following us for seven years. You keep telling me that he's going to be dealt with! Deal with him!"

Abigail hung up the phone with enough force that Renee was surprised the base didn't fall off of the wall. Abigail then walked towards the liquor cabinet, pulled out a bottle of brandy & poured herself a healthy amount to calm her nerves. Once Abigail calmed down, she turned to Renee, took a deep breath & acknowledged that her lover was home.

"Hi Renee, sorry you had to hear me like that."

"Don't be sorry, just tell me what's wrong."

"Fucking Detective Rinaldo Fucking Porzio. That's what's fucking wrong."

"Again?"

"Yeah Renee, again. One of our assets in the DPD has been his partner for the last year or so. This afternoon, he reported to his handler that the detective is reopening a bunch of his off the books, gut feeling cases to weed out the unamerican elements in society. Which means that he's looking into us again. You know Alex, my handler back in New York, he wouldn't have let this shit stand. If he were here, the detective would have been dealt with in fifty-two."

Renee then followed Abigail into the living room where Abigail sat down on the couch, exhausted.

"How was your day, Renee?"

"I think that it's a good thing that you are sitting down."

Abigail got nervous.

"What happened Renee?"

"Well, you remember how I've been looking to hire someone because we were shorthanded even before Martha went on maternity leave?"

"Yeah, did something happen?"

"Well, in between crowds of customers, a woman walked in looking for a job. When I was interviewing her, she seemed grateful that I was giving her the time of day since apparently a lot of employers aren't interested in hiring a Black woman in a tight dress."

"Fuck I hate the fifties. Go on."

"Well, after she found out that I don't have any men working for me, I think that she started flirting with me, telling me that men would be too distracted by me to focus on work."

"Well she's not wrong Renee. Maintaining my cover was always hard around you because I couldn't think straight."

Renee smiled.

"As true as that might be, it got weird after that. When I asked her about her experience, she looked around to make sure that we were alone & said something to me in a language that I don't recognize."

Abigail got concerned. She stood up, took Renee's hand in her own & looked her in the eye.

"Renee, can you repeat what this woman said to you as best as you can, I have an idea about what it might be."

Closing her eyes, Renee worked to remember the moment as best as she could. Ruby sitting across from her, her dress looking like it was about to give out against the bust it was stretched over, & the words that Ruby had said in that strange language.

"Zdes'… bezopasno… govorit'."

"Fucking Hell!"

Renee opened her eyes in alarm.

"What does it mean?"

"It's Russian, she was asking if it was safe to talk."

"Was she a Soviet spy?"

"I doubt it. Not on the day that the good detective is opening up his off the book's investigations. I bet that she's either an informant of his, or somebody that he's paying off or blackmailing to try & prove that you're a queer Soviet agent, here to spread communism & feminism to the good Americans."

"Mon Dieu! What do we do now?"

"Now, I call up Ash, or maybe even Director Strand, & tell them that either they deal with Rinaldo, or I will.

Renee then watched as Abigail stormed into the kitchen & ripped the phone off of its base to start dialing one of her emergency numbers.

May 12th, 1959

Detective Rinaldo Porzio unlocked his front door & walked inside, fuming over the day's events. He couldn't fault his partner for finding that lead. It wasn't his fault that the two of them had to spend the last two days on a stakeout, waiting for a suspect that never showed. Still, it meant two days where he couldn't do anything about his suspects.

Listening to his informant Ruby try to extract information from the Rodin girl had been embarrassing. She had been in there for all of twenty seconds before she started clumsily flirting & speaking in Russian. His one informant that speaks fluent commie & she blew it like a rank amateur. Now the Rodin girl & her partner were probably suspicious that something was going on.

Picking up his mail, he walked into the kitchen & opened his fridge to pull out a can of beer. Downing the beer in a matter of seconds, he grabbed another can & headed for the living room where he would begin plotting his next move.

That was when he felt dizzy. Leaning on the wall for a moment, he felt his whole world spinning. For a moment, he was able to resist it, but then he felt his body relaxing to the point that his muscles gave out. He then slumped to the floor with a thud & fell over, staring up at his ceiling.

For a moment, he just lay there, his mind feeling sluggish when the back door opened & his partner walked in. Standing over him, his partner poked him with his foot for a moment. He then called out to someone else.

"He's down. He's not out yet, but he's down."

Confused, Rinaldo could do nothing but lay there as more people walked into his house. First, he saw three of the biggest guys that he had ever seen. They looked like they were identical triplets, &

like their fathers were gorillas. Behind the three grunts in suits, Abigail Oldman walked into his living room to stand over him.

With his mind clouding over, he tried to ask what the hell was going on, but what he got out was some whispered gibberish. As Abigail stood over him, glaring at him, his partner turned to the three massive grunts that looked like they each could bench press a bus.

"Delta 3, did you get the beer cans from his trash."

One of them held up a bag full of empty beer cans.

"Good, spread those around his kitchen like a drunk that doesn't give a fuck. You, Delta 2, do you have the heroin?"

Another of the grunts lifted a duffle bag & grunted something that sounded like a yes.

"Good, put it on the kitchen table, remember to open one of the bricks & spill it around."

He grunted & preceded to the kitchen.

"Delta 1, once agent Abigail gets everything about her & Renee, you spread out the evidence we got from the precinct for those drug trafficking cases."

The third man grunted as Abigail sorted through all of the files, grabbing up everything to do with her & Renee. Summoning up the last of his strength, Rinaldo managed to grunt out enough passable English to be understood.

"W... Why... are you... What are... you... doing...?"

"Sorry Rinaldo, you're a good guy, relative to society, but you got too curious & you wouldn't leave well enough alone."

Rinaldo couldn't manage anything else. He fought to stay awake, but he was fading fast. When Abigail came back to where he was slumped, he could barely understand what she was saying.

"So where ... ... going ... end up?"

"He couldn't understand what his partner said as he slipped into the darkness."

May 19th, 1959

The air was hot & dry & somewhere nearby, a fan was blowing in a futile attempt to cool the room down a bit. Rinaldo Porzio opened his eyes & felt the massive throbbing of a pounding headache that was quickly fading as he came too.

Looking around, he quickly figured out that he was in a hospital room. What he couldn't explain was why he was alone in a room with six beds & why he was handcuffed to the bed. Looking at his hand, it seemed weird, odd, like the hand of an old man. As he sat there contemplating the strange appearance of his hand & the empty ward around him, a doctor walked in.

"Ah good, you're finally awake. You had a lot of people worried there for a moment."

"Sorry about that, how did I get here?"

"We'll cover that in a moment."

The doctor then leaned over the bed & had Rinaldo follow his finger & preform a few other basic tests.

"Alright, that seems to be working fine. Can you tell me your name?"

"Officer Rinaldo Porzio."

"Excellent. Now Mr. Porzio, can you tell me where you are?"

"I seem to be in a hospital, not exactly sure where this is."

"Understandable, you are a long way from home. You're in Del Rio, Texas. You've been here for a few days now."

"Texas! How did I get to Texas?"

"That's not entirely clear. Now, can you tell me what the date is, month & year please?"

"If it's only been a few days like you said, then it should still be late July 1931."

The doctor looked at him incredulously.

"Are you certain about that sir?"

"Pretty certain, but maybe it's August."

"Mr. Porzio, it's May 19th, 1959."

"What!"

Rinaldo sat upright.

"You're messing with me doctor, you said that it's only been a few days. It can't be 1959."

"I'm afraid that it is. You disappeared from your home in Detroit a week ago. Then a few days ago, you were found wondering the outskirts of town, naked & confused."

Rinaldo couldn't believe what he was hearing until he caught sight of a small mirror on the bedside table. Grabbing it with his uncuffed hand, he looked at his reflection & saw the image of an old man, a far cry from the young buck he recalled seeing in the mirror before he went to bed the night before.

"Doctor… What the hell is going on here? How can I not remember the last… … twenty-eight years? Did I hit my head?"

"There was no evidence of head trauma that we could find. Perhaps it's something that you took."

"Will my memories come back."

"If you're telling the truth, they might."

"What do you mean? Why would I be lying about that?"

"For the same reason that you're handcuffed to the bed there, son. There are some federal agents waiting outside that would like a word with you."

"Why do some G-men want to talk to me?"

"Something about stolen police evidence & piles of narcotics found in your home in Detroit, that you supposedly don't remember. If you'll excuse me, I'm going to tell them that your awake."

Chapter 20
June 2nd, 1961

Renee's day was perfect. The sun was shining, the customers at work had been pleasant enough & in two days, it was going to be her birthday. There was nothing better than when her birthday fell on a weekend because it meant that Abigail would be home with her all day. The last time that her birthday had been on a Saturday, they had spent the whole day in bed together, naked.

Sure this time around it was on a Sunday, which meant that she would have to spend a part of her morning talking to her handler. But that just meant that she would want to make it up to Renee when she got home. Visions of strip teases, loving caresses, probing fingers & entwined bodies flooded her mind.

Coming up on the house that she had shared with Abigail for the last sixteen years, she saw her neighbor Brian washing his car, again. Ever since he had retired almost a year ago, he had been spending ridiculous amounts of time working on his lawn, his garden & his car. Now that summer had rolled around, it was always something to see him working on his car. Abigail called him a man who's run out of fucks to give. Renee believed it.

At sixty-six years old, he was washing his car, shirtless, while grooving to the Monkees singing I'm a believer on the radio. His wife was constantly going on about how he's become a teenager that forgot to grow up. Judging by the way he was constantly smacking her rear & the smile that it always brought to her lips, she wasn't complaining. Renee walked up to him.

"Looks like retirement is treating you well."

"That it is Renee. That it is. You know, I got to retire at the perfect time. 1960, best time in the world to finish working."

"Is that so?"

"That it is. Good music on the radio, easy ways to travel around the world with the love of my life & I can watch men go to space from the comfort of my living room."

"That was something, wasn't it? A man in space."

"It sure was Renee. You know, when I was a boy, maybe eight or nine years old, I remember hearing my father talk about the wright brothers first flight. Now my grandchildren will remember me talking about the first spaceflight. Incredible. I never thought that I would live to see the day that men made it into space."

"I know the feeling. I never thought that I would live to see something like that."

Brain laughed.

"I think that you might still be a bit young to be saying that Renee, even if you're hitting the big three five on Sunday."

"Yeah, thirty-five, where do the years go."

Renee kicked herself mentally. Saying that she never thought that she would live to see spaceflight was perfectly fine for someone who was turning fifty-five like she really was. But to the rest of the world, she was turning thirty-five.

"So, any big plans for the birthday girl?"

"Not really. I'll probably just stay home & wonder why I'm still single & on my way to becoming a spinster."

"What happened to the handsome fella that took you out on the town a few weeks ago? Wasn't he a doctor?"

Renee remembered the agent that Abigail's handler had arranged to take her out. He had been handsome, for a man. He was working as a surgeon so that the agency could have access to a hospital. Working as a surgeon & a spy from the future had left little time for him to date, so she had gone out with him so that they could both cut down the rumors around them.

"He was a trauma surgeon. Turns out that he was married."

"Oh, I'm sorry to hear that."

"I am as well. He knew what he was doing."

Brain grinned a bit at the insinuation that Renee had done more than just seen some movies with him.

"I wouldn't go mentioning that to some of our other neighbors."

"Oh, that's right, I keep forgetting that American women aren't supposed to have that kind of fun without a ring on their finger."

"A real shame if you ask me."

As they laughed, they were interrupted by the sound of car honking as someone pulled into Renee's driveway. Turning around, Renee saw Abigail driving a new light blue, Oldsmobile Starfire into the driveway with the top down. Renee & Brain were both stunned by the site of the new convertible. Abigail got out of the new car, took her sunglasses off & walked over to Renee & Brain.

"What do you think?"

Brian was the first to speak up.

"It's beautiful. What brought this on?"

"It seemed like a good idea. I mean, we've been living in the motor city for the better part of twenty years, I figured it was high time to get a car. I was going to get something a little more economical, but when I saw this beauty in the lot, she called out to me."

"I can understand that. Must have cost a pretty penny."

"That it did. Renee, you aren't saying anything."

Renee was staring at the car intensely, almost as if she were mesmerized by it.

"Sorry Abigail, that car just seems familiar for some reason, like I saw it a long time ago."

"I don't see how, this is a new model, an Oldsmobile Starfire. Just came out this year. Don't tell me you don't like it."

"I love it. It's incredible. But I swear that I've seen it somewhere before."

Brian had walked around the car twice. Nodding his head in approval of the blue beauty.

"It looks like a dream Abigail. The kind of car that someone in the movies would be riding off into the sunset in."

As Abigail laughed, Renee suddenly remembered her visions from when Abigail lit the beacon in 1935. It was from one of her visions of the future where they were driving off to San Francisco together. The vision from twenty-six years ago had been brief, but it was coming back to her. The sleek curves, the white interior, the wind blowing through their hair as they followed the setting sun into San Francisco.

Of all of the possible futures that she had seen that day, this was the one that she had been hoping for. Her & the woman that she loved, riding off into the sunset to chase a better world.

January 9th, 1963

Abigail couldn't deny what she was seeing in the mirror anymore. They had definitely started to sag a bit. Seeing herself in the mirror, she had been surprised to see that she looked different from how she saw herself. It was as if a hint of her youthful glow had faded away.

Convinced that what that jackass had said was just some bullshit, Abigail had stripped down to her birthday suit so that she could get a good look at her body. She wasn't entirely happy by what she saw.

The 1950s hadn't been quite as rough as the 1930s had been in most ways, but the last decade & a half had begun to take a bit of a toll. Her raven black hair didn't seem quite as dark as it had a decade ago. There was no signs of grey hair, it just seemed a shade lighter. Her hands & her face seemed to be a bit darker than the rest of her pale body, a result of the sun having dealt its damage to the parts of her skin that it could kiss. Her once tight stomach seemed to have just a bit of looseness to it, as if it were preparing to start giving up in a few more years.

She was by no possible measure old; she was certain of that. Still, it wasn't too difficult to see that her last rejuvenation treatment had been eighteen years ago. For a moment, she contemplated what she would look like if she had never had that treatment. What she would look like if she were fifty-eight instead of thirty-eight. It made her feel better about what she was seeing in her reflection, although it didn't make her feel young again.

Without bothering to put anything on, Abigail walked out of her bedroom & headed downstairs to the kitchen where Renee was sitting at the table with a pen in hand over some notes that she was jotting down.

"Renee, do you think that I look old or tired?"

"What was that Abigail… Mon Dieu."

Renee had been so distracted by her task that she had barely noticed that Abigail had walked into the room. Seeing her nude lover standing there, on display was not what she had been expecting to see. It took a few seconds for her brain to catch up to the situation.

"Curtains! Christ au-dessus."

Renee rushed to the large kitchen window & pulled the curtains shut in the hopes that the back neighbor hadn't accidentally looked into their kitchen to see Abigail presenting herself.

"Abigail, we have neighbors. What if they had seen you?"

"Relax Abigail, it's after eight. The people behind us, like most of the street, have already gone to bed."

"Still. You can't just go parading around naked with the curtains open."

"Another reason that I don't like this century."

"Abigail… what brought this on? Not that I'm complaining, but why are you naked in our kitchen?"

"Brentwood."

"Wait? The new assistant manager at your work? How is he involved in this?"

"Between running late this morning & being slammed at work, I never really had a chance to do my normal makeup. I figured that it'd be alright if I looked almost all natural since I work in the back, away from customers."

"Okay Abigail, I am with you so far."

"Then that prick came around back to flirt with the girls & when he saw me, he had a fucking opinion about my how I looked."

"Oh boy. What did the fool say?"

"He said that I had better find a husband soon because I'm starting to look old & tired."

"So where did you bury his body?"

Abigail smiled.

"Seriously Renee, do I look like I'm getting old?"

Renee then took a second to look Abigail up & down. She then started walking around Abigail as if she were an inspector looking for imperfections. Abigail stood there; a bit nervous about what the verdict might be. When Renee came back around, she gave Abigail's body one last top to bottom glance.

"You look beautiful. Stunning. Like the woman of my dreams. You look good for thirty-eight & you look damn good for fifty-eight. If this is what getting old looks like, then I'll happily grow old with you."

Abigail smiled from ear to ear.

"Thanks Renee. So what are you up top in here? What did I interrupt when I came in her for you to stare at?"

"I was writing a letter to my family back home in France."

"Oh. Sorry Renee. If I had known it was family time, I would have put some clothes on. Some underwear at least."

"It's alright. The truth is that I needed a distraction. I was writing down some notes on how I was going to lie & tell them that I'm feeling a bit under the weather lately. That way in two years…"

Ignoring the fact that she was still buck naked, Abigail stepped forward & wrapped her arms around Renee. It would only be about another two years until Renee had to send her last letter to her family. Even though she hadn't seen some of them since she had been a child, & even though she had never actually met most of them, Abigail knew it was going to be hard for her.

Renee's extended family was all that she really had left from her past. Once that connection was gone, she would be a little further from them every day as she followed Abigail into the world of the future. Even if Renee ran home to France right that moment, she still wouldn't be able to be with her family because she would have to come up with an excuse for why she looked younger than some of her nieces. These letters were her connection to her family & she was lying though her teeth in them to prepare for the last one.

"I know that this can't be easy for you Renee. Is there anything that I can do to help?"

"Well, you could start parading around the house naked & asking me to stare at you. That would really help."

Abigail chuckled.

"Do you want to sit down & talk about it?"

"I would like that, Abigail."

"Do you want me to put some clothes on?"

"No."

January 24th, 1965

The weather was being less than agreeable. The snow & wind would have been fine if they were cuddled up on the couch drinking hot chocolate, or even better, if they were curled up in bed. Instead they were driving to a restaurant in a nasty little blizzard.

Renee was certain that she knew what was going on. It was just like twenty years ago. They only had six months left in their assignment in Detroit, & she was being asked to attend a meeting with Renee's handler in some agency-controlled restaurant where they could talk freely. They were going to be getting their new orders. Abigail pulled the Starfire into a parking lot that had a surprising number of cars in it since it was supposed to be closed.

"Are you sure this is the right place Abigail? There are a lot of people here."

"It's closed for a private event. An agent was sent back with orders for a lot of people who are getting new directives & reassignments today. Now that we own a bunch of properties like this, we don't have to have muted conversation in cafes. We can just say that the restaurant is hosting a private event."

"So everybody in there is an agent?"

"An agent, a handler, or a trusted civilian."

Walking inside, they shook the snow from their boots & coats. A robust woman in black jeans with a tight white blouse met them. She spoke with a smoky voice as she looked over her clipboard.

"Reservation?"

Abigail pulled a small card that they had received in the mail out of her purse.

"Oldman for three, confirmation skull candy."

"Right this way."

She then led them past a number of tables where they saw agents talking openly about music, shows, sims & games that Renee had never heard of & that Abigail remembered fondly. When they reached their table, they found that Ash Bailey was already there, waiting for them.

"Abigail, Renee, glad that the two of you could make it despite the snow. Have a seat, it'll be our turn as soon as the new agent is finished with the gentleman over there in the grey suit."

They both sat down as he poured them some water.

"Renee, I haven't seen you in ages. How are you doing?"

"I'm doing alright. Getting a bit tired of driving in this snow. I've got people coming into the bakery looking to escape the cold, no interest in what I'm baking."

"At least you only have to put up with it for a few more months."

"True. How are you doing Ash?"

"Old. My body is passed retirement age, but I've still got to work at the pawn shop for another two or three years. I hope my next assignment is something that requires me to be young. Like college young. My advice, if they ever give you a choice, choose a mission that doesn't involve reaching your mid-sixties."

"I'll keep that in mind. I'll be turning thirty-nine again in a few months & I can already feel a bit worn out. I can't imagine how I'd feel if I was turning fifty-nine like I should be."

"You would feel like crap. Here comes our fourth now."

The young woman that had been talking to the man in the grey suit approached them & stood at their table. Renee had never seen a woman who looked conservative in a dress that only went down to her knees. Still, the slender brunette with the hourglass figure & the perfect complexion stood at their table as Ash introduced her.

"Ladies, this is Agent Mollie Stoneman. She'll be telling you about your new assignments & if all goes according to plan, she'll be elected to the Senate in the 1986."

"Only if I can convince half a million people in Oklahoma to vote for a woman in the middle of the Reagan administration. I told the powers that be I wanted a challenge & they've come through."

Mollie took a seat across from Abigail & reached into her purse to pull out what looked like nothing more than a pair of brochures to ordinary people.

"Pleasure to meet you agent Oldman, I've heard so much about you & miss Rodin."

"Everyone has. I imagine that we're being uprooted in a few months."

"Indeed. Official orders are to relocate on July 1st. The two of you will get your treatments at a safe house just outside of town. Then you'll un-age in a safehouse near Sacramento before reporting to San Francisco."

"California. Sunshine, sandy beaches, the future heart of queer culture. All that I have to do now is convince Renee to wear a bikini."

"Good luck with that Abigail. I'm not even sold on what passes for skirts these days."

Mollie laughed as she watched the couple joke with each other.

"I'm glad that you like the idea of California because your next assignment might get extended. It will most likely be a standard twenty years, but we may have to extend it to thirty-five years."

"So it might be a retirement gig that only ends at the turn of the millennium. Any idea on how likely that is?"

"Not very likely. I just figured that I should mention it just in case. We'll have a definite answer for you by 1980."

"Alright, so if I might be extended, does that mean that I'm still just going to be copying financial information?"

"While you will continue to provide us with financial intelligence, you'll also be taking on some new responsibilities, such as opening & managing agency accounts for other agents. You'll have a few other small responsibilities as well; you can find the information in these."

Mollie then handed over the brochures which actually contained the vital information that she would need without looking like dossiers. Mollie then turned her attention to Renee while Abigail looked through the information in the brochures.

"Miss Rodin, before we begin setting up your next life, can I assume that you'll be willing to work in another bakery? We can create another cover for you if you'd like, perhaps something in welding."

"A woman welder wouldn't stand out too much?"

"It would be noticeable, but California in the 60s & 70s, most people would be too distracted by the constant waves of protests, marches, demonstrations, bra burnings & free love movements to care that one woman is welding."

"Wow. That sounds like it's going to be a crazy time."

"Oh it will be."

"Can I have some time to think about it?"

"Sure, we'll only really need an answer by April, otherwise we'll just assume it's a go ahead on the bakery."

"Fair enough. Can I ask you a question?"

"Sure, that's one of the reason why I'm here today. What's on your mind Renee?"

"Abigail keeps telling me that in the future, we'll be able to get married, but we still have to hide from our neighbors. With everything that's supposed to happen in the next twenty years, will we be able to stop hiding?"

Mollie smiled.

"I don't know if you'll want to go around announcing your relationship to the world, but even if none of our plans pan out, in about ten to fifteen years, gays & lesbians will start getting some protections under California law. So I don't know if it'll be safe enough for you two to be out before 85, but in a few more years, it won't be the end of the world if people figure out that you're more than just close roommates."

Renee felt Abigail's hand in her own. Turning to Abigail, she smiled as she truly thought of her as her future wife for the first time.

July 1st, 1965

With most of their belongings already on the way to San Francisco in a moving truck being driven by another agent, all that was left for them to pack was their clothing & their most precious possessions. Photo albums, letters from Renee's extended family, precious little Knick-knacks that they had acquired together over the last twenty-five years together.

With the trunk full of clothes & things they would need, their boxes were now taking up the back seat where Abigail was tying them down & making sure the boxes were securely closed so that nothing would be lost as they drove with the top down.

As Abigail applied another strip of tape to the boxes sitting on the back seat, she thought back to six days ago, to when she walked out of her office with a small box full of her personal possessions. She had given her notice to her manager at the bank in the first week of June & two weeks later, they had had a small lunch party to say goodbye to her.

A part of her was going to miss some of her coworkers. She had known that from experience. There were still times that she missed Grace, Molly, Sandra, Jasmin & Bess from the bank she worked at in New York. As she realized that those girls must be around retirement age by now, she realized one of the major drawbacks to her chosen career as a time spy. She would never get to catch up with the friends that she had left behind.

Renee took one last walk around their now empty house. They had made so many memories in this house. Reading pulp sci-fi books together. Watching the news while Abigail told her how unfolding events would play out. Preparing for their fake dates & waiting for the others to come back home. Celebrating their 30th anniversary together six weeks early by making sweet, passionate love in every room of the house.

The hardest part had been telling Martha & Sandra that she was moving back to France to help her family. It was almost identical to the lie that she had told her friends in the Brooklyn Naval Yard twenty years earlier.

The looks on their faces had been priceless when she told them that she was transferring ownership of the bakery to them. When they asked her why she would do that instead of selling it, she told them that it wouldn't be fair to trust their jobs to whoever bought the place after almost twenty years of working for her.

As Renee emerged from the house for the very last time, Brian came up to them to wish them well. Invoking Abigail's imaginary brother, Gary Oldman, they had told Brian & all of their neighbours that he had moved to New York & opened a clinic there. They were moving there because he had secured them both some good jobs with good hours which might allow them to finally find some husbands. They both ignored the looks from some of their neighbours that subtly said, at your age.

"All ready to go to New York?"

Abigail smiled.

"I think that we are Brian. I'm going to miss this place."

"That's understandable. It's a great place with great neighbours."

Abigail laughed.

"True. Our neighbours are wonderful. I can think of one in particular that's been pretty incredible."

"We'll all miss the two of you. Best of luck in New York."

Abigail & Renee then both hugged him goodbye.

"Have you got everything Renee?"

"Yes. I suppose I'm ready to go."

Abigail then walked up to the front door, locked it, & slipped their keys though the mail slot for the next owner.

"That's that. I guess we don't live here anymore."

As Abigail turned around, she saw a bunch of their neighbours standing in their yards or on the sidewalk. Retirees & housewives that didn't have to be at work on a Thursday afternoon. Abigail & Renee both waived to all of them & shouted goodbye as they climbed into their blue convertible.

Abigail started up the car. As the V-8 skyrocket engine roared to life, Abigail took one last look around at her neighbours for the last time. She regretted that they were going to miss this year's fourth of July block party. It was even going to be on a Sunday. Reaching for the gear shifter, she turned to Renee.

"Ready to go?"

"Almost, there's just one last thing that I want to do."

Before Abigail could ask her what she wanted to do, Renee grabbed her shirt collar & pulled her forward. Abigail suddenly felt Renee's lips against hers, right there, in full display of their neighbours. It was exhilarating & passionate. One of the best kisses of her life. When their lips finally parted, they were both grinning like idiots.

"I've wanted to do that since 1935."

"Me too Renee. Let's get out of here."

As soon as they turned away from each other, they could both tell which neighbours had figured out that they were more than roommates & which ones hadn't. The few that had suspected it were the only ones that weren't slack jawed.

Abigail then slid the transmission into drive, & turned onto the street, leaving the last twenty years behind & driving them both to a rejuvenation treatment & twenty years that would hopefully allow them to share more kisses together in public.

The End.

www.ingramcontent.com/pod-product-compliance
Lightning Source LLC
Chambersburg PA
CBHW061010120726
47910CB00006B/1865